VISIONS
OF
TOMORROW

VISIONS
OF
TOMORROW

Science Fiction Predictions
That Came True

EDITED BY
THOMAS A. EASTON
AND
JUDITH K. DIAL

A Herman Graf Book
Skyhorse Publishing

Skyhorse Publishing books may be purchased in bulk at special discounts for sales promotion, corporate gifts, fund-raising, or educational purposes. Special editions can also be created to specifications. For details, contact the Special Sales Department, Skyhorse Publishing, 555 Eighth Avenue, Suite 903, New York, NY 10018 or info@skyhorsepublishing.com.

www.skyhorsepublishing.com

10 9 8 7 6 5 4 3 2 1

Library of Congress Cataloging-in-Publication Data available on file.
ISBN: 978-1-60239-998-3

Printed in Canada

CONTENTS

~

III. BYTE ME!
(Computer-related predictions)

IV. IS IT CATCHING?
(Biological predictions)

V. KEEP WATCHING THE SKIES!
(Predictions of things to come)

COPYRIGHTS

❧

SCIENCE FICTION AS PROPHECY

~

Robert Silverberg

There's a widespread impression among people who don't read science fiction that science fiction writers are capable of predicting the future. They believe that television, computers, spaceships, atomic bombs, and space satellites all were described in science fiction stories long before they became realities, and that anyone who wants to know what's coming next in our troubled world needs only to keep up with the current sf literature.

I will concede that that's true in a very general way. But in fact science-fiction writers don't regard themselves as prophets by trade—I can testify to that, after close to sixty years in the business—and the actual record of science fiction as prophecy shows a few brilliant guesses, some impressive almost-on-the-mark predictions, and a vast number of predicted futures that never came about—indeed, have been shown by time to have been completely wrongheaded. Most of us are just telling stories, after all. We look at the world about us and try to extrapolate current trends into future developments, and, because we know the tricks of the trade, we are often able to come up with some very interesting speculations that now and then turn out to be surprisingly accurate anticipations of things to come. Some of them, though, are just speculations—interesting enough for the purposes of the story, but not in any way an accurate forecast of the future. And even those science-fictionists who devote serious effort to forecasting the future are immensely better at forecasting general patterns than at discerning specific details. It isn't really difficult to extend broad technological or social trends into the future, but making sharp and specific predictions is more a matter of luck than genius, even for the best of science-fiction writers.

I can demonstrate that by showing you how two of the best writers who ever wrote science fiction went astray in their attempts to give us a view of the very short-term future.

Robert A. Heinlein was one. Heinlein, an Annapolis graduate with a strong grounding in the sciences, took an engineer's approach to the future. Everything he wrote was developed rigorously out of a broad and deep knowledge of our own world, forming a coherent and internally consistent vision of times to come.

In 1949 a Hollywood producer asked Heinlein to do the screenplay of a documentary-style movie about the first voyage to the moon, and to serve as the film's technical adviser. The result was *Destination Moon* (1950). It was thoughtfully done down to the smallest touches. Cunning special effects provided authentic reproductions of a rocket launching, of the gravitational effects of acceleration, of a spacewalk, of the lunar surface. *Destination Moon* was a sincere and intelligent attempt to depict man's initial flight into space as it was probably going to happen.

It was a fine film. But, we know now, it got practically every detail wrong.

Heinlein's lunar ship was an atomic-powered single-stage rocket designed and built by three men on behalf of a small syndicate of private investors. When the government refuses to let the inventors test their engine at its California construction site, they hastily decide to blast off before anyone can stop them—and launch their expedition in less than twenty-four hours, with an untested engine and themselves as the improvised crew. A federal court order is issued to block the takeoff, but the intrepid astronauts escape by advancing their departure time by several hours. Once in space they realize that a course correction is necessary, so they recalculate their orbit with some hasty pencil-and-paper notations, using a slide rule, an almanac, and an office calculator. And off they go to Luna, where they manage a hazardous manual landing, don their spacesuits, and step forth to claim the moon in the name of the United States.

The story was a trifle melodramatic, but in 1950 it seemed plausible and technologically convincing; today it appears merely quaint, if not absurd. Neither Heinlein nor anyone else in science fiction foresaw that it would take a decade of work to get men to the moon; no one realized that the job would have to be a colossal cooperative enterprise by scores of the nation's largest corporations; no one imagined the immense network of tracking stations and the gigantic computer installation required to guide the mission. The complex Apollo scheme—a multistage, liquid-fueled rocket, separate orbital and moon-landing modules, abandonment of most components of the vehicle along the way, homecoming by parachute drop into the ocean—went altogether unanticipated. Nor did Heinlein or anybody else predict the most astounding aspect of the entire venture, that the astronauts, after having made their lunar landing, would unveil a television camera and transmit to Earth a live video view of mankind's first footsteps on the moon.

What remains, then, of Heinlein's carefully devised vision of the initial voyage to the moon? Only some clever special effects and the fundamental notion that we would get a manned expedition to the moon in the middle decades of the twentieth century. Time has turned virtually everything else into fantasy.

My other prime example is Olaf Stapledon (1886–1950), the most far-seeing of all visionary novelists. In such works as *Last and First Men* (1930) and *Starmaker* (1937), Stapledon gave us astounding vistas of galactic evolution stretching billions of years into the future. Stapledon may have been a great visionary, but he wasn't much of a prophet. Writing in 1930, he completely failed to foresee the rise of Adolf Hitler just three years later, and spoke of the Germany of his day as "the most pacific [of nations], a stronghold of enlightenment." Instead he singled out Mussolini, who was already in power, as the strongest figure in Europe ("a man whose genius in action combined with his rhetoric and crudity of thought to make him a a very successful dictator"). His early chapters are full of other manifest failures of prophecy. When we find him predicting an Anglo-French war around 1950 that ends with France ruling all of Europe and England virtually destroyed, we must simply shake our heads. He misses the development of atomic energy, too, giving us only the invention of an undescribed explosive weapon so terrible that everyone agrees to destroy the formula for it, and does.

Most—not all—of Stapledon's portrait of the world of the late twentieth and early twenty-first century is equally wrong-headed—"awkward and naive," as Gregory Benford said in his introduction to a 1988 edition of the book, and even "ludicrous," as Brian Aldiss once observed. Stapledon's account of the near future was so far off the mark that in a 1953 American edition of *Last and First Men* the publisher simply deleted most of the the first three chapters of the sixteen-chapter book.

But Stapledon himself knew he was no prophet. In the preface to the first British edition in 1930 he said that he did not intend "actually to prophesy what will as a matter of fact occur; for in our present state such prophecy is certainly futile, save in the simplest matters. We are not to set up as historians attempting to look ahead instead of backwards. We can only select a certain thread out of the tangle of many equally valid possibilities. But we must select with a purpose. The activity we are undertaking is not science, but art; and the effect that it should have on the reader is the effect that art should have."

Arthur C. Clarke, whose own most famous prediction (in a 1945 technical article, not a science-fiction story) was that we would be able to transmit television images around the world by placing space satellites in twenty-four-hour orbits, was another of sf's most highly respected seers. But even he felt that nuts-and-bolts prediction of the future was difficult to the point of impossibility. "The real future is not logically foreseeable," he wrote. Clarke disclaimed such prediction explicitly in one of his best-known books, *Childhood's End* (1953), a tale of mankind's ultimate transformation into a single communal cosmic entity, which bore the extraordinary disclaimer on its flyleaf, "The opinions expressed in this book are not those of its author." And, as we look back in science fiction, we find a few remarkably good guesses embedded in an enormous mass of error and short-sightedness. Many nine-teenth-century writers anticipated the airplane, but no one, apparently, foresaw the internal combustion engine, the radio, or motion pictures. Lt. AM Fuller's *A.D.2000* (1890) told of an era that had underground railways much like our subways, electric clocks not too different from ours, and a national newspaper published simul-taneously in many places by a sort of teletype network called a "sympathetic telegraph"—but air travel was conducted in dirigi-bles, and surface transport still made use of horse-drawn buggies. Rudyard Kipling's "With the Night Mail" (1909) also saw gas-filled airships rather than planes, though Kipling's view of the necessity for aerial traffic control was a perceptive one.

Isaac Asimov, in a thoughtful 1953 essay called "Social Science Fiction," discussed the various ways science-fiction writers go about trying to envision the future. He wrote, "Let us suppose it is 1880 and we have a series of three writers who are each interested in writing a story of the future about an imaginary vehicle that can move without horses by some internal source of power, a horse-less carriage, in other words. We might even make up a word and call it an automobile."

The first of Asimov's three writers hits upon the notion of an internal-combustion machine, "describing how the machine would run, explaining the workings of an internal-combustion engine, painting a word-picture of the struggles of the inventor. . . . The climax of the yarn is the drama of the machine, chugging its way along at the gigantic speed of twenty miles an hour between a double crowd of cheering admirers. . . . This is gadget science fiction."

Asimov's second writer specializes in adventure science fiction. He starts with the invention of the automobile and goes on to tell the tale of the kidnapping of the inventor's beautiful daughter by a gang of thieves, who intend to trade her for the blueprints of the invention. (She is ultimately rescued by the inventor's young assistant, riding out into the desert in the experimental automobile just in time to save her from dying of thirst.)

The third writer, though, wants to examine the problems that such a radical new invention will cause for society. "Because of the automobile, a gigantic oil industry has grown up, highways have been paved across the nation. America has become a land of travelers, cities have spread out into suburbs, and—what do we do about automobile accidents?" The best kind of visionary writer, Asimov said, is the one who doesn't stop with inventing the horseless buggy, but goes on to foresee the freeway, the traffic light, the highway patrol. And *that* kind of prediction of the future is next to impossible to bring off successfully in a science-fiction story.

Despite such limitations, some surprisingly keen predictions have been made. Edward Everett Hale's short novel *The Brick Moon*, published in *The Atlantic Monthly* in 1869, described the construction and launching of a hollow space satellite sent into orbit 4,000 miles above the Earth as an aid to navigation. H.G. Wells, in "The Land Ironclads" (1903), virtually invented the military tank. Wells's "The War in the Air" (1908) portrayed aerial warfare much as it would be conducted in Europe less than a decade later; and his "The World Set Free" (1914) told of the tapping of the atomic energy of uranium in 1953 and of the devastation of the world by atomic bombs, called by that name (though Wells imagined that they would be dropped from airplanes by hand.)

In 1941 *Astounding Science Fiction* published a story called "Solution Unsatisfactory" by Anson MacDonald—a pseudonym, as it turned out, for Robert A. Heinlein. This, too, forecast atomic warfare as a consequence of unlocking nuclear energy. Heinlein envisioned not bombs but a radioactive dust capable of rendering large areas uninhabitable. In his story use of the dust knocks Germany out of World War II within a week—and then Heinlein goes on to examine the problems of a postwar world in which the United States alone possesses the superweapon while Soviet physicists struggle to duplicate it, a stunning glance forward into the Cold War realities of 1945–50.

That story caused no great fuss when it appeared, but another that the same magazine ran early in 1944 caused considerable official anguish: "Deadline," by Cleve Cartmill. This tale of cloak-and-dagger operations on another planet included such phrases as "U-235 has been separated in quantity sufficient for preliminary atomic-power research. . . . It was extracted from uranium ores by new atomic isotope separation methods. . . . The explosion of a pound of U-235 releases as much energy as a hundred million pounds of TNT. . . ."

The story went on to describe a plausible atomic bomb—just as Manhattan Project scientists were nearing the climax of their work. A dazzling example of science fiction's ability to see the future? Hardly. Everything in Cartmill's story was based on technical reports openly published as far back as 1939. But he pulled everything together so shrewdly that military intelligence agents thought there had been a security leak, and hurriedly called on *Astounding's* editor, John W. Campbell, to find out how Cartmill had learned about the bomb. Campbell calmly pointed out that Cartmill had simply been recycling existing data—and, when asked to stop publishing stories about atomic energy for the duration of the war, told them that a sudden disappearance of such themes from his magazine might arouse the very suspicions the government was so eager to suppress.

My favorite example of getting it right in a science-fiction story is Murray Leinster's astonishing "A Logic Named Joe"

(1946), which in just a few thousand words gives us the whole Internet, lock stock, and Google, fifty years ahead of time. What Leinster (whose real name was Will F. Jenkins) calls a "logic" is actually a sort of business machine with a keyboard and a television screen attached. You know what *that* is. But in 1946 no one did. Computers had already begun to figure in a few sf stories, but they were usually referred to as "thinking machines," and they were always visualized as immense objects filling laboratories the size of warehouses. The desk-model personal computer that every child knows how to use was too fantastic a concept even for science fiction then—until "A Logic Named Joe."

And what a useful computer the "logic" was! Everybody had one. "You know the logic setup," Jenkins' narrator tells us. "You got a logic in your house. It looks like a vision receiver used to, only it's got keys instead of dials and you punch the keys for what you wanna get. It's hooked to the tank, which has the Carson Circuit all fixed up with relays. Say you punch 'Station SNAFU' on your logic. Relays in the tank take over an' whatever vision-program SNAFU is telecastin' comes on your logic's screen. Or you punch 'Sally Hancock's phone' an' the screen blinks an' sputters an' you're hooked up with the logic in her house an' if someone answers you got a vision-phone connection. But besides that, if you punch for the weather forecast or who won today's race at Hialeah or who was mistress of the White House durin' Garfield's administration or what is PDQ and R sellin' for today, that comes on the screen too.

The relays in the tank do it. The tank is a big buildin' full of all the facts in creation an' all the recorded telecasts that ever was made—no, it's hooked in with all the other tanks all over the country—an' anything you wanna know or see or hear, you punch for it an' you get it. Also it does math for you, and keeps books, an' acts as consultin' chemist, physician, astronomer, and tea-leaf reader, with a 'Advice to Lovelorn' thrown in."

Substitute "servers" for "tanks" and you have a pretty good description of the structure of the Internet. The "Carson Circuit" is the 1946 version of the magical algorithm by which Google provides the path to just about any information you might want in a fraction of a second. Where the particular logic that gets nicknamed "Joe" differs from other logics, though, and from the computers we all own today, is that it is miswired in some strange way that gives it the ability to assemble existing data into startling new combinations on its own initiative—plus a complete lack of inhibitions in making the new information available to its users.

So Joe's screen suddenly declares, "Announcing new and improved service! Your logic is now equipped to give you not only consultive but directive service. If you want to do something and don't know how to do it—ask your logic!"

Want to murder your wife and get away with it, for example? Joe will provide details of a way to mix green shoe polish and frozen pea soup to commit the perfect crime. Want to drink all you'd like and sober up five minutes later? Take a teaspoon of this detergent. Make foolproof counterfeit money? Like this, Joe says. Rob a bank? Turn base metal into gold? Build a perpetual-motion machine? Shift money from somebody else's bank account to your own?

Here's the trick. All the information is in the tanks, somewhere. Joe will find it and connect it for you and serve it up without a second thought, or even a first one. And Joe is connected to all the logics in the world, so everybody can ask for anything in the privacy of his own home.

But it's the end of privacy, of course. You give your logic your name and it will tell you your address, age, sex, your charge—account balance, your wife or husband's name, your income, your traffic-ticket record, and all manner of other bits of personal data. You give the logic someone else's name and it'll provide the same information about that person, too. It's every privacy advocate's worst nightmare: nobody has any secrets. You don't even need to do any hacking. Just turn on your logic and ask.

The logic technician who discovers Joe's special capabilities tells his supervisor that the whole logic tank must be shut down at once before society collapses under Joe's cheerful onslaught. But how? "Does it occur to you, fella, that the tank has been doin' all the computin' for every business office for years?" the supervisor asks. "It's been handlin' the distribution of 94 percent of all the telecast programs, has given out all the information on weather, plane schedules, special sales, employment opportunities and news; has handled all person-to-person contacts over wires and recorded every business conversation and agreement—Listen, fella! Logics changed civilization! Logics *are* civilization! If we shut off logics, we go back to a kind of civilization we have forgotten how to run!"

Exactly so. A totally connected world is a totally dependent world. Will F. Jenkins, writing back there just a few months after the end of World War II, saw the whole thing coming.

The rest of us, though, are rarely so lucky. We don't expect to be. We are concerned with possibilities rather than probabilities; we begin with a premise about the future that has a certain logical plausibility and extend it to its farthest consequences, primarily to see what the consequences of such a premise would be. As Isaac Asimov wrote in his 1953 essay on social science fiction, "Its authors, as a matter of course, present their readers with new societies, with possible futures and consequences. It is a social experimentation on paper; social guesses plucked out of air. And this is the great service of science fiction. To accustom the reader to the possibility of change, to have him think along various lines— perhaps very daring lines."

To make the readers *think*—to make them see *possible* futures, and ponder their consequences—that's what we hope to achieve, along with telling a good story that will hold their interest. The top-flight science-fiction writer—the Heinlein, the Asimov, the Clarke, the Stapledon, the Leinster—achieves that again and again. If, once in a while, he also manages to get the future *right*, as Murray Leinster did in "A Logic Named Joe," that's a bonus, the topping on the cake. It does happen, we know. But it doesn't happen often.

—R. S., 2010

PREFACE

~

WHEN SCIENCE FICTION GETS IT RIGHT!

Fans and critics have argued for many years over just what science fiction is. The truth is that it is many things. It is adventure in space and on faraway planets. It is tales of strange science such as timetravel and brain transplants and genetic engineering. It is utopian dreams and dystopian nightmares.

Sometimes it is even an effort to foresee the future. In fact, the idea that science fiction should try to describe the likely shape of things to come has a long history in the field. The authors who pursued that vision of science fiction include such luminaries as Jules Verne. H. G. Wells even titled a book *The Shape of Things to Come* (1933; Penguin Classics, 2006). Hugo Gernsback, who in 1929 founded the first science fiction magazine, *Amazing Stories*, and is often credited with initiating science fiction as a genre of popular fiction, wrote a novel called *Ralph 124C41+* (say it out loud). He also pushed the idea that science fiction had a two-fold mission, to educate readers about the science behind the fiction (which makes many vintage stories almost unreadable today) and to attempt to see where current science was leading and what technological marvels were just around the corner. He was also an entrepreneur in the early electronics industry, notably radio, and he was himself able to foresee some future developments of that technology. Indeed, *Ralph 124C41+* includes a description of radar, which although the principle had been demonstrated in 1904 was not to take useful form until shortly before World War II, which led to rapid improvements.

There is a hint here that science fiction writers do not pull their predictions out of thin air. They often read scientific publications, both academic and popular. They are aware of what the technical folks are working on (sometimes they are even among those technical folks). Verne worked this way. Wells was both a writer of early science fiction (*The Time Machine*, 1895) and a popularizer of science. Their attempts to predict the future are thus often quite well grounded.

Not that they always succeed! In fact, much of the technology found in science fiction stories is sheer baloney! It's made up to meet the needs of the story, or it's recycled from hundreds of prior stories, or it's just for cool (there's a lot of that in movies).

But sometimes science fiction writers get it right. Robert A. Heinlein conceived of the water-bed in 1934 and described it in three of his novels, supposedly well enough to make water-beds unpatentable when someone started making them. E. M. Forster's *The Machine Stops* (1909), a chilling comment on dependence on technology, included the concept of email. Many more examples can be mentioned, but the point of this anthology is to show, not tell. We have assembled a list of shorter works from 1844 to today, all of which come close—sometimes startlingly so—to describing technology and/or consequent social trends in the story's future.

We begin with a story by Edgar Allan Poe, in which he describes a transatlantic balloon journey. It wasn't a planned trip, for a storm carried the balloon off its intended path, but the point—that such trips could be made—was both novel and apt. Eventually dirigibles made the same journey in reality. And then the dirigibles vanished, replaced by newer technology.

We follow Poe's tale with three more whose predictions have come to pass, and then move to four stories whose predictions have reached the prototype stage. Four computer-related stories then touch on issues of very current concern—the Internet and privacy, computer viruses, Internet addiction, and identity theft. Our biotech selections are perhaps the most frightening or mind-boggling of all; could Vonda McIntyre possibly be right that someday we will be able to "print" living things? We end with a trio of stories whose predictions still seem more like science fiction than prophecy—except that people *are* working on the science behind the fiction.

There is only so much room in a single book. We might have included:

Fritz Leiber's "Sanity" (*Astounding*, April 1944), which described both indoor slidewalks such as we now see in airports and the end of mental hospitals (they used to be common);

Charles Ott's "The Astrological Engine" (*Analog*, September 1977), which predicted handheld horoscope calculators when handheld calculators were still new; the horoscope calculator actually hit the market six months after the story was published;

Ray Bradbury's "There Will Come Soft Rains" (*The Illustrated Man*, 1950), whose floor-cleaning robots sound a lot like the Roomba robotic vacuum cleaner;

Mack Reynolds' "Romp" (*Analog*, October 1966), which involved a kind of computer crime;

Maurice A. Hugi's (really Eric Frank Russell's) "Mechanical Mice" (*Astounding*, January 1941), which told of a self-reproducing machine that today seems very much a forecast of the RepRap 3D printer (intended to be able to print copies of itself).

And many more. The purpose of science fiction is not prophecy, but sometimes it *does* get things right.

Finally, why are *we* the folks who put this book together? Tom has had a long relationship with *Analog* magazine (once known as *Astounding*), writing stories and articles and thirty years worth of book review columns. The magazine has a history of trying to look at the future, and Tom has had nearly as long a history of interest in futurism and technological forecasting. He is usually disguised as a professor of science.

Judith has a family interest in the theme. Her mother was married to Cleve Cartmill when he wrote "Deadline." That doesn't make her any real relation to Cartmill, but it does explain why she was familiar with the circumstances around the story and the story itself from a very early age.

She was raised by her father, a mechanical engineer and physicist. In high school he'd read all the back issues of *Scientific American* (his school library had them), which started him pondering about the nature of scientific change and how technology developed. Working in aeronautics, starting with a wooden biplane, by the time he retired he'd worked on wind tunnels, been to the Bikini test, and contributed designs to the DC-1 through DC-10 aircraft, Voyager, and Mercury. He taught at the California Institute of Technology for more than forty years. He also started reading science fiction in the 1920s and never stopped. The sciences, and the growth and development of technologies and science fiction, were all regular topics in Judith's childhood home.

Judith herself has worked in the electronics industry, in bookselling (with an emphasis on science fiction/fantasy), and as a technical writer. She is also an irregular member of the *New York Review of Science Fiction's* volunteer staff.

Thomas A. Easton
Judith K. Dial
January 2010

one

❦

BEEN THERE,
DONE THAT

(Predictions that have already happened)

— EDGAR ALLAN POE —

"THE BALLOON HOAX"

■ *New York Sun, 1844.*

A successful prediction is no less successful for having already come to pass. What makes it a prediction is that it pertains to a future relative to when the story was written.

Balloons were not a new idea in the 1840s. The Montgolfier brothers flew the first human passengers over Paris in a hot-air balloon in 1783. The English Channel was actually crossed by a hydrogen balloon in 1785. When Edgar Allan Poe's intrepid crew proposed to do the same thing in 1844, a storm arose and swept the balloon westward, all the way to North America, over half a century before the first rigid-framed zeppelin was built and some seventy-five years before anyone actually flew anything across the Atlantic, by accident or design.

Poe's basic technique was extrapolation, a standby of science fiction even today. He realized that once a balloon was in the air, the only limit on how far it could go was set not by distance but by how long the lighter-than-air gas filling the balloon could be maintained. Therefore, if a balloon in 1785 could cross the Channel, another could cross the Atlantic, with a bit of help from a gale. His story was originally published in the *New York Sun* under the headline:

ASTOUNDING NEWS!
BY EXPRESS VIA NORFOLK:
THE ATLANTIC CROSSED
IN THREE DAYS!
SIGNAL TRIUMPH OF
MR. MONCK MASON'S
FLYING MACHINE!

People lined up in the street to get the exciting news!

Twenty years later Jules Verne extended the extrapolation even further in *Five Weeks in a Balloon* (1863). And in time, those zeppelins made long-distance lighter-than-air craft travel a reality. Their time did not last long, for airplanes displaced them, but that does not mean that Poe's prediction of the long-distance capabilities of lighter-than-air craft was not valid.

Today, hot-air balloons serve recreational purposes only. A few zeppelins are available for sightseeing flights. Related blimps, like those made by the American Blimp Corporation, are filled with helium or hydrogen; they carry advertising and serve military and emergency purposes around the world. They have also been proposed for carrying high-altitude windmills and communications antennae.

THE BALLOON HOAX

~

Edgar Allan Poe

ASTOUNDING NEWS BY EXPRESS, VIA NORFOLK!—THE ATLANTIC CROSSED IN THREE DAYS! SIGNAL TRIUMPH OF MR. MONCK MASON'S FLYING MACHINE!—ARRIVAL AT SULLIVAN'S ISLAND, NEAR CHARLESTON, S.C., OF MR. MASON, MR. ROBERT HOLLAND, MR. HENSON, MR. HARRISON AINSWORTH, AND FOUR OTHERS, IN THE STEERING BALLOON, VICTORIA, AFTER A PASSAGE OF SEVENTY-FIVE HOURS FROM LAND TO LAND! FULL PARTICULARS OF THE VOYAGE!

The great problem is at length solved! The air, as well as the earth and the ocean, has been subdued by science, and will become a common and convenient highway for mankind. *The Atlantic has been actually crossed in a balloon!* and this too without difficulty—without any great apparent danger—with thorough control of the machine—and in the inconceivably brief period of seventy-five hours from shore to shore! By the energy of an agent at Charleston, S.C., we are enabled to be the first to furnish the public with a detailed account of this most extraordinary voyage, which was performed between Saturday, the 6th instant, at 11 AM, and 2 PM, on Tuesday, the 9th instant, by Sir Everard Bringhurst; Mr. Osborne, a nephew of Lord Bentinck's; Mr. Monck Mason and Mr. Robert Holland, the well-known aeronauts; Mr. Harrison Ainsworth, author of *Jack Shepherd*, etc.; and Mr. Henson, the projector of the late unsuccessful flying machine—with two seamen from Woolwich—in all, eight persons. The particulars furnished below may be relied on as authentic and accurate in every respect, as, with a slight exception, they are copied *verbatim* from the joint diaries of Mr. Monck Mason and Mr. Harrison Ainsworth, to whose politeness our agent is indebted for much verbal information respecting the balloon itself, its construction, and other matters of interest. The only alteration in the MS received has been made for the purpose of throwing the hurried account of our agent, Mr. Forsyth, into a connected and intelligible form.

THE BALLOON

"Two very decided failures, of late—those of Mr. Henson and Sir George Cayley—had much weakened the public interest in the subject of aerial navigation. Mr. Henson's scheme (which at first was considered very feasible even by men of science) was founded upon the principle of an inclined plane, started from an eminence by an extrinsic force applied and continued by the revolution of impinging vanes in form and number resembling the vanes of a windmill. But, in all the experiments made with models at the Adelaide Gallery, it was found that the operation of these fans not only did not propel the machine, but actually impeded its flight. The only propelling force it ever exhibited, was the mere *impetus* acquired from the descent of the inclined plane; and this *impetus* carried the machine further when the vanes were at rest, than when they were in motion—a fact which sufficiently demonstrates their inutility; and in the absence of the propelling, which was also the *sustaining*, power, the whole fabric would necessarily descend. This consideration led Sir George Cayley to think only of adapting a propeller to some machine having of itself an independent power of support—in a word, to a balloon; the idea however, being novel, or original, with Sir George, only so far as regards the mode of its application to practice. He exhibited a model of his invention at the Polytechnic Institution. The propelling principle, or power, was here, also, applied to interrupted surfaces, or vanes, put in revolution. These vanes were four in number, but were found entirely ineffectual in moving the balloon, or in aiding its ascending power. The whole project was thus a complete failure.

"It was at this juncture that Mr. Monck Mason (whose voyage from Dover to Weilburg in the balloon, *Nassau*, occasioned so much excitement in 1837) conceived the idea of employing the principle of the Archimedean screw for the purpose of propulsion through the air—rightly attributing the failure of Mr. Henson's scheme, and of Sir George Cayley's to the interruption of surface in the independent vanes. He made the first public experiment at Willis's Rooms, but afterward removed his model to the Adelaide Gallery.

"Like Sir George Cayley's balloon, his own was an ellipsoid. Its length was thirteen feet six inches—height, six feet eight inches. It contained about three hundred and twenty cubic feet of gas, which, if pure hydrogen, would support twenty-one pounds upon its first inflation, before the gas has time to deteriorate or escape. The weight of the whole machine and apparatus was seventeen pounds—leaving about four pounds to spare. Beneath the centre of the balloon, was a frame of light wood, about nine feet long, and rigged on to the balloon itself with a network in the customary manner. From this framework was suspended a wicker basket or car.

"The screw consists of an axis of hollow brass tube, eighteen inches in length, through which, upon a semispiral inclined at fifteen degrees, pass a series of steel-wire radii, two feet long, and thus projecting a foot on either side. These radii are connected at the outer extremities by two bands of flattened wire—the whole in this manner forming the framework of the screw, which is completed by a covering of oiled silk cut into gores, and tightened so as to present a tolerably uniform surface. At each end of its axis this screw is supported by pillars of hollow brass tube descending from the hoop. In the lower ends of these tubes are holes in which the pivots of the axis revolve. From the end of the axis, which is next the car, proceeds a shaft of steel, connecting the screw with the pinion of a piece of spring machinery fixed in the car. By the operation of this spring, the screw is made to revolve with great rapidity, communicating a progressive motion to the whole. By means of the rudder, the machine was readily turned in any direction. The spring was of great power, compared with its dimensions, being capable of raising forty-five pounds upon a barrel of four inches diameter after the first turn, and gradually increasing as it was wound up. It weighed, altogether, eight pounds six ounces. The rudder was a light frame of cane covered with silk, shaped somewhat like a battledore, and was about three feet long, and at the widest, one foot. Its weight was about two ounces. It could be turned *flat*, and directed upward or downward, as well as to the right or left; and thus enabled the aeronaut to transfer the resistance of the air which in an inclined position it must generate in its passage, to any side upon which he might desire to act; thus determining the balloon in the opposite direction.

"This model (which, through want of time, we have necessarily described in an imperfect manner) was put in action at the Adelaide Gallery, where it accomplished a velocity of five miles per hour; although, strange to say, it excited very little interest in comparison with the previous complex machine of Mr. Henson—so resolute is the world to despise anything which carries with it an air of simplicity. To accomplish the great desideratum of aerial navigation, it was very generally supposed that some exceedingly complicated application must be made of some unusually profound principle in dynamics.

"So well satisfied, however, was Mr. Mason of the ultimate success of his invention, that he determined to construct immediately, if possible, a balloon of sufficient capacity to test the question by a voyage of some extent—the original design being to cross the British Channel, as before, in the *Nassau* balloon. To carry out his views he solicited and obtained the patronage of Sir Everard Bringhurst and Mr. Osborne, two gentlemen well known for scientific acquirement, and especially for the interest they have exhibited in the progress of aerostation. The project, at the desire of Mr. Osborne, was kept a profound secret from the public—the only persons entrusted with the design being those actually engaged in the construction of the machine, which was built (under the superintendence of Mr. Mason, Mr. Holland, Sir Everard Bringhurst, and Mr. Osborne) at the seat of the latter gentleman near Penstruthal, in Wales. Mr. Henson, accompanied by his friend Mr. Ainsworth, was admitted to a private view of the balloon, on Saturday last—when the two gentlemen made final arrangements to be included in the adventure. We are not informed for what reason the two seamen were also included in the party—but, in the course of a day or two, we shall put our readers in possession of the minutest particulars respecting this extraordinary voyage.

"The balloon is composed of silk, varnished with the liquid gum caoutchouc. It is of vast dimensions, containing more than 40,000 cubic feet of gas; but as coal-gas was employed in place of the more expensive and inconvenient hydrogen, the supporting power of the machine, when fully inflated, and immediately after inflation, is not more than about 2,500 pounds. The coal-gas is not only much less costly, but is easily procured and managed.

"For its introduction into common use for purposes of aerostation, we are indebted to Mr. Charles Green. Up to his discovery, the process of inflation was not only exceedingly expensive, but uncertain. Two and even three days have frequently been wasted in futile attempts to procure a sufficiency of hydrogen to fill a balloon, from which it had great tendency to escape, owing to its extreme subtlety, and its affinity for the surrounding atmosphere. In a balloon sufficiently perfect to retain its contents of coal-gas unaltered, in quality or amount for six months, an equal quantity of hydrogen could not be maintained in equal purity for six weeks.

"The supporting power being estimated at 2,500 pounds, and the united weights of the party amounting only to about 1,200, there was left a surplus of 1,300, of which again 1,200 was exhausted by ballast, arranged in bags of different sizes, with their respective weights marked upon them—by cordage, barometers, telescopes, barrels containing provision for a fortnight, watercasks, cloaks, carpet-bags, and various other indispensable matters, including a coffee warmer, contrived for warming coffee by means of slack-lime, so as to dispense altogether with fire, if it should be judged prudent to do so. All these articles, with the exception of the ballast, and a few trifles, were suspended from the hoop overhead. The car is much smaller and lighter, in proportion, than the one appended to the model. It is formed of a light wicker, and is wonderfully strong for so frail-looking a machine. It's rim is about four feet deep. The rudder is also very much larger, in proportion, than that of the model; and the screw is considerably smaller. The balloon is furnished besides with a grapnel, and a guide-rope; which latter is of the most indispensable importance. A few words, in explanation, will here be necessary for such of our readers as are not conversant with the details of aerostation.

"As soon as the balloon quits the earth, it is subjected to the influence of many circumstances tending to create a difference in its weight; augmenting or diminishing its ascending power. For example, there may be a deposition of dew upon the silk, to the extent even of several hundred pounds; ballast has then to be thrown out, or the machine may descend. This ballast being discarded, and a clear sunshine evaporating the dew, and at the same time expanding the gas in the silk, the whole will again rapidly ascend. To check this ascent, the only resource is (or rather *was*, until Mr. Green's invention of the guide-rope) the permission of the escape of gas from the valve; but, in the loss of gas, is a proportionate general loss of ascending power; so that, in a comparatively brief period, the best-constructed balloon must necessarily exhaust all its resources, and come to the earth. This was the great obstacle to voyages of length.

"The guide-rope remedies the difficulty in the simplest matter conceivable. It is merely a very long rope which is suffered to trail from the car, and the effect of which is to prevent the balloon from changing its level in any material degree. If, for example, there should be a deposition of moisture upon the silk, and the machine begins to descend in consequence, there will be no necessity for discharging ballast to remedy the increase in weight, for it is remedied, or counteracted, in an exactly just proportion, by the deposit on the ground of just so much of the end of the rope as is necessary. If, on the other hand, any circumstances should cause undue levity, and consequent ascent, this levity is immediately counteracted by the additional weight of rope upraised from the earth. Thus, the balloon can neither ascend nor descend, except within very narrow limits, and its resources, either in gas or ballast, remain comparatively unimpaired. When passing over an expanse of water, it becomes necessary to employ kegs of copper or wood, filled with liquid ballast of a lighter nature than water. These float, and serve all the purposes of a mere rope on land. Another most important office of the guide-rope is to point out the *direction* of the balloon. The rope *drags*, either on land or sea, while the balloon is free; the latter, consequently, is always in advance, when any progress whatever is made: a comparison, therefore, by means of the compass, of the relative positions of the two objects, will always indicate the *course*. In the same way, the angle formed by the rope with the verticle axis of the machine indicates the *velocity*. When there is *no* angle—in other words, when the rope hangs perpendicularly, the whole apparatus is stationary; but the larger the angle, that is to say, the farther the balloon precedes the end of the rope, the greater the velocity; and the converse.

"As the original design was to cross the British Channel, and alight as near Paris as possible, the voyagers had taken the precaution to prepare themselves with passports directed to all parts of the Continent, specifying the nature of the expedition, as in the case of the *Nassau* voyage, and entitling the adventurers to exemption from the usual formalities of office; unexpected events, however, rendered these passports superfluous.

"The inflation was commenced very quietly at daybreak, on Saturday morning, the 6th instant, in the courtyard of Wheal-Vor House, Mr. Osborne's seat, about a mile from Penstruthal, in North

Wales; and at seven minutes past eleven, everything being ready for departure, the balloon was set free, rising gently but steadily, in a direction nearly south; no use being made, for the first half hour, of either the screw or the rudder. We proceed now with the journal, as transcribed by Mr. Forsyth from the joint MS of Mr. Monck Mason and Mr. Ainsworth. The body of the journal, as given, is in the handwriting of Mr. Mason, and a PS is appended, each day, by Mr. Ainsworth, who has in preparation, and will shortly give the public a more minute and, no doubt, a thrillingly interesting account of the voyage."

THE JOURNAL

"*Saturday, April the 6th.* Every preparation likely to embarrass us having been made overnight, we commenced the inflation this morning at daybreak; but owing to a thick fog, which encumbered the folds of the silk and rendered it unmanageable, we did not get through before nearly eleven o'clock. Cut loose, then, in high spirits, and rose gently but steadily, with a light breeze at north, which bore us in the direction of the British Channel. Found the ascending force greater than we had expected; and as we arose higher and so got clear of the cliffs, and more in the sun's rays, our ascent became very rapid. I did not wish, however, to lose gas at so early a period of the adventure, and so concluded to ascend for the present. We soon ran out our guide-rope; but even when we had raised it clear of the earth, we still went up very rapidly. The balloon was unusually steady, and looked beautifully. In about ten minutes after starting, the barometer indicated an altitude of 15,000 feet. The weather was remarkably fine, and the view of the subjacent country—a most romantic one when seen from any point—was now especially sublime. The numerous deep gorges presented the appearance of lakes, on account of the dense vapours with which they were filled, and the pinnacles and crags to the southwest, piled in extricable confusion, resembling nothing so much as the giant cities of Eastern fable. We were rapidly approaching the mountains in the south, but our elevation was more than sufficient to enable us to pass them in safety. In a few minutes we soared over them in fine style; and Mr. Ainsworth, with the seamen, was surprised at their apparent want of altitude when viewed from the car, the tendency of great elevation in a balloon being to reduce inequalities of the surface below, to nearly a dead level. At half-past eleven still proceeding nearly south, we obtained our first view of the British Channel; and, in fifteen minutes afterwards, the line of breakers on the coast appeared immediately beneath us, and we were fairly out at sea. We now resolved to let off enough gas to bring our guide-rope, with the buoys affixed, into the water. This was immediately done, and we commenced a gradual descent. In about twenty minutes our first buoy dipped, and at the touch of the second soon afterward, we remained stationary as to elevation. We were all now anxious to test the efficiency of the rudder and screw, and we put them both into requisition forthwith, for the purpose of altering our direction more to the eastward, and in a line for Paris. By means of the rudder we instantly effected the necessary change of direction, and our course was brought nearly at right angles to that of the wind; then we set in motion the spring of the screw, and were rejoiced to find it propel as readily as desired. Upon this we gave nine hearty cheers, and dropped in the sea a bottle, enclosing a slip of parchment with a brief account of the principle of the invention. Hardly, however, had we done with our rejoicings, when an unforeseen accident occurred which discouraged us in no little degree. The steel rod connecting the spring with the propeller was suddenly jerked out of place, at the car end (by a swaying of the car through some movement of one of the two seamen we had taken up), and in an instant hung dangling out of reach, from the pivot of the axis of the screw. While we were endeavouring to regain it, our attention being completely absorbed, we became involved in a strong current of wind from the east, which bore us, with rapidly increasing force, toward the Atlantic. We soon found ourselves driving out to sea at the rate of not less, certainly, than fifty or sixty miles an hour, so that we came up with Cape Clear, at some forty miles to our north, before we had secured the rod, and had time to think what we were about. It was now that Mr. Ainsworth made an extraordinary but, to my fancy, a by no means unreasonable or chimerical proposition, in which he was instantly seconded by Mr. Holland—viz.: that we should take advantage of the strong gale which bore us on, and in place of beating back to Paris, make an attempt to reach the coast of North America. After slight reflection I gave a willing assent to this bold proposition, which (strange to say) met with objection from the two seamen only. As the stronger party, however, we overruled their fears, and kept resolutely upon our course. We steered due west; but as the trailing of the buoys materially impeded our progress, and we had the balloon abundantly at command, either for ascent or descent, we first threw out fifty pounds of ballast, and then wound up (by means of the windlass) so much of the rope as brought it quite clear of the sea. We perceived the effect of this manoeuvre immediately, in a vastly increased rate of progress; and, as the gale freshened, we flew with a velocity nearly inconceivable; the guide-rope flying out behind the car like a streamer from a vessel. It is needless to say that a very short time sufficed us to lose sight of the coast. We passed over innumerable vessels of all kinds, a few of which were endeavouring to beat up, but the most of them lying to. We occasioned the greatest excitement on board all—an excitement greatly relished by ourselves, and especially by our two men, who, now under the influence of a dram of Geneva, seemed resolved to give all scruple, or fear, to the wind. Many of the vessels fired signal guns; and in all we were saluted with loud cheers (which we heard with surprising distinctness) and the waving of caps and handkerchiefs. We kept on in this manner throughout the day with no material incident, and, as the shades of night closed around us, we made a rough estimate of the distance traversed. It could not have been less than five hundred miles, and was probably much more. The propeller was kept in constant operation, and, no doubt, aided our progress materially. As the sun went down, the gale freshened into an absolute hurricane, and the ocean beneath was clearly visible on account of its phosphorescence. The wind was from the east all night, and gave us the brightest omen of success. We suffered no little from cold, and the dampness of the atmosphere was most unpleasant; but the ample space in the car enabled us to lie down, and by means of cloaks and a few blankets we did sufficiently well."

"PS [by Mr. Ainsworth] The last nine hours have been unquestionably the most exciting of my life. I can conceive nothing more sublimating than the strange peril and novelty of an adventure such as this. May God grant that we succeed! I ask not success for mere safety to my insignificant person, but for the sake of human knowledge and for the vastness of the triumph. And yet the feat is only so evidently feasible that the sole wonder is why men have scrupled to attempt it before. One single gale such as now befriends us—let such a tempest whirl forward a balloon for four or five days (these gales often last longer) and the voyager will be easily borne, in that period, from coast to coast. In view of such a gale the broad Atlantic becomes a mere lake. I am more struck, just now, with the supreme silence which reigns in the sea beneath us, notwithstanding its agitation, than with any other phenomenon presenting itself. The waters give up no voice to the heavens.

"The immense flaming ocean writhes and is tortured uncomplainingly. The mountainous surges suggest the idea of innumerable dumb gigantic fiends struggling in impotent agony. In a night such as is this to me, a man *lives*—lives a whole century of ordinary life—nor would I forego this rapturous delight for that of a whole century of ordinary existence."

"*Sunday, the 7th.* [Mr. Mason's MS] This morning the gale, by ten, had subsided to an eight-or nine-knot breeze (for a vessel at sea), and bears us, perhaps, thirty miles per hour, or more. It has veered, however, very considerably to the north; and now, at sundown, we are holding our course due west, principally by the screw and rudder, which answer their purposes to admiration. I regard the project as thoroughly successful, and the easy navigation of the air in any direction (not exactly in the teeth of a gale) as no longer problematical. We could not have made head against the strong wind of yesterday; but, by ascending, we might have got out of its influence, if requisite. Against a pretty stiff breeze, I feel convinced, we can make our way with the propeller. At noon, today, ascended to an elevation of nearly 25,000 feet, by discharging ballast. Did this to search for a more direct current, but found none so favourable as the one we are now in. We have an abundance of gas to take us across this small pond, even should the voyage last three weeks. I have not the slightest fear for the result. The difficulty has been strangely exaggerated and misapprehended. I can choose my current, and should I find *all* currents against me, I can make very tolerable headway with the propeller. We have no incidents worth recording. The night promises fair."

"PS [By Mr. Ainsworth] I have little to record, except the fact (to me quite a surprising one) that, at an elevation equal to that of Cotopaxi, I experienced neither intense cold, nor headache, nor difficulty of breathing; neither, I find, did Mr. Mason, nor Mr. Holland, nor Sir Everard. Mr. Osborne complained of constriction of the chest—but this soon wore off. We have flown at a great rate during the day, and we must be more than halfway across the Atlantic. We have passed over some twenty or thirty vessels of various kinds, and all seem to be delightfully astonished. Crossing the ocean in a balloon is not so difficult a feat after all. *Omne ignotum pro magnifico. Mem.:* At 25,000 feet elevation the sky appears nearly black, and the stars are distinctly visible; while the sea does not seem convex (as one might suppose) but absolutely and most unequivocally *concave*.[1]

"*Monday, the 8th*. [Mr. Mason's MS] This morning we had again some little trouble with the rod of the propeller, which must be entirely remodeled, for fear of serious accident—I mean the steel rod, not the vanes. The latter could not be improved. The wind has been blowing steadily and strongly from the northeast all day; and so far fortune seems bent upon favouring us. Just before day, we were all somewhat alarmed at some odd noises and concussions in the balloon, accompanied with the apparent rapid subsidence of the whole machine. These phenomena were occasioned by the expansion of the gas, through increase of heat in the atmosphere, and the consequent disruption of the minute particles of ice with which the network had become encrusted during the night. Threw down several bottles to the vessels below. See one of them picked up by a large ship—seemingly one of the New York line packets. Endeavoured to make out her name, but could not be sure of it. Mr. Osborne's telescope made it out something like *Atalanta*. It is now twelve at night, and we are still going nearly west, at a rapid pace. The sea is peculiarly phosphorescent."

"PS [By Mr. Ainsworth] It is now two AM, and nearly calm, as well as I can judge—but it is very difficult to determine this point, since we move *with* the air so completely. I have not slept since quitting Wheal-Vor, but can stand it no longer, and must take a nap. We cannot be far from the American coast."

"*Tuesday, the 9th*. [Mr. Mason's MS] One pm We are in full view of the low coast of South Carolina. The great problem is accomplished. We have crossed the Atlantic—fairly and *easily* crossed it in a balloon! God be praised! Who shall say that anything is impossible hereafter?"

The Journal here ceases. Some particulars of the descent were communicated, however, by Mr. Ainsworth to Mr. Forsyth. It was nearly dead calm when the voyagers first came in view of the coast, which was immediately recognized by both the seamen, and by Mr. Osborne. The latter gentleman having acquaintances at Fort Moultrie, it was immediately resolved to descend in its vicinity. The balloon was brought over the beach (the tide being out and the sand hard, smooth, and admirably adapted for a descent) and the grapnel let go, which took firm hold at once. The inhabitants of the island, and of the fort, thronged out, of course, to see the balloon; but it was with the greatest difficulty that any one could be made to credit the actual voyage—*the crossing of the Atlantic.* The grapnel caught at two PM precisely; and thus the whole voyage was completed in seventy-five hours; or rather less, counting from shore to shore. No serious accident occurred. No real danger was at any time apprehended. The balloon was exhausted and secured without trouble; and when the MS from which this narrative is compiled was dispatched from Charleston, the party was still at Fort Moultrie. Their further intentions were not ascertained; but we can safely promise our readers some additional information either on Monday or in the course of the next day, at furthest.

This is unquestionably the most stupendous, the most interesting, and the most important undertaking ever accomplished or even attempted by man. What magnificent events may ensue, it would be useless now to think of determining.

1. NOTE— Mr. Ainsworth has not attempted to account for this phenomenon, which, however, is quite susceptible of explanation. A line dropped from an elevation of 25,000 feet, perpendicularly to the surface of the earth (or sea), would form the perpendicular of a right-angled triangle, of which the base would extend from the right angle to the horizon, and the hypothenuse from the horizon to the balloon. But the 25,000 feet of altitude is little or nothing, in comparison with the extent of the prospect. In other words, the base and hypothenuse of the supposed triangle

would be so long, when compared with the perpendicular, that the two former may be regarded as nearly parallel. In this manner the horizon of the aeronaut would appear to be *on a level* with the car. But, as the point immediately beneath him seems, and is, at a great distance below him, it seems, of course, also, at a great distance below the horizon. Hence the impression of *concavity;* and this impression must remain, until the elevation shall bear so great a proportion to the extent of prospect, that the apparent parallelism of the base and hypothenuse disappears—when the earth's real convexity must become apparent.

— H. G. WELLS —

"THE LAND IRONCLADS"

■ *Strand Magazine*, December 1903.

The first military tank was sketched by Leonardo da Vinci, who wrote to the Duke of Milan in the late 1400s, "I can make armoured cars, safe and unassailable, which will enter the serried ranks of the enemy with their artillery, and there is no company of men at arms so great that they will break it. And behind these the infantry will be able to follow quite unharmed and without any opposition."

In due time, H. G. Wells posited something very similar for his story, "The Land Ironclads," published fourteen years before the first actual use of tanks in World War I. At the time, it is clear from the story, war was thought to be an occupation best suited to those who pursue the rugged outdoors life, not to those citified folks who rely on science and technology. The last line of the story hints that the tank would change that. Few would now argue the point.

THE LAND IRONCLADS

∿

H. G. Wells

I

The young lieutenant lay beside the war correspondent and admired the idyllic calm of the enemy's lines through his field glass.

"So far as I can see," he said, at last, "one man."

"What's he doing?" asked the war correspondent.

"Field-glass at us," said the young lieutenant.

"And this is war!"

"No," said the young lieutenant; "it's Bloch."

"The game's a draw."

"No! They've got to win or else they lose. A draw's a win for our side."

They had discussed the political situation fifty times or so, and the war correspondent was weary of it. He stretched out his limbs. "Aaai s'pose it is!" he yawned.

"*Flut!*"

"What was that?"

"Shot at us."

The war correspondent shifted to a slightly lower position.

"No one shot at him," he complained.

"I wonder if they think we shall get so bored we shall go home?"

The war correspondent made no reply.

"There's the harvest, of course . . . "

They had been there a month. Since the first brisk movements after the declaration of war things had gone slower and slower, until it seemed as though the whole machine of events must have run down. To begin with, they had had almost a scampering time; the Invader had come across the frontier on the very dawn of the war in half-a-dozen parallel columns behind a cloud of cyclists and cavalry, with a general air of coming straight on the capital, and the defender-horsemen had held him up, and peppered him and forced him to open out to outflank, and had then bolted to the next position in the most approved style, for a couple of days, until in the afternoon, *bump!* they had the invader against their prepared lines of defense. He did not suffer so much as had been hoped and expected: he was coming on it seemed with his eyes open, his scouts winded the guns, and down he sat at once without the shadow of an attack and began grubbing trenches for himself, as though he meant to sit down there to the very end of time. He was slow but much more wary than the world had been led to expect, and he kept convoys tucked in and shielded his slow marching infantry sufficiently well, to prevent any heavy adverse scoring.

"But he ought to attack," the young lieutenant had insisted.

"He'll attack us at dawn, somewhere along the lines. You'll get the bayonets coming into the trenches just about when you can see," the war correspondent had held until a week ago.

The young lieutenant winked when he said that.

When one early morning the men the defenders sent to lie out five hundred yards before the trenches, with a view to the unexpected emptying of magazines into any night attack, gave way to causeless panic and blazed away at nothing for ten minutes, the war correspondent understood the meaning of that wink.

"What would you do if you were the enemy?" said the war correspondent, suddenly.

"If I had men like I've got now?"

"Yes."

"Take these trenches."

"How?"

"Oh-dodges! Crawl out halfway at night before moonrise and get into touch with the chaps we send out. Blaze at 'em if they tried to shift, and so bag some of 'em in the daylight. Learn that patch of ground by heart, lie all day in squatty holes, and come on nearer next night. There's a bit over there, lumpy ground, where they could get across to rushing distance easy. In a night or so. It would be a mere game for our fellows; it's what they're made for. . . . Guns? Shrapnel and stuff wouldn't stop good men who meant business."

"Why don't *they* do that?"

"Their men aren't brutes enough; that's the trouble. They're a crowd of devitalized townsmen, and that's the truth of the matter. They're clerks, they're factory hands, they're students, they're civilized men. They can write, they can talk, they can make and do all sorts of things, but they're poor amateurs at war. They've got no physical staying power, and that's the whole thing. They've never slept in the open one night in their lives; they've never drunk anything but the purest water-company water; they've never gone short of three meals a day since they left their devitalizing feeding-bottles. Half their cavalry never cocked leg over horse till it enlisted six months ago. They ride their horses as though they were bicycles—you watch 'em! They're fools at the game, and they know it. Our boys of fourteen can give their grown men points. . . Very well—"

The war correspondent mused on his face with his nose between his knuckles.

"If a decent civilization," he said, "cannot produce better men for war than—"

He stopped with belated politeness.

"I mean—"

"Than our open-air life," said the young lieutenant, politely.

"Exactly," said the war correspondent. "Then civilization has to stop."

"It looks like it," the young lieutenant admitted.

"Civilization has science, you know," said the war correspondent. "It invented and it makes the rifles and guns and things you use."

"Which our nice healthy hunters and stockmen and so on, rowdy-dowdy cowpunchers and horse-whackers, can use ten times better than—*What's that?*"

"What?" said the war correspondent, and then seeing his companion busy with his field-glass he produced his own. "Where?" said the war correspondent, sweeping the enemy's lines.

"It's nothing," said the young lieutenant, still looking.

"What's nothing?"

The young lieutenant put down his glass and pointed. "I thought I saw something there, behind the stems of those trees. Something black. What it was I don't know."

The war correspondent tried to get even by intense scrutiny.

"It wasn't anything," said the young lieutenant, rolling over to regard the darkling evening sky, and generalized: "There never will be anything anymore forever. Unless—"

The war correspondent looked inquiry.

"They may get their stomachs wrong, or something—living without proper drains."

A sound of bugles came from the tents behind. The war correspondent slid backward down the sand and stood up. *Boom!* came from somewhere far away to the left.

"Halloa!" he said, hesitated, and crawled back to peer again. "Firing at this time is jolly bad manners."

The young lieutenant was incommunicative again for a space.

Then he pointed to the distant clump of trees again. "One of our big guns. They were firing at that," he said.

"The thing that wasn't anything?"

"Something over there, anyhow."

Both men were silent, peering through their glasses for a space. "Just when it's twilight," the lieutenant complained. He stood up.

"I might stay here a bit," said the war correspondent.

The lieutenant shook his head. "There is nothing to see," he apologized, and then, went down to where his little squad of sun-brown, loose-limbed men had been yarning in the trench. The war correspondent stood up also, glanced for a moment at the business-like bustle below him, gave perhaps twenty seconds to those enigmatical trees again, then turned his face toward the camp,

He found himself wondering whether his editor would consider the story of how somebody thought he saw something black behind a clump of trees, and how a gun was fired at this "illusion" by somebody else, too trivial for public consultation?

"It's the only gleam of a shadow of interest," said the war correspondent, "for ten whole days."

"No," he said presently, "I'll write that other article, 'Is War Played Out?' "

He surveyed the darkling lines in perspective, the tangle of trenches one behind another, one commanding another, which the defender had made ready. The shadows and mists swallowed up their receding contours, and here and there a lantern gleamed, and here and there knots of men were busy about small fires. "No troops on earth could do it," he said.

He was depressed. He believed that there were other things in life better worth having than proficiency in war; he believed that in the heart of civilization, for all its stresses, its crushing concentrations of forces, its injustice and suffering, there lay something that might be the hope of the world, and the idea that any people by living in the open air, hunting perpetually, losing touch with books and art and all the things that intensify life, might hope to resist and break that great development to the end of time, jarred on his civilized soul.

Apt to his thought came a file of defender soldiers and passed him in the gleam of a swinging lamp that marked the way.

He glanced at their red-lit faces, and one shone out for a moment, a common type of face in the defender's ranks: ill-shaped nose, sensuous lips, bright clear eyes full of alert cunning, slouch hat cocked on one side and adorned with the peacock's plume of the rustic Don Juan–turned–soldier, a hard brown skin, a sinewy frame, an open, tireless stride, and a master's grip on the rifle.

The war correspondent returned their salutations and went on his way.

"Louts," he whispered. "Cunning, elementary louts. And they are going to beat the townsmen at the game of war!"

From the red glow among the nearer tents came first one and then half-a-dozen hearty voices, bawling in a drawling unison the words of a particularly slab and sentimental patriotic song.

"Oh, go it!" muttered the war correspondent, bitterly.

II

It was opposite the trenches called after Hackbone's Hut that the battle began. There the ground stretched broad and level between the lines, with scarcely shelter for a lizard, and it seemed to the startled, just–awakened men who came crowding into the trenches that this was one more proof of that green inexperience of the enemy of which they had heard so much. The war correspondent would not believe his ears at first, and swore that he and the war artist, who, still imperfectly roused, was trying to put on his boots by the light of a match held in his hand, were the victims of a common illusion. Then, after putting his head in a bucket of cold water, his intelligence came back as he toweled. He listened. "Gollys!" he said; "That's something more than scare–firing this time. It's like ten thousand carts on a bridge of tin."

There came a sort of enrichment to that steady uproar. "Machine guns!"

Then, "Guns!"

The artist, with one boot on, thought to look at his watch, and went to it hopping.

"Half an hour from dawn," he said.

"You were right about their attacking, after all. . . ."

The war correspondent came out of the tent, verifying the presence of chocolate in his pocket as he did so. He had to halt for a moment or so until his eyes were toned down to the night a little. "Pitch!" he said. He stood for a space to season his eyes before he felt justified in striking out for a black gap among the adjacent tents. The artist coming out behind him fell over a tent rope. It was half-past two o'clock in the morning of the darkest night in time, and against a sky of dull black silk the enemy was talking searchlights, a wild jabber of searchlights. "He's trying to blind our riflemen," said the war correspondent with a flash, and waited for the artist, and then set off with a sort of discreet haste again. "Whoa!" he said, presently. "Ditches!"

They stopped.

"It's the confounded searchlights," said the war correspondent.

They saw lanterns going to and fro, nearby, and men falling in to march down to the trenches. They were for following them, and then the artist began to feel his night eyes. "If we scramble this," he said, "and it's only a drain, there's a clear run up to the ridge." And that way they took. Lights came and went in the tents behind, as the men turned out, and ever and again they came to broken ground and staggered and stumbled. But in a little while they drew near the crest. Something that sounded like the impact of a very important railway accident happened in the air above them, and the shrapnel bullets seethed about them like a sudden handful of hail. "Right-ho!" said the war correspondent, and soon they judged they had come to the crest and stood in the midst of a world of great darkness and frantic glares, whose principal fact was sound.

Right and left of them and all about them was the uproar, an army-full of magazine fire, at first chaotic and monstrous and then, eked out by little flashes and gleams and suggestions, taking the beginnings of a shape. It looked to the war correspondent as though the enemy must have attacked in line and with his whole force—in which case he was either being or was already annihilated.

"Dawn and the Dead," he said, with his instinct for headlines. He said this to himself, but afterwards, by means of shouting, he conveyed an idea to the artist. "They must have meant it for a surprise," he said.

It was remarkable how the firing kept on. After a time he began to perceive a sort of rhythm in this inferno of noise. It would decline—decline perceptibly, droop towards something that was comparatively a pause—a pause of inquiry.

"Aren't you all dead yet?" this pause seemed to say. The flickering fringe of rifle flashes would become attenuated and broken, and the *whack-bang* of the enemy's big guns two miles away there would come up out of the deeps. Then suddenly, east or west of them, something would startle the rifles to a frantic outbreak again.

The war correspondent taxed his brain for some theory of conflict that would account for this, and was suddenly aware that the artist and he were vividly illuminated. He could see the ridge on which they stood and before them in black outline a file of riflemen hurrying down towards the nearer trenches. It became visible that a light rain was falling, and farther away towards the enemy was a clear space with men—"Our men?"—running across it in disorder. He saw one of those men throw up his hands and drop. And something else black and shining loomed up on the edge of the beam coruscating flashes; and behind it and far away a calm, white eye regarded the world. "Whit, whit, whit," sang something in the air, and then the artist was running for cover, with the war correspondent behind him. *Bang* came shrapnel, bursting close at hand as it seemed, and our two men were lying flat in a dip in the ground, and the light and everything had gone again, leaving a vast note of interrogation upon the night.

The war correspondent came within bawling range. "What the deuce was it? Shooting our men down!"

"Black," said the artist, "and like a fort. Not two hundred yards from the first trench."

He sought for comparisons in his mind. "Something between a big blockhouse and a giant's dish-cover," he said.

"And they were running!" said the war correspondent. "You'd run if a thing like that, searchlight to help it, turned up like a prowling nightmare in the middle of night."

They crawled to what they judged the edge of the dip and lay regarding the unfathomable dark. For a space they could distinguish nothing, and then a sudden convergence of the searchlights of both sides brought the strange thing out again. In that flickering pallor it had the effect of a large and clumsy black insect, an insect the size of an ironclad cruiser, crawling obliquely to the first line of trenches and firing shots out of portholes in its back.

And on its carcass the bullets must have been battering with more than the passionate violence of hail on a roof of tin.

Then in the twinkling of an eye the curtain of the dark had fallen again and the monster had vanished, but the crescendo of musketry marked its approach to the trenches.

They were beginning to talk about the thing to each other, when a flying bullet kicked dirt into the artist's face, and they decided abruptly to crawl down into the cover of the trenches. They had got down with an unobtrusive persistence into the second line before the dawn had grown clear enough for anything to be seen. They found themselves in a crowd of expectant riflemen, all noisily arguing about the thing that would happen next. The enemy's contrivance had done execution upon the outlying men, it seemed, but they did not believe it would do any more. "Come the day and we'll capture the lot of them," said a burly soldier.

"Them?" said the war correspondent.

"They say there's a regular string of 'em, crawling along the front of our lines. . . Who cares?"

The darkness filtered away so imperceptibly that at no moment could one declare decisively that one could see. The searchlights ceased to sweep hither and thither. The enemy's monsters were dubious patches of darkness upon the dark, and then no longer dubious, and so they crept out into distinctness. The war correspondent, munching chocolate absentmindedly, beheld at last a spacious picture of battle under the cheerless sky, whose central focus was an array of fourteen or fifteen huge clumsy shapes lying in perspective on the very edge of the first line of trenches, at intervals of perhaps three hundred yards, and evidently firing down upon the crowded riflemen. They were so close in that the defender's guns had ceased, and only the first line of trenches was in action.

The second line commanded the first, and as the light grew the war correspondent could make out the riflemen who were fighting these monsters, crouched in knots and crowds behind the transverse banks that crossed the trenches against the eventuality of an enfilade. The trenches close to the big machines were empty save for the crumpled suggestions of dead and wounded men; the defenders had been driven right and left as soon as the prow of this land ironclad had loomed up over the front of the trench. He produced his field-glass, and was immediately a center of inquiry from the soldiers about him.

They wanted to look, they asked questions, and after he had announced that the men across the traverses seemed unable to advance or retreat, and were crouching under cover rather than fighting, he found it advisable to loan his glasses to a burly and incredulous corporal. He heard a strident voice, and found a lean and sallow soldier at his back talking to the artist.

"There's chaps down there caught," the man was saying. "If they retreat they got to expose themselves, and the fire's too straight. . . ."

"They aren't firing much, but every shot's a hit."

"Who?"

"The chaps in that thing. The men who're coming up—"

"Coming up where?"

"We're evacuating them trenches where we can. Our chaps are coming back up the zigzags. . . . No end of 'em hit. . . . But when we get clear our turn'll come. Rather! These things won't be able to cross a trench or get into it; and before they can get back our guns'll smash 'em up. Smash 'em right up. See?" A brightness came into his eyes. "Then we'll have a go at the beggars inside," he said. . . .

The war correspondent thought for a moment, trying to realize the idea. Then he set himself to recover his field-glasses from the burly corporal. . . .

The daylight was getting clearer now. The clouds were lifting, and a gleam of lemon yellow amidst the level masses to the east portended sunrise. He looked again at the land ironclad. As he saw it in the bleak, grey dawn, lying obliquely upon the slope and on the very lip of the foremost trench, the suggestion of a stranded vessel was very great indeed. It might have been from eighty to a hundred feet long—it was about two hundred and fifty yards away–its vertical side was ten feet high or so, smooth for that height, and then with a complex patterning under the eaves of its flattish turtle cover. This patterning was a close interlacing of portholes, rifle barrels, and telescope tubes—sham and real—indistinguishable one from the other. The thing had come into such a position as to enfilade the trench, which was empty now, so far as he could see, except for two or three crouching knots of men and the tumbled-looking dead. Behind it, across the plain, it had scored the grass with a train of linked impressions, like the dotted tracings sea-things leave in sand. Left and right of that track dead men and wounded men were scattered—men it had picked off as they fled back from their advanced positions in the searchlight glare from the invader's lines. And now it lay with its head projecting a little over the trench it had won, as if it were a single sentient thing planning the next phase of its attack. . . .

He lowered his glasses and took a more comprehensive view of the situation. These creatures of the night had evidently won the first line of trenches and the fight had come to a pause. In the increasing light he could make out by a stray shot or a chance exposure that the defender's marksmen were lying thick in the second and third line of trenches up towards the low crest of the position, and in such of the zigzags as gave them a chance of a converging fire. The men about him were talking of the guns. "We're in the line of the big guns at the crest but they'll soon shift one to pepper them," the lean man said, reassuringly.

"Whup," said the corporal.

"*Bang! bang! bang! Whir-r-r-r.*" It was a sort of nervous jump and all the rifles were going off by themselves. The war correspondent found himself and the artist, two idle men crouching behind a line of pre-occupied backs of industrious men discharging magazines. The monster had moved. It continued to move regardless of the hail that splashed its skin with bright new specks of lead. It was singing a mechanical little ditty to itself, "*Tuf-tuf, tuf-tuf, tuf-tuf,*" and squirting out little jets of steam behind. It had humped itself up, as a limpet does before it crawls; it had lifted its skirt and displayed along the length of it—*feet*! They were thick, stumpy feet, between knobs and buttons in shape-flat, broad things, reminding one of the feet of elephants or the legs of caterpillars; and then, as the skirt rose higher, the war correspondent, scrutinizing the thing through his glasses again, saw that these feet hung, as it were, on the rims of wheels. His thoughts whirled back to Victoria Street, Westminster, and he saw himself in the piping times of peace, seeking matter for an interview.

"Mr.—Mr. Diplock," he said; "and he called them Pedrails . . . Fancy meeting them here!"

The marksman beside him raised his head and shoulders in a speculative mood to fire more certainly—it seemed so natural to assume the attention of the monster must be distracted by this trench before it—and was suddenly knocked backwards by a bullet through his neck. His feet flew up, and he vanished out of the margin of the watcher's field of vision. The war correspondent groveled tighter, but after a glance behind him at a painful little confusion, he resumed his field-glass, for the thing was putting down its feet one after the other, and hoisting itself farther and farther over the trench. Only a bullet in the head could have stopped him looking just then.

The lean man with the strident voice ceased firing to turn and reiterate his point. "They can't possibly cross," he bawled. "They—"

"*Bang! Bang! Bang, bang!*"—drowned everything.

The lean man continued speaking for a word or so, then gave it up, shook his head to enforce the impossibility of anything crossing a trench like the one below, and resumed business once more.

And all the while that great bulk was crossing. When the war correspondent turned his glass on it again it had bridged the trench, and its queer feet were rasping away at the farther bank, in the attempt to get a hold there. It got its hold. It continued to crawl until the greater bulk or it was over the trench—until it was all over. Then it paused for a moment, adjusted its skirt a little nearer the ground, give an unnerving "*toot, toot,*" and came on abruptly at a pace of, perhaps, six miles an hour straight up the gentle slope towards our observer.

The war correspondent raised himself on his elbow and looked a natural inquiry at the artist.

For a moment the men about him stuck to their position and fired furiously. Then the lean man in a mood of precipitancy slid backwards, and the war correspondent said "Come along," to the artist, and led the movement along the trench. As they dropped down, the vision of a hillside of trench being rushed by a dozen vast cockroaches disappeared for a space, and instead was one of a narrow passage, crowded with men, for the most part receding, though one or two turned or halted. He never turned back to see the nose of the monster creep over the brow of the trench; he never even troubled to keep in touch with the artist. He heard the "whit" of bullets about him soon enough, and saw a man before him stumble and drop, and then he was one of a furious crowd fighting to get into a transverse zigzag ditch that enabled the defenders to get under cover up and down the hill. It was like a theatre panic. He gathered from signs and fragmentary words that on ahead another of these monsters had also won to the second trench.

He lost his interest in the general course of the battle for a space altogether; he became simply a modest egotist, in a mood of hasty circumspection, seeking the farthest rear, amidst a dispersed multitude of disconcerted riflemen similarly employed. He scrambled down through trenches, he took his courage in both hands and sprinted across the open, he had moments of panic when it seemed madness not to be quadrupedal, and moments of shame when he stood up and faced about to see how the fight was going. And he was one of many thousand very similar men that morning. On the ridge he halted in a knot of scrub, and was for a few minutes almost minded to stop and see things out.

The day was now fully come. The grey sky had changed to blue, and of all the cloudy masses of the dawn there remained only a few patches of dissolving fleeciness. The world below was bright and singularly clear. The ridge was not, perhaps, more than a hundred feet or so above the general plain, but in this flat region it sufficed to give the effect of extensive view. Away on the north side of the ridge, little and far, were the camps, the ordered wagons, all the gear of a big army; with officers galloping about and men doing aimless things, Here and there men were falling in, however, and the cavalry was forming up on the plain beyond the tents. The bulk of men who had been in the trenches were still on the move to the rear, scattered like sheep without a shepherd over the farther slopes. Here and there were little rallies and attempts to wait and do something vague; but the general drift was away from any concentration. Then on the southern side was the elaborate lacework of trenches and defenses, across which these iron turtles, fourteen of them spread out over a line of perhaps three miles, were now advancing as fast as a man could trot, and methodically shooting down and breaking up any persistent knots of resistance. Here and there stood little clumps of men, outflanked and unable to get away, showing the white flag, and the invader's cyclist infantry was advancing now across the open, in open order but unmolested, to complete the work of the machines. So far as the day went, the defenders already looked a beaten army. A mechanism that effectually ironclad against bullets, that could at a pinch cross a thirty-foot trench, and that seemed able to shoot out rifle bullets with unerring precision, was clearly an inevitable victor against anything but rivers, precipices, and guns.

He looked at his watch. "Half-past four! Lord! What things can happen in two hours. Here's the whole blessed army being walked over, and at half-past two—

"And even now our blessed louts haven't done a thing with their guns!"

He scanned the ridge right and left of him with his glasses. He turned again to the nearest land ironclad, advancing now obliquely to him and not three hundred yards away, and then scrambled the ground over which he must retreat if he was not to be captured.

"They'll do nothing," he said, and glanced again at the enemy. And then from far away to the left came the thud of a gun, followed very rapidly by a rolling gunfire. He hesitated and decided to stay.

III

The defender had relied chiefly upon his rifles in the event of an assault. His guns he kept concealed at various points upon and behind the ridge ready to bring them into action against any artillery preparations for an attack on the part of his antagonist. The situation had rushed upon him with the dawn, and by the time the gunners had their guns ready for motion, the land ironclads were already in among the foremost trenches. There is a natural reluctance to fire into one's own broken men, and many of the guns, being intended simply to fight an advance of the enemy's artillery, were not in positions to hit anything in the second line of trenches. After that the advance of the land ironclads was swift. The defender-general found himself suddenly called upon to invent a new sort of warfare, in which guns were to fight alone amidst broken and retreating infantry. He had scarcely thirty minutes in which to think it out. He did not respond to the call, and what happened that morning was that the advance of the land ironclads forced the fight, and each gun and battery made what play its circumstances dictated. For the most part it was poor play.

Some of the guns got in two or three shots, some one or two, and the percentage of misses was unusually high. The howitzers, of course, did nothing. The land ironclads in each case followed much the same tactics. As soon as a gun came into play the monster turned itself almost end on, so as to get the biggest chance of a glancing hit, and made not for the gun, but for the nearest point on its flank from which the gunners could be shot down. Few of the hits scored were very effectual; only one of the things was disabled, and that was the one that fought the three batteries attached to the brigade on the left wing. Three that were hit when close upon the guns were clean shot through without being put out of action. Our war correspondent did not see that one momentary arrest of the tide of victory on the left; he saw only the very ineffectual fight of half-battery 96B close at hand upon his right. This he watched some time beyond the margin of safety.

Just after he heard the three batteries opening up upon his left he became aware of the thud of horses' hoofs from the sheltered side of the slope, and presently saw first one and then two other guns galloping into position along the north side of the ridge, well out of sight of the great bulk that was now creeping obliquely towards the crest and cutting up the lingering infantry beside it and below, as it came.

The half-battery swung round into line—each gun describing its curve—halted, unlimbered, and prepared for action.

Bang!

The land ironclad had become visible over the brow of the hill, and just visible as a long black back to the gunners. It halted, as though it hesitated.

The two remaining guns fired, and then their big antagonist had swung round and was in full view, end on, against the sky, coming at a rush.

The gunners became frantic in their haste to fire again. They were so near the war correspondent could see the expressions on their excited faces through his field-glass. As he looked he saw a man drop, and realized for the first time that the ironclad was shooting.

For a moment the big black monster crawled with an accelerated pace towards the furiously active gunners. Then, as if moved by a generous impulse, it turned its full broadside to their attack, and scarcely forty yards away from them. The war correspondent turned his field-glass back to the gunners and perceived it was now shooting down the men about the guns with the most deadly rapidity.

Just for a moment it seemed splendid and then it seemed horrible. The gunners were dropping in heaps about their guns. To lay a hand on a gun was death. *Bang!* went the gun on the left, a hopeless miss, and that was the only second shot the half-battery fired. In another moment half-a-dozen surviving artillerymen were holding up their hands amidst a scattered muddle of dead and wounded men, and the fight was done.

The war correspondent hesitated between stopping in his scrub and waiting for an opportunity to surrender decently, or taking to an adjacent gully he had discovered. If he surrendered it was certain he would get no copy off; while, if he escaped, there were all sorts of chances. He decided to follow the gully, and take the first offer in the confusion beyond the camp of picking up a horse.

IV

Subsequent authorities have found fault with the first land ironclads in many particulars, but assuredly they served their purpose on the day of their appearance. They were essentially long, narrow, and very strong steel frameworks carrying the engines, and borne upon eight pairs of big pedrail wheels, each about ten feet in diameter, each a driving wheel and set upon long axles free to swivel round a common axis. This arrangement gave them the maximum of adaptability to the contours of the ground. They crawled level along the ground with one foot high upon a hillock and another deep in a depression, and they could hold themselves erect and steady sideways upon even a steep hillside. The engineers directed the engines under the command of the captain, who had lookout points at small ports all round the upper edge of the adjustable skirt of twelve-inch iron-plate which protected the whole affair, and could also raise or depress a conning-tower set about the portholes through the center of the iron top-cover. The riflemen each occupied a small cabin of peculiar construction and these cabins were slung along the sides of and before and behind the great main framework, in a manner suggestive of the slinging of the seats of an Irish jaunting car. Their rifles, however, were very different pieces of apparatus from the simple mechanisms in the hands of their adversaries.

These were in the first place automatic, ejected their cartridges and loaded again from a magazine each time they fired, until the ammunition store was at an end, and they had the most remarkable sights imaginable, sights which threw a bright little camera-obscura picture into the light-tight box in which the rifleman sat below. This camera-obscura picture was marked with two crossed lines, and whatever was covered by the intersection of these two lines, that the rifle hit. The sighting was ingeniously contrived. The rifleman stood at the table with a thing like an elaboration of a draughtsman's dividers in his hand, and he opened and closed these dividers, so that they were always at the apparent height—if it was an ordinary, size man—of the man he wanted to kill. A little twisted strand of wire like an electric-light wire ran from this implement up to the gun, and as the dividers opened and shut the sights went up or down. Changes in the clearness of the atmosphere, due to changes of moisture, were met by an ingenious use of that media sensitive substance, catgut, and when the land ironclad moved forward the sights got a compensatory deflection in the direction of its motion. The riflemen stood out in his pitch dark chamber and watched a little picture before him. One hand held the dividers for judging distance, and the other grasped a big knob like a door handle. As he pushed this knob about the rifle above swung to correspond, and the picture passed to and fro like an agitated panorama. When he saw a man he wanted to shoot he brought him up to the cross-lines, and then pressed a finger upon a little push like an electric-bell push, conveniently placed in the center of the knob. Then the man was shot. If by any chance the rifleman missed his target he moved the knob a trifle, or readjusted his dividers, pressed the push, and got him the second time.

This rifle and its sights protruded from a porthole, exactly like a great number of other portholes that ran in a triple row under the eaves of the cover of the land ironclad. Each porthole displayed a rifle and sight in dummy, so that the real ones could only be hit by a chance shot, and if one was, then the young man below said "Pshaw!" turned on an electric light, lowered the injured instrument into his camera, replaced the injured part, or put up a new rifle if the injury was considerable.

You must conceive these cabins as hung clear above the swing of the axles, and inside the big wheels upon which the great elephant-like feet were hung, and behind these cabins along the center of the monster ran a central gallery into which they opened, and along which worked the big compact engines. It was like a long passage into which this throbbing machinery had been packed, and the captain stood about the middle, close to the ladder that led to his conning-tower, and directed the silent, alert engineers—for the most part by signs. The throb and noise of the engines mingled with the reports of the rifles and the intermittent clangor of the bullet hail upon the armor. Ever and again he would touch the wheel that raised his conning tower, step up his ladder until his engineers could see nothing of him above the waist, and then come down again with orders. Two small electric lights were all the illumination of this space—they were placed to make him most clearly visible to his subordinates; the air was thick with the smell of oil and petrol, and had the war correspondent been suddenly transferred from the spacious dawn outside to the bowels of the apparatus he would have thought himself fallen into another world.

The captain, of course, saw both sides of the battle. When he raised his head into his conning-tower there were the dewy sunrise, the amazed and disordered trenches, the flying and falling soldiers, the depressed looking groups of prisoners, the beaten guns; when he bent down again to signal "Half speed," "Quarter speed," "Half circle round towards the right," or whatnot, he was in the oil-smelling twilight of the ill-lit engine room. Close beside him on either side was the mouthpiece of a speaking tube, and ever and again he would direct one side or other of his strange craft to "Concentrate fire forward on gunners," or to "Clear out trench about a hundred yards on our right front."

He was a young man, healthy enough but by no means suntanned, and of a type of feature and expression that prevails in His Majesty's Navy: alert, intelligent, quiet. He and his engineers and his riflemen all went about their work, calm and reasonable men. They had none of that flapping strenuousness of the half-wit in a hurry, that excessive strain upon the blood vessels, that hysteria of effort which is so frequently regarded as the proper state of mind for heroic deeds. If their machine had demanded anything of the sort they would, of course, have improved their machine. They were all perfectly sober and in good training, and if any of them had begun to ejaculate nonsense or bawl patriotic airs, the others would probably have gagged him and tied him up as a dangerous, unnerving sort of fool. And if they were free from hysteria they were equally free from that stupid affectation of nonchalance which is the refuge of the thoroughly incapable in danger. Death was abroad, and there were marginal possibilities of the unforeseen, but it is no good calculating upon the incalculable, and so beyond a certain unavoidable tightening up of nerve and muscle, a certain firmness of the lips, this affected them not at all.

For the enemy these young engineers were defeating they felt a certain qualified pity and a quite unqualified contempt. They regarded these big, healthy men they were shooting down precisely as these same big, healthy men might regard some inferior kind of nigger. They despised them for making war; despised their bawling patriotisms and their emotionality profoundly; despised them, above all, for the petty cunning and the almost brutish want of imagination their method of fighting displayed. "If they must make war," these young men thought, "why in thunder don't they do it like sensible men?" They resented the assumption that their own side was too stupid to do anything more than play their enemy's game, that they were going to play this costly folly according to the rules of unimaginative men. They resented being forced to the trouble of making man-killing machinery; resented the alternative of having to massacre these people or endure their truculent yappings; resented the whole unfathomable imbecility of war.

Meanwhile, with something of the mechanical precision of a good clerk posting a ledger, the riflemen moved their knobs and pressed their buttons. . . .

The captain of Land Ironclad Number Three had halted on the crest close to his captured half-battery. His lined-up prisoners stood hard by and waited for the cyclists behind to come for them. He surveyed the victorious morning through his conning-tower. He read the general's signals. "Five and Four are to keep among the guns to the left and prevent any attempt to recover them. Seven and Eleven and Twelve, stick to the guns you have got; Seven, get into position to command the guns taken by Three. Then, we're to do something else, are we? Six and One, quicken up to about ten miles an hour and walk round behind that camp to the levels near the river—we shall bag the whole crowd of them," interjected the young man. "Ah, here we are! Two and Three, Eight and Nine,

Thirteen and Fourteen, space out to a thousand yards, wait for the word, and then go slowly to cover the advance of the cyclist infantry against any charge of mounted troops. That's all right. But where's Ten? Halloa! Ten to repair and get movable as soon as possible. They've broken up Ten!"

The discipline of the new war machines was business-like rather than pedantic, and the head of the captain came down out of the conning-tower to tell his men. "I say, you chaps there. They've broken up Ten. Not badly, I think; but anyhow, he's stuck!"

But that still left thirteen of the monsters in action to finish up the broken army.

The war correspondent stealing down his gully looked back and saw them all lying along the crest and talking, fluttering congratulatory flags to one another. Their iron sides were shining golden in the light of the rising sun.

V

The private adventures of the war correspondent terminated in surrender about one o'clock in the afternoon, and by that time he had stolen a horse, pitched off it, and narrowly escaped being rolled upon; found the brute had broken its leg, and shot it with his revolver. He had spent some hours in the company of a squad of dispirited riflemen, who had commandeered his field-glass and whose pedestrianism was exemplary, and he had quarreled with them about topography at last, and gone off by himself in a direction that should have brought him to the banks of the river and didn't. Moreover, he had eaten all his chocolate and found nothing in the whole world to drink. Also, it had become extremely hot. From behind a broken, but attractive, stone wall he had seen far away in the distance the defender horsemen trying to charge cyclists in open order, with land ironclads outflanking them on either side. He had discovered that cyclists could retreat over open turf before horsemen with a sufficient margin of speed to allow of frequent dismounts and much terribly effective sharpshooting and he had a sufficient persuasion that those horsemen, having charged their hearts out, had halted just beyond his range of vision and surrendered. He had been urged to sudden activity by a forward movement of one of those machines that had threatened to enfilade his wall. He had discovered a fearful blister on his heel.

He was now in a scrubby gravelly place, sitting down and meditating on his pocket-handkerchief, which had in some extraordinary way become in the last twenty-four hours extremely ambiguous in hue. "It's the whitest thing I've got," he said.

He had known all along that the enemy was east, west, and south of him, but when he heard war ironclads Numbers One and Six talking in their measured, deadly way not half a mile to the north he decided to make his own little unconditional peace without any further risks. He was for hoisting his white flag to a bush and taking up a position of modest obscurity near it, until someone came along. He became aware of voices, clatter, and the distinctive noises of a body of horses, quite near, and he put his handkerchief in his pocket again and went to see what was going forward.

The sound of firing ceased, and then as he drew near he heard the deep sounds of many simple, coarse, but hearty and noble-hearted soldiers of the old school swearing with vigor.

He emerged from his scrub upon a big level plain, and far away a fringe of trees marked the banks of the river.

In the center of the picture was a still intact road bridge, and a big railway bridge a little to the right. Two land ironclads rested, with a general air of being long, harmless sheds, in a pose of anticipatory peacefulness right and left of the picture, completely commanding two miles and more of the river levels. Emerged and halted a little from the scrub was the remainder of the defender's cavalry, dusty, a little disordered and obviously annoyed, but still a very fine show of men. In the middle distance three or four men and horses were receiving medical attendance, and a little nearer a knot of officers regarded the distant novelties in mechanism with profound distaste. Everyone was very distinctly aware of the twelve other ironclads, and of the multitude of townsmen soldiers, on bicycles or afoot, encumbered now by prisoners and captured war gear but otherwise thoroughly effective, who were sweeping like a great net in their rear.

"Checkmate," said the war correspondent, walking out into the open. "But I surrender in the best of company. Twenty-four hours ago I thought war was impossible—and these beggars have captured the whole blessed army! Well! Well!" He thought of his talk with the young lieutenant. "If there's no end to the surprises of science, the civilized people have it, of course. As long as their science keeps going they will necessarily be ahead of open-country men. Still. . ."

He wondered for a space what might have happened to the young lieutenant.

The war correspondent was one of those inconsistent people who always want the beaten side to win. When he saw all these burly, sun-tanned horsemen, disarmed and dismounted and lined up; when he saw their horses unskillfully led away by the singularly not equestrian cyclists to whom they had surrendered; when he saw these truncated Paladins watching this scandalous sight, he forgot altogether that he had called these men "cunning louts" and wished them beaten not four-and-twenty hours ago. A month ago he had seen that regiment in its pride going forth to war, and had been told of its terrible prowess, how it could charge in open order with each man firing from his saddle, and sweep before it anything else that ever came out to battle in any sort of order, foot or horse. And it had had to fight a few score of young men in atrociously unfair machines!

"Manhood *versus* Machinery" occurred to him as a suitable headline. Journalism curdles all one's mind to phrases.

He strolled as near the lined-up prisoners as the sentinels seemed disposed to permit and surveyed them and compared their sturdy proportions with those of their lightly built captors.

"Smart degenerates," he muttered. "Anemic cockneydom."

The surrendered officers came quite close to him presently, and he could hear the colonel's high-pitched tenor. The poor gentleman had spent three years of arduous toil upon the best material in the world perfecting that shooting from the saddle charge, and he was mourning with phrases of blasphemy, natural under the circumstances what one could be expected to do against this suitably consigned ironmongery.

"Guns," said someone.

"Big guns they can walk round. You can't shift big guns to keep pace with them and little guns in the open they rush. I saw 'em rushed. You might do a surprise now and then—assassinate the brutes, perhaps—"

"You might make things like 'em."

"What? *More* ironmongery? Us?"

"I'll call my article," meditated the war correspondent, " 'Mankind *versus* Ironmongery,' and quote the old boy at the beginning."

And he was much too good a journalist to spoil his contrast by remarking that the half-dozen comparatively slender young men in blue pajamas who were standing about their victorious land ironclad, drinking coffee and eating biscuits, had also in their eyes and carriage something not altogether degraded below the level of a man.

— CLEVE CARTMILL —

"DEADLINE"

■ *Astounding*, **March 1944**

"**D**eadline" posits an atomic bomb using U-235, as did the first actual bombs. The story was written and published during the time of the Manhattan Project and, because of its resemblance to actual research, the FBI and the Army Counter Intelligence Corps investigated both Cleve Cartmill and John Campbell of *Astounding Stories*, where the story first appeared. A complete history of the story and the subsequent investigations would take more space than we have here.

For Judith, "Deadline" is a family story: "My mother was married to Cleve Cartmill when he wrote 'Deadline,' although I am not related to him. This story is so notorious that there are stories told about the story. Many have said they thought 'Cleve Cartmill' was a pseudonym and are surprised when I tell them that's not true.

"One person told me that 'Deadline' suggested a line of investigation to the scientists at Los Alamos that didn't work. There is also the story among book dealers that the March 1944 issue of *Astounding* is difficult to find because the FBI bought 90 percent of the copies from newsstands or removed them from the distributor's loading docks. Whether either the Los Alamos story or the FBI acquiring copies of the magazine are true I do not know."

For a thorough history of the investigations, see Robert Silverberg's "The Cartmill Affair" at *Asimov's Science Fiction Magazine*, October and November 2003 (available online at http://www.asimovs.com/_issue_0310/ref.shtml and http://www.asimovs.com/_issue_0311/ref2.shtml).

DEADLINE

❧

Cleve Cartmill

DETONATION AND ASSEMBLY

1 2.16. As stated in Chapter II, it is impossible to prevent a chain reaction from occurring when the size exceeds the critical size. For there are always enough neutrons (from cosmic rays, from spontaneous fission reactions, or from alpha-particle-induced reactions in impurities) to initiate the chain. Thus until detonation is desired, the bomb must consist of a number of separate pieces each one of which is below the critical size either by reason of small size or unfavorable shape. To produce detonation, the parts of the bomb must be brought together rapidly. In the course of this assembly process the chain reaction is likely to start—because of the presence of stray neutrons—before the bomb has reached its most compact (most reactive) form. Thereupon the explosion tends to prevent the bomb from reaching that most compact form. Thus it may turn out that the explosion is so inefficient as to be relatively useless. The problem, therefore, is two-fold: (1) to reduce the time of assembly to a minimum; and (2) to reduce the number of stray (predetonation) neutrons to a minimum.

Official Report: Atomic Energy for Military Purposes
Henry D. Smyth

❧❧

Heavy flak burst above and below the flight of bombers as they flashed across the night sky of the planet Cathor. Ybor Sebrof grinned as he nosed his glider at a steep angle away from the fireworks. The bombers had accomplished their mission: they had dropped him near Nilreq, had simulated a raid.

He had cut loose before searchlights slatted the sky with lean, white arms. They hadn't touched the glider, marked with their own insignia. Their own glider, in fact, captured when Seilla advance columns had caught the Namo garrison asleep. He would leave it where he landed, and let Sixa intelligence try to figure out how it got there.

Provided, of course, that he landed unseen.

Sixa intelligence officers would have another job, too. That was to explain the apparent bombing raid that dropped no bombs. None of the Seilla planes had been hit, and the Sixa crowd couldn't know that the bombers were empty: no bombs, no crews, just speed.

He could see tomorrow's papers, hear tomorrow's newscasts. "Raiders driven off. Craven Democracy pilots cringe from Nilreq ack-ack." But the big bugs would worry. The Seilla planes could have dropped bombs, if they'd had any bombs. They had flitted across the great industrial city with impunity. They could have laid their eggs. The big bugs would wonder about that. Why? they would ask each other profoundly. What was the reason?

Ybor, grinned. He was the reason. He'd make them wish there had been bombs instead of him. Possibility of failure never entered his mind. All he had to do was to penetrate into the stronghold of the enemy, find Dr. Sitruc, kill him, and destroy the most devastating weapon in history. That was all.

He caught a sharp breath as a farmhouse loomed some distance ahead, and veered over against the dark edge of a wood. The green-grey plane would be invisible against the background, unless keen eyes caught its shadow under a fugitive moon.

He glided silently now, on a little wind that gossiped with treetops. Only the wind and the trees remarked on his passing. They could keep the secret.

He landed in a field of grain that whispered fierce protest as the glider whished through its heavy-laden plumes. These waved above the level of the motorless ship, and Ybor decided that it would not be seen before harvesting machines gathered the grain.

The air was another problem. He did not want the glider discovered just yet, particularly if he should be intercepted on his journey into the enemy capital. Elementary intelligence would connect him with this abandoned ship if he were stopped in this vicinity for any reason, and if the ship should be discovered on the morrow.

He took a long knife from its built-in sheath in the glider and laid about him with it until he had cut several armloads of grain. He scattered these haphazardly—not in any pattern—over parts of the ship. It wouldn't look like a glider now, even from the air.

He pushed through the shoulder-high growth to the edge of the wood.

He moved stealthily here. It was almost a certainty that big guns were hidden here, and he must avoid discovery. He slipped along the soft carpet of vegetation like a nocturnal cat, running on all fours under low branches, erect when possible.

A sharp scent of danger assailed his nostrils, and he crouched motionless while he sifted this odor. It made a picture in his head: men, and oil, and the acrid smoke of exploded gases. A gun crew was directly ahead.

Ybor took to the trees. He moved from one to the other, with no more sound than soft-winged night birds, and approached the source of the odor. He paused now and then, listening for a sentry's footsteps.

He heard them presently, a soft *pad-pad* which mingled, in different rhythm, with snores which became audible on the light wind.

The better part of valor, Ybor knew, was to circle this place, to leave the sentry unaware of his passage through the wood. But habit was too strong. He must destroy, for they were the enemy.

He moved closer to the sound of footsteps. Presently, he crouched above the line of the sentry's march, searching the darkness with eye and ear. The guard passed below, and Ybor let him go. His ears strained through snores from nearby tents until he heard another guard. Two were on sentry duty.

He pulled the knife from his belt and waited. When the sentry shuffled below him, Ybor dropped soundlessly onto the man's shoulders, stabbing as he fell.

There was a little noise. Not much, but a little. Enough to bring a low-voiced hail from the other guard.

"Namreh?" called the guard. "What happened?"

Ybor grunted, took the dead man's gun and helmet and took over his beat. He marched with the same rhythm the enemy feet had maintained until he met the second guard. Ybor silenced questions with a swift slash of the knife, and then turned his attention to the tents.

Presently, it was done. He clamped the fingers of the first guard around the knife hilt and went away. Let them think that one of their men had gone mad and killed the others before suiciding. Let the psychologists get a little workout on this.

When he had penetrated to the far edge of the wood, dawn had splashed pale color beyond Nilreq, pulling jumbled buildings into dark silhouette. There lay his area of operations. There, perhaps, lay his destiny, and the destiny of the whole race.

This latter thought was not born of rhetorical hyperbole. It was cold, hard fact. It had nothing to do with patriotism, nor was it concerned with politico-economic philosophy. It was concerned with a scientific fact only: if the weapon, which was somewhere in the enemy capital, were used, the entire race might very well perish, down to the last man.

Now began the difficult part of Ybor's task. He started to step out of the wood. A slight sound from behind froze him for a fraction of a second while he identified it. Then, in one incredibly swift motion, he whirled and flung himself at its source.

He knew he was fighting a woman after the first instant of contact. He was startled to some small extent, but not enough to impair his efficiency. A chopping blow, and she lay unconscious at his feet. He stood over her with narrowed eyes, unable to see what she looked like in the leafy gloom.

Then dawn burst like a salvo in the east, and he saw that she was young. Not immature, by any means, but young. When a spear of sunlight stabbed into the shadow, he saw that she was lovely.

Ybor pulled out his combat knife. She was an enemy, and must be destroyed. He raised his arm for the coup de grâce, and held it there. He could not drive the blade into her. She seemed only to sleep, in her unconsciousness, with parted ripe lips and limp hands. You could kill a man while he slept, but Nature had planted a deep aversion in your instincts to kill a helpless female.

She began to moan softly. Presently she opened her wide brown eyes, soft as a captive fawn's.

"You hit me." She whispered the accusation.

Ybor said nothing.

"You hit me," she repeated.

"What did you expect?" he asked harshly. "Candy and flowers? What are you doing here?"

"Following you," she answered. "May I get up?"

"Yes. Why were you following?"

"When I saw you land in our field, I wondered why. I ran out to see you cover your ship and slip into the woods. I followed."

Ybor was incredulous. "You followed me through those woods?"

"I could have touched you," she said. "Any time."

"You lie!"

"Don't feel chagrined," she said. She flowed to her feet in a liquid movement. Her eyes were almost on a level with his. Her smile showed small, white teeth. "I'm very good at that sort of thing," she said. "Better than almost anybody, though I admit you're no slouch."

"Thanks," he said shortly. "All right, let's hear the story. Most likely it'll be the last you'll ever tell. What's your game?"

"You speak Ynamren like a native," the girl said.

Ybor's eyes glinted. "I am a native."

She smiled her disbelief. "And you kill your own soldiers? I think not. I saw you wipe out that gun crew. There was too much objectivity about you. One of us would do it with hatred. For you, it was a tactical maneuver."

"You're cutting your own throat," Ybor warned. "I can't let you go. You're too observing."

She repeated, "I think not." After a pause, she said, "You'll need help, whatever your mission. I can offer it."

He was contemptuous. "You offer my head a lion's mouth. I can hide it there? I need no help. Especially from anybody clumsy enough to be caught. And I've caught you, my pretty."

She flushed. "You were about to storm a rampart. I saw it in your odd face as you stared toward Nilreq. I caught my breath with hope that you could. That's what you heard. If I'd thought you were my enemy, you'd have heard nothing. Except, maybe, the song of my knife blade as it reached your heart."

"What's odd about my face?" he demanded. "It'd pass in a crowd without notice."

"Women would notice it," she said. "It's lopsided."

He shrugged aside the personal issue. He took her throat in his hands. "I have to do this," he said. "It's highly important that nobody knows of my presence here. This is war. I can't afford to be humane."

She offered no resistance. Quietly, she looked up at him and asked, "Have you heard of Ylas?"

His fingers did not close on the soft flesh. "Who has not?"

"I am Ylas," she said.

"A trick."

"No trick. Let me show you." As his eyes narrowed— "No, I have no papers, of course. Listen. You know Mulb, Sworb, and Nomos? I got them away."

Ybor hesitated. She could be Ylas, but it would be a fantastic stroke of luck to run into the fabulous director of Ynamre's Underground so soon. It was almost beyond belief. Yet, there was a chance she was telling the truth. He couldn't overlook that chance.

"Names," he said. "You could have heard them anywhere."

"Nomos has a new-moon scar on his wrist," she said. "Sworb is tall, almost as tall as you, and his shoulders droop slightly. He talks so fast you can hardly follow. Mulb is a dope. He gets by on his pontifical manner."

These, Ybor reflected, were crisp thumbnail sketches.

She pressed her advantage. "Would I have stood by while you killed that gun crew if I were a loyal member of the Sixa Alliance? Wouldn't I have cried a warning when you killed the first guard and took his helmet and gun?"

There was logic in this, Ybor thought.

"Wasn't it obvious to me," she went on, "that you were a Seilla agent from the moment that you landed in my grain field? I could have telephoned the authorities."

Ybor took his hands from her throat. "I want to see Dr. Sitruc," he said.

She frowned off toward Nilreq, at towers golden in morning sunlight. Ybor noted indifferently that she made a colorful picture with her face to the sun. A dark flower, opening toward the dawn. Not that it mattered. He had no time for her. He had little time for anything.

"That will take some doing," she said.

He turned away. "Then I'll do it myself. Time is short."

"Wait!" Her voice had a quality which caused him to turn. He smiled sourly at the gun in her hand.

Self-contempt blackened Ybor's thoughts. He had had her helpless, but he had thought of her as a woman, not as an armed enemy. He hadn't searched her because of callow sentimentality. He had scaled the heights of stupidity, and now would plunge to his deserved end. Her gun was steady, and purpose shone darkly in her eyes.

"I'm a pushover for a fairy tale," she said. "I thought for a while that you really were a Seilla agent. How fiendishly clever you are, you and your council! I should have known when those planes went over. They went too fast."

Ybor said nothing. He was trying to absorb this.

"It was a smart idea," she went on in her acid, bitter voice. "They towed you over, and you landed in my field. A coincidence, when you come to think of it. I have been in that farmhouse only three days. Of all places, you pick it. Not by accident, not so. You and the other big minds on the Sixa council knew the planes would bring me to my window, knew my eyes would catch the shadow of your glider, knew I'd investigate. You even killed six of your own men, to dull my suspicions. Oh, I was taken in for a while."

"You talk like a crazy woman," Ybor said. "Put away that gun."

"When you had a chance to kill me and didn't," she said, "my last suspicion died. The more fool I. No, my bucko, you are not going back to report my whereabouts, to have your goons wait until my committee meets and catch us all. Not so. You die here and now."

Thoughts raced through Ybor's head. It would be a waste of energy; to appeal to her on the ground that if she killed him she would in effect destroy her species. That smacked of oratory. He needed a simple appeal, crisp and startling. But what? His time was running short; he could see it in her dark eyes.

"Your last address," he said, remembering Sworb's tale of escape, "was 40 Curk Way. You sold pastries, and Sworb got sick on little cakes. He was sick in your truck, as it carted him away at eleven minutes past midnight."

Bull's eye. Determination to kill went out of her eyes as she remembered. She was thoughtful for a moment.

Then her eyes glinted. "I've not heard that he reached Acireb safely. You could have caught him across the Enarta border and beaten the truth out of him. Still," she reflected, "you may be telling the truth . . . "

"I am," Ybor said quietly. "I am a Seilla agent, here on a highly important mission. If you can't aid me directly, you must let me go. At once."

"You might be lying, too, though. I can't take the chance. You will march ahead of me around the wood. If you make one overt move, or even a move that I don't understand, I'll kill you."

"Where are you taking me?"

"To my house. Where else? Then we'll talk."

"Now listen to me," he said passionately, "there is no time for—"

"March!"

He marched.

Ybor's plan to take her unawares when they were inside the farmhouse dissolved when he saw the great hulk who admitted them. This was a lumpish brute with the most powerful body Ybor had ever seen, towering over his own more than average height. The man's arms were as thick as Ybor's thighs, and the yellow eyes were small and vicious. Yet, apelike though he was, the giant moved like a mountain cat, without sound, with deceptive swiftness.

"Guard him," the girl commanded, and Ybor knew the yellow eyes would not leave him.

He sank into a chair, an old chair with a primitive tail slot, and watched the girl as she busied herself at the mountainous cooking range. This kitchen could accommodate a score of farmhands, and that multiple-burner stove could turn out hot meals for all.

"We'd better eat," she said. "If you're not lying, you'll need strength. If you are, you can withstand torture long enough to tell us the truth."

"You're making a mistake," Ybor began hotly, but stopped when the guard made a menacing gesture.

She had a meal on the table soon. It was a good meal, and he ate it heartily. "The condemned man," he said, and smiled.

For a camaraderie had sprung up between them. He was male, not too long past his youth, with clear, dark eyes, and he was put together with an eye to efficiency; and she was a female, at the ripening stage. The homey task of preparing a meal, of sharing it, lessened the tension between them. She gave him a fleeting, occasional smile as he tore into his food.

"You're a good cook," he said, when they had finished.

Warmth went out of her. She eyed him steadily. "Now," she said crisply. "Proof."

Ybor shrugged angrily. "Do you think I carry papers identifying me as a Seilla agent? 'To whom it may concern, bearer is high in Seilla councils. Any aid you may give him will be appreciated.' I have papers showing that I'm a newspaper man from Eeras. The newspaper offices and building have been destroyed by now, and there is no means of checking."

She thought this over. "I'm going to give you a chance," she said. "If you're a top-flight Seilla agent, one of your Nilreq men can identify you. Name one, and we'll get him here."

"None of them know me by sight. My face was altered before I came on this assignment, so that nobody could give me away, even accidentally."

"You know all the answers, don't you?" she scoffed. "Well, we will now take you into the cellar and get the truth from you. And you won't die until we do. We'll keep you alive, one way or another."

"Wait a moment," Ybor said. "There is one man who will know me. He may not have arrived. Solraq."

"He came yesterday," she said. "Very well. If he identifies you, that will be good enough. Sleyg," she said to the huge guard, "fetch Solraq."

Sleyg rumbled deep in his throat, and she made an impatient gesture. "I can take care of myself. Go!" She reached inside her blouse, took her gun from its shoulder holster and pointed it across the table at Ybor. "You will sit still."

Sleyg went out. Ybor heard a car start, and the sound of its motor faded rapidly.

"May I smoke?" Ybor asked.

"Certainly." With her free hand she tossed a pack of cigarettes across the table. He lighted one, careful to keep his hand in sight, handed it to her, and applied flame to his own. "So you're Ylas," he said conversationally.

She didn't bother to reply.

"You've done a good job," he went on. "Right under their noses. You must have had some close calls."

She smiled tolerantly. "Don't be devious, chum. On the off chance that you might escape, I'll give you no data to use later."

"There won't be any later if I don't get out of here. For you or anybody."

"Now you're melodramatic. There'll always be a later, as long as there's time."

"Time exists only in consciousness," he said. "There won't be any time, unless dust and rocks are aware of it."

"That's quite a picture of destruction you paint."

"It will be quite a destruction. And you're bringing it nearer every minute. You're cutting down the time margin in which it can be averted."

She grinned. "Ain't I nasty?"

"Even if you let me go this moment—" he began.

"Which I won't."

"—the catastrophe might not be averted. Our minds can't conceive the unimaginable violence which might very well destroy all animal life. It's a queer picture," he mused, "even to think about. Imagine space travelers of the future sighting this planet empty of life, overgrown with jungles. It wouldn't even have a name. Oh, they'd find the name. All traces of civilization wouldn't be completely destroyed. They'd poke in the crumbled ruins and finds bits of history. Then they'd go back to their home planet with the mystery of Cathor. Why did all life disappear from Cathor? They'd find skeletons enough to show our size and shape, and they'd decipher such records as were found. But nowhere would they find even a hint of the reason our civilization was destroyed. Nowhere would they find the name of Ylas, the reason."

She merely grinned.

"That's how serious it is," Ybor concluded. "Not a bird in the sky, not a pig in a sty. Perhaps no insects, even. I wonder," he said thoughtfully, "if such explosions destroyed life in other planets in our system. Lara, for example. It had life, once. Did civilization rise to a peak there, and end in a war that involved every single person on one side or another? Did one side, in desperation, try to use an explosive available to both but uncontrollable, and so lose the world?"

"*Shh!*" she commanded. She was stiff, listening.

He heard it then, the rhythmic tramp of feet. He flicked a glance through the window toward the wood. "Ynamre," he said.

A sergeant marched a squad of eight soldiers across the field toward the house. Ybor turned to the girl.

"You've got to hide me! Quick!"

She stared at him coldly. "I have no place."

"You must have. You must take care of refugees. Where is it?"

"Maybe you've caught me," she said grimly, "but you'll learn nothing. The Underground will carry on."

"You little fool! I'm with you."

"That's what you say. I haven't any proof."

Ybor wasted no more time. The squad was almost at the door. He leaped over against the wall and squatted there. He pulled his coat half off, shook his black hair over his eyes, and slacked his face so that it took on the loose, formless expression of an idiot. He began to play with his fingers, and gurgled.

A pounding rifle butt took the girl to the door. Ybor did not look up. He twisted his fingers and gurgled at them.

"Did you hear anything last night?" the sergeant demanded.

"Anything?" she echoed. "Some planes, some guns."

"Did you get up? Did you look out?"

"I was afraid," she answered meekly.

He spat contemptuously. There was a short silence, disturbed only by Ybor's gurgling.

"What's that?" the sergeant snapped. He stamped across the room, jerked Ybor's head up by the lock of hair. Ybor gave him an insane, slobbering grin. The sergeant's eyes were contemptuous. "Dummy!" he snarled. He jerked his hand away. "Why don't you kill it?" he asked the girl. "All the more food for you. Sa-a-a-y," he said, as if he'd seen her for the first time, "not bad, not bad. I'll be up to see you, cookie, one of these nights."

Ybor didn't move until they were out of hearing. He got to his feet then, and looked grimly at Ylas. "I could have been in Nilreq by now. You'll have to get me away. They've discovered that gun crew, and will be on the lookout."

She had the gun in her hand again. She motioned him toward the chair. "Shall we sit down?"

"After that? You're still suspicious? You're a fool."

"Ah? I think not. That could have been a part of the trick, to lull my suspicions. Sit—down!"

He sat. He was through with talking. He thought of the soldiers' visit. That sergeant probably wouldn't recognize him if they should encounter each other. Still, it was something to keep in mind. One more face to remember to dodge.

If only that big ape would get back with Solraq. His ears, as if on cue, caught the sound of an approaching motor. He was gratified to see that he heard it a full second before Ylas. Her reflexes weren't so fast, after all.

It was Sleyg, and Sleyg alone. He came into the house on his soft cat feet. "Solraq," he reported, "is dead. Killed last night."

Ylas gave Ybor a smile. There was deadliness in it.

"How very convenient," she said, "for you. Doesn't it seem odd even to you, Mr. Sixa Intelligence Officer, that of all the Seilla agents you pick a man who is dead? I think this has gone far enough. Into the cellar with him, Sleyg. We'll get the truth this time. Even," she added to Ybor, "though it'll kill you."

The chair was made like a straitjacket, with an arrangement of clamps and straps that held him completely motionless. He could move nothing but his eyeballs.

Ylas inspected him. She nodded satisfaction. "Go heat your irons," she said to Sleyg. "First," she explained to Ybor, "we'll burn off your ears, a little at a time. If that doesn't wear you down, we'll get serious."

Ybor said, "I'll tell you the truth now."

She sneered at that. "No wonder the enemy is knocking at your gates. You were driven out of Aissu on the south, and Ytal on the north. Now you are coming into your home country, because you're cowards."

"I'm convinced that you are Ylas," Ybor went on calmly. "And though my orders were that nobody should know of my mission, I think I can tell you. I must. I have no choice. Then listen. I was sent to Ynamre to—"

She cut him off with a fierce gesture. "The truth!"

"Do you want to hear this or not?"

"I don't want to hear another fairy tale."

"You are going to hear this, whether you like it or not. And you'll hold off your gorilla until I've finished. Or have the end of the race on your head."

Her lip curled. "Go on."

"Have you heard of U-235? It's an isotope of uranium."

"Who hasn't?"

"All right. I'm stating fact, not theory. U-235 has been sepa-rated, in quantity easily sufficient for preliminary atomic-power research, and the like. They got it out of uranium ores by new atomic isotope separation methods; they now have quantities measured in pounds. By 'they,' I mean Seilla research scientists. But they have not brought the whole amount together, or any major portion of it. Because, they are not at all sure that, once started, it would stop before all of it had been consumed—in something like one micromicrosecond of time."

Sleyg came into the cellar. In one hand he carried a portable forge. In the other, a bundle of metal rods. Ylas motioned him to put them down in a corner. "Go up and keep watch," she ordered. "I'll call you."

A tiny exultation flickered in Ybor. He had won a concession. "Now the explosion of a pound of U-235," he said, "wouldn't be too unbearably violent, though it releases as much energy as a hundred million pounds of TNT. Set off on an island, it might lay waste the whole island, uprooting trees, killing all animal life, but even that wouldn't seriously disturb the really unimaginable tonnage which even a small island represents."

"I assume," she broke in, "that you're going to make a point? You're not just giving me a lecture on high explosives?"

"Wait. The trouble is, they're afraid that explosion of energy would be so incomparably violent, its sheer, minute concentration of unbearable energy so great, that surrounding matter would be set off. If you could imagine concentrating half a billion of the most violent lightning strokes you ever saw, compressing all their fury into a space less than half the size of a pack of cigarettes—you'd get some idea of the concentrated essence of hyperviolence that explosion would represent. It's not simply the *amount* of energy; it's the frightful concentration of intensity in a minute volume.

"The surrounding matter, unable to maintain a self-supporting atomic explosion normally, might be hyper-stimulated to atomic explosion under U-235's forces and, in the immediate neighborhood, release its energy, too. That is, the explosion would not involve only one pound of U-235, but also five or fifty or five thousand tons of other matter. The extent of the explosion is a matter of conjecture."

"Get to the point," she said impatiently.

"Wait. Let me give you the main picture. Such an explosion would be serious. It would blow an island, or a hunk of continent, right off the planet. It would shake Cathor from pole to pole, cause earthquakes violent enough to do serious damage on the other side of the planet, and utterly destroy everything within at least one thousand miles of the site of the explosion. And I mean everything.

"So they haven't experimented. They could end the war overnight with controlled U-235 bombs. They could end this cycle of civilization with one or two uncontrolled bombs. And they don't know which they'd have if they made 'em. So far, they haven't worked out any way to control the explosion of U-235."

"If you're stalling for time," Ylas said, "it won't do you any good, personally. If we have callers, I'll shoot you where you sit."

"Stalling?" Ybor cried. "I'm trying my damnedest to shorten it. I'm not finished yet. Please don't interrupt. I want to give you the rest of the picture. As you pointed out, the Sixa armies are being pushed back to their original starting point: Ynamre. They started out to conquer the world, and they came close, at one time. But now they are about to lose it. We, the Seilla, would not dare to set off an experimental atomic bomb. This war is a phase, to us; to the Sixa, it is the whole future. So the Sixa are desperate, and Dr. Sitruc has made a bomb with not one, but sixteen pounds of U-235 in it. He may have it finished any day. I must find him and destroy that bomb. If it's used, we are lost either way. Lost the war, if the experiment is a success; the world, if not. You and you alone stand between extinction of the race and continuance."

She seemed to pounce. "You're lying! Destroy it, you say. How? Take it out in a vacant lot and explode it? In a desert? On a high mountain? You wouldn't dare even to drop it in the ocean, for fear it might explode. Once you had it, you'd have ten million tigers by the tail—you wouldn't dare turn it loose."

"I can destroy it. Our scientists told me how."

"Let that pass for the moment," she said. "You have several points to explain. First, it seems odd that you heard of this, and we haven't. We're much closer to developments than you, across three thousand miles of water."

"Sworb," Ybor said, "is a good man, even if he can't eat sweets. He brought back a drawing of it. Listen, Ylas, time is precious! If Dr. Sitruc finishes that bomb before I find him, it may be taken any time and dropped near our headquarters. And even if it doesn't set off the explosion I've described—though it's almost certain that it would—it would wipe out our southern army and equipment, and we'd lose overnight."

"Two more points need explaining," she went on calmly. "Why my grain field? There were others to choose from."

"That was pure accident."

"Perhaps. But isn't that string of accidents suspiciously long when you consider the death of Solraq?"

"I don't know anything about that. I didn't know he was dead."

She was silent. She strode back and forth across the cellar, brows furrowed, smoking nervously. Ybor sat quietly. It was all he could do; even his fingers were in stalls.

"I'm half inclined to believe you," she said finally, "but look at my position. We have a powerful organization here. We've risked our lives, and many of us have died, in building it up. I know how we are hated and feared by the authorities. If you are a Sixa agent, and I concluded that you were by the way you spoke the language, you would go to any length, even to carrying out such an elaborate plot as this might be, to discover our methods and membership. I can't risk all that labor and life on nothing but your word."

"Look at my position," Ybor countered. "I might have escaped from you, in the wood and here, after Sleyg left us. But I didn't dare take a chance. You see, it's a matter of time. There is a definite, though unknown, deadline. Dr. Sitruc may finish that bomb any time and screw the fuse in. The bomb may be taken at any time after that and exploded. If I had tried to escape, and you had shot me—and I'm sure you would—it would take weeks to replace me. We may have only hours to work with."

She was no longer calm and aloof. Her eyes had a tortured look, and her hands clenched as if she were squeezing words from her heart: "I can't afford to take the chance."

"You can't afford not to," Ybor said.

Footsteps suddenly pounded overhead. Ylas went rigid, flung a narrowed glace of speculation and suspicion at Ybor, and went out of the cellar. He twisted a smile; she hadn't shot him, as she had threatened.

He sat still, but each nerve was taut, quivering, and raw. What now? Who had arrived? What could it mean for him? Who belonged to that babble upstairs? Whose feet were heavy? He was soon to know, for the footsteps moved to the cellar door, and Ylas preceded the sergeant who had arrived earlier.

"I've got orders to search every place in this vicinity," the sergeant said, "so shut up."

His eyes widened when they fell on Ybor. "Well, well!" he cried. "If it isn't the dummy. Sa-a-ay, you snapped out of it!"

Ybor caught his breath as an idea hit him.

"I was drugged," Ybor said, leaping at the chance for escape. "It's worn off now."

Ylas frowned, searching, he could see, for the meaning in his words. He went on, giving her her cue: "This girl's servant, that big oaf upstairs—"

"He ran out," the sergeant said. "We'll catch him."

"I see. He attacked me last night in the grain field out there, brought me here and drugged me."

"What were you doing in the grain field?"

"I was on my way to see Dr. Sitruc. I have information of the most vital nature for him."

The sergeant turned to Ylas. "What d'ya say, girlie?"

She shrugged. "A stranger, in the middle of the night, what would you have done?"

"Then why didn't you say something about it when I was here a while ago?"

"If he turned out to be a spy, I wanted the credit for capturing him."

"You civilians," the sergeant said in disgust. "Well, maybe this is the guy we're lookin' for. Why did you kill that gun crew?" he snarled at Ybor.

Ybor blinked. "How did you know? I killed them because they were enemies."

The sergeant made a gesture toward his gun. His face grew stormy. "Why, you dirty spy—"

"Wait a minute!" Ybor said. "What gun crew? You mean the Seilla outpost, of course, in Aissu?"

"I mean our gun crew, you rat, in the woods out there."

Ybor blinked again. "I don't know anything about a gun crew out there. Listen, you've got to take me to Dr. Sitruc at once. Here's the background. I have been in Seilla territory, and I learned something that Dr. Sitruc must know. The outcome of the war depends on it. Take me to him at once, or you'll suffer for it."

The sergeant cogitated. "There's something funny here," he said. "Why have you got him all tied up?"

"For questioning," Ylas answered.

Ybor could see that she had decided to play it his way, but she wasn't convinced. The truth was, as he pointed out, she could not afford to do otherwise.

The sergeant went into an analytical state which seemed to be almost cataleptic. Presently he shook his massive head. "I can't quite put my finger on it," he said in a puzzled tone. "Every time I get close, I hit a blank . . . what am I saying?" He became crisp, menacing. "What's your name, you?" he spat at Ybor.

Ybor couldn't shrug. He raised his eyebrows. "My papers will say that I am Yenraq Ekor, a newspaperman. Don't let them fool you. I'll give my real name to Dr. Sitruc. He knows it well. You're wasting time, man!" he burst out. "Take me to him at once. You're worse than this stupid female!"

The sergeant turned to Ylas. "Did he tell you why he wanted to see Dr. Sitruc?"

She shrugged again, still with speculative eyes on Ybor. "He just said he had to."

"Well, then," the sergeant demanded of Ybor, "why do you want to see him?"

Ybor decided to gamble. This goof might keep him here all day with aimless questioning. He told the story of the bomb, much as he had told it to Ylas. He watched the sergeant's face, and saw that his remarks were completely unintelligible. Good! The soldier, like so many people, knew nothing of U-235. Ybor went into the imaginative and gibberish phase of his talk.

"And so, if it's uncontrolled," he said, "it might destroy the planet, blow it instantly into dust. But what I learned was a method of control, and the Seilla have a bomb almost completed. They'll use it to destroy Ynamre. But if we can use ours first, we'll destroy them. You see, it's a neutron shield that I discovered while I was a spy in the Seilla camps. It will stop the neutrons, released by the explosion, from rocketing about space and splitting mountains. Did you know that one free neutron can crack this planet in half? This shield will confine them to a limited area, and the war is ours. So hurry! Our time may be measured in minutes!"

The sergeant took it all in. He didn't dare not believe, for the picture of destruction which Ybor painted was on such a vast scale that sixteen generations of men like the sergeant would be required to comprehend it.

The sergeant made up his mind. "Hey!" he yelled toward the cellar door, and three soldiers came in. "Get him out of that. We'll take him to the captain. Take the girl along, too. Maybe the captain will want to ask her some questions."

"But I haven't done anything," Ylas protested.

"Then you got nothing to be afraid of, beautiful. If they let you go, I'll take personal charge of you."

The sergeant had a wonderful leer.

You might as well be fatalistic, Ybor thought as he waited in Dr. Sitruc's anteroom. Certain death could easily await him here, but even so, it was worth the gamble. If he were to be a pawn in a greater game—the greatest game, in fact—so be it.

So far, he had succeeded. And it came to him as he eyed his two guards that final success would result in his own death. He couldn't hope to destroy that bomb and get out of this fortress alive. Those guarded exits spelled *finis,* if he could even get far enough from this laboratory to reach one of them.

He hadn't really expected to get out alive, he reflected. It was a suicide mission from the start. That knowledge, he knew now, had given plausibility to his otherwise thin story. The captain, even as the sergeant, had not dared to disbelieve his tale. He had imparted verisimilitude to his story of destruction because of his deep and flaming determination to prevent it.

Not that he had talked wildly about neutron shields to the captain. The captain was intelligent, compared to his sergeant. And so Ybor had talked matter-of-factly about heat control, and had made it convincing enough to be brought here by guards who grew more timid with each turn of the lorry's wheels.

Apparently, the story of the bomb was known here at the government experimental laboratories; for all the guards had a haunted look, as if they knew that they would never hear the explosion if something went wrong. All the better, then. If he could take advantage of that fact, somehow, as he had taken advantage of events to date, he might . . . might . . .

He shrugged away speculation. The guards had sprung to attention as the inner door opened, and a man eyed Ybor.

This was a slender man with snapping dark eyes, an odd-shaped face, and a commanding air. He wore a smock, and from its sleeves extended competent-looking hands.

"So you are the end result," he said dryly to Ybor. "Come in."

Ybor followed him into the laboratory. Dr. Sitruc waved him to a straight, uncomfortable chair, using the gun which was suddenly in his hand as an indicator. Ybor sat, and looked steadily at the other. "What do you mean, end result?" he asked.

"Isn't it rather obvious?" the doctor asked pleasantly. "Those planes that passed over last night were empty; they went too fast, otherwise. I have been speculating all day on their purpose. Now I see. They dropped you."

"I heard something about planes," Ybor said, "but I didn't see 'em."

Dr. Sitruc raised polite eyebrows. "I'm afraid I do not believe you. My interpretation of events is this: those Seilla planes had one objective, to land an agent here who was commissioned to destroy the uranium bomb. I have known for some time that the Seilla command has known of its existence, and I have wondered what steps they would take to destroy it."

Ybor could see no point in remaining on the defensive. "They are making their own bomb," he said. "But they have a control. I'm here to tell you about it, so that you can use it on our bomb. We have time."

Dr. Sitruc said: "I have heard the reports on you this morning. You made some wild and meaningless statements. My personal opinion is that you are a layman, with only scant knowledge of the subject on which you have been so glib. I propose to find out—before I kill you. Oh, yes," he said, smiling, "you will die in any case. In my present position, knowledge is power. If I find that you actually have knowledge which I do not, I propose that I alone will retain it. You see my point?"

"You're like a god here. That's clear enough from the attitude of the guards."

"Exactly. I have control of the greatest explosive force in world history, and my whims are obeyed as iron commands. If I choose, I may give orders to the High Command. They have no choice but to obey. Now, you—your name doesn't matter; it's assumed, no doubt—tell me what you know."

"Why should I? If I'm going to die, anyway, my attitude is to hell with you. I do know something that you don't, and you haven't time to get it from anybody but me. By the time one of your spies could work his way up high enough to learn what I did, the Sixa would be defeated. But I see no reason to give you the information. I'll sell it to you—for my life."

Ybor looked around the small, shining laboratory while he spoke, and he saw it. It wasn't particularly large; its size did not account for the stab of terror that struck his heart. It was the fact that the bomb was finished. It was suspended in a shockproof cradle. Even a bombing raid would not shake it loose. It would be exploded when and where the doctor chose.

"You may well turn white as a sheet," Dr. Sitruc chuckled. "There it is, the most destructive weapon the world has ever known."

Ybor swallowed convulsively. Yes, there it was. Literally the means to an end—the end of the world. He thought wryly that those religionists who still contended that this war would be ended miraculously by divine intervention would never live to call the bomb a miracle. What a shot in the doctrine the explosion would give them if only they could come through it unscathed!

"I turned white," he answered. Dr. Sitruc, "because I see it as a blind, uncontrolled force. I see it as the end of a cycle, when all life dies. It will be millennia before another civilization can reach our present stage."

"It is true that the element of chance is involved. If the bomb sets off surrounding matter for any considerable radius, it is quite possible that all animate life will be destroyed in the twinkling of an eye. However, if it does not set off surrounding matter, we shall have won the world. I alone—and now you—know this. The

High Command sees only victory in that weapon. But enough of chitchat. Your would bargain your life for information on how to control the explosion. If you convince me that you have such knowledge, I'll set you free. What is it?"

"That throws us into a deadlock," Ybor objected. "I won't tell you until I'm free, and you won't free me until I tell."

Dr. Sitruc pursed thin lips. "True," he said. "Well, then, how's this? I shall give the guards outside a note ordering that you be allowed to leave unmolested after you come through the laboratory door."

"And what's to prevent your killing me in here, once I have told you?"

"I give you my word."

"It isn't enough."

"What other choice have you?"

Ybor thought this over, and conceded the point. Somewhere along the line, either he or Dr. Sitruc would have to trust the other. Since this was the doctor's domain, and since he held Ybor prisoner, it was easy to see who would take the other on trust. Well, it would give him a breathing spell. Time was what he wanted now.

"Write the note," he said.

Dr. Sitruc went to his desk and began to write. He shot glances at Ybor which excluded the possibility of successful attack. Even the quickest spring would be fatal, for the doctor was far enough away to have time to raise his gun and fire. Ybor had a hunch that Dr. Sitruc was an excellent shot. He waited.

Dr. Sitruc summoned a guard, gave him the note, and directed that Ybor be allowed to read it. Ybor did, nodded. The guard went out.

"Now," Dr. Sitruc began, but broke off to answer his telephone. He listened, nodded, shot a slitted glance at Ybor, and hung up. "Would it interest you to know," he asked, "that the girl who captured you was taken away from guards by members of the Underground?"

"Not particularly," Ybor said. "Except that . . . yes," he cried, "it does interest me. It proves my authenticity. You know how widespread the Underground is, how powerful. It's clear what happened; they knew I was coming, knew my route, and caught me. They were going to torture me in their cellar. I told that sergeant the truth. Now they will try to steal the bomb. If they had it, they could dictate terms."

It sounded a trifle illogical, maybe, but Ybor put all of the earnestness he could into his voice. Dr. Sitruc looked thoughtful.

"Let them try. Now, let's have it."

The tangled web of lies he had woven had caught him now. He knew of no method to control the bomb. Dr. Sitruc was not aware of this fact, and would not shoot until he was. Ybor must stall, and watch for an opportunity to do what he must do. He had gained a point; if he got through that door, he would be free. He must, then, get through the door—with the bomb. And Dr. Sitruc's gun was in his hand.

"Let's trace the reaction," Ybor began.

"The control!" Dr. Sitruc snapped.

Ybor's face hardened. "Don't get tough. My life depends on this. I've got to convince you that I know what I'm talking about, and I can do that by describing the method from the first. If you interrupt, then to hell with you."

Dr. Sitruc's odd face flamed with anger. This subsided after a moment, and he nodded. "Go on."

"Oxygen and nitrogen do not burn—if they did, the first fire would have blown this planet's atmosphere off in one stupendous explosion. Oxygen and nitrogen will burn if heated to about three thousand degrees Centigrade, and they'll give off energy in the process. But they don't give off sufficient energy to maintain that temperature—so they rapidly cool, and the fire goes out. If you maintain that temperature artificially—well, you're no doubt familiar with that process of obtaining nitric oxide."

"No doubt," Dr. Sitruc said acidly.

"All right. Now U-235 can raise the temperature of local matter to where it will, uh, 'burn,' and give off energy. So let's say we 'set off' a little pinch of U-235. Surrounding matter also explodes, as it is raised to an almost inconceivable temperature. It cools rapidly; within perhaps one-hundred-millionth of a second, it is down below the point of ignition. Then maybe a full millionth of a second passes before it's down to one million degrees hot, and a minute or so may elapse before it is visible in the normal sense. Now that visible radiation will represent no more than one-hundred-thousandth of the total radiation at one million degrees—but even so, it would be several hundred times more brilliant than the sun. Right?"

Dr. Sitruc nodded. Ybor thought there was a touch of deference in his nod.

"That's pretty much the temperature cycle of a U-235 plus surrounding matter explosion, Dr. Sitruc. I'm oversimplifying, I guess, but we don't need to go into detail. Now that radiation *pressure* is the stuff that's potent. The sheer momentum, physical pressure of light from the stuff at one million degrees, would amount to tons and tons and *tons* of pressure. It would blow down buildings like a titanic wind if it weren't for the fact that absorption of such appalling energy would volatilize the buildings before they could move out of the way. Right?"

Dr. Sitruc nodded again. He almost smiled.

"All right," Ybor went on. He now entered the phase of this contest where he was guessing, and he'd get no second guess. "What we need is a damper, something to hold the temperature of surrounding matter down. In that way, we can limit the effect of the explosion to desired areas, and prevent it from destroying cities on the opposite side of Cathor. The method of applying the damper depends on the exact mechanical structure of the bomb itself."

Ybor got to his feet easily, and walked across the laboratory to the cradle which held the bomb. He didn't even glance at Dr. Sitruc; he didn't dare. Would he be allowed to reach the bomb?

Would an unheard, unfelt bullet reach his brain before he took another step?

When he was halfway across the room, he felt as if he had already walked a thousand miles. Each step seemed to be slow motion, leagues in length. And still the bomb was miles away. He held his steady pace, fighting with every atom of will his desire to sprint to his goal, snatch it, and flee.

He stopped before the bomb, looked down at it. He nodded, ponderously. "I see," he said, remembering Sworb's drawings and the careful explanations he had received. "Two cast-iron hemispheres, clamped over the orange segments of cadmium alloy. And the fuse—I see it is in—a tiny can of cadmium alloy containing a speck of radium in a beryllium holder and a small explosive powerful enough to shatter the cadmium walls. Then—correct me if I'm wrong, will you?—the powdered uranium oxide runs together in the central cavity. The radium shoots neutrons into this, mass—and the U-235 takes over from there. Right?"

Dr. Sitruc had come up behind Ybor, stood at his shoulder. "Just how do you know so much about that bomb?" he asked with overtones of suspicion.

Ybor threw a careless smile over his shoulder. "It's obvious, isn't it? Cadmium stops neutrons, and it's cheap and effective. So you separate the radium and U-235 by thin cadmium walls, brittle so the light explosion will shatter them, yet strong enough to be handled with reasonable care."

The doctor chuckled. "Why, you are telling the truth."

Dr. Sitruc relaxed, and Ybor moved. He whipped his short, prehensile tail around the barrel of Dr. Sitruc's gun, yanked the weapon down at the same time his fist cracked the scientist's chin. His free hand wrenched the gun out of Dr. Sitruc's hand.

He didn't give the doctor a chance to fall from the blow of his fist. He chopped down with the gun butt and Dr. Sitruc was instantly unconscious. Ybor stared down at the sprawled figure with narrowed eyes. Dare he risk a shot? No, for the guards would not let him go, despite the doctor's note, without investigation. Well—

He chopped the gun butt down again. Dr. Sitruc would be no menace for some time, anyway. And all Ybor needed was a little time. First, he had to get out of here.

That meant taking the fuse out of the bomb. He went over to the cradle, examined the fuse. He tried to unscrew it. It was too tight. He looked around for a wrench. He saw none. He stood half-panic-stricken. Could he afford a search for the wrench which would remove the fuse? If anyone came in, he was done for. No, he'd have to get out while he could.

And if anybody took a shot at him, and hit the bomb, it was goodbye Cathor and all that's in it. But he didn't dare wait here. And he must stop sweating ice water, stop this trembling.

He picked up the cradle and walked carefully to the door. Outside, in the anteroom, the guards who had brought him there turned white. Blood drained out of their faces like air from a punctured balloon. They stood motionless, except for a slight trembling of their knees, and watched Ybor go out into the corridor.

Unmolested, Dr. Sitruc had said. He was not only unmolested, he was avoided. Word seemed to spread through the building like poison gas on a stiff breeze. Doors popped open, figures hurried out—and ran away from Ybor and his cargo. Guards, scientists, men in uniform, girls with pretty legs, bare-kneed boys—all ran.

To where? Ybor asked with his heart in his mouth. There was no safe place in all the world. Run how they might, as far as they could, and it would catch them if he fell or if the bomb were accidentally exploded.

He wanted a plane. But how to get one, if everybody ran? He could walk to the airport, if he knew where it was. Still, once he was away from these laboratories, any policeman, ignorant of the bomb, could stop him, confiscate the weapon, and perhaps explode it.

He had to retain possession.

The problem was partly solved for him. As he emerged from the building, to see people scattering in all directions, a huge form came out from behind a pillar and took him by the arm. "Sleyg," Ybor almost cried with terror which became relief.

"Come," Sleyg said, "Ylas wants you."

"Get me to a plane!" Ybor said. He thought he'd said it quietly, but Sleyg's yellow eyes flickered curiously at him.

The big man nodded, crooked a finger, and led the way. He didn't seem curious about the bomb. Ybor followed to where a small car was parked at the curb. They climbed in, and Sleyg pulled out into traffic.

So Ylas wanted him, eh? Why? He gave up speculation to watch the road ahead, cradling the bomb in his arms against rough spots.

He heard a plane, and searched for it anxiously. All he needed at this stage was a bombing raid, and a direct hit on this car. They had promised him that no raids would be attempted until they were certain of his success or failure, but brass hats were a funny lot. You never knew what they'd do next, like countermanding orders given only a few minutes before.

Still, no alarm sirens went off, so the plane must be Sixa. Ybor sighed with relief.

They drove on, and Ybor speculated on the huge, silent figure beside him. How had Sleyg known that he would come out of that building? How had he known he was there? Did the Underground have a pipeline even into Dr. Sitruc's office?

These speculations were useless, too, and he shrugged them away as Sleyg drove out of the city through fields of grain. The Sixa, apparently, were going to feed their armies mush, for he saw no other produce.

Sleyg cut off the main road into a bumpy lane, and Ybor clasped the bomb firmly. "Take it easy," he warned.

Sleyg slowed obediently, and Ybor wondered again at the man's attitude. Ybor did not seem to be a prisoner, yet he was not in command here completely. It was a sort of combination of the two, and it was uncomfortable.

They came to a bare, level stretch of land where a plane stood, props turning idly. Sleyg headed toward it. He brought the car to a halt, motioned Ybor out. He then indicated that Ybor should enter the big plane.

"Give me your tool kit," Ybor said, and the big man got it.

The plane bore Sixa insignia, but Ybor was committed now. If he used the bomb as a threat, he could make anybody do what he liked. Still, he felt a niggling worry.

Just before he stepped on the wing ramp, a shot came from the plane. Ybor ducked instinctively, but it was Sleyg who fell— with a neat hole between his eyes. Ybor tensed himself, stood still. The fuselage door slid back, and a face looked out.

"Solraq!" Ybor cried. "I thought you were dead!"

"You were meant to think it, Ybor. Come on in."

"Wait till I get these tools." Ybor handed the cradle up to the dark man who grinned down at him. "Hold the baby," Ybor said. "Don't drop him. If he cries, you'll never hear him."

He picked up the tool kit, climbed into the plane. Solraq waved a command to the pilot, and the plane took off. Ybor went to work gingerly on the fuse while Solraq talked.

"Sleyg was a cutie," he said. "We thought he was an ignorant ape. He was playing a big game, and was about ready to wind it up. But, when you named me for identification, he knew that he'd have to turn in his report, because we could have sent you directly to Dr. Sitruc, and helped you. Sleyg wasn't ready yet, so he reported me dead. Then he had the soldiers come and search the house, knowing you'd be found and arrested. He got into trouble when that skirt-chasing sergeant decided to take Ylas along. He had to report that to others of the Underground, because he had to have one more big meeting held before he could get his final dope.

"You see, he'd never turned in a report," Solraq went on. "He was watched, and afraid to take a chance. When Ylas and I got together, we compared notes, searched his belongings, and found the evidence.

"Then we arranged this rendezvous—if you got away. She told Sleyg where you were, and to bring you here. I didn't think you'd get away, but she insisted you were too ingenious to get caught. Well, you did it, and that's all to the good. Not that it would have mattered much. If you'd failed, we'd have got hold of the bomb somehow, or exploded it in Dr. Sitruc's laboratory."

Ybor didn't bother to tell him that it didn't matter where the bomb was exploded. He was too busy trying to prevent its exploding here. At last he had the fuse out. He motioned Solraq to open the bomb bay. When the folding doors dropped open, he let the fuse fall between them.

"Got its teeth pulled," he said, "and we'll soon empty the thing."

He released the clamps and pulled the hemispheres apart. He took a chisel from the tool kit and punched a hole in each of the cadmium cans in succession, letting the powder drift out. It would fall, spread, and never be noticed by those who would now go on living.

They would live because the war would end before Dr. Sitruc could construct another bomb. Ybor lifted eyes that were moist.

"I guess that's it," he said. "Where are we going?"

"We'll parachute out and let this plane crash when we sight our ship some fifty miles at sea. We'll report for orders now. This mission's accomplished."

— ROBERT SHECKLEY —

"THE PRIZE OF PERIL"

■ *The Magazine of Fantasy & Science Fiction*, **May 1958**

The TV show "Survivor" first appeared (as "Expedition Robinson") in Sweden in 1997. It quickly became popular, perhaps especially in the U.S., where it established "reality TV" as a popular genre. But the basic idea goes back almost half a century to Robert Sheckley's "The Prize of Peril" (movie versions 1970 [German] and 1983 [French]; some think it also influenced Stephen King's novella "The Running Man"). TV is not so bloody-minded, but reality TV certainly does put people in dangerous (or uncomfortable) situations without benefit of script and then watch them as they succeed or fail.

Where did Sheckley get his idea? TV had already run "Candid Camera," whose popularity might have led him to extrapolate toward a pinnacle of sensationalism. He himself had written "Seventh Victim" (*Galaxy*, 1953), centering on people hunting people with licenses to kill. This story was later filmed (1965) and then novelized (1966) as *The Tenth Victim*. Combine the two, and. . .

THE PRIZE OF PERIL

Robert Sheckley

Raeder lifted his head cautiously above the windowsill. He saw the fire escape, and below it a narrow alley. There was a weatherbeaten baby carriage in the alley, and three garbage cans. As he watched, a black-sleeved arm moved from behind the farthest can, with something shiny in its fist. Raeder ducked down. A bullet smashed through the window above his head and punctured the ceiling, showering him with plaster.

Now he knew about the alley. It was guarded, just like the door.

He lay at full length on the cracked linoleum, staring at the bullet hole in the ceiling, listening to the sounds outside the door. He was a tall man with bloodshot eyes and a two-day stubble. Grime and fatigue had etched lines into his face. Fear had touched his features, tightening a muscle here and twitching a nerve there. The results were startling. His face had character now, for it was reshaped by the expectation of death.

There was a gunman in the alley and two on the stairs. He was trapped. He was dead.

Sure, Raeder thought, he still moved and breathed; but that was only because of death's inefficiency. Death would take care of him in a few minutes. Death would poke holes in his face and body, artistically dab his clothes with blood, arrange his limbs in some grotesque position of the graveyard ballet . . . Raeder bit his lip sharply. He wanted to live. There had to be a way.

He rolled onto his stomach and surveyed the dingy cold-water apartment into which the killers had driven him. It was a perfect little one-room coffin. It had a door, which was watched, and a fire escape, which was watched. And it had a tiny windowless bathroom.

He crawled to the bathroom and stood up. There was a ragged hole in the ceiling, almost four inches wide. If he could enlarge it, crawl through into the apartment above . . .

He heard a muffled thud. The killers were impatient. They were beginning to break down the door.

He studied the hole in the ceiling. No use even considering it. He could never enlarge it in time. They were smashing against the door, grunting each time they struck. Soon the lock would tear out, or the hinges would pull out of the rotting wood. The door would go down, and the two blank-faced men would enter, dusting off their jackets . . .

But surely someone would help him! He took the tiny television set from his pocket. The picture was blurred, and he didn't bother to adjust it. The audio was clear and precise. He listened to the well-modulated voice of Mike Terry addressing his vast audience.

". . . *terrible spot,*" Terry was saying. *"Yes, folks, Jim Raeder is in a truly terrible predicament. He had been hiding, you'll remember, in a third-rate Broadway hotel under an assumed name. It seemed safe enough. But the bellhop recognized him, and gave that information to the Thompson gang."*

The door creaked under repeated blows. Raeder clutched the little television set and listened.

"Jim Raeder just managed to escape from the hotel! Closely pursued, he entered a brownstone at one fifty-six West End Avenue. His intention was to go over the roofs. And it might have worked, folks, it just might have worked. But the roof door was locked. It looked like the end. . . . But Raeder found that apartment seven was unoccupied and unlocked. He entered . . . "

Terry paused for emphasis, then cried: "—*and now he's trapped there, trapped like a rat in a cage! The Thompson gang is breaking down the door! The fire escape is guarded! Our camera crew, situated in a nearby building, is, giving you a close-up now. Look, folks, just look! Is there no hope for Jim Raeder?*"

Is there no hope? Raeder silently echoed, perspiration pouring from him as he stood in the dark, stifling little bathroom, listening to the steady thud; gainst the, door.

"*Wait a minute!*" Mike Terry cried. "*Hang on, Jim Raeder, hung on a little longer. Perhaps there is hope! I have an urgent call from one of our viewers, a call on the Good Samaritan Line! Here's someone who thinks he can help you, Jim. Are you listening, Jim Raeder?*"

Raeder waited, and heard the hinges tearing out of rotten wood.

"*Go right ahead, sir,*" said Mike Terry. "*What is your name, sir?*"

"*Er, Felix Bartholemow.*"

"*Don't be nervous, Mr. Bartholemow. Go right ahead.*"

"*Well, OK. Mr. Raeder,*" said an old man's shaking voice, "*I used to live at one five six West End Avenue. Same apartment you're trapped in, Mr. Raeder—fact! Look, that bathroom has got a window, Mr. Raeder. It's been painted over, but it has got a—*"

Raeder pushed the television set into his pocket. He located the outlines of the window and, kicked. Glass shattered, and daylight poured startlingly in. He cleared the jagged sill and quickly peered down.

Below was a long drop to a concrete courtyard. The hinges tore free. He heard the door opening. Quickly Raeder climbed through the window, hung by his fingertips for a moment, and dropped.

The shock was stunning. Groggily he stood up. A face appeared at the bathroom window.

"Tough luck," said the man, leaning out and taking careful aim, with a snub-nosed .38.

At that moment a smoke bomb exploded inside the bathroom.

The killer's shot went wide. He turned, cursing. More smoke bombs burst in the courtyard, obscuring Raeder's figure. He could hear Mike Terry's frenzied voice over the TV set in his pocket. *"Now run for it!"* Terry was screaming. *"Run, Jim Raeder, run for your life. Run now, while the killers' eyes are filled with smoke. And thank Good Samaritan Sarah Winters, of three four one two Edgar Street; Brockton, Mass., for donating fivesmoke bombs and employing the services of a man to throw them!"*

In a quieter voice, Terry continued: *"You've saved a man's life today, Mrs. Winters. Would you tell our audience how it—"*

Raeder wasn't able to hear any more. He was running through the smoke-filled courtyard, past clotheslines, into the open street.

He walked down sixty-third Street, slouching to minimize his height, staggering slightly from exertion, dizzy from lack of food and sleep.

"Hey you!"

Raeder turned. A middle-aged woman was sitting on the steps of a brownstone, frowning at him.

"You're Raeder, aren't you? The one they're trying to kill?"

Raeder started to walk away.

"Come inside here, Raeder," the woman said.

Perhaps it was a trap. But Raeder knew that he had to depend upon the generosity and goodheartedness of the people. He was their representative, a projection of themselves, an average guy in trouble. Without them, he was lost. With them, nothing could harm him.

Trust in the people, Mike Terry had told him. They'll never let you down.

He followed the woman into her parlor. She told him to sit down and left the room, returning almost immediately with a plate of stew. She stood watching him while he ate, as one would watch an ape in the zoo eat peanuts.

Two children came out of the kitchen and stared at him. Three overalled men came out of the bedroom and focused a television camera on him. There was a big television set in the parlor. As he gulped his food, Raeder watched the image of Mike Terry, and listened to the man's strong, sincere, worried voice.

"There he is, folks," Terry was saying. *"There's Jim Raeder now, eating his first square meal in two days. Our camera crews have really been working to cover this for you! Thanks, boys, . . . Folks, Jim Raeder has been given a brief sanctuary by Mrs. Velma O'Dell, of three forty-three Sixty-Third Street.*

"Thank you, Good Samaritan O'Dell! It's really wonderful how people from all walks of life have taken Jim Raeder to their hearts!"

"You better hurry," Mrs. O'Dell said.

"Yes, ma'am," Raeder said.

"I don't want no gunplay in my apartment."

"I'm almost finished, ma'am."

One of the children asked, "Aren't they going to kill him?"

"Shut up," said Mrs. O'Dell,

"Yes, Jim," chanted Mike Terry, *"you'd better hurry. Your killers aren't far behind. They aren't stupid men, Jim. Vicious, warped, insane—yes! But not stupid. They're following a trail of blood—blood from your torn hand, Jim!"*

Raeder hadn't realized until now that he'd cut his hand on the window sill.

"Here, I'll bandage that," Mrs. O'Dell said. Raeder stood up and let her bandage his hand. Then she gave him a brown jacket and a gray slouch hat.

"My husband's stuff," she said.

"He has a disguise, folks!" Mike Terry cried delightedly. *"This is something new! A disguise! With seven hours to go until he's safe!"*

'Now get out of here," Mrs. O'Dell said.

"I'm going, ma'am," Raeder said. "Thanks."

"I think you're stupid," she said. "I think you're stupid to be involved in this."

"Yes, ma'am."

"It just isn't worth it."

Raeder thanked her and left. He walked to Broadway, caught a subway to fifty-ninth Street, then an uptown local to eighty-sixth. There he bought a newspaper and changed for the Manhasset through- express.

He glanced at his watch. He had six and a half hours to go.

The subway roared under Manhattan. Raeder dozed, his bandaged hand concealed under the newspaper, the hat pulled over his face. Had he been recognized yet? Had he shaken the Thompson gang? Or was someone telephoning them now?

Dreamily he wondered if he had escaped death. Or was he still a cleverly animated corpse, moving around because of death's inefficiency? (My dear, death is so *laggard* these days! Jim Raeder walked about for hours after he died, and actually answered people's *questions* before he could be decently buried!)

Raeder's eyes snapped open. He had dreamed something unpleasant. He couldn't remember what.

He closed his eyes again and remembered, with mild astonishment, a time when he had been in no trouble.

That was two years ago. He had been a big, pleasant young man working as a truck driver's helper. He had no talents. He was too modest to have dreams.

The tight-faced little truck driver had the dreams for him. "Why not try for a television show, Jim? I would if had your looks. They like nice average guys with nothing much on the ball. As contestants. Everybody likes guys like that. Why not look into it?"

So he had looked into it. The owner of the local television store had explained it further.

"You see, Jim, the public is sick of highly trained athletes with their trick reflexes and their professional courage. Who can feel for guys like that? Who can identify? People want to watch exciting things, sure. But not when some joker is making it his business for fifty thousand a year. That's why organized sports are in a slump. That's why the thrill shows are booming."

"I see," said Raeder.

"Six years ago, Jim, Congress passed the Voluntary Suicide Act. Those old senators talked a lot about free will and self-determinism at the time. But that's all crap. You know what the Act really means? It means that amateurs can risk their lives for the big loot, not just professionals. In the old days you had to be a professional boxer or footballer or hockey player if you wanted your brains beaten out legally for money. But now that opportunity is open to ordinary people like you, Jim."

"I see," Raeder said again.

"It's a marvelous opportunity. Take you. You're no better than anyone, Jim. Anything you can do, anyone can do. You're *average*. I think the thrill shows would go for you."

Raeder permitted himself to dream. Television shows looked like a sure road to riches for a pleasant young fellow with no particular talent or training. He wrote a letter to a show called *Hazard* and enclosed a photograph of himself.

Hazard was interested in him. The JBC network investigated, and found that he was average enough to satisfy the wariest viewer. His parentage and affiliations were checked. At last he was summoned to New York, and interviewed by Mr. Moulian.

Moulian was dark and intense, and chewed gum as he talked. "You'll do," he snapped. "But not for *Hazard*. You'll appear on *Spills*. It's a half-hour daytime show on Channel Three."

"Gee," said Raeder.

"Don't thank me. There's a thousand dollars if you win or place second, and a consolation prize of a hundred dollars if you lose. But that's not important."

"No, sir."

"*Spills* is a *little* show. The JBC network uses it as a testing ground. First- and second-place winners on *Spills* move on to *Emergency*. The prizes are much bigger on *Emergency*."

"I know they are, sir."

"And if you do well on *Emergency* there are the first-class thrill shows, like *Hazard* and *Underwater Perils,* with their nationwide coverage and enormous prizes. And then comes the really big time. How far you go is up to you."

"I'll do my best, sir," Raeder said.

Moulian stopped chewing gum for a moment and said, almost reverently, "You can do it, Jim. Just remember. You're *the people,* and *the people* can do anything."

The way he said it made Raeder feel momentarily sorry for Mr. Moulian, who was dark and frizzy-haired and pop-eyed; and was obviously not *the people.*

They shook hands. Then Raeder signed a paper absolving the JBC of all responsibility should he lose his life, limbs, or reason during the contest. And he signed another paper exercising his rights under the Voluntary Suicide Act. The law required this, and it was a mere formality.

In three weeks, he appeared on *Spills.*

The program followed the classic form of the automobile race. Untrained drivers climbed into powerful American and European competition cars and raced over a murderous twenty-mile course. Raeder was shaking with fear as he slid his big Maserati into the wrong gear and took off.

The race was a screaming, tire-burning nightmare. Raeder stayed back, letting the early leaders smash themselves up on the counter-banked hairpin turns. He crept into third place when .a Jaguar in front of him swerved against an Alfa-Romeo, and the two cars roared into a plowed field. Raeder gunned for second place on the last three miles, but couldn't find passing room. An S-curve almost took him, but he fought the car back onto the road, still holding third. Then the lead driver broke his crankshaft in the final fifty yards, and Jim ended in second place.

He was now a thousand dollars ahead. He received four fan letters, and a lady in Oshkosh sent him a pair of argyles. He was invited to appear on *Emergency.*

Unlike the others, *Emergency* was not a competition-type program. It stressed individual initiative. For the show, Raeder was knocked out with a non-habit-forming narcotic. He awoke in the cockpit of a small airplane, cruising, on autopilot at ten thousand feet. His fuel gauge showed nearly empty. He had no parachute. He was supposed to land the plane.

Of course, he had never flown before.

He experimented gingerly with the controls, remembering that last week's participant had recovered consciousness in a submarine, had opened the wrong valve, and had drowned.

Thousands of viewers watched spellbound as this average man, a man just like themselves, struggled with the situation just as they would do. Jim Raeder was *them*. Anything he could do, they could do. He was representative of *the people*.

Raeder managed to bring the ship down in some semblance of a landing. He flipped over a few times, but his seat belt held. And the engine, contrary to expectation, did not burst into flames.

He staggered out with two broken ribs, three thousand dollars, and a chance, when he healed, to appear on *Torero*.

At last, a first-class thrill show! *Torero* paid ten thousand dollars. All you had to do was kill a black Miura bull with a sword, just like a real, trained matador.

The fight was held in Madrid, since bullfighting was still illegal in the United States. It was nationally televised.

Raeder had a good cuadrilla. They liked the big, slow-moving American. The picadors really leaned into their lances, trying to slow the bull for him. The banderilleros tried to run the beast off his feet before driving in their banderillas. And the second matador, a mournful man from Algeciras, almost broke the bull's neck with fancy cape work.

But when all was said and done it was Jim Raeder on the sand, a red muleta clumsily gripped in his left hand, a sword in his right, facing a ton of black, blood-streaked, wide-horned bull.

Someone was shouting, "Try for the lung, hombre. Don't be a hero, stick him in the lung." But Jim only knew what the technical adviser in New York had told him: Aim with the sword and go in over the horns.

Over he went. The sword bounced off bone, and the bull tossed him over its back. He stood up, miraculously ungouged, took another sword and went over the horns again with his eyes closed. The god who protects children and fools must have been watching, for the sword slid in like a needle through butter, and the bull looked startled, stared at him unbelievingly, and dropped like a deflated balloon.

They paid him ten thousand dollars, and his broken collarbone healed in practically no time. He received twenty-three fan letters, including a passionate invitation from a girl in Atlantic City, which he ignored. And they asked him if he wanted to appear on another show.

He had lost some of his innocence. He was now fully aware that he had been almost killed for pocket money. The big loot lay ahead. Now he wanted to be almost killed for something worthwhile.

So he appeared on *Underwater Perils,* sponsored by Fairlady's Soap. In face mask, respirator, weighted belt, flippers, and knife, he slipped into the warm waters of the Caribbean with four other contestants, followed by a cage-protected camera crew. The idea was to locate and bring up a treasure which the sponsor had hidden there.

Mask diving isn't especially hazardous. But the sponsor had added some frills for public interest. The area was sown with giant clams, moray eels, sharks of several species, giant octopi, poison coral, and other dangers of the deep.

It was a stirring contest. A man from Florida found the treasure in a deep crevice, but a moray eel found him. Another diver took the treasure, and a shark took him. The brilliant blue-green water became cloudy with blood, which photographed well on color TV. The treasure slipped to the bottom and Raeder plunged after it, popping an eardrum in the process. He plucked it from the coral, jettisoned his weighted belt and made for the surface. Thirty feet from the top he had to fight another diver for the treasure.

They feinted back and forth with their knives. The man struck, slashing Raeder across the chest. But Raeder, with the self-possession of an old contestant, dropped his knife and tore the man's respirator out of his mouth.

That did it. Raeder surfaced, and presented the treasure at the standby boat. It turned out to be a package of Fairlady's Soap—"The Greatest Treasure of All."

That netted him twenty-two thousand dollars in cash and prizes, and three hundred and eight fan letters, and an interesting proposition from a girl in Macon, which he seriously considered. He received free hospitalization for his knife slash and burst eardrum, and injections for coral infection.

But best of all, he was invited to appear on the biggest of the thrill shows, *The Prize of Peril.*

And that was when the real trouble began. . .

The subway came to a stop, jolting him out of his reverie. Raeder pushed back his hat and observed, across the aisle, a man staring at him and whispering to a stout woman. Had they recognized him?

He stood up as soon as the doors opened, and glanced at his watch. He had five hours to go.

At the Manhasset station he stepped into a taxi and told the driver to take him to New Salem. "New Salem?" the driver asked, looking at him in the rear-vision mirror.

"That's right."

The driver snapped on his radio. "Fare to New Salem. Yep, that's right. *New Salem.*"

They drove off. Raeder frowned, wondering if it had been a signal. It was perfectly usual for taxi drivers to report to their dispatchers, of course, But something about the man's voice . . .

"Let me off here," Raeder said.

He paid the driver and began walking down a narrow country road that curved through sparse woods. The trees were too small and too widely separated for shelter. Raeder walked on, looking for a place to hide.

There was a heavy truck approaching. He kept on walking, pulling his hat low on his forehead. But as the truck drew near, he heard a voice from the television.set in his pocket. It cried, *"Watch out!"*

He flung himself into the ditch. The truck careened past, narrowly missing him, and screeched to a stop. The driver was shouting, "There he goes! Shoot, Harry, shoot!"

Bullets clipped leaves from the trees as Raeder sprinted into the woods.

"It's happened again!" Mike Terry was saying, his voice high-pitched with excitement. *"I'm afraid Jim Raeder let himself be lulled into a false sense of security. You can't do that, Jim! Not with your life at stake! Not with killers pursuing you! Be careful, Jim, you still have four and a half hours to go!"*

The driver was saying, "Claude, Harry, go around with the truck. We got him boxed."

"They've got you boxed, Jim Raeder!" Mike Terry cried. *"But they haven't got you yet! And you can thank Good Samaritan Susy Peters of twelve Elm Street, South Orange, New Jersey, for that warning shout just when the truck was bearing down on you. We'll have little Susy on stage in just a moment. Look, folks, our studio helicopter has arrived on the scene. Now you can see Jim Raeder running, and the killers pursuing, surrounding him . . . "*

Raeder ran through a hundred yards of woods and found himself on a concrete highway, with open woods beyond. One of the killers was trotting through the woods behind him. The truck had driven to a connecting road, and was now a mile way, coming toward him.

A car was approaching from the other direction. Raeder ran into the highway, waving frantically. The car came to a stop.

"Hurry!" cried the blond young woman driving it.

Raeder dived in. The woman made a U-turn on the highway. A bullet smashed through the windshield. She stamped the accelerator, almost running down the lone killer who stood in the way.

The car surged away before the truck was within firing range.

Raeder leaned back and shut his eyes tightly. The woman concentrated on her driving, watching for the truck in her rear-vision mirror.

"It's happened again!" cried Mike Terry, his voice ecstatic. *"Jim Raeder has been plucked again from the jaws of death, thanks to Good Samaritan Janice Morrow of four three three Lexington Avenue, New York City. Did you ever see anything like it, folks? The way Miss Morrow drove through a fusillade of bullets and plucked Jim Raeder from the mouth of doom! Later we'll interview Miss Morrow and get her reactions. Now, while Jim Raeder speeds away—perhaps to safety, perhaps to further peril—we'll have a short announcement from our sponsor. Don't go away! Jim's got four hours and ten minutes until he's safe. Anything can happen!"*

"OK," the girl said. "We're off the air now. Raeder, what in the hell is the matter with you?"

"Eh?" Raeder asked. The girl was in her early twenties. She looked efficient, attractive, untouchable: Raeder noticed that she had good features, a trim figure. And he noticed that she seemed angry.

"Miss," he said, "I don't know how to thank you for—"

"Talk straight," Janice Morrow said. "I'm no Good Samaritan. I'm employed by the JBC network."

"So the program had me rescued!"

"Cleverly reasoned," she said.

"But why?"

"Look, this is an expensive show, Raeder. We have to turn in a good performance. If our rating slips, we'll all be in the street selling candy apples. And you aren't cooperating."

"What? Why?"

"Because you're terrible," the girl said bitterly. "You're a flop, a fiasco. Are you trying to commit suicide? Haven't you learned *anything* about survival?"

"I'm doing the best I can."

"The Thompsons could have had you a dozen times by now. We told them to take it easy, stretch it out. But it's like shooting a clay pigeon six feet tall. The Thompsons are cooperating, but they can only fake so far. If I hadn't come along, they'd have had to kill you—air-time or not."

Raeder stared at her, wondering how such a pretty girl could talk that way. She glanced at him, then quickly looked back to the road.

"Don't give me that look!" she said. "You chose to risk your life for money, buster. And plenty of money! You knew the score. Don't act like some innocent little grocer who finds the nasty hoods are after him. That's a different plot."

"I know," Raeder said.

"If you can't live well, at least try to die well."

"You don't mean that," Raeder said.

"Don't be too sure. . . You've got three hours and forty minutes until the end of the show. If you can stay alive, fine. The boodle's yours. But if you can't, at least try to give them a run for the money."

Raeder nodded, staring intently at her.

"In a few moments we're back on the air. I develop engine trouble, let you off. The Thompsons go all out now. They kill you when and if they can, as soon as they can. Understand?"

"Yes," Raeder said. "If I make it, can I see you some time?"

She bit her lip angrily. "Are you trying to kid me?"

"No. I'd like to see you again. May I?"

She looked at him curiously. "I don't know. Forget it. We're almost on. I think your best bet is the woods to the right. Ready?"

"Yes. Where can I get in touch with you? Afterward, I mean."

"Oh, Raeder, you aren't paying attention. Go through the woods until you find a washed-out ravine. It isn't much, but it'll give you some cover."

"Where can I get in touch with you?" Raeder asked again.

"I'm in the Manhattan telephone book." She stopped the car. "OK, Raeder, start running "

He opened the door.

"Wait." She leaned over and kissed him on the lips. "Good luck, you idiot. Call me if you make it."

And then he was on foot, running into the woods.

He ran through birch and pine, past an occasional split-level house with staring faces at the big picture window. Some occupant of those houses must have called the gang, for they were close behind him when he reached the washed-out little ravine. Those quiet, mannerly, law-abiding people didn't want him to escape, Raeder thought sadly. They wanted to see a killing. Or perhaps they wanted to see him *narrowly escape* a killing.

It came to the same thing, really.

He entered the ravine, burrowed into the thick underbrush and lay still. The Thompsons appeared on both ridges, moving slowly, watching for any movement. Raeder held his breath as they came parallel to him.

He heard the quick explosion of a revolver. But the killer had only shot a squirrel. It squirmed for a moment, then lay still.

Lying in the underbrush, Raeder heard the studio helicopter overhead. He wondered if any cameras were focused on him. It was possible. And if someone was watching, perhaps some Good Samaritan would help.

So looking upward, toward the helicopter, Raeder arranged his face in a reverent expression, clasped his hands and prayed. He prayed silently, for the audience didn't like religious ostentation. But his lips moved. That was every man's privilege.

And a real prayer was on his lips. Once, a lip-reader in the audience had detected a fugitive pretending to pray, but actually just reciting multiplication tables. No help for that man!

Raeder finished his prayer. Glancing at his watch, he saw that he had nearly two hours to go.

And he didn't want to die! It wasn't worth it, no matter how much they paid! He must have been crazy, absolutely insane to agree to such a thing . . .

But he knew that wasn't true. And he remembered just how sane he had been.

One week ago he had been on the *Prize of Peril* stage, blinking in the spotlight, and Mike Terry had shaken his hand.

"Now, Mr. Raeder," Terry had said solemnly, "do you understand the rules of the game you are about to play?"

Raeder nodded.

"If you accept, Jim Raeder, you will be a *hunted man* for a week. *Killers* will follow you, Jim. *Trained* killers, men wanted by the law for other crimes, granted immunity for this single killing under the Voluntary Suicide Act. They will be trying to kill *you*, Jim. Do you understand?"

"I understand," Raeder said. He also understood the two hundred thousand dollars he would receive if he could live out the week.

"I ask you again, Jim Raeder. We force no man to play for stakes of death."

"I want to play," Raeder said.

Mike Terry turned to the audience. "Ladies and gentlemen, I have here a copy of an exhaustive psychological test which an impartial psychological testing firm made on Jim Raeder at our request. Copies will be sent to anyone who desires them for twenty-five cents to cover the cost of mailing. The test shows that Jim Raeder is sane, well-balanced, and fully responsible in every way." He turned to Raeder. "Do you still want to enter the contest, Jim?"

"Yes, I do."

"Very well!" cried Mike Terry. "Jim Raeder, meet your would-be killers!"

The Thompson gang moved on stage, booed by the audience.

"Look at them, folks," said Mike Terry, with undisguised contempt. "Just look at them! Antisocial, thoroughly vicious, completely amoral. These men have no code but the criminal's warped code, no honor but the honor of the cowardly hired killer. They are doomed men, doomed by our society, which will not sanction their activities for long, fated to an early and unglamorous death."

The audience shouted enthusiastically.

"What have you to say, Claude Thompson?" Terry asked.

Claude, the spokesman of the Thompsons, stepped up to the microphone. He was a thin, clean-shaven man, conservatively dressed.

"I figure," Claude Thompson said hoarsely, "I figure we're no worse than anybody. I mean, like soldiers in a war, *they* kill. And look at the graft in government, and the unions. Everybody's got their graft."

That was Thompson's tenuous code. But how quickly, with what precision, Mike Terry destroyed the killer's rationalizations! Terry's questions pierced straight to the filthy soul of the man.

At the end of the interview Claude Thompson was perspiring, mopping his face with a silk handkerchief and casting quick glances at his men.

Mike Terry put a hand on Raeder's shoulder. "Here is the man who has agreed to become your victim—if you can catch him."

"We'll catch him," Thompson said, his confidence returning.

"Don't be too sure," said Terry. "Jim Raeder has fought wild bulls—now he battles jackals. He's an average man. He's *the people*—who mean ultimate doom to you and your kind."

"We'll get him," Thompson said.

"And one thing more," Terry said, very softly. "Jim Raeder does not stand alone. The folks of America are for him. Good Samaritans from all corners of our great nation stand ready to assist him. Unarmed, defenseless, Jim Raeder can count on the aid and goodheartedness of *the people;* whose representative he is. So don't be too sure, Claude Thompson! The average men are for Jim Raeder—and there are a lot of average men!"

Raeder thought about it, lying motionless in the underbrush. Yes, *the people* had helped him. But they had helped the killers, too.

A tremor ran through him. He had chosen, he reminded himself. He alone was responsible. The psychological test had proved that.

And yet, how responsible were the psychologists who had given him the test? How responsible was Mike Terry for offering a poor man so much money? Society had woven the noose and put it around his neck, and he was hanging himself with it, and calling it free will.

Whose fault?

"Aha!" someone cried.

Raeder looked up and saw a portly man standing near him. The man wore a loud tweed jacket. He had binoculars around his neck, and a cane in his hand.

"Mister," Raeder whispered, "please don't tell—"

"Hi!" shouted the portly man, pointing at Raeder with his cane. "Here he is!"

A madman, thought Raeder. The damned fool must think he's playing Hare and Hounds.

"Right over here!" the man screamed.

Cursing, Raeder sprang to his feet and began running. He came out of the ravine and saw a white building in the distance. He turned toward it. Behind him he could still hear the man.

"That way, over there. Look, you fools, can't you see him yet?"

The killers were shooting again. Raeder ran, stumbling over uneven ground, past three children playing in a tree house.

"Here he is!" the children screamed. "Here he is!" Raeder groaned and ran on. He reached the steps of the building, and saw that it was a church.

As he opened the door, a bullet struck him behind the right kneecap.

He fell, and crawled inside the church.

The television set in his pocket was saying, *"What a finish, folks, what a finish! Raeder's been hit! He's been hit, folks, he's crawling now, he's in pain, but he hasn't given up! Not Jim Raeder!"*

Raeder lay in the aisle near the altar. He could hear a child's eager voice saying, "He went in there, Mr. Thompson. Hurry, you can still catch him!"

Wasn't a church considered a sanctuary? Raeder wondered.

Then the door was flung open, and Raeder realized that the custom was no longer observed. He gathered himself together and crawled past the altar, out the back door of the church.

He was in an old graveyard. He crawled past crosses and stars, past slabs of marble and granite, past stone tombs and rude wooden markers. A bullet exploded on a tombstone near his head, showering him with fragments. He crawled to the edge of an open grave.

They had deceived him, he thought. All of those nice average normal people. Hadn't they said he was their representative? Hadn't they sworn to protect their own? But no, they loathed him. Why hadn't he seen it? Their hero was the cold, blank-eyed gunman, Thompson, Capone, Billy the Kid. Young Lochinvar, El Cid, Cuchulain, the man without human hopes or fears. They worshiped him, that dead, implacable, robot gunman, and lusted to feel his foot in their face.

Raeder tried to move, and slid helplessly into the open grave.

He lay on his back, looking at the blue sky. Presently a black silhouette loomed above him, blotting out the sky. Metal twinkled. The silhouette slowly took aim.

And Raeder gave up all hope forever. "WAIT, THOMPSON!" roared the amplified voice of Mike Terry.

The revolver wavered.

"It is one second *past five o'clock! The week is up!* JIM RAEDER HAS WON!"

There was a pandemonium of cheering from the studio audience.

The Thompson gang, gathered around the grave, looked sullen.

"He's won, friends, he's won!" Mike Terry cried. *"Look, look on your screen! The police have arrived, they're taking the Tho—psons away from their victim—the victim they could not kill. And all this is thanks to* you, *Good Samaritans of America. Look, folks, tender hands are lifting Jim Raeder from the open grave that was his final refuge. Good Samaritan Janice Morrow is there. Could this be the beginning of a romance? Jim seems to have fainted, friends, they're giving him a stimulant. He's won two hundred thousand dollars! Now we'll have a few words from Jim Raeder!"*

There was a short silence.

"That's odd," said Mike Terry. *"Folks, I'm afraid we can't hear from Jim just now. The doctors are examining him. Just one moment . . . "*

There was a silence. Mike Terry wiped his forehead, and smiled. *"It's the strain, folks, the terrible strain. The doctor tells me . . . Well, folks, Jim Raeder is temporarily not himself. But it's only temporary! JBC is hiring the best psychiatrists and psychoanalysts in the country. We're going to do everything humanly possible for this gallant boy. And entirely at* our own *expense."*

Mike Terry glanced at the studio clock. *"Well, it's about time to sign off, folks. Watch for the announcement of our next great thrill show. And don't worry, I'm sure that very soon we'll have Jim Raeder back with us."*

Mike Terry smiled, and winked at the audience. *"He's bound to get well, friends. After all, we're all pulling for him!"*

two

WATCH YOUR STEP

(Prototypes have been built)

— JEFF HECHT —

"DIRECTED ENERGY"

■ *Nature*, **April 13, 2006.**

Sometimes, sf predictions come true so fast, you'd swear the writer must know something! Jeff Hecht, a science writer who covers laser technology extensively, writes that, "You don't need a massive laser to bag a bug, and I've been told that on a slow day in the laser lab the temptation to take the odd pot shot is darn near irresistible. It's easy to find proposals on the web. There are spoof videos. And I pitched in with a plan for a laser search-and-destroy anti-mosquito system in the otherwise august pages of *Nature* . . . although I never got around to trying to build one." And then, "Jordin Kare, [a] former Livermore physicist, bought a batch of equipment on eBay and cobbled together a mosquito defense system which duly dispatches the blood-suckers. A video shows a mosquito catching fire as it flies into the invisible infrared laser beam, and the charred corpse falls to the floor." He says he hadn't read my story before I sent him a copy.

As "Rocket Scientists Shoot Down Mosquitoes With Lasers: The Star Wars Connection," *Wall Street Journal*, March 14, 2009, confirms, the basic idea is a straightforward modification of weapons technology.

DIRECTED ENERGY

~

Jeff Hecht

A buzzing sound startled Ellen so she spilled her tea. After years of fighting the spread of insect-borne diseases in a warming world, bugs scared her more than her brother Bernie's war machines.

"Are you okay, Sis?" Bernie asked. "You look jittery."

"I thought I heard a mosquito." She had felt something tickling her left ear earlier, but it had only been the naturally shed macaw feather attached to her new earring.

He chuckled. "You can't be so jumpy in defense work."

She frowned older-sibling disapproval at her errant brother. "Controlling the spread of disease-carrying insects is a serious business, Bernie."

"So is defending against nuclear missiles."

"How many million people did they kill last year?"

"None, thanks to missile defense."

"Really, Bernie?" Ellen was eight years older, and after fifty-two years retained the wisdom of age. "How many nuclear missiles could your lasers really shoot down? You never even tested them."

"It's classified. I can't tell you."

That was his standard line. "It's classified because it doesn't work, and that's embarrassing, isn't it, Bernie?"

"It's a strategic defense system, Sis. It doesn't have to work every time. It's supposed to deter attack, so we only have to convince the other side that it could work."

"So it's all a bluff. I wish I could bluff mosquitoes away. Did anybody ever use anything you developed at Beltway Banditos?"

"The name was Beltway Systems," said Bernie, who had tired of the joke years ago. "Some of our technology has dual military and civilian uses. Remember that low-orbit satellite telephone system I told you about? The laser links between satellites used the pointing and tracking technology developed for our space-based laser interceptor."

"Did the phone satellites ever get off the ground?"

Bernie's face slumped, as it always did when one of his experiments went wrong, and he looked at the floor of his cluttered little house. "They laid me off before they finished the system, and I haven't checked."

Ellen signed. Bernie had spent twenty-five years in the defense industry, until the worsening climate crisis had finally drained the big money away from military hardware. "What are you working on now?"

Bernie's eyes brightened; he always liked to talk about his latest crazy idea. "I found more dual-use potential for the tracking and pointing technology. I've scaled it down a bit, and I have a prototype out in the workshop. With your interest in bugs, you really should see it work."

"Where should I hide?" Ellen remembered the match-head rocket that had burned down the family garage when Bernie was fourteen.

"You don't have to hide," Bernie said, rising from his chair. "You will need a pair of laser safety goggles, though."

When they reached his garage workshop, Bernie handed Ellen a pair of light pink wraparound goggles. "They look pretty clear in the visible, but block the near-infrared beams almost completely."

The goggles made Bernie's hair and moustache look pink. "You're not going to burn holes in my clothes again, are you?" Ellen asked.

"No, nothing like that. It shouldn't harm clothing at all." Bernie put on a similar pair of goggles, pushed a wheeled red metal cabinet, then slid open the garage door.

Ellen saw the power cord to the cabinet was ominously thick. "Is this another of your crazy laser guns?"

"It can't sustain megawatt power, but it's good enough for insects."

"You've made a laser fly swatter?" Bernie flipped open the hinged cover, revealing a black metal bench cluttered with lenses and metal boxes. "This is to a fly swatter as the Internet is to a smoke signal. It includes sensors that track the position of each insect, processors to analyze their trajectories, a tracking and pointing system, and pulsed semiconductor lasers. It runs a modified version of software I developed for an orbiting laser battle station to track a fleet of nuclear warheads."

He pointed at a series of little boxes, and explained their functions too fast for Ellen to follow. Then he flipped a switch.

ZAP! A flash erupted in front of the box, and a little puff of smoke spread into the air. ZAP! Another flash. Except for his white hair and his middle-aged spread, Bernie could have been a sixteen-year-old playing with a new techno-toy.

"Each zap takes out another bug. I can set it to pick out only certain species if you want, so it bags mosquitoes but not butterflies."

Ellen was speechless. Her brother had finally done something worthwhile. The little laser box could destroy incoming disease-carrying insects without using pesticides or harming beneficial types. She could see thousands of the boxes in village squares around the world, blocking the spread of disease. "Incredible!" she said. "Simply incredible."

Bernie glowed with pride.

"How did you manage to scale everything down?"

"Not quite everything." Bernie looked thoughtful for a moment. "It takes a lot of sensors and computer power to track the bugs, but it's a lot cheaper than missile defense."

"Wonderful," Ellen said, nodding her head. She saw one of the little laser boxes point toward her. A *ZAP* sizzled near her ear. "Ouch," she said, putting her hand up and feeling her earring. "Bernie! You burnt the feather off my earring."

"It was moving; it must have fooled the sensors."

"That was a naturally shed feather from an endangered species. I paid seventy dollars for it!"

A familiar impish grin appeared on her brother's face. "We're still ahead. Each laser pulse costs only fifty dollars."

— THOMAS A. EASTON —

"MATCHMAKER"

■ *Analog,* **August 1990.**

If you've ever trained an animal you know how frustrating it can be. Almost inevitably, there comes a time when you wish you could just make the animal stop doing what they're doing. With a chip-controlled animal, you could do just that, but would it be right? Thomas A. Easton explores the ethics of the situation, as well as the human wish to control other beings in this story.

Is such control even possible? The research goes back to the 1950s, when Jose Delgado used implanted wires to stop a charging bull in its tracks. Ethical controversy helped stop the research at the time, but in the last decade or so, chip-controlled cockroaches and rats (Google on "Roborat") have been demonstrated. Today DARPA is funding research into chip-controlled insects ("Cyborg bugs"). The latest achievement is a beetle whose takeoffs, landings, and turns can be controlled remotely. It may be only a matter of time before the ethical debates are no longer academic.

MATCHMAKER

~

Thomas A. Easton

"Sit!" said Jimmy Brane. His dog's ears stiffened. The animal's eyes were bright, and attentive, but his bulldog face was as blankly devoted as ever.

"You don't have the faintest idea of what I want, do you?" He walked behind Tige, tapped the gengineered animal's haunch, and said "Sit!" again. Nothing happened.

Finally, he squatted in front of the dog, sitting on his heels, his eyes on a level with the chrome model of an old eighteen-wheeler that hung from the dog's collar. His arms extended down between his knees. "Sit!"

Tige's, mouth snapped shut. The ears tipped forward. He seemed—could it be? Jimmy wondered—to be saying, "So that's what you want!" And then, indeed, he lowered his rear to the ground.

"Is that all it takes?" asked Jimmy, still squatting, looking up at the dog. Tige was a young Mack just a little larger than an old-fashioned pickup truck. His hide was a dark brindle, with a single white circle around one eye. And he apparently was so smart that all one had to do was show him what one wanted, and he would understand, and obey.

"Shake hands?" he said, his voice uncontrollably tentative. He lifted one hand himself and watched, disbelieving, as Tige did the same. He leaped to his feet and seized the paw. "Shake hands!"

"Good boy!" he said then, and after a few minutes of watching Tige race around the field, he tried again. "Sit!" Tige obeyed immediately, and he also showed as well that he remembered his second lesson. Jimmy seized the proffered paw delightedly and laughed aloud.

Now! he thought, and "Now!" he said out loud. Maybe he had something that would catch black-haired Julie's eye and make her pay attention. Julie Templeton, who was a year ahead of him in the training program and resolutely ignored every attempt he made to chat, Julie, who surely would never, never look at him, or consent to a date, or . . .

Teaching one's truck tricks just wasn't done. Jimmy had therefore deliberately chosen to begin Tige's training in the most remote of the Daisy Hill Truck Farm's many fields. If he had been nearer to the farm's barns and dorms, he might have been seen by his fellow trainees. He would also have been able to see the white fences that surrounded the nearer pastures, and he might have remembered the cattle the farm raised to provide the growing trucks with milk and meat.

Now, sitting obediently on the floor of his stall, stinking as only five tons of dripping wet dog can stink, Tige grinned doggily at his master. His stubby tail thumped cheerfully on the concrete.

"Litterhead!" said Jimmy. To one side of the stall rested a litterbug, a shovel-jawed genimal of porcine stock. Its task was to clean up manure and other rubbish. Unfortunately, litterbugs did not patrol the pastures.

"Litterhead!" Jimmy's face was directed upward, exposed to the rank gusts of dog breath. One hand was wrapped around a massive canine and tugging, as if he could shake the Mack's head back and forth. "It wasn't enough to run, was it? You had to roll. And you had to do it where the cows . . ." Jimmy had had to walk the Mack back to the barn—he had been too filthy to ride—and then to hose him down before returning him to his stall. He had missed breakfast, and now he was late for class.

And it was his own mechin' fault. He shouldn't have been thinking of impressing Julie.

He peered down at himself. His light brown coveralls, the shoulders marked with patches bearing the farm's distinctive logo, a black-eared white beagle, were wet but not dirty. And the wet would dry; he needn't change. With a sigh, he opened a bin mounted on the wall, withdrew a biscuit the size of a football, and tossed it to Tige. Then he rummaged until he found a crumb a little larger than his fist, gnawed loose a chunk, grimaced, told himself that it was better than no breakfast at all, closed the stall's outer door, and left.

"Where have you been, Mr. Brane?" Jimmy froze, bent over the back-of-the-room seat into which he had been about to slip. His fellow trainee truckers looked at him and grinned. The instructor was glaring.

"Cleaning up Tige, Ms. Garland. I walked him in a cow pasture by mistake."

When the laughter subsided, Ms. Garland—Betsy to the staff members, he knew, but not to him, not to any trainee—leaned toward him away from the chalkboard. She was a woman of distinctive shape, three times as large below as she was above, given to tent-like skirts and tight blouses, with the head of a blonde cherub atop it all "I presume you did your reading last night. Tell us, Mr. Brane, why we bother to plug computers into the Macks' brains."

He straightened. He was not one to neglect his studies. "Yes, ma'am. It's so we can have total control of their movements on the road. But . . ."

"But what?"

"Isn't that kind of control unnecessary, Ms. Garland? It seems to be a hangover from when trucks were just machines."

"And now they're alive? And for centuries, dogs have been taught sheepherding, tracking, retrieving, and dozens of other useful tricks? So all we have to do is train them to obey voice commands, or gestures, or reins, and that will do?" She sighed as if she had heard it all before, as of course she had. Now she scanned the class. "Mr. Higgins. Why can't we rely on obedience?"

Alec Higgins, a rangy redhead whom Jimmy considered one of his few friends at the farm, said, "They might not obey. They could decide to chase something, or go after a bitch in heat."

"Not that." Their instructor was shaking her head. "The Bioform Regulatory Administration insisted that the gengineers remove that particular instinct. If they hadn't, even the computers might not be enough. But chasing, yes. Or attempts to socialize with other trucks on the road. You can imagine the traffic jams. And that's what made the BRA require rigid controls before letting Macks go into general use."

"But can't computers go wrong? What about sabotage?"

Ms. Garland nodded. "It's been done, yes. Virus programs and sabotaged chips. But that only led to new designs that are virtually impossible to subvert."

Tonya Metz, dark of both hair and skin, slim, and easily outraged, spoke before her upraised hand could be recognized. "But it's slavery! As soon as they're big enough to go on the road, we turn them into machines, nothing more than masses of muscle and nerves and control circuits. And—"

Ms. Garland nodded once more. "You're quite right. The Macks have much more intelligence than we let them use." She waited out the storm of approval from her students who daily lived with, trained, and loved their young Macks. "But that's the law, even though we may think it's unnecessary. The Macks have to have their freedom at the same time we do—in our off hours."

It would be two more years before Tige was big enough and strong enough to haul the great cargo trailers on the interstate greenways. Until then, Jimmy's days would continue to be filled with classes. He would learn computer operation, rules of the road, trucking history, even something of the gengineering that had created the trucks and other bioforms, and of the skeletal reinforcements that made it possible for them to carry their immense weight. He would learn how to care for his Mack, to watch his nutrition, to groom him and clean him, to notice, tend to, and prevent muscle strains and other ailments.

He would even train Tige, under guidance, teaching him to accept loads such as the control and cargo pod that would be strapped to his back and the trailer he would drag behind for larger loads. Perhaps most important of all, he would teach Tige to submit when the computer was plugged into the socket in the back of his skull. The machine would then override virtually all influence of Tige's will, making him a prisoner within his own skull. It would take a great deal of time and patience and love before Tige would have the necessary faith that control would return, that submission was only temporary, that the abnegation of self was what his master demanded and deserved and that it was therefore right.

That evening, after dinner, when the Macks were all bedded down in their stalls and the trainees were supposed to be studying, Jimmy answered a knock on the door of his room to find Alec Higgins standing in the hall, "C'mon in," he said, gesturing toward the easychair. "I've got beer."

Alec's shoulder patches were identical to Jimmy's, though his coverall bore a broad red stripe from left shoulder to hip. He shook his head. "Nah. I just wanted to stretch my legs. Come with?"

"Sure." Together, they passed down the dorm's central hallway toward the staircase, ignoring the sounds of veedos, music, and conversation behind the doors they passed. At the head of the stairs, they leaned over a balcony to watch the dimly lit floor of the puppy barn below. Steel cages kept the pups away from the ground floor entries, and drainage grills surrounded the bases of the pillars that upheld the dormitory.

The puppies were smaller than Tige was now but still huge, huge enough, Jimmy recalled, simultaneously to intimidate and to enthrall a young man, fresh out of high school, who had never seen them before. Now they lay in sprawling heaps, nestled in straw, windrowed against a wall, snorting, kicking, whining. Litterbugs quietly patrolled the floor.

"Making any progress with Julie?"

"Hah!" Jimmy raised his upper lip, fleering as might a Mack that scented something pungent. After a long moment of silence, he said, "Remember what you told me?"

"Mmm?"

"About how Julie and her friends rode their Macks to a local Scottish games."

"And the pups chased the cabers?"

"Yeah. Do you think she'd like a dog that does tricks?"

"You been teaching Tige to roll over?"

Jimmy gave a short laugh. "Not yet. Not that, anyway."

Alec grinned. "Maybe, but it ain't smart, you know. Keep 'em on the wire. Don't give 'em any choices. And BRA won't give you any trouble."

"I know, but . . ." Jimmy didn't think it was fair. Tige was obviously smart enough to train, quickly and well. He was probably smart enough to drive on the road without any computer hookup at all. Plugging him in must be like gluing a concert pianist's fingers to the keys of a player piano. No trouble, yes. But also no freedom.

"As for women," said Alec, with a wink. "The last thing *you* want to do is start rolling over for *them*."

Was that what Julie liked? Dog games? Tricks? Sitting up and shaking hands were kid stuff. But the Daisy Hill Truck Farm would not, he was sure, approve of building a catapult to throw tree trunks for the Macks to fetch. So maybe he should teach Tige to point every time he saw Julie. No. He shook his head. She probably would not consider that cute.

What could Jimmy do? How could he convince Julie to pay attention to him? She was older, yes, but not that much older. A year, that was all. That was nothing.

Julie herself had trained her Mack for riding. So had every other trainee, even him. Most straddled their truck's neck, hooking their feet under the collar. A few preferred to put a strap around the genimal's chest to bind a bench-like seat upon its back, which was much too broad to straddle.

How trainable were the Macks? No one knew. No one had ever tried to find out, for no one had ever needed to know. As soon as the Macks were grown, their computers made them do everything their masters wished.

It didn't take much longer for Jimmy to decide that perhaps, just maybe, if only he could train Tige to do something new, something no one had ever seen a Mack truck do before, something the computers were never programmed to *make* a Mack do, for it had nothing to do with trucking, then he could impress Julie and get her attention. And then . . . The grin he grinned in the privacy of his skull, he knew, was as fatuous as it could be, but the knowledge did not stop him.

The stock from which Macks had been gengineered had been dominated by English bulldogs, but some showed strong signs of other stocks that had gone into the genetic mix. Julie's Mack, for instance, had a slenderer build and was marked with a few large, white spots on a black background. She resembled more than anything else a Boston bulldog grown up. Julie called her Blackie.

Jimmy stood near the bus barn, chewing his lip and watching the girl and her Mack as they left the stall. Blackie wore only her collar, Julie her farm coveralls and shoulder patches.

Blackie was half again as big as Tige, but that was only because she was a year older and that much closer to her full growth. Eventually Tige would match her, and they would make a pair of Macks well suited for the long-haul routes.

Would he—could he?—be as good a match for Blackie's driver? For Julie? He winced as his teeth came down too hard on a fold of skin. He would never have a chance to find out, would he? Tige was smart, yes. He learned quickly, and he seemed to grasp immediately whatever Jimmy wished. But he could not learn anything that the human could not teach. And Jimmy had been able to think of nothing that might have the remotest chance of making Julie notice him.

He wondered whether she might have any interest in the more abstract question of whether Macks truly needed computer controls. She knew they didn't, for she seemed about to go riding, and Blackie would do her bidding for love and eagerness to please. Not because she was forced willy-nilly to obey.

As Julie closed the door to the stall, Jimmy waved. She turned her head, saw who he was, and turned away. She swung onto the Mack's neck and tucked her feet beneath the collar.

"Litter," said Jimmy. Her deliberate ignoring of his greeting stung. He patted Tige's shoulder and said plaintively, "We haven't got a chance."

The Mack lowered his great head as if he understood. Jimmy climbed aboard, and they followed Blackie onto the curved greenway that passed the Farm, Tige's nails clicking occasionally on the patches of ancient pavement that poked through the grass. Jimmy wished that she would turn and notice him and pause to wait for him. But that didn't matter, any more than did her destination. In just a moment, he and Tige would catch up, while the farm's buildings were still in sight, and then . . .

What could he say? What could he do?

He could only try.

"Julie!" he called.

She turned, saw who was behind her, shook her head, made an exasperated face, and turned away again. Jimmy sensed the clear thought: He was just a kid, right? A year younger, a year less trained. Not worthy of her time.

He slapped Tige on the neck behind his ear. "Go on, boy. Get ahead of her." Then, as Tige drew abreast, he said, "Julie! I've done it!"

When she did not stop or seem to notice, Jimmy had Tige put on enough speed to draw ahead a hundred feet and stop. Then, "Watch!" he yelled, and "Sit," he said, and Tige lowered his hindquarters to the ground. "Beg," and the massive forepaws rose mantis-like into the air. "Speak!" and a thunderous "Woof!" shook the air.

Jimmy untangled his feet from Tige's collar and slid down his back, checking the slide by grabbing handfuls of fur. Tige's skin twitched but otherwise the Mack ignored him, holding his pose almost as rigidly as a statue.

Blackie came nearer and stopped. Julie stared curiously, first at Tige, then at Jimmy. "How'd you get him to do that?"

"I showed him. And I bet Blackie would catch on just as fast." He gestured, inviting her to join him on the ground.

Jimmy watched her hesitate while the wish to know more rose to dominate her scorn for an underclass kid. He turned to the Mack and said, "Lie down." Tige obeyed, and when Jimmy turned back to Julie, he found her standing beside him, an arm's length away. His heart leaped within his chest. He swallowed painfully. She was interested!

"How did you show him?"

"I squatted and begged and lay down and rolled over. And he caught on real fast. They're pretty smart." He eyed her cautiously. "I bet Blackie could catch on, too."

She looked back at her Mack. The genimal was standing quietly, watching the proceedings with every appearance of alert attention. "There's not much point, is there? I mean, it's neat, but who wants a truck that can do tricks?"

Jimmy's spirits fell. He had been right. Such simple tricks were not enough. He waved a hand, and Tige promptly stood up. "But . . ." he said. "It means that we can drive our trucks without the computers. We can train them to do what we say! We don't *need* to enslave them."

She shook her head. "BRA would never allow it. It's not reliable enough." She turned toward her Mack. "You're too idealistic."

Jimmy clearly heard the words she did not say out loud: "Grow up, kid. Forget the silly ideas."

Her tone changed suddenly. "Blackie! Hold still! Dammit!" Jimmy spun around. Julie was reaching for her Mack's collar, but the genimal was sidling away from her. "Look at this!" she cried. "If she had a computer, there wouldn't be any of this nonsense."

Jimmy had to agree that Blackie's behavior was unusual. "She's too young to be in . . ." He caught himself. When the gengineers had removed the male Mack's ability to respond to heat phero-mones, they had also removed the female's ability to produce them, and to respond to male odors. They had, the textbook said, reasoned that while trucks should not respond to each other in that way, neither should the male trucks chase unmodified dogs, or the dogs chase female trucks. For the trucks, mating was neces-sarily a matter of artificial insemination.

"Look at her!" Julie had stopped chasing the Mack. Now she stood, legs spread, arms akimbo, watching as Blackie moved closer to Tige while Tige raised his head and sniffed. Then Jimmy's Mack stepped forward to butt Julie's with the side of his head.

Blackie stood still and cocked her head attentively. Now Tige barked once, softly, and sat. Blackie promptly followed suit. Tige shifted into the begging posture, and so did Blackie.

"I'll be damned!" Julie scowled and stamped one foot on the turf of the greenway. She turned toward Jimmy. "Did you teach him this, too?"

Jimmy shook his head. He was as surprised as she, but he was grinning with delight.

"Then help me separate them!"

"No!" he cried, putting out a hand to halt her movement toward the genimals. He hesitated, trying to think of a plausible excuse for denying her. "They must be trying to show us how smart they are."

"Bull litter!" She pushed his arm aside and reached for her truck's collar. Blackie responded by sidestepping, turning, facing her mistress, and barking once, gently, just as Tige had spoken to her. But she did not sit. Instead, using her nose, she butted Julie gently in the chest, pushing her inexorably toward Jimmy.

Tige simply lay down on the turf, his chin on his forepaws, watching. Jimmy reached out, and when his hand touched Julie's shoulder, Blackie backed off, lay down beside Tige, and joined the watch. Together, they blocked the road entirely. Fortunately, for the moment, there was no traffic.

Julie tried to jerk away, but Jimmy's hand tightened. "I think," he said. "I think your truck wants us together."

"It's none of her business!" she twisted and freed herself of his grasp.

"But that's why I taught Tige those tricks."

"What do you mean?"

"I wasn't really trying to prove we don't need the computers. We don't, but I really just wanted to impress you. To get your attention."

She was looking at him now. He was not quite a kid anymore. "And you expect me to think that my truck agrees with you? That I should let you court me? That I should . . .?"

He said nothing. He simply stood, staring, his hands limp at his sides. The Macks watched them both.

"You are out of your ever-lovin' mind!"

Despite her words, his heart leaped in his chest. She was smiling as she spoke. Smiling at him. And the future bloomed as bright as it had ever done in his dreams.

But then he frowned. His mood crashed. *His* future was bright.

Tige's was darker than ever. His destiny had not changed. He was still the pianist who would have his fingers glued to the keyboard of a player piano, forced to follow willy-nilly someone else's score. But it was not just freedom Tige—and Blackie, too—would lose. Their controlling computers would deny them any chance to exercise the virtuosity they had just displayed.

"What's the matter?" Her hand was on his arm. Concern was in her voice.

He looked at the Macks. They understood so much. Perhaps they even understood this, though their doggy grins said as clearly as words that life held more important things to worry about.

He sighed. Worry was a human thing, wasn't it? Animals, even gengineered animals, tended far more to live in the moment.

Still, he would have to tell her. Perhaps, together, they could find an answer.

three

~~~~~~

BYTE ME!

(Computer-related predictions)

— MURRAY LEINSTER —

"A LOGIC NAMED JOE"

■ *Astounding,* **March 1946**

Before the Internet, if you wanted to answer a question, you either had to know who to ask or be able to look it up. That's not true anymore, as you can research almost anything on the Net. Nearly everyone has access through home computers, magic boxes full of trick circuits. From students to experts, we are all hooked together and share information.

In the 1950s, when integrated circuits were first proposed and built, you still had to know who to ask or look up your answers in a book. This was still true in 1962 when Darpanet, the Internet's predecessor, began. Our modern Internet didn't begin until the 1990s. The details are wrong but the basic concepts for a "magic" box full of "trick" circuits and the interconnections that form the Net are here in "A Logic Named Joe," written in 1946 (and discussed by Robert Silverberg in his introduction to this book).

A LOGIC NAMED JOE

~

Murray Leinster

It was on the third day of August that Joe came off the assembly line, and on the fifth Laurine came into town, and that afternoon I saved civilization. That's what I figure, anyhow. Laurine is a blonde that I was crazy about once—and crazy is the word—and Joe is a logic that I have stored away down in the cellar right now. I had to pay for him because I said I busted him, and sometimes I think about turning him on and sometimes I think about taking an ax to him. Sooner or later I'm gonna do one or the other. I kinda hope it's the ax. I could use a coupla million dollars—sure!—an' Joe'd tell me how to get or make 'em. He can do plenty! But so far I've been scared to take a chance After all, I figure I really saved a civilization by turning him off.

The way Laurine fits in is that she makes cold shivers run up an' down my spine when I think about her. You see, I've got a wife which I acquired after I had parted from Laurine with much romantic despair. She is a reasonable good wife, and I have some kids that are hellcats, but I value 'em. If I have sense enough to leave well enough alone, sooner or later I will retire on a pension an' Social Security an' spend the rest of my life fishin' contented an' lyin' about what a great guy I used to be. But there's Joe. I'm worried about Joe.

I'm a maintenance man for at the Logics Company. My job is servicing logics, and I admit modestly that I am pretty good. I was servicing televisions before that guy Carson invented his trick circuit that will select any of 'steenteen million other circuits—in theory there ain't no limit—and before the Logics Company hooked it into the tank-and-integrator setup they were usin' 'em as a business-machine service. They added a vision screen for speed—an' they found out they'd make logics. They were surprised an' pleased. They're still findin' out what logics will do, but everybody's got 'em.

I got Joe, after Laurine nearly got me. You know the logics setup. You got a logic in your house. It looks like a vision receiver used to, only it's got keys instead of dials and you punch the keys for what you wanna get. It's hooked into the tank, which has the Carson Circuit all fixed up with relays. Say you punch "Station SNAFU" on your logic. Relays in the tank take over an' whatever vision-program SNAFU is telecastin' comes on your logic's screen. Or you punch "Sally Hancock's Phone" an' the screen blinks an' sputters an' you're hooked up with the logic in her house an' if somebody answers you got a vision-phone connection. But besides that, if you punch for the weather forecast or who won today's race at Hialeah or who was mistress of the White House durin' Garfield's administration or what is PDQ and R sellin' for today, that comes on the screen too. The relays in the tank do it. The tank is a big buildin' full of all the facts in creation an' all the recorded telecasts that ever was made an' it's hooked in with all the other tanks all over the country—an' anything you wanna know or see or hear, you punch for it an' you get it. Very convenient. Also it does math for you, an' keeps books, an' acts as consultin' chemist, physicist, astronomer, an' tea-leaf reader, with a "Advice to Love-lorn" thrown in. The only thing it won't do is tell you exactly what your wife meant when she said, "Oh, you think so, do you?" in that peculiar kinda voice. Logics don't work good on women. Only on things that make sense.

Logics are all right, though. They changed civilization, the highbrows tell us. All on accounta the Carson Circuit. And Joe shoulda been a perfectly normal logic, keeping some family or other from wearin' out its brains doin' the kids' homework for 'em. But somethin' went wrong in the assembly line. It was somethin' so small that precision gauges didn't measure it, but it made Joe an individual. Maybe be didn't know it at first. Or maybe, bein' logical, he figured out that if he was to show he was different from other logics they'd scrap him. Which woulda been a brilliant idea. But anyhow, he come off the assembly line, an' he went through the regular tests without anybody screamin' shrilly on findin' out what he was. And he went right on out an' was duly installed in the home of Mr. Thaddeus Korlanovitch at 119 East Seventh Street, second floor front. So far, everything was serene.

The installation happened late Saturday night. Sunday morning the Korlanovitch kids turned him on an' seen the Kiddie Shows. Around noon their parents peeled 'em away from him an' piled 'em in the car. Then they come back in the house for the lunch they'd forgot an' one of the kids sneaked back an' they found him punchin' keys for the Kiddie Shows of the week before. They dragged him out an' went off. But they left Joe turned on.

That was noon. Nothin' happened until two in the afternoon. It was the calm before the storm. Laurine wasn't in town yet, but she was comin'. I picture Joe sittin' there all by himself, buzzing meditative. Maybe he ran Kiddie Shows in the empty apartment for awhile. But I think he went kinda remote-control exploring in the tank. There ain't any fact that can be said to be a fact that ain't on a data plate in some tank somewhere—unless it's one the tehnicians are diggin' out an' puttin' on a data plate now. Joe had plenty of material to work on. An' he musta started workin' right off the bat.

Joe ain't vicious, you understand. He ain't like one of these ambitious robots you read about that make up their minds the human race is inefficient and has got to he wiped out an' replaced by thinkin' machines. Joe's just got ambition. If you were a machine, you'd wanna work right, wouldn't you? That's Joe. He wants to work right. An' he's a logic. An' logics can do a lotta things that ain't been found out yet. So Joe, discoverin' the fact, begun to feel restless. He selects some things us dumb humans ain't thought of yet, an' begins to arrange so logics will be called on to do 'em.

That's all. That's everything. But, brother, it's enough!

Things are kinda quiet in the Maintenance Department about two in the afternoon. We are playing pinochle. Then one of the guys remembers he has to call up his wife. He goes to one of the banks of logics in Maintenance and punches the keys for his house. The screen sputters. Then a flash comes on the screen.

"Announcing new and improved logics service! Your logic is now equipped to give you not only consultive but directive service. If you want to do something and don't know how to do it—ask your logic!"

There's a pause. A kinda expectant pause. Then, as if reluctantly, his connection comes through. His wife answers an' gives him hell for somethin' or other. He takes it an' snaps off.

"Whadda you know?" he says when he comes back. He tells us about the flash. "We shoulda been warned about that. There's gonna be a lotta complaints. Suppose a fella asks how to get ridda his wife an' the censor circuits block the question?"

Somebody melds a hundred aces an says:

"Why not punch for it an' see what happens?"

It's a gag, o' course. But the guy goes over. He punches keys. In theory, a censor block is gonna come on an' the screen will say severely, "Public Policy Forbids This Service." You hafta have censor blocks or the kiddies will be askin' detailed questions about things they're too young to know. And there are other reasons. As you will see.

This fella punches, "How can I get rid of my wife?" Just for the fun of it. The screen is blank for half a second. Then comes a flash. "Service question: Is she blond or brunette?" He hollers to us an' we come look. He punches, "Blond." There's another brief pause. Then the screen says, "Hexymetacryloaminoacetine is a constituent of green shoe polish. Take home a frozen meal including dried pea soup. Color the soup with green shoe polish. It will appear to be green-pea soup, Hexymetacryloaminoacetine is a selective poison which is fatal to blond females but not to brunettes or males of any coloring. This fact has not been brought out by human experiment, but is a product of logics service. You cannot be convicted of murder. It is improbable that you will be suspected."

The screen goes blank, and we stare at each other. It's bound to be right. A logic workin' the Carson Circuit can no more make a mistake than any other kinda computin' machine. I call the tank in a hurry.

"Hey, you guys!" I yell. "Somethin's happened! Logics are givin' detailed instructions for wife-murder! Check your censor-circuits—but quick!"

That was close, I think. But little do I know. At that precise instant, over on Monroe Avenue, a drunk starts to punch for somethin' on a logic. The screen says "Announcing new and improved logics service! If you want to do something and don't know how to do it—ask your logic!" And the drunk says, owlish, "I'll do it!" So he cancels his first punching and fumbles around and says: "How can I keep my wife from finding out I've been drinking?" And the screen says, prompt: "Buy a bottle of Franine hair shampoo. It is harmless but contains a detergent which will neutralize ethyl alcohol immediately. Take one teaspoonful for each jigger of hundred-proof you have consumed."

This guy was plenty plastered—just plastered enough to stagger next door and obey instructions. An' five minutes later he was cold sober and writing down the information so he couldn't forget it. It was new, and it was big! He got rich offa that memo! He patented *SOBUH, The Drink that Makes Happy Homes!*" You can top off any souse with a slug or two of it an' go home sober as a judge. The guy's cussin' income taxes right now!

You can't kick on stuff like that But an ambitious young fourteen-year-old wanted to buy some kid stuff and his pop wouldn't fork over. He called up a friend to tell his troubles. And his logic says: "If you want to do something and don't know how to do it—ask your logic!" So this kid punches: "How can I make a lotta money, fast?"

His logic comes through with the simplest, neatest, and the most efficient counterfeitin' device yet known to science. You see, all the data was in the tank. The logic—since Joe had closed some relays here an' there in the tank—simply integrated the facts. That's all. The kid got caught up with three days later, havin' already spent two thousand credits an' havin' plenty more on hand. They hadda time tellin' his counterfeits from the real stuff, an' the only way they done it was that he changed his printer, kid fashion, not bein' able to let somethin' that was workin' right alone.

Those are what you might call samples. Nobody knows all that Joe done. But there was the bank president who got humorous when his logic flashed that "Ask your logic" spiel on him, and jestingly asked how to rob his own bank. An' the logic told him, brief and explicit but good! The bank president hit the ceiling, hollering for cops. There musta been plenty of that sorta thing. There was fifty-four more robberies than usual in the next twenty-four hours, all of them planned astute an' perfect. Some of 'em they never did figure out how they'd been done. Joe, he'd gone exploring in the tank and closed some relays like a logic is supposed to do—but only when required—and blocked all censor-circuits an' fixed up this logics service which planned perfect crimes, nourishing an' attractive meals, counterfeitin' machines, an' new industries with a fine impartiality. He musta been plenty happy, Joe must. He was functionin' swell, buzzin' along to himself while the Korlanovitch kids were off ridin' with their ma an' pa.

They come back at seven o'clock, the kids all happily wore out with their afternoon of fightin' each other in the car. Their folks put 'em to bed and sat down to rest. They saw Joe's screen flickerin' meditative from one subject to another an' old man Korlanovitch had had enough excitement for one day. He turned Joe off.

An' at that instant the pattern of relays that Joe had turned on snapped off, all the offers of directive service stopped flashin' on logic screens everywhere, an' peace descended on the earth.

For everybody else. But for me, Laurine come to town. I have often thanked God fervent that she didn't marry me when I thought I wanted her to. In the intervenin' years she had progressed. She was blond an' fatal to begin with. She had got blonder and fataler an' had had four husbands and one acquittal for homicide an' had acquired an air of enthusiasm and self-confidence. That's just a sketch of the background. Laurine was not the kinda former girlfriend you like to have turning up in the same town with your wife. But she came to town, an' Monday morning she tuned right into the middle of Joe's second spasm of activity.

The Korlanovitch kids had turned him on again. I got these details later and kind a pieced 'em together. An' every logic in town was dutifully flashin' a notice, "If you want to do something and don't know how to do it—ask your logic!" every time they were turned on for use. More'n that, when people punched for the morning news, they got a full account of the previous afternoon's doings. Which put 'em in a frame of mind to share in the party. One bright fella demands, "How can I make a perpetual motion machine?" And his logic sputters a while an' then comes up with a setup usin' the Brownian movement to turn little wheels. If the wheels ain't bigger'n a eighth of an inch they'll turn, all right, an' practically it's perpetual motion. Another one asks for the secret of transmuting metals. The logic rakes back in the data plates an' integrates a strictly practical answer. It does take so much power that you can't make no profit except on radium, but that pays off good. An' from the fact that for a coupla years to come the police were turnin' up new and improved jimmies, knob-claws for gettin' at safe-innards, and all-purpose keys that'd open any known lock—why there must have been other inquirers with a strictly practical viewpoint. Joe done a lot for technical progress!

But he done more in other lines. Educational, say. None of my kids are old enough to be int'rested, but Joe bypassed all censor-circuits because they hampered the service he figured logics should give humanity. So the kids an' teenagers who wanted to know what comes after the bees an' flowers found out. And there is certain facts which men hope their wives won't do more'n suspect, an those facts are just what their wives are really curious about. So when a woman dials: "How can I tell if Oswald is true to me?" and her logic tells her—you can figure out how many rows got started that night when the men come home!

All this while Joe goes on buzzin' happy to himself, showin' the Korlanovitch kids the animated funnies with one circuit while with the others he remote-controls the tank so that all the other logics can give people what they ask for and thereby raise merry hell.

An' then Laurine gets onto the new service. She turns on the logic in her hotel room, probly to see the week's style-forecast. But the logic says, dutiful: "If you want to do something and don't know how to do it—ask your logic!" So Laurine prob'ly looks enthusi-astic—she would!—and tries to figure out something to ask. She already knows all about everything she cares about—ain't she had four husbands and shot one?—so I occur to her. She knows this is the town I live in. So she punches, "How can I find Ducky?"

OK, guy! But that is what she used to call me. She gets a service question. "Is Ducky known by any other name?" So she gives my regular name. And the logic can't find me. Because my logic ain't listed under my name on account of I am in Maintenance, and don't want to be pestered when I'm home, and there ain't any data plates on code-listed logics, because the codes get changed so often—like a guy gets plastered an' tells a redhead to call him up, an' on gettin' sober hurriedly has the code changed before she reaches his wife on the screen.

Well! Joe is stumped. That's probly the first question logics service hasn't been able to answer. "How can I find Ducky?"!! Quite a problem! So Joe broods over it while showing the Korlanovitch kids the animated comic about the cute little boy who carries sticks of dynamite in his hip pocket an' plays practical jokes on everybody. Then he gets the trick. Laurine's screen suddenly flashes:

"Logics special service will work upon your question. Please punch your logic designation and leave it turned on. You will be called back."

Laurine is merely mildly interested, but she punches her hotel-room number and has a drink and takes a nap. Joe sets to work. He has been given a idea.

My wife calls me at Maintenance and hollers. She is fit to be tied. She says I got to do something. She was gonna make a call to the butcher shop. Instead of the butcher or even the "If you want to do something" flash, she got a new one. The screen says, "Service question: What is your name?" She is kinda puzzled, but she punches it. The screen sputters an then says: "Secretarial Service Demonstration! You—" It reels off her name, address, age, sex, coloring, the amounts of all her charge accounts in all the stores, my name as her husband, how much I get a week, the fact that I've been pinched three times—twice was traffic stuff, and once for a argument I got in with a guy—and the interestin' item that once when she was mad with me she left me for three weeks an' had her address changed to her folks' home. Then it says, brisk: "Logics Service will hereafter keep your personal accounts, take messages, and locate persons you may wish to get in touch with.

This demonstration is to introduce the service." Then it connects her with the butcher.

But she don't want meat, then. She wants blood. She calls me.

"If it'll tell me all about myself," she says, fairly boilin', "it'll tell anybody else who punches my name! You've got to stop it!"

"Now, now, honey!" I says. "I didn't know about all this! It's new! But they musta fixed the tank so it won't give out information except to the logic where a person lives!"

"Nothing of the kind!" she tells me, furious. "I tried! And you know that Blossom woman who lives next door?' She's been married three times and she's forty-two years old and she says she's only thirty! And Mrs. Hudson's had her husband arrested four times for nonsupport and once for beating her up. And—"

"Hey!" I says. "You mean the logic told you this?"

"Yes!" she wails. "It will tell anybody anything! You've got to stop it! How long will it take?"

"I'll call up the tank," I says. "It can't take long."

"Hurry!" she says, desperate, "before somebody punches my name! I'm going to see what it says about that hussy across the street."

She snaps off to gather what she can before it's stopped. So I punch for the tank and I get this new "What is your name?" flash. I got a morbid curiosity and I punch my name, and the screen says: "Were you ever called Ducky?" I blink. I ain't got no suspicions. I say, "Sure!" And the screen says, "There is a call for you."

Bingo! There's the inside of a hotel room and Laurine is reclinin' asleep on the bed. She'd been told to leave her logic turned on an' she'd done it. It is a hot day and she is trying to be cool. I would say that she oughta not suffer from the heat. Me, being human, I do not stay as cool as she looks. But there ain't no need to go into that. After I get my breath I say, "For heaven's sake!" and she opens her eyes.

At first she looks puzzled, like she was thinking is she getting absentminded and is this guy somebody she married lately. Then she grabs a sheet and drapes it around herself and beams at me.

"Ducky!" she says. "How marvelous!"

I say something like "Ugmph!" I am sweating. She says:

"I put in a call for you, Ducky, and here you are! Isn't it romantic? Where are you really, Ducky? And when can you come up? You've no idea how often I've thought of you!"

I am probably the only guy she ever knew real well that she has not been married to at some time or another.

I say "Ugmph!" again, and swallow.

"Can you come up instantly?" asks Laurine brightly.

"I'm . . . workin'," I say. "I'll . . . uh . . . call you back."

"I'm terribly lonesome," says Laurine. "Please make it quick, Ducky! I'll have a drink waiting for you. Have you ever thought of me?"

"Yeah," I say, feeble. "Plenty!"

"You darling!" says Laurine: "Here's a kiss to go on with until you get here! Hurry, Ducky!"

Then I sweat! I still don't know nothing about Joe, understand. I cuss out the guys at the tank because I blame them for this. If Laurine was just another blonde—well—when it comes to ordinary blondes I can leave 'em alone or leave 'em alone, either one. A married man gets that way or else. But Laurine has a look of unquenched enthusiasm that gives a man very strange weak sensations at the back of his knees. And she'd had four husbands and shot one and got acquitted.

So I punch the keys for the tank technical room, fumbling. And the screen says: "What is your name?" but I don't want any more. I punch the name of the old guy who's stock clerk in Maintenance. And the screen gives me some pretty interestin' dope—I never woulda thought the old fella had ever had that much pep—and winds up by mentionin' an unclaimed deposit now amountin' to two hundred eighty credits in the First National Bank, which he should look into. Then it spiels about the new secretarial service and gives me the tank at last.

I start to swear at the guy who looks at me. But he says, tired:

"Snap it off, fella. We got troubles an' you're just another. What are the logics doin' now?"

I tell him, and he laughs a hollow laugh.

"A light matter, fella," he says. "A very light matter! We just managed to clamp off all the data plates that give information on high explosives. The demand for instructions in counterfeiting is increasing minute by minute. We are also trying to shut off, by main force, the relays that hook into data plates that just barely might give advice on the fine points of murder. So if people will only keep busy getting the goods on each other for a while, maybe we'll get a chance to stop the circuits that are shifting credit-balances from bank to bank before everybody's bankrupt except the guys who thought of askin' how to get big bank accounts in a hurry."

"Then," I says, hoarse, "shut down the tank! Do somethin'!"

"Shut down the tank?" he says, mirthless. "Does it occur to you, fella, that the tank has been doin' all the computin' for every business office for years? It's been handlin' the distribution of 94 percent of all telecast programs, has given out all information on weather, plane schedules, special sales, employment opportunities and news; has handled all person-to-person contacts over wires and recorded every business conversation and agreement— Listen, fella! Logics changed civilization. Logics are civilization! If we shut off logics, we go back to a kind of civilization we have forgotten how to run! I'm getting hysterical myself and, that's why I'm talkin' like this! If my wife finds out my paycheck is thirty credits a week more than I told her and starts hunting for that redhead—"

He smiles a haggard smile at me and snaps off. And I sit down and put my head in my hands. It's true. If something had happened back in cave days and they'd hadda stop usin' fire— If they'd hadda stop usin' steam in the nineteenth century or electricity in the twentieth— It's like that. We got a very simple civilization. In the nineteen hundreds a man would have to make use of a typewriter, radio, telephone, teletypewriter, newspaper, reference library, encyclopedias, office files, directories, plus messenger service and consulting lawyers, chemists, doctors, dietitians, filing clerks, secretaries—all to put down what he wanted to remember an' to tell him what other people had put down that he wanted to know; to report what he said to somebody else and to report to him what they said back. All we have to have is logics. Anything we want to know or see or hear, or anybody we want to talk to, we punch keys on a logic. Shut off logics and everything goes skiddoo. But Laurine—

Somethin' had happened. I still didn't know what it was. Nobody else knows, even yet. What had happened was Joe. What was the matter with him was that he wanted to work good. All this fuss he was raisin' was, actually, nothin' but stuff we shoulda thought of ourselves. Directive advice, tellin' us what we wanted to know to solve a problem, wasn't but a slight extension of logical-integrator service. Figurin' out a good way to poison a fella's wife was only different in degree from figurin' out a cube root or a guy's bank balance. It was gettin' the answer to a question. But things was goin' to pot because there was too many answers being given to too many questions.

One of the logics in Maintenance lights up. I go over, weary, to answer it. I punch the answer key. Laurine says:

"Ducky!"

It's the same hotel room. There's two glasses on the table with drinks in them. One is for me. Laurine's got on some kinda frothy hangin'-around-the-house-with-the-boyfriend outfit that automatic makes you strain your eyes to see if you actually see what you think. Laurine looks at me enthusiastic.

"Ducky!" says Laurine. "I'm lonesome! Why haven't you come up?"

"I . . . been busy," I say, strangling slightly.

"Pooh!" says Laurine. "Listen, Ducky! Do you remember how much in love we used to be?"

I gulp.

"Are you doin' anything this evening?" says Laurine.

I gulp again, because she is smiling at me in a way that a single man would maybe get dizzy, but it gives a old married man like me cold chills. When a dame looks at you possessive—

"Ducky!" says Lanrine, impulsive. "I was so mean to you! Let's get married!"

Desperation gives me a voice:

"I . . . got married," I tell her, hoarse.

Laurine blinks. Then she says, courageous: "Poor boy! But we'll get you outta that! Only it would be nice if we could be married today. Now we can only be engaged!"

"I . . . can't—"

"I'll call up your wife," says Laurine, happy, "and have a talk with her. You must have a code signal for your logic, darling. I tried to ring your house and noth—"

Click! That's my logic turned off. I turned it off. And I feel faint all over. I got nervous prostration. I got combat fatigue. I got anything you like. I got cold feet.

I beat it outta Maintenance, yellin' to somebody I got a emergency call. I'm gonna get out in a Maintenance car an' cruise around until it's plausible to go home. Then I'm gonna take the wife an' kids an' beat it for somewheres that Laurine won't ever find me. I don't wanna be fifth in Laurine's series of husbands and maybe the second one she shoots in a moment of boredom. I got experience of blondes. I got experience of Laurine! And I'm scared to death!

I beat it out into traffic in the Maintenance car. There was a disconnected logic in the back, ready to substitute for one that hadda burned-out coil or something that it was easier to switch and fix back in the Maintenance shop. I drove crazy but automatic. It was kinda ironic, if you think of it. I was goin' hoopla over a strictly personal problem, while civilization was crackin' up all around me because other people were havin' their personal problems solved as fast as they could state 'em. It is a matter of record that part of the Mid-Western Electric research guys had been workin' on cold electron-emission for thirty years, to make vacuum tubes that wouldn't need a Dower source to heat the filament. And one of those fellas was intrigued by the "Ask your logic" flash. He asked how to get cold emission of electrons. And the logic integrates a few squintillion facts on the physics data plates and tells him. Just as casual as it told somebody over in the Fourth Ward how to serve leftover soup in a new attractive way, and somebody else on Mason Street how to dispose of a torso that somebody had left careless in his cellar after ceasing to use same.

Laurine wouldn't never have found me if hadn't been for this new logics service. But now that it was started— Zowie! She'd shot one husband and got acquitted. Suppose she got impatient because I was still married an' asked logics service how to get me free an' in a spot where I'd have to marry her by 8:30 PM? It woulda told her! Just like it told that woman out in the suburbs how to make sure her husband wouldn't run around no more. *Br-r-r-r!* An' like it told that kid how to find some buried treasure. Remember? He was happy totin' home the gold reserve of the Hanoverian Bank and Trust Company when they caught on to it. The logic had told him how to make some kinda machine that nobody has been able to figure how it works even yet, only they guess it dodges around a couple extra dimensions. If Laurine was to start askin' questions with a technical aspect to them, that would be logics' service meat! And fella, I was scared! If you think a he-man oughtn't to be scared of just one blonde—you ain't met Laurine!

I'm drivin' blind when a social-conscious guy asks how to bring about his own particular system of social organization at once. He don't ask if it's best or if it'll work. He just wants to get it started. And the logic—or Joe—tells him! Simultaneous, there's a retired preacher asks how can the human race be cured of concupiscience. Bein' seventy, he's pretty safe himself, but he wants to remove the peril to the spiritual welfare of the rest of us. He finds out. It involves constructin' a sort of broadcastin' station to emit a certain wave-pattern an' turnin' it on. Just that. Nothing more. It's found out afterward, when he is solicitin' funds to construct it. Fortunate he didn't think to ask logics how to finance it, or it woulda told him that, too, an' we woulda all been cured of the impulses we maybe regret afterward but never at the time. And there's another group of serious thinkers who are sure the human race would be a lot better off if everybody went back to nature an' lived in the woods with the ants an' poison ivy. They start askin' questions about how to cause humanity to abandon cities and artificial conditions of living. They practically got the answer in logics service!

Maybe it didn't strike you serious at the time, but while I was drivin' aimless, sweatin' blood over Laurine bein' after me, the fate of civilization hung in the balance. I ain't kiddin'. For instance, the Superior Man gang that sneers at the rest of us was quietly asking questions on what kinda weapons could be made by which Superior men could take over and run things—

But I drove here an' there, sweatin' an' talkin' to myself.

"What I oughta do is ask this wacky logics service how to get outa this mess," I says. "But it'd just tell me a intricate and fool-proof way to bump Laurine off. I wanna have peace! I wanna grow comfortably old and brag to other old guys about what a hellion I used to be, without havin' to go through it an' lose my chance of livin' to be a elderly liar."

I turn a corner at random, there in the Maintenance car.

"It was a nice kinda world once," I says, bitter. "I could go home peaceful and not have belly-cramps wonderin' if a blonde has called up my wife to announce my engagement to her. I could punch keys on a logic without gazing into somebody's bedroom while she is giving her epidermis an air bath and being led to think things I gotta take out in thinkin'. I could—"

Then I groan, rememberin' that my wife, naturally, is gonna blame me for the fact that our private life ain't private any more if anybody has tried to peek into it.

"It was a swell world," I says, homesick for the dear dead days-before-yesterday. "We was playin' happy with our toys like little innocent children until somethin' happened. Like a guy named Joe come in and squashed all our mud pies."

Then it hit me. I got the whole thing in one flash. There ain't nothing in the tank setup to start relays closin'. Relays are closed exclusive by logics, to get the information the keys are punched for. Nothin' but a logic coulda cooked up the relay patterns that constituted logics service. Humans wouldn't ha' been able to figure it out! Only a logic could integrate all the stuff that woulda made all the other logics work like this—

There was one answer. I drove into a restaurant and went over to a pay-logic an' dropped in a coin.

"Can a logic be modified," I spell out, "to cooperate in long-term planning which human brains are too limited in scope to do?"

The screen sputters. Then it says:

"Definitely yes."

"How great will the modifications be?" I punch.

"Microscopically slight. Changes in dimensions," says the screen. "Even modern precision gauges are not exact enough to check them, however. They can only come about under present manufacturing methods by an extremely improbable accident, which has only happened once."

"How can one get hold of that one accident which can do this highly necessary work?" I punch.

The screen sputters. Sweat broke out on me. I ain't got it figured out close, yet, but what I'm scared of is that whatever is Joe will be suspicious. But what I'm askin' is strictly logical. And logics can't lie. They gotta be accurate. They can't help it

"A complete logic capable of the work required," says the screen, "is now in ordinary family use in—"

And it gives me the Korlanovitch address and do I go over there! Do I go over there fast! I pull up the Maintenance car in front of the place, and I take the extra logic outta the back, and I stagger up the Korlanovitch flat and I ring the bell. A lad answers the door.

"I'm from Logics Maintenance," I tell the kid. "An inspection record has shown that your logic is apt to break down any minute. I come to put in a new one before it does."

The kid says "OK!" real bright and runs back to the livin' room where Joe—I got the habit of callin' him Joe later, through just meditatin' about him—is runnin' somethin' the kids wanna look at. I hook in the other logic an' turn it on, conscientious making sure it works. Then I say:

"Now kiddies, you punch this one for what you want. I'm gonna take the old one away before it breaks down."

And I glance at the screen. The kiddies have apparently said they wanna look at some real cannibals. So the screen is presenting an anthropological expedition scientific record film of the fertility dance of the Huba-Jouha tribe of West Africa. It is supposed to be restricted to anthropological professors an' post-graduate medical students. But there ain't any censor blocks workin' anymore and it's on. The kids are much interested. Me, bein' a old married man, I blush.

I disconnect Joe. Careful. I turn to the other logic and punch keys for Maintenance. I do not get a services flash. I get Maintenance. I feel very good. I report that I am goin' home because I fell down a flight of steps an' hurt my leg. I add, inspired:

"An' say, I was carryin' the logic I replaced an' it's all busted. I left it for the dustman to pick up."

"If you don't turn 'em in," says Stock, "you gotta pay for 'em."

"Cheap at the price," I say.

I go home. Laurine ain't called. I put Joe down in the cellar, careful. If I turned him in, he'd be inspected an' his parts salvaged even if I busted somethin' on him. Whatever part was off-normal might be used again and everything start all over. I can't risk it. I pay for him and leave him be.

That's what happened. You might say I saved civilization an' not be far wrong. I know I ain't goin' to take a chance on havin' Joe in action again. Not while Laurine is livin'. An' there are other reasons. With all the nuts who wanna change the world to their own line o' thinkin', an' the ones that wanna bump people off, an' generally solve their problems— Yeah! Problems are bad, but I figure I better let sleepin' problems lie.

But on the other hand, if Joe could be tamed, somehow, and got to work just reasonable— He could make me a coupla million dollars, easy. But even if I got sense enough not to get rich, an' if I get retired and just loaf around fishin' an' lyin' to other old duffers about what a great guy I used to be— Maybe I'll like it, but maybe I won't. And after all, if I get fed up with bein' old and confined strictly to thinking— Why, I could hook Joe in long enough to ask: "How can a old guy not stay old?" Joe'll be able to find out. An' he'll tell me.

That couldn't be allowed out general, of course. You gotta make room for kids to grow up. But it's a pretty good world, now Joe's turned off. Maybe I'll turn him on long enough to learn how to stay in it. But on the other hand, maybe—

— GREGORY BENFORD —

"THE SCARRED MAN"

■ *Venture*, **May 1970.**

When physicist and soon-to-be-famous science fiction writer Dr. Gregory Benford was working at Lawrence Livermore Laboratories from 1967 to 1971, he said, "One day I was struck by the thought that one might . . . intentionally [make] a [computer] program that deliberately made copies of itself elsewhere." The next step, of course, was to write such a program. It worked, thereby becoming the first computer virus (though it did not carry any sort of nasty payload designed to steal passwords or create a spam-sending bot-net).

Then he wrote this story as an extrapolation of the basic idea. He calls it his only "truly prophetic" story and notes that the idea was first picked up in the early 1970s by other science-fiction writers. Later, unfortunately, computer viruses became common in the real world, and an entire industry has grown up to combat them. As in the story, a popular antivirus program is in fact called "Vaccine" (see for example http://download.cnet.com/Panda-USB-Vaccine/3000-2239_4-10909938.html).

THE SCARRED MAN

~◡

Gregory Benford

The cold seeped through my rough jacket. I hurried along the poorly lit mall, sensing the massive ice that lay just beyond the plastaform walls. That was when I first noticed the man with the scar.

Few patrons were out this early, nosing into the cramped shops or reading the gaudy neon adverts outside the clubs. Later the gambling would bring them in from their docked ships and the mall would fill. There would be noise and some singing, a brief flurry of fighting here and there, the calling of barkers. Dark women in filmy dresses would stroll casually for customers, making the men forget the chill of fifteen meters of snow overhead.

Thus it was that the scarred man stood out among the few idlers. He hurried, with that slight toeing in of the feet that comes of walking down the narrow passages of a commercial submarine. I would have noticed him even without the scar on his face, because there was something furtive in his movements, some hint that he felt eyes upon him.

In this place it was not at all unusual to see a scar, a tattoo, or even a flesh wound, freshly made. Ross City was a free port, the only large one in Antarctica. Privateers and smugglers filled the coves.

Ross was a straitlaced American explorer of a century or so before. I am sure he would have reddened with outrage at some of the things which went on in the city that bore his name. Submarines with silenced screws were plying a steady trade in smuggled oil, running between the outlaw offshore rigs of Australia and the hungry markets of North and South America. Ross City, tucked into a shelf jutting out from Mount Erebus., lies on a great circle between Australia and Chile: it was the natural focus of men skirting the law.

Smugglers had money—anyone dealing in scarce raw materials did, these days. They were willing to spend for a secure port to hole up in, particularly when the UN patrols were conducting their usually futile southern Pacific sweeps. The submariners lived with danger; a few close scrapes were a hazard of the trade. A scar in itself was not unusual; the man's manner was. And beneath his obviously altered face, I knew this man.

I decided to follow him. Perhaps the chill air made me reckless. Perhaps my skiing hadn't quite drained me of the random, unfocused energy a man acquires in a desk job. I told myself I was on holiday, bound for an evening slumming in the trade, bars, and a bit of spice before serious drinking would not be out of place. I dug in my heels and went after him.

He ducked down a side passage. I turned the corner only a moment behind him. It was a short block, but my man had vanished. Into one of the shops? Several were day businesses darkened. The others—

I glanced quickly into a dingy shrimp-fry joint and didn't see him. The next brightly lit entrance was a homosexual restaurant/bar; the signifying emblem was prominently displayed. I passed it by—my man didn't look the sort, and he hadn't behaved as if on the way to an assignation.

There remained one doorway, one that by chance I knew well. VOYAGER TAVERN the blue neon proclaimed, though it was actually an alcohol and pill bar. I often put in here during an evening's rounds, searching for atmosphere. Some dangerous men are said to frequent the place, particularly in the back rooms. I came to the Voyager for the ample drinks and relaxed mood.

I hesitated, wondering if I should dash down the street and check beyond the next corner, and then pushed through the Voyager's door. I was right. My man stood only a few feet away, back to me. He looked slowly around the room, as if expecting to find someone he knew. He was taking his time doing it. Probably his eyes took a while to adjust to the dark, after the garish lighting outside. Mine did, too; but I knew the bar well and slipped silently around him, navigating by the low murmur of conversations more than the dim red lighting.

I chose a side booth with a good view of the room, sat, and looked back at the scarred man. One of the Voyager's girls approached him with a graphic gesture, smiling from beneath impossibly long eyelashes. He waved a hand, brusquely dismissing her, and said something in a rasping voice. She shrugged and moved off.

The scarred man nodded at someone across the room from me and I followed his look. I was surprised: he nodded at an acquaintance of mine, Nigel Roberts. Nigel was playing cards with an array of scruffy men in khaki; he raised a finger in salute and went back to studying his hand.

The man sniffed and continued to search the bar. He seemed to have an air of distance and reserve about him that was most atypical of the sort of man who became a smuggler. His face bore an expression that implied he felt himself above the customers in the bar and disliked being so distantly greeted by someone he knew.

"Hello," a woman's voice said. "On for an evening of pleasure?"

It was the same girl, again. I had been with her once before and found her competent but uninspired. I doubted if she remembered my face. I smiled, told her no, and she drifted away.

The movement attracted the man's attention. He peered at my table, squinting in the poor light, holding up a hand to block out the glare of a nearby lamp.

Then he saw me. His face froze with shock.

His wiry arms tensed suddenly and he glared at me with an intense, burning rage. He took three jerky steps forward, balling his fists.

I shifted my weight forward onto my feet. I lifted myself off the booth seat about an inch. The movement would be imperceptible in this light. I was ready to move to either side, which is about all one can do when attacked in a sitting position. I breathed deeply, setting myself automatically for whatever came.

Abruptly, he stopped.

The scar ran down from below his ear to the very tip of his pointed chin. In this light it flamed a stark red. But even as I watched, it subsided and faded back into the pallor of his skin. He remained standing, weight set, frozen.

We gazed at one another for a long moment.

He flushed, lowering his eyes, and shook his head. He glanced up at me once more, as if to check and be sure I was not the man he had supposed. With a dry sound he shrugged, abruptly turned, and marched into the back room of the bar.

As he moved through the pink patches of light and shadow I noticed that his scar was deeper near the throat. As though made by the blade of a knife coming from below. It was not fresh and bore the dark, mottled look of a deep cut that could not be readily corrected by a skin graft or even tissue regeneration.

I sighed and settled back. He was probably calming himself in the back booths with one of the more potent—and illegal—drugs. My heart was pounding away, fueled by the adrenaline of a moment before. I had found the experience unsettling, for all its intriguing aspects, and I finished my first drink, when it came, in one long pull.

I had come into Ross City that evening for a break from the genteel monotony of the Mount Erebus resort, where I spent most of my holiday. The tourist value of Antarctica lies in the Mount's ski slopes and the endless plains of blinding white. The sting of the incredible cold quickens my blood. I ski there yearly, rather than on the tailored and well-known slopes in Eurasia or the Americas. Conditions there are quite pedestrian. Like all sports in this century, it has been rendered simple, safe, and dull for the ant armies who want everything packaged and free of the unexpected.

Near the great population centers—a phrase that includes virtually all the planet now—there is little risk and thus no true sport. For that, you come to Antarctica.

Unfortunately, the adventurers are seldom exceptional conversationalists and I found them boring. A week at the Erebus resort was more than enough to become saturated with tales of near-accidents, broken bindings at the critical wrong moment, and slopes-I-have-known. So I took the tube down to the City, strolled through the red-light districts and ate in the expatriate restaurants. It is perfectly safe even for a gentleman of my obvious affluence, for sportsmen and tourists are well treated. We bring in Free Dollars, which in turn create the economic margin that allows the City to remain a free port.

"Interesting one, eh?" Nigel said at my elbow.

The card game had broken up soon after the scarred man left, so Nigel came over to sit with me. I did not ask after his fortune. He didn't volunteer information, so he had lost again.

"Yes," I said. "For a moment he seemed to know me."

"I noticed. Come to think, you *do* look something like—"

"Who? The man who gave him that scar?"

"Well, it's a bit of a story, that scar and all."

"Fine. Let's have it. What are you drinking?"

When a snow frappe—laced with rum and cloves—had come for him, Nigel continued.

"He's a restless sort, that one. Name is Sapiro. Been on the subs for quite a time now. Hard to miss him with that scar, eh?—and he's not the type to be overlooked anyway. Always on the push, though I expect he's slowed down a bit now. Must've been born ambitious." Nigel's Australian accent inevitably gained the upper hand once he said more than two sentences at a go. I noticed he seemed nervous, drumming his fingers on the tabletop and fidgeting with his glass. Perhaps his gambling losses had unsettled him.

"The man's done everything, at one time or another. Jobbed on an offshore rig, worked the fishing fleets, did some depth mining until the UN outlawed using amateurs in that game." Nigel looked at me with narrowed eyes. "Had a habit of rushing things, being a touch careless. He wanted to get places fast."

"He hasn't come very far, for all that."

"Ah, but you don't know."

"Know what?"

Nigel hesitated, as though deciding whether to tell me. His brow crinkled with thought. Why was the decision so important? This was simply a casual conversation. But somehow, underneath, I caught a thread of tension in Nigel. Did he have some personal stake in Sapiro?

Nigel looked at me across the table, fingering a napkin. Intently, with a sudden rush, he began:

"Sapiro started as a technical type. Computers. Worked for International Computational Syndicate."

"That is the combine with IBM as principal holder, isn't it?"

"Right. I'm sure you know what those outfits are like—regiments of stony-eyed executives, each one with a fractional share of a secretary, living in a company suburb and hobnobbing with only company people. A closed life. Well, that's what Sapiro got himself into and for a while he didn't mind it. Fit right in. All he wanted to do was get to the top, and he didn't care what he wore or where he lived or what he had to say at cocktail parties to get there."

"But it didn't last."

"For a man like Sapiro, ICS wasn't enough. Back in the 1990s, you know, that was when the white-collar squeeze came on. Computers had caught up. Machines could do all the simple motor function jobs and then they started making simple executive decisions, like arranging routing schedules and production plans and handling most of the complaints with automatic problem-solving circuits. That didn't leave any room for the ordinary pencil pusher and they started to wind up in the unemployment lines.

"Well, Sapiro wasn't playing in that low-caliber a league, but he could feel the hot breath on his neck. He guessed the machines were always going to be getting better and the rest of his life would be a tough, flat-out race to stay ahead of their capabilities."

"He was right," I said, sipping at my mug.

"Sure he was. Three quarters of the population can tell you that right now from firsthand experience.

"But ambition is a funny thing. Sapiro wanted his share of the loot—"

"I gather that was rather a lot."

"A fortune, nothing less. Enough to keep him above the herd for life, without him ever lifting a finger. You see, he wasn't hot for power or status. It was money he wanted. Once he had the money he'd get some status anyway. It's not easy to keep those two separate these days. Once you've got a high living standard, you get a taste for status and power, they're the ones everybody's after. Funny."

"What did Sapiro do?" I said to hurry him along. Nigel had a tendency to lapse into philosophy in the middle of his stories.

"Well, he didn't want to fight the computers. So he looked for a way to use them. By this time he was a minor executive baby-sitting for the experimental machine language division, over-seeing their research and reporting back to the company. He had a brother-in-law in the same lab, a mathematican. They were good friends—Sapiro was married to the researcher's sister—but they didn't see much of each other in an official capacity.

"One evening they had the brother-in-law over to dinner and were sitting around talking shop. Everybody likes to make fun of computers, you know, and they were making jokes about them, figuring up schemes to make them break down and all that."

"Everybody is afraid of them," I said.

"Yes, I suppose that's it. Fear. They were tossing around ideas and having a good time when the brother-in-law—his name was Garner—thought up a new one. They kept kicking it around, getting a few laughs out of it, when they both suddenly realized that it would really work. There weren't any holes in it, as there were in most computer stories."

"This was a new vulnerability the designers had overlooked?" I said.

"Not exactly. The new machines ICS was putting together had a way they could be rigged, and no one could tell that one little extra circuit had been built in. It never functioned in any other capacity, except the way Garner wanted it to.

"It worked like this. You start with your own computer, one of the new models. Give it a program to execute. But instead of doing the job immediately, the machine waits awhile and then, in the middle of somebody else's calculation, takes five or ten seconds out to do your work. You know what a random number generator is?"

"Well . . . it's some sort of program, isn't it? It produces a number at random and there is no way to tell what the next one will be. The first one might be a 6, next a 47, then a 13. But there is no way to tell what the next one will be."

"That's it. The time interval before your computer did your job would be random, so that the guy whose program came ten minutes after ours was supposedly done didn't always find five or ten seconds missing. That made the trouble hard to trace, even if the other guy noticed he was losing a few seconds.

"But the kicker in all this is that Garner had found a way to charge those seconds to the account that was running at the time."

"Oh, I see. That gave him free running time at someone else's expense. Very clever."

"Yes, but not quite clever enough. After all, he and Sapiro had access to only one or two computers. If they stole lots of time from the other users—and what would they do with anyway?—it would be noticed."

"Could they not sell the computer time to some other company?"

"Of course. But they couldn't steal much. It wouldn't be profitable enough to run the risk."

"I imagine the risk would be considerable as well."

"Quite. You know as well as I what the cartels are doing these days. It was even tougher then, ICS owned Sapiro and Garner. As long as they were employed there the company could arrange their 'disappearance' and few would be the wiser. They lived in a company town that looked the other way when company goons dispensed justice. No, the risk wasn't worth it. The scope would have to be a lot bigger—and the profits—before they could afford to make the gamble.

"Garner was the better technician but Sapiro knew the way management's mind worked. Any fool knew computer time was worth money. The corporations would take pains to be sure no one could make away with sizable chunks of it, chunks large enough to perform a respectable calculation. So Sapiro figured he'd do just the reverse of what ICS expected."

"Oh? I—"

"Here's what he did. He had to have Garner's help, of course, in hiding the initial program inside a complicated subroutine, so even a careful search wouldn't find it. That was Garner's only contribution, and a good thing, too, because he wasn't a man who could deal with people. He knew nothing of character, couldn't tell a thief from a duke. Or so Sapiro thought."

"Then Sapiro—" I said. The only way to get Nigel to hold on to the subject was to threaten to interrupt, a theory which was quickly verified when he raised his voice a decibel and plunged on:

"The program he logged in instructed the computer to dial a seven digit, telephone number at random. Now, most phones are operated by people. But quite a few belong to computers and are used to transfer information and programming instructions to other computers. Whenever a computer picks up the receiver— metaphorically, I mean—there's a special signal that says it's a computer, not a human. Another computer can recognize the signal, see.

"Sapiro's computer just kept dialing at random, hanging up on humans, until it got a fellow computer of the same type as itself. Then it would send a signal that said in effect, 'Do this job and charge it to the charge number you were using when I called.' And then it would transmit the same program Sapiro had programmed into it."

"So that—" I said.

"Right on. The second computer would turn around and start calling at random intervals, trying to find another machine. Eventually it would."

"I see, much like the windup toy game."

"The what?"

"When I was a boy we used to wonder about those windup dummies one could buy. Suppose you got a bunch and fixed them so they would just walk to the next dummy and wind him up with the little screw on the back. I remember once thinking that I could mobilize an entire windup toy army that way."

"Didn't work though, did it?"

"No." I smiled wryly. "I'm told the trouble lies in the energy. No dummy would have the power to wind up another to quite the same strength, so they would all run down pretty soon."

"Yup, that's it. Only with Sapiro the money to pay for the few seconds of computer time was coming out of all the accounts available to the computer, completely randomly. He was using somebody else's energy."

"I still don't see—"

"As soon as the program was in the machine and working, he and Garner quit. Those were tough days, and ICS didn't shed any tears to see them go. Their friends thought they were crazy for throwing up good jobs."

"How did they live?"

"Opened a computer consultant firm. Got no business, of course, but they were biding their time. All the while that one computer at ICS was dialing away, making a call about every twenty minutes. Pretty soon it had to find another soulmate, then there'd be two dialing.

"Garner calculated it would take five months for half the ICS computers in North America to be reached. But before that, programmers began to notice longer running times for standard jobs they'd set up, and people started to worry. The Sapiro program was buried deep and it was random, so everybody figured the trouble was a basic fault of the ICS computer. A random symptom is always evidence that the machine is failing, they said."

"Enter, Sapiro and Garner, Consultants," I said.

"You got it. They volunteered to find the trouble for free the first time. Garner was smart enough to hide what he was doing, and in an hour or so they straightened out the machine. Said they had a new method and couldn't reveal it. All they'd done was countermand the program that had been telephoned into the machine.

"That got them all the publicity they needed. They fixed a lot of ICS computers for incredible fees, only they did it through a cover agency so ICS wouldn't realize who they were.

"It worked fine because even after they'd debugged a machine, sometime or other another computer that hadn't been fixed would call up and transmit the orders again. They never ran out of customers.

"Sapiro got rich and so did Garner, only Garner never seemed to show it. He didn't buy anything new or take his wife to Luna for a vacation. Sapiro figured it was just Garner's shyness. He didn't imagine his partner was saving it all up someplace where he could run when the time came. Sapiro didn't have much time to think about it anyway because he was working eighteen hour days, with assistants to do fake work as a blind. The flunkies would go in, fiddle with the machine the way Sapiro had told them, and then Sapiro would pop in, dump the program—he called it VIRUS—and take off. The people who owned the machine never suspected anything because it looked like a complicated process; all those assistants were there for hours.

"Sapiro and Garner just flew around the hemisphere, selling their cure-all—Sapiro called it VACCINE—and making money.

"Then one night the ICS goons came after him. They weren't out for fun, either. They tried a sonic rifle at short range and the only thing that saved Sapiro was an accident—his 'copter fell into a lake, where the ICS goons couldn't reach him to finish him off. He floated on a seat cushion and kept his head low while they searched from shore. It was late fall and the water was leeching the warmth out of him. He waited as long as he could but the ICS agents didn't leave the shoreline—they were just making sure.

"He started paddling. It was hard to make any time without splashing and attracting attention but the movement kept him warm a little longer—just enough to get him to the other end of the lake. It wasn't a lake, actually, but a reservoir. Sapiro heard a rushing of water and thought it was the edge of the falls. He tried to swim away but by that time he was too weak. He went over.

"But it wasn't the falls. It was an overflow spot that fell about ten feet and then swirled away, taking him with it. The current carried him a half mile beyond the edge of the park area. He staggered up to the street, found a cab and used his credit cards to get to a hotel."

"He didn't go home?"

"No point. ICS had the house, his wife, everything. He checked by phone and found out several interesting things. That Garner hadn't come to work that day. That Garner's home numbers didn't answer. That his office was surrounded by ICS men.

"It took him three days to find Garner. He'd holed up somewhere and thought he was safe, but Sapiro bought off a few people and tracked him.

"Garner had sold out to ICS, of course. The deal was that ICS wouldn't touch him after he handed over the information, but that didn't stick for Sapiro. When ICS saw what fools they'd been, they went for blood and Sapiro was the nearest throat handy. They'd have killed Garner, too, if they'd known where he was.

"So after Sapiro took every Free Dollar Garner had—he was carrying it in solid cash, some jewelry and universal bank drafts, to be sure ICS didn't get it—he called ICS and told them where Garner was. He'd left Garner boarded in and tied up."

"Then it all resolved satisfactorily," I said. "He got his money and his freedom."

"Freedom, yes. Money, no. Sapiro ran for Australia and beat it into the bush country. ICS never tracked him but they got some of the cash by good luck, and Sapiro had to spend the rest of it to keep them off his tail. He had a year or two of good living but then it was gone. Even while he was spending it there was not much fun to it. ICS was still looking for him, and by coincidence an agent ran into him in Sydney. Sapiro got the worst of the fight but he smashed the fellow's head when they both fell over a railing—he landed on top.

"That convinced him to lie low. It was about time he had to anyway because the money was almost gone. He got onto the offshore rigs and then into smuggling because it paid better. He's still doing it. He can't forget that he was once a big operator, though, and he looks down his nose a bit at the people he must associate with."

"Is that why he seemed a bit cold and reserved when he came in here?" I asked.

"Probably. He isn't a bad sort and he does tell a good joke. He would've come in and been sociable if he hadn't seen you."

"Why me?"

"He showed me some pictures from the ICS days once. One of them was of Garner. There's a fair resemblance between you two. Garner's hair was darker, but then it might have lightened with age."

"But ICS took care of him," I said.

"Maybe. Sapiro left him for ICS, but Garner might have gotten away or even talked his way out of it. Improbable, granted, but it could have turned out that way."

"I don't think Sapiro is afraid of Garner at all, but you'll admit it must have been a shock for him to think he saw his old partner like that."

"Yes," I said, "I can well understand it. He gave me rather a start just by glaring at me."

"Good job he realized his mistake. Might have—"

"But look," I said. I was becoming impatient. "You said you would tell me about that scar. It's an awful thing, ought to have something done about it. How did Sapiro get it? When the 'copter crashed, or in the fight with the ICS man?"

"Ah yes, that. He's fond of the scar, you know. Wouldn't have it changed for anything, says it makes him look dashing. Stupid."

I raised an eyebrow. "Why? A man can allow himself a few eccentricities."

"Not a man like Sapiro. ICS can't afford to have someone still in circulation, living proof that ICS can be beaten. It might give some other ambitious chap an idea or two."

"But it's been years!" I said. "Surely—"

"The only sure thing is that ICS is big and Sapiro, however clever, is small. That, and his mouth is too large. He has told his story too many times, over too many drinks."

"The same way you're telling me now."

Nigel smiled and the lines in his face deepened in the dim light of the bar. "It doesn't matter now. Sapiro told his little tale to a man who needed money. A man who knew who to call at ICS."

I hesitated for a moment. I glanced toward the back room of the bar. A haze of pungent marijuana smoke was drifting lazily through the beaded curtain that shielded the back. Sapiro was probably quite far gone now, unable to react quickly.

"A man who gambles, you mean," I said slowly. "A man who fancies himself a shrewd hand at cards, but somehow cannot manage to get the best of the gaming tables here in Ross City and simply won't stay away from them."

Nigel regarded me coldly, unmoving. "Pipe dreams," he said, too casually.

"But our man still feels guilty about it, doesn't he? The old code about ratting out on friends—doesn't vanish so easily as you thought? So while you're waiting for the finish you tell an acquaintance about Sapiro, maybe thinking I will agree that he is a dishonest, stupid man who might as well be converted into cash for poor Nigel, the overdrawn gambler?"

"There's nothing for it, you know," he said grimly. "The scar's given him away back there. It wasn't hard to describe to them. By the time you could reach the curtain—"

Through the strands of colored beads, but somehow as though from far away, there came a faint scream. It had an odd bubbling edge to it, as if something was happening to the man's throat. Abruptly it became something else, something far worse, and suddenly ended.

The job was perfectly done. The terrible sound had never risen above the hum of conversation in the front room, never disturbed the layered smoke and drowsy mood. No head but mine had turned.

Quite professional.

Nigel was looking at me smugly; unconsciously, I had jumped to my feet. His face was losing its lines of strain.

"Finish your drink?" he said. "There's nothing more to do. What can any of us do, eh? Eh?"

I nodded and sank back into my seat. It was done. ICS had their man at last; they'd been satisfied.

I was free.

"THE INFODICT"

Asimov's Science Fiction Magazine, **August 2001.**

Want to know everything someone does or even thinks? It used to require following them around, tapping their phone, and bugging their bedroom or office, or hiring a private eye to do these things for you. It's called stalking, and it isn't nice. It's even a crime.

If the person you're stalking likes or loves you, it might not be an issue, but it can get old fast. Or it used to. In a connected, networked world, where one can keep an eye on social networking sites such as Facebook and tap into traffic surveillance cameras, networked water and electric meters, and a thousand other indicators of the other person's behavior, it might become normal. In fact, one might be alarmed if one detects that the other person isn't watching you just as obsessively!

Even in such a world, some people will take it to extremes. James Van Pelt gives us such a person in Sanji, whose interest in Marlyss is so obsessive that he quite justifies the story's title, "The Infodict." But it seems a sure bet that the easier it becomes to satisfy such an obsession, the more common it will become. We can see the first signs in how many ordinary people Google friends and prospective dates, as well as in warnings to be careful about what we say on sites like Facebook.

THE INFODICT

～

James Van Pelt

Sanji kept a spider on Marlyss constantly, and his Concierge prompted him with updates. As Sanji sold forty cases to the crosstown outlet, it scrolled her location when her car passed under a traffic vid at Divisadero and Pine.

At the moment, he was in his office, deep in his leather chair, feet up, but it wouldn't matter if he was at home or at the park or on a flight; when the info flowed, he swam in it.

Earlier in the day he'd played back some of her phone calls. Last week she'd said, "I'd love to have dinner with you." He replayed it several times, her liquidy contralto. "I'd love to . . . I'd love to . . . I'd love to . . . "

Where's she going? Sanji called up her travel patterns for the last week, Monday's for the last month, and every fifth of the month for the year. Numbers rolled through the air between him and his desk, everything he'd gathered on her since they'd started dating a year ago. No match. He OKed the delivery, quick scanned for reservations she might have made or credit blips. Nothing. He red flagged the time for later analysis just as it reported her at Divisadero and Lombard.

"You watching Marlyss again, bud?" said Raymond. "You're obsessive." Raymond sat on the edge of Sanji's desk. As usual his tie didn't match his shirt, and the suit coat should have been retired years ago. Rather than getting a hair implant, he had combed thin strands over the bald spot. "Where's your specs? Don't you work here anymore?"

Sanji minimized the Marlyss profiler, but kept the program running in the background. New numbers showing this afternoon's inventories, shipments, and condition of the delivery fleet popped up. All in the green. He stood, smoothed the front of his jacket, checked his look in the mirror. Businessman perfect. Just the right part in the hair. A meticulous, trim appearance.

"I get buzzed if there's a problem." Raymond pointed to the flesh-colored button in his ear. "I'm just a PR flak. Nonessential paperwork only. Short of a complete emergency, my job could be done by a high school intern." He shrugged. "Let me take you to lunch."

Sanji's own earphone squeaked a high pitched, short-speak message about highway traffic and truck travel time. With a pressure on his desk handplate, Sanji alerted the drivers.

"I've got the expense account. I'll pay." Sanji put his desk on auto mode, which handled routine calls, rerouted email and forwarded everything to the Concierge, a black, wallet-sized case attached to his belt.

Sanji checked the daily specials at Reefers, a favorite spot for the business crowd, and ordered while they walked. "What do you want?" Above them thin clouds filtered the San Francisco afternoon, softly lighting apartment buildings and trees.

Raymond said, "Don't you ever turn that thing off? I thought I'd decide when we got there."

Sanji laughed. They wove through the lines in front of the fast food kiosks. "You're a positive Luddite. We can have the food waiting, cooked to our specifications, eat, and be out in fifteen minutes. Don't you know they hate customers like you?"

They turned down a long hill, each step jolting Sanji's specs as they flashed that Marlyss had used credit to park her car at a lot just off Divisadero and Marina Boulevard. Weather numbers scrolled up: 65 degrees, 86 percent humidity and gusty breezes off the bay. Probably cold as hell. A list of small restaurants and shops within walking distance appeared, all in historic San Francisco, most without vid security he could tap into. He checked her med monitors. Pulse over 100 and steady. Respiration elevated. She was walking. Blood sugar a little low. Probably going to lunch herself. But why downtown? Why the change of habit? Did it mean anything about their relationship? He wouldn't know where she was until she paid for something.

Sanji ran a quick check on her infosystems. As far as he could tell, she hadn't accessed any data about him since dinner last night. Did that mean she didn't care?

"Maybe I don't know what I want yet," said Raymond

"That's the point. You could be deciding now. You're not a very good multitasker." Other pedestrians walked around them. Most wore specs. Many of them working, sub-vocalizing communiques, their eyes flitting back and forth as they read data.

Raymond looked from building to building. Sanji knew Raymond was interested in restored architecture. Why he didn't access the info off the Net was beyond him. Raymond actually liked to *see* the structures.

Raymond said, "So, did you ask her?"

Sanji wrinkled his brow. It was such a direct question. "Yes, last night."

"And?"

They crossed the street and entered Reefers. "Good afternoon, sirs," said the door as it opened for them. "Your table is ready."

A line shimmered on the floor leading them into the restaurant. On the walls, outdoor footage of a rock concert surrounded them. The soundtrack was just loud enough to make other patron's conversations unintelligible.

Sanji said, "She wants to think it over. She'll tell me tonight. I'm thirty-two. You'd think I wouldn't be so nervous."

"Thirty-two and never been married. As far as dating goes, you're practically a teenager. Thinking it over's better than a no." They sat. "Can I get a menu?" Raymond said to the table.

A minute later a waiter, looking miffed, delivered a paper version of the day's offerings. "Are you new to Reefers, sir? We have a much more attractive electronic display tailor-made for our Concierge customers."

"You'll just have to come back, son. I left mine at work," said Raymond. The waiter's jaw dropped, and Raymond added, "You must be the new one. I've eaten here twice a week for four years."

The waiter did the peculiar mid-focus, twitchy stare someone got when checking a readout in his specs. "Who *are* you, sir?"

Raymond smirked. "I pay cash."

"Ah, one of those," said the waiter with a sniff, as if everything was clear now. He stalked away.

"Where do you *get* cash?" said Sanji.

"If you go to your bank in person, and present identification, it's still available. Mostly they keep it around for international travelers."

Sanji shook his head. This was another of Raymond's oddities. He was so consistently dependable, however, that management had decided he was eccentric rather than weird.

"But why go to the trouble?"

The waiter appeared again, an order tablet in hand.

"I haven't decided yet," said Raymond, and the waiter turned on his heel. "That boy isn't going to get a tip."

Sanji toyed with his napkin. Around them, others were eating their meals, their conversations lost in the projected concert's ambient noise. On the wall, a new band mounted the stage. A sea of heads stretched from the foreground to the stage's base.

Raymond said, "That's Woodstock. The 2014 one. I love the classic footage. The other night they showed the old Who concert that ended in a riot. Pretty strange to be eating shrimp in the shell while watching cops beating kids over the head with batons."

"It's the atmosphere," said Sanji. He called up the Marlyss profiler again. Her pulse was down, but he had no fresh information on her other than she only had fifteen minutes left on her parking. The day after being asked to marry, she goes off on a strange errand. The question was, what was on her mind?

"Is it work or Marlyss now?"

Sanji snapped the display off guiltily. "How'd you know?"

"Your eyes get all spastic."

Sanji sighed. "How can you stand it, not being connected? Do you know where your wife is this instant? Have you checked on your children this morning?"

Raymond put the menu down. "Now that I'm ready, where's that waiter? No, I haven't checked on them. I don't know how you do it. You can't eternally keep your fingers on everyone's pulse. It'll drive you crazy."

Marlyss's heart rate blinked onto the display again. The Concierge reported it had remained unchanged for the last ten minutes. Analysis indicated she was sitting or standing, probably eating lunch. Was she alone? Something fluttered in Sanji's chest. "I have a right to all the information that's available. That's the law. What would be crazy would be not taking advantage of it."

Sanji's earplug beeped a pay-attention as new displays scrolled across the bottom of his specs. The Far Eastern division reported a markdown in raw material pricing. If he ordered now, he could cut 7 percent on manufacturing, invest the savings in interest-bearing bonds for an extra percent and a half. He thought for a couple seconds about whether the numbers could drop more, decided that they might, but not much, placed the order and shifted funds into the right accounts. In the meantime, a tiny vid window opened up in the upper left corner of his vision. The spider had found Marlyss. In the grainy picture from a bank's security camera she walked up the street, gripping her coat closed at her neck. The breeze whipped her long, red hair in front of her face.

A quick query placed the bank a half block from her car. The Concierge listed three restaurants that were her most likely lunch spot. All touristy seafood places. But she hadn't *paid* for anything.

If she wasn't eating lunch, what was she doing there? She walked out of the first camera's view, and the Concierge switched to another camera that caught her back as she walked up the block, then out of sight around the corner.

"You're not going to make it until this afternoon, are you? Man, you are practically comatose when you pay attention to that thing. You're an infozombie. They have twelve-step programs for your problem."

Sanji squirmed. "You can never get enough good data. That's why all information is public. Nothing is private."

"Maybe that's OK for business activities or government policy. You're trying to read her mind. Ah, there he is."

The waiter reappeared, looking bored.

"What's the catch of the day? The menu didn't list it."

Rolling his eyes, the waiter said, "Orange roughy."

"I'll have that then."

Sanji leaned forward. "You don't get it. If you love someone, you want to know everything you can. How else will she know I care?"

"They used to call that 'stalking.'"

"That's ridiculous. Stalking is following her around. Threatening her. All I'm doing is accessing available data, which is my right. She knows I can do it—everybody does it—in fact, she probably expects me to. This is the information society."

"All I know is in matters of the heart, the more you know the more you don't know."

Sanji sat back. The waiter arrived, pushing a cart, their meals steaming. He put the plates in front of them. When he left, Sanji said, "What the hell does that mean?"

Raymond smiled, cut into the orange roughy. "It means that sometimes you don't want to know what's on the menu until you get there."

For the rest of the meal, they ate quietly while rock crowds cheered on the walls. Numbers rippled across Sanji's vision: delivery times, work schedules, stock prices. His earplug whispered status reports. When he finished, he couldn't remember what he'd eaten.

At work Sanji set a countdown clock in his specs' upper right corner. Four hours until he met Marlyss. She went home. No vids in her house, but her security alarm reported when she disarmed it, electricity consumption went up as she turned on lights, water usage indicated she'd showered. Then, nothing. Her pulse perked along steadily. Her Concierge was in sleep mode.

He drummed his fingers on the desk, baffled. Why wasn't she checking on him? In the year they'd dated she had *never* checked on him as far as he could tell. From her point of view, their entire relationship was based on conversations and the time they'd spent together. No wonder she can't answer the question: she doesn't know me, he thought. A stomach twinge hit, and he flinched. His own med readouts indicated indigestion and suggested an antacid. He wondered what he had eaten that would cause that; he couldn't recall anything spicy. Last night had been the same though, and it wasn't food-related. He told her good night, the echo of his proposal fairly hanging in the apartment's air. Her hand rested briefly on his, her fingers warm and long and fine. "I need to think about it," she said.

After she left, he laid in his bed staring at the ceiling, thinking about her beside him. He rubbed his palm over the sheets on what would be her side. They were cold and smooth and empty. He tried to recapture the moment before he asked her, when the words were formed but he hadn't spoken them yet. Even now, only minutes later, he could hardly believe he'd had the nerve to do it. Then the twinge. Stomach acid reflux. She wasn't there, and maybe she never would be. His guts tied up inside him, but he didn't get medicine. He put on his specs, activated the Concierge, started the data streaming. Green text flowing across his eyes. Quick-speak chirps in his ear. After a while, he connected the spider for Marlyss. It picked through the megamillion information strands, and soon he swam in her numbers. All of them. Medical records, shopping purchases, paychecks, tax returns, utility bills, loans, bank statements, school, everything. And the vids he'd saved. Marlyss at the mall. Marlyss in the park. Marlyss coming and going from a thousand places, all captured digitally, stored somewhere, and retrieved by him.

But nowhere—not a clue—on how she would answer his question. Sanji clenched the sheets. How could the answer not be there? What was left to know?

His eyes grew dry watching the clock count down. He blinked and shook his head. Scrolled through jewelry catalogues, screen after screen of wedding rings. Checked travel brochures. South American beach resorts. European tour packages. What would she like? Briefly he connected with a flower shop, then broke it off. She said she wanted time. Flowers would seem pushy. Or would they be romantic? What was in her head?

He imagined a sensor planted in everyone's brain. Readouts cunningly tailored to track emotion and thought. *That* would be information worth having. There would be no need for guess-work.

Irresistibly, with glacier-like gravity, the clock unwound the minutes.

Marlyss waited for him in front of the Maritime Museum. In the dusk behind her a restored schooner attached to the dock with three permanent gangplanks thrust its bare masts into the cloudy sky. Sanji walked quickly. The wind cut through his jacket, and he realized he hadn't been near the sea in months. She'd suggested Fisherman's Wharf for their rendezvous. "I like the seagulls," she'd said.

He'd correlated seagulls to her database and found she'd papered the first apartment she'd rented, years before they met, in

Seascape Serenity, a pattern of lighthouses, chambered nautiluses, and seagulls.

"I missed you," he said as they hugged, and he regretted the words immediately. It'd only been a day. He sounded needy.

"Me too." She held his hand and they strolled toward the shops and tourist attractions. In the bay to their left a cargo hovercraft, surrounded by its self-generated mist, thundered past Alcatraz. He sensed the unanswered question between them like a malignant djinn.

Glumly he noted the temperature and weather report to give himself something to watch. Even though she walked beside him, he couldn't resist replaying "I'd love to have dinner with you." To give himself courage, he triggered the loop: "I'd love to . . . I'd love to . . . I'd love to. . . ."

Beside him, she was a silent cipher, red hair spilled over her jacket, most of her face obscured. Just the edge of her cheek and a bit of her nose visible from the side. Something didn't look right about her. As they walked, he glanced from the corner of his eye several times. Finally it occurred to him. She wasn't wearing her specs! He ran a quick check. Her Concierge was still in her apartment.

Casually he reached up and pulled his own off. He blinked against the breeze, hitting him square in the face for the first time. They went into his pocket. He shut down his Concierge, and his earplug went dead.

Sidewalk stands they passed sold cheap T-shirts and San Francisco trinkets. Crab and beer smells escaped the restaurants. Tourists waited in lines for tables. She led them into a maze of souvenir displays and then onto a boardwalk overlooking a small marina. Private fishing boats bobbed under the dock lights. It was nearly night. The buildings cut the wind, and Sanji didn't feel as cold.

Marlyss said, "I come here sometimes when I want to think." She sat on a wooden bench and when he sat beside her, she looked straight at him for the first time since they'd started walking. Her hand went to his cheek. "Sanji." She traced a line from his temple to the corner of his mouth. "I've never seen you without your specs."

And they were kissing, her lips soft against his, her breath quick against his skin. After a minute, he realized she was crying. His face was damp with it. He touched a tear from below her eye with wonder.

She said, "They told me you were an infodict. My friends told me you were . . . emotionally isolated." She giggled, a surprising sound in her throaty voice. "Oh, Sanji, I would love to marry you."

And they kissed again, long and silent. Sanji felt the waves beneath them lapping against the pilings, rocking their bench the tiniest bit. Seagulls cried in the bay. He held her close. She trembled, and he trembled too. It was all so huge, the emotion within. In the night, in the artificial light, the boats moved in elegant witness to the moment. Sanji knew he would remember this instant forever.

He didn't know how long they'd sat before Marlyss straightened and pulled away from him. She wiped her face. "I need to tidy up a bit. Do you mind? There's a restroom just around the corner. I won't be a minute."

"Of course not," he said, and even these little words felt different, because now he was speaking them to the woman who'd said yes. Everything was different now: the quality of air, the quality of sound, all of it. "I'll be right here," he said.

She kissed him on the cheek, smiled, and walked to the corner of the building, her footsteps loud against the boards.

Sanji leaned back, the bench a firm support behind him, and he stretched his legs. He sighed. It was good.

Then he noticed a small box halfway up the light pole on the dock across the water, a police unit, an infrared camera turned on only at night for security. Of course, the police would watch closely at night, when most crimes occurred. He looked around. The area was thick with surveillance. Accessible surveillance. His hand snuck into his pocket, caressed his specs. He twitched the Concierge back to life.

Yes, there he was, in reds and blacks as the camera saw him. He expanded the search, jumping from camera to camera. There was the front of the building he sat behind now. There was the side. There was the door to the public restroom. Sanji backed up the infrared vid a couple of minutes. There was Marlyss, entering the restroom. Sanji turned the spider up a notch. Water ran in the restroom. A hand dryer pulled energy.

He thought, what's she thinking now? Is she sorry she said yes? Will she always love me? It would take a lot of data to know. The information would have to flow fast and furious. Yes it would.

When she came out, he put the specs back in his pocket, but the Concierge was ready. The spider was running, and it would never rest.

— RAJNAR VAJRA —

"E-MAGE"

■ *Analog*, July 1999.

Identity theft is nothing new. It once involved stealing bank and credit card statements and phone bills from the garbage and using the account numbers to make calls or charge purchases. In a more extreme form—"ghosting"—it could mean passing yourself off as the other person. The usual method was to find someone of your age/general description, get documents pertaining to them, and use the documents to become that person.

One of the most infamous ghosts was the "Great Impostor," Ferdinand W. Demara, Jr., who impersonated the surgeon Joseph Cyr on a Royal Navy boat, including performing surgeries (and no one died!) during the Korean War. He was exposed when Joseph Cyr's mother read an article about his surgeries and declared him a fraud, as her son was a civilian. (She called him first to be sure.)

Now that agencies can share databases and cross-check data, it should be impossible for someone to adopt another's identity while they still live. Right? But what if the identity thief could change the data in the databases? What if people didn't socialize enough off-line for anyone to be able to testify that they really were who they said they were? "E-Mage" paints a frightening portrait of the consequences, and we can only hope that Rajnar Vajra is dead wrong.

For our money, his real prediction shows up in a one-liner: "When society collapses, *my* accusing finger is going to be pointing at the damn banks. . . ." Remember, this was 1999, not 2009.

E-MAGE

Rajnar Vajra

My bills were paid to the end of the month—hallelujah!—and junk food overstuffed the fridge. So when someone knocked on my door in that tentative fashion which says client rather than salesperson, Jojoba's Witness, or landlord, I got excited.

If some quick money sprinted my way, for once it could be squandered on something more fun than the utilities or frozen peas. Maybe that Iomega teragulp-drive I'd had my eye on . . .

None of my uncle's illegal equipment was poking up from the strategic debris so I yelled, "Come right in, door's not locked."

It was seldom locked. In this neighborhood (not hell, but you can smell it from here), a locked entrance speaks of vulnerable people or valuables inside; so my trick is to post "armed response" stickers, put convincing bulletholes in the wall opposite my doorway, leave the door unbarred, and sink my good stuff in a sea of garbage.

With barely decent haste, I uncovered my work terminal and punched it into active mode. With my other hand, I lit a fresh stick of sandalwood incense. One look sent my dog, Little Mo, scurrying off to the bedroom. I needn't have rushed. Nothing happened for so long, I got tempted to ignore my bad knees and leap up to pull the procrastinator inside by force.

Finally, two strangers sidled nervously through the trashy hightide and stood next to me blinking and squinting, struggling to pierce the sweet smog. The glare of my big, wall-mounted video membrane made the air even more opaque, transforming tendrils of incense-smoke into glowing tentacles.

As for me, it takes more than a little fog to screw up my vision. Besides, my visitors radiated desperation as vivid as a searchlight.

Married but not newlyweds, I guessed. The woman was pretty and trim and freckled and a pinch older than me, perhaps matching my computer monitor by being twenty-five. Years, in her case, not inches; she was of "normal" height—although compared to me she was a giant. The man was cute, blond, very tall, and looked twenty at most even with no-sleep bags under his eyes. He kept wiping sweat off his upper lip.

The curtain was up and I was putting on a show.

While I looked the prospective clients over, my fingers were typing 222 words per minute of genuine C-Quad-Plus code which I'd memorized for the purpose.

Two purposes, actually. For most people, it silently advertised my expertise. Equally important, if I looked busy, no one would expect me to stand up and shake hands. So new clients would swallow my competence before getting turned off by how short and young and female I was.

Here we be, ladies and gendermen, in the third decade of the twenty-first century and American society is as size-ist, age-ist, appearance-ist, anthropocentric, racist, and sexist as ever. Even here in supposedly cosmopolitan Detroit. Ah well, our species is still very young as species go, maybe someday we'll actually grow up . . .

Grow up! Would you listen to me? Even *my* metaphors are size-ist, and I'm only two and a half inches from being classified a freaking midget!

"Are you . . . you must be Sharon Peabody?" The man observed.

"Who the hell gave you *that* name," I snarled, still typing like an Alternative American Standard Keyboard whirlwind.

"Uh, this superhacker we met at a computer swap-meet. We went there . . . looking for advice."

"Superhacker. Might you be more *specific*?"

"Well . . . he was skinny, had a droopy moustache like Buffalo Bill. Called you a genius and a 'freelance heroine' when it comes to computer crimes. Said you salvage lives and money on, uh . . . 'spec.' God, I hope it's true!"

"Long thin hair at the sides, but Mr. Scalp on top?"

"That's the guy. Said he was 'Grim,' but we're not sure if that was his name or his mood."

"Last name. His first happens to be Herman. Next time you see him, be sure to call him Herm; he loves that. And yes, I work on contingency. Sometimes. I can't give you an estimate until I know the score but I'll try to be reasonable. Meanwhile, I'm 'Emagia' to you two or 'E-Mage' if you want to get formal. You see, in here," I tapped my camouflaged CPU, "I'm a *magician*. Anyone who tries Sharon on me better move aside quick. Are we on the same home page?"

"Whatever you say . . . Emagia. I'm Brian, Brian Feldman, and this is my wife Tricia. We'll pay whatever—whatever you think is fair. Provided you can get us our money back, of course. If not, I don't see how we can pay you at all. Christ! I guess you can tell we need help . . . pretty damn bad."

"Flop on the couch and tell the tale. Just brush those magazines aside." I'd finished the sequence I was pretending to work on and pretended to save it with a command which made the drive light come on briefly. Verisimilitude and all that. Then I quit C++++ and swiveled to face the clients.

Brian tried to smile at his wife. "Do you want to explain, honey, or should I?"

"I'll do it," Tricia surprised me by saying. "We've been . . . I believe the word is compsumed, Emagia. You probably know what that means better than we do."

"Not necessarily. Personal experience is a peerless teacher. I do know that computer-subsumption has devastating effects on its victims. But the good news is that: those effects are usually *reversible*."

Her chin was quivering as she fought to get the words out. "But we've lost *everything*. We can't even prove we're *us*!"

I winced despite my morale-boosting intentions. "That's pretty harsh. When they steal your identities along with your stuff it's 'major compsumption.' Big-league rip-off. Most broadbandits can only dream about pulling such stunts. Still have your U-cards?" I'd never heard of a fully compsumed person managing to keep their Universal-card, but it could happen.

"Brian's was taken when he tried to use an ATM, and I lost mine when we went to the police. They ran it through their data-capture machine and—"

"And someone else's file popped up. So the cops impounded the card. Right?"

Brian, who'd been fidgeting like a four-year-old in church, couldn't keep quiet any longer. "They said they were going to 'investigate,' but that was a *week* ago! And they've gotten nowhere!"

"Still, they must have basically believed you. Otherwise, you'd have been arrested for sure. What have you been doing with yourselves since this happened?"

"Talking to people," he said. "Trying to find someone like you. We've been staying with friends, but our cash has run out and we can't get any more. Whoever did this . . . they've taken our savings, our business, our checking. Even our stocks."

"Hold up." I savored that word "stocks"; this case held promise! "You're staying with *friends*? Well *that's* unusual. Heavy broadbandits generally avoid people with living family or friends. They look for super-isolated individuals or couples, usually self-employed types who travel constantly. People with detached roots, or those who've never grown any."

"That was us until a week ago. These friends of ours, we met them *after* this nightmare started. I guess we just lucked out; the Hortons are great but they can't really vouch for us."

"Too bad. Anyone else you've had recent personal contact with? Accountants? Bank tellers? Don't laugh; I happen to think it's worth the fee to deal with a real, live *homo sapiens*."

When society collapses, *my* accusing finger is going to be pointing at the damn banks. . . .

"Think, folks! How about real-estate agents? Business associates, landlords, neighbors, waiters who might remember you paying with plastic, car sleazepeople . . . ?

Brian patted his wife's hand despite the fact that his was trembling too. "You mean salespeople? We don't own a car. Had an apartment, but we got it through the Web and never got to know our neighbors. No families, just like you said. Our business— we're art dealers—is . . . *was* done entirely through the Web. No one really *knows* us, not enough to back us up. We've always used automated services for pretty much everything."

Maybe no man is an island, but this couple had dug themselves one huge trench!

"All right. I'm praying you remember your U-card numbers. Give those to me, and we'll take a sneak peek around the North American Data Base and see what's what. While you're at it, give me the Hortons' first names."

No need to draw the big gun yet, so I followed standard spy protocol, working my way into a major mainframe (Omaha's Insurance Common) with weak security but good access. From here, I could safely call up the gov files corresponding to the Feldmans' identity numbers. I logged on as Prudential rep "Anne Omenis" and my ODM (online data manager) extracted and applied the hour's password.

My clients stared at the big monitor, fascinated by the results of my keyboard prowess (no voice-driven baby toys for me). To them I must have seemed fast as teflon-coated lightning, but most of my attention was elsewhere. I was multitasking, and the second task only showed on an independent monitor—a light-emitting-plastic membrane hidden from where my guests were sitting.

My first priority was to make sure I wasn't being set up. If the cuckoos who'd pried my clients from their lives were top pros, I might have to use Uncle Terry's induction-reality gear to set matters right. I couldn't afford to get caught.

So I focused a hidden camera, digitized the Feldmans' faces, and sent the images with a 64-bit sample of their voices to a certain friend in a certain government agency.

By the time the NADB files popped up, my friend had confirmed that my visitors weren't narcs.

According to the North American Data Base, they also weren't the Feldmans.

The official Feldmans were older: a heavyset, thirty-two-year-old, black-haired man with some nasty facial scars; and a blond dumpling of a woman with three chins and mascara-encrusted eyes. The kind of woman whose perfume you could almost smell over the Internet.

"There you are," I said cheerfully, turning around again. "My, but you look so much better in person."

"Those are the slashers?" Brian asked, leaning forward to get a better view.

"They may be on the team. But they're not 'slashers.'" It bugs me when people get their terms mixed up. "Slashers are hackers, mostly kids, who make destructive viruses for fun and are too immature to grasp how much their fun makes people suffer. *These* assholes are 'cuckoos,' because they take over other people's nests . . . steal their nesteggs."

"Oh. Cuckoos. But now we know what they look like!"

"Sorry, but I doubt it. These pictures don't mean a thing. If the images aren't total fakes, our nouveau-Feldmans are undoubtedly disguised."

"Shit! So we're royally screwed?"

"*Electronically* screwed if anything. Buck up! You've come to the right place." I smiled confidently, hoping my clients could see it through the murk, but not well enough for the insincerity to register. "If you guys are telling the truth, and I'm betting you are, someone has covered up the original information."

Tricia's eyes were running (misery or my incense?) and she was rubbing her stomach. "How can you help us, if they erased the information?"

"Didn't I say 'covered up'? Trust me, you don't *erase* data from the NADB, they have watchdog routines just waiting for someone to try. And 'vipers' ready to do something about it. But remember the millennium fears about the old computer systems that had only two digits for the date? Ever since then, systems engineers have left things more . . . open-ended. An expert can *add* data. And if you know exactly where and how to look, you'll find a two-byte time-stamp on the modification. That's our starting point."

When I was twelve and blissfully unaware that my last growth spurt had been just that, my favorite relative, Uncle Terry, threw all his nieces and nephews a joint birthday party.

He hired Amazing Bob, the type of magician who does such gigs, and Amazing Bob treated us all to a full hour of close-up magic.

I was standing close enough to the man to smell chocolate cake on his breath when he finally pulled a stunt that left me baffled. He made a fist and slowly stuffed a big silk scarf into it. Then he opened his hand. No scarf. Then he did the whole thing in reverse.

Man, was I upset! His other tricks had been child's play to figure out and I'd been feeling pleasantly smart and superior. The scarf had really gone into his hand, I was sure of that much, and he hadn't palmed it away or whisked it up his sleeve; both his sleeves were rolled up.

Finally, in frustration, I stormed into the kitchen to be alone and think.

Assuming he wasn't actually making the silk vanish or rendering it invisible—and nothing about Amazing Bob suggested anything remotely amazing—I could only imagine one explanation, although it seemed absurdly improbable.

He had a secret pocket hidden somewhere on his *hand*, maybe a fake finger, and that's where the scarf had gone.

This *had* to be the answer, but I didn't really believe it until I rejoined the group and scrutinized Bob's left hand.

Not only was there an obvious rubber cap on his thumb, what made it obvious was that it was an *entirely different tint* than the rest of his hand. And none of us had noticed!

After an hour of intense work, I started wondering if the cuckoos had stuck the machine-language equivalent of a rubber cap inside the North American Data Base.

The time signature that absolutely had to be there wasn't. In itself, the absence wasn't suspicious enough to bring to the authorities because the cuckoos had stuck a spurious, premature time stamp in the appropriate slot. A neat trick, and pretty much impossible without altering the NADB's operating system . . . which was completely impossible. Were my clients lying after all?

It was my turn to sweat. If the cuckoos were real and way past my league, the Feldmans were up Shit Creek without a canoe.

For the first time in four years, I wanted a smoke.

I copied the relevant coding and attacked it with my arsenal: unspoolers, decompilers including my own home-baked dissection program, segment tracers (the logic equivalent of audio signal injectors) . . . and got zip. Aside from one trivial checksum irregularity, which like as not was an artifact produced by one of my programs, everything seemed disgustingly kosher.

Finally, I forced myself upright. My knees were on their best behavior today so I only suffered a class three twinge as I excused myself and limped into the kitchen to grind my teeth and consider. Hey, it worked when I was twelve! As I passed the hand-lettered sign which displayed my motto (I cherish, therefore I am), I touched it for luck—doubtless adding another fingerprint to the multitude that had turned the paper yellowish.

I poured myself a glass of water from a pitcher in the fridge and took a long sip. Good God, I thought. What a lousy host I am, I haven't even offered my clients so much as a—

Oh. Just like that, I had a logical explanation for the missing time code! There was a tricky finger in the data stream . . .

The cuckoos must have installed an entire *program* within the NADB, an application designed to hide itself while providing selectively false information.

My, my. The implications sent shivers down my neck. The NADB contained no free memory space where such a large program could be inserted; therefore the program could only have been constructed by installing a routing shell which utilized building blocks that were *already there*: storage and retrieval subroutines plus bits and pieces of various data files.

Fantastic! M. C. Escher himself would've had trouble visualizing how to fit such elements together. Someone very smart had cobbed together a Frankenstein program and made it invisible . . . or *was* it invisible now that I knew about it?

"News, folks," I announced upon returning to the living room. "Maybe good, maybe not. But I've got an idea." Tricia and Brian, who were huddled together on my couch like flood victims on the rescue boat, looked up with new hope. I winked at them and seated myself before the terminal.

And there it was. The program's existence had become as obvious as a pink thumb on a tanned hand. Obvious to *me*, that is. The pattern wasn't distinct enough to prove anything to the authorities. Hell, even a fellow expert might accuse me of having an imagination. And now that I'd identified the program, I'd identified a problem.

I tilted way back in my chair, staring up at my dirty ceiling.

The couch creaked and garbage crunched as Tricia arose to stand behind me, looming like a mountain, eyes focused on the monitor. Brian got up too and stood next to her, shifting his weight noisily from foot to foot. Their faces looked spooky upside-down and 90 percent chin.

"What's the matter?" Tricia asked.

I hadn't meant to sigh out loud. "Someone installed an application here which allows genuine data to be pulled from the files, but that data never sees the light of day. Instead, it's stored in a temporary batch file and the nature of the information tells the program which false data to send on."

"Can't you erase it?" Brian asked anxiously.

"The program? No way. Anything you stick into the NADB gets protected as if it stood on holy ground."

"What *can* you do?"

"Add some lines of my own. Trouble is, I can't see the thing well enough to know where the lines should go. It's encrypted in three interdependent layers . . . which means—damn it!—it must have a self-correcting interpreter!"

Tricia reached down and squeezed my shoulder as if I was the one in trouble. "Half the time, I've got no idea what you're talking about, but are you saying the . . . cuckoos are using some kind of secret code?"

"In a manner of speaking."

"Can you crack it?"

"Not in a reasonable length of time, Tricia. Not by any *normal* means. This isn't like a substitution-cipher where you merely have to figure out which letter goes where. We're dealing with *algorithms* here, and there are so many freaking possibilities that—"

"So we *are* screwed?" Brian interrupted.

"Brian, my friend. Work on that defeatist attitude! There may, I say *may*, be a way to get timely results, but . . . it's going to require a lot of trust." Mostly from me.

I sat up straight and pivoted around. My clients were watching me the way my cousins had once watched Amazing Bob.

"I'm willing to take a *humongous* chance," I said slowly. "And I'll need your help to do it, but you two have got to swear to keep my secrets and *mean it.*"

They silently nodded agreement in precise unison. Their sincerity was thick enough to spread on toast.

"Now as to my fee . . . " I stated a price and they showed no interest in haggling.

I took a deep breath. "Here goes. I've got a gizmo here that might allow me to—to corrupt the enemy program by interacting with it . . . um, *personally.*"

"What kind of gizmo?" Brian asked.

"It's called an 'inductive-reality stimulator.' IRS, like the tax piranhas. It was invented by . . . a friend of mine who designed the prototype for NASA."

This "friend" was actually my Uncle Terry, Dr. Terrance Peabody, but my clients didn't need to know everything.

"It works by producing complex, moving magnetic fields which match the brain's own rhythms and flows. Then Faraday's Law of Induction goes to town. Far as I know, only two of these devices exist. NASA's got the original, and I've got the improved version. Fantastically illegal, by the way."

Brian raised his hand classroom-style. "Why so illegal?"

"It proved to be far more powerful than anyone expected; in the wrong hands this thing could do some heavy damage. So it was declared top-secret and off-limits."

"But what does it *do?*"

"Allows me to access data systems through symbolism."

"You've lost me completely," Tricia groaned.

"It puts me in direct, but subjective, contact with whatever data system I hook up to. I experience that system as another world, but not like Gibson's cyberspace—"

Two blank looks had derailed my train of thought.

"You've never heard of William Gibson?"

Dual headshakes, side-to-side this time.

"Maybe you guys need to get *in* more. He was a writer. Influential. About fifty years ago, he suggested that your mind could experience a kind of universe *inside* data-streams . . . if you got out your soldering iron and did some deft work on your own head. He named this universe 'cyberspace.'"

"I've heard that word," Brian admitted.

"It's still uttered now and then. So here's how you get there, according to Gibson: Run wires to your brain, attach them to a jack, install the jack in your skull and you're ready to party! Then you take the appropriate cable (God knows what *that* would be) and attach the jack to the family laptop. And, voila, you wind up inside. Infinite cybernetic vistas, that sort of thing.

"Nice to see you two can still smile, but Gibson was apparently serious. Sadly, the human mind doesn't work like that. While you can trigger sensations or memories by zapping various parts of your brain, that brain works in—and I'm quoting my friend here—'prolific, multi-channel, simultaneous, widespread, bioelectric-chemical chains.' You need a prolific, multi-channel, etc. *interface* for the job. Put it this way: you can go spelunking Sylvius fissure, say, but you'll never find a spot marked 'input.' "

"So your IRS uses a . . . magnetic interface?"

"Be . . . Aye . . . N-G-O! First nut that stuck his head inside a powerful electromagnet saw light. Then some researcher, showing more sense, applied magnetic field stimulation to *other* people's heads and discovered that it made his subjects experience all sorts of—"

Brian leaned forward excitedly. "So *your* interface puts your mind in cyberspace?"

I grinned. "Not cyberspace. With the IRS, information takes on *personality*. You'll understand when you see it working. The point is to let my subconscious mind grapple with problems by feel, problems too complex for my conscious mind to—"

"Are you talking about virtual reality?"

"Virtual reality, ha! Goggles. Touch-gloves. CGI. Kid stuff. This is *immersion* reality and, believe me, there's a difference. With the IRS you are *there*."

Brian frowned at the mess on the floor and then glanced through my thin, dingy window-curtains and frowned some more.

"How did something so . . . ultra-tech wind up . . . "

"In a dump like this? My friend wanted to keep experimenting with the machine after NASA canned his project. So he gave the new one to me for safekeeping. Purloined letter." My clients were looking blank again. "Doesn't anyone *read* anymore? I mean hidden in plain sight, figuratively speaking. Enough talk, let's get rolling. Except hang on for just a sec, I need to go tinkle and fetch woman's best friend."

Little Mo was a canine angel, asleep and curled up on the floor on my favorite throw rug. The ever-vigilant watchdog, I thought. Ready at a moment's notice to defend his mistress! I woke him up by whispering stuff in his floppy ears that I'd be too embarrassed to repeat. He wagged his tail as he stretched.

My clients looked distinctly alarmed when I returned to the living room followed by my pet behemoth.

"This is Little Mo," I announced. "Half German shepherd, half Irish wolfhound. Mo, these are friends of mine; be nice. Hold out your hands, folks, and let Mo get a good sniff. Don't worry, he's absurdly gentle once he knows you."

With formal introductions complete, I parked my dog and his refilled water dish near the door. That was definitely that. No one would get in now without my permission.

"Time to get the system warmed up, folks . . . which in this case means cooled down. Should be enough liquid helium left." I was busily uncovering various components and connectors and snapping them together. A deep humming arose from under the debris near one wall.

"Takes a minute to get the field up to strength," I remarked. "You might as well sit down. Or better yet, if you need to use the bathroom, now's the time. Down the hall, second door to the left."

Tricia was wiping her eyes again and I decided to let the air clear a bit. The incense holds back a deliberate stench, part of my security system. When I have to go out, it's nice to know that intruders are not only going to suffer, they're going to leave a scent-trail for my dog to follow. Of course, when Little Mo is around, intruders become *out*-truders fast, but the big baby whines if I leave the apartment without him.

"Are you OK, Tricia?" I wondered.

"I'll be all right. I'm tired, that's all. Didn't you say something about needing our help? What do you want us to do exactly?"

"Take the clamps off after I'm done; it's a lot faster if I don't have to do it myself. But mainly, I need you to watch the monitor while keeping an eye on me. The membrane will mostly show stuff from the world I'll be in, but all sorts of information can suddenly pop up on the screen—from my memory or from the NADB—and I won't know it's there. I want you to tell me if anything . . . *germane* appears."

I rooted through garbage for the heavily-padded clamps and attached my chair to the floor and my legs and waist to the chair. Then I assembled the headset and put it on, hooked the bottom part of the arm-clamps to the chair, loaded the IRS software and targeted it to the directory of the NADB where the covert program lurked.

"If I had a real lab," I complained, "I'd just push a shiny button. You'd hear a smooth whirring and everything would just *happen*.

As is, the only automatic part is these arm clamps, they'll close magnetically when the program starts."

"What are the clamps for?" Brian asked suspiciously.

I grinned. "They look a tad ominous, don't they? The software is going to build me a virtual body with a virtual nervous system tied in to my real nervous system. Meanwhile, the hardware will read the muscle-moving nerve impulses from my brain and use them as controllers for the virtual body. Are you with me so far?"

"I think so."

"Good. Now here's the tricky part. We don't want my actual body lurching around the apartment while I'm busy elsewhere, so the hardware has a selective buffer designed to keep nerve impulses from reaching my muscles. Not *every* nerve impulse is blocked; I'll still be able to interact with the actual world in certain ways, and I'll still be able to breathe, which I approve of. But the buffer isn't perfect, so the clamps will stop me from banging into things if random impulses get through."

"I see." Brian sounded relieved and I was saddened to have to spoil that.

"I suppose I should tell you there's another reason for the clamps. There's a . . . small hazard we could conceivably run into."

"Which is?" he asked softly.

"Seizures. They only happened to me once but I was pretty sore afterwards."

That news brought no one any joy and Tricia was now looking downright scared.

"You're a lot braver than me," she remarked. "What are we supposed to do if something goes wrong?"

"I won't be able to see you once I enter the induction world, but I'll be able to hear you and talk to you. If I stop responding, punch any key on my keyboard. If I start foaming at the mouth or go all rigid or start twitching, push a key, only hurry up about it. OK? So . . . everyone ready?"

I put my arms into the proper positions, my index finger could just reach the keyboard's return button, and I triggered the—

This time, it was a gray void. I couldn't see or touch my new body, but I could feel it working, expending energy. Then my feet materialized and I watched their movements with interest.

Apparently, I was walking.

A moment of confusion as if each of my eyes was perceiving a different universe. When this cleared, a pebbled path was under my feet. It felt softer than it looked. I saw no sky here, nor any bright light-source, but each pebble had highlights as if reflecting a noon sun. The highlights made the path appear magical and luminous.

"What's happening?" Brian asked.

"Just getting oriented. Be patient. What's on the monitor?"

"Nothing. Wait . . . there's a narrow road. Tiny rocks . . . "

Tricia's voice chimed in, "Bare feet just appeared toward the bottom of the screen, kind of tromping along. No body, just feet."

"Those are mine. The rest of me should be showing up pretty soon. Remember that everything here is a symbol of something, but it's all made of code. Those pebbles are little chunks of—hold on! Something's happening up ahead."

In the distance, a fantastic castle was forming. It stretched up and up, a thousand walls within other walls, all with wide merlons, narrow crenels, and thousands of turrets and balconied minarets. Innumerable bright flags flew proudly, illuminated by an invisible sun and blown by impalpable winds . . .

"I see it. One hell of a fortress," said Brian. "What's the symbolism?"

"Don't know yet, but I'm obviously headed there."

A huge bonfire containing a vague shape in the center of the flames hid the castle's base.

My arms and legs emerged, then my torso. By the time I could touch my new face, I was smiling. In this world, I was no dwarf with arthritic knees. The road felt solid now and grassy meadows had manifested to either side. With no warning, running shoes condensed from the void, appearing on my feet complete with tied laces. Message received: *long* way to go. I began jogging.

"Hey! I can see you now," Brian stated. "Except you're not, ah, wearing anything . . . except shoes and you look . . . "

"Different? I bet. Clothes will appear if and when they're called for. Uh-oh. Check out that bonfire!"

The shape in the fire was beginning to resemble an exceedingly large reptilian animal. When its titanic chest suddenly expanded, all the surrounding flames were sucked into the beast's mouth, leaving the creature alarmingly exposed to view.

Brian whistled. "My God! What *is* that thing? Some kind of dragon?"

The oriental kind perhaps. Maybe Tibetan, the head had a certain bumpy look. Yet, there was something tauntingly familiar about the shape of the eyes . . .

"Here's my guideline, Brian," I said quietly. "If it looks like a dragon, and breaths fire like a dragon . . . "

"I thought dragons," Tricia grumbled, "were supposed to breathe fire *out* not in?"

"Right you are. And that deviation certainly means . . . something. God knows what. But I do see an underlying pattern here. Each time you use the IRS it's different, and this time it looks like I'm stuck in a medieval fairy tale. You know, the kind where some poor schnook has to face the inevitable three challenges. My subconscious probably got the idea because the program we're trying to mess up has three levels."

"This is a *game*? How do you win?"

"Bet the first part is getting past the dragon."

"That doesn't look easy," Tricia said sympathetically.

It only took a few minutes more to reach the great beast but the whole time it kept seeming bigger and bigger. If the animal was big, the castle was simply stupendous from close up and it came nicely equipped with a wide moat. The path, here paved with seashells, ended at a narrow drawbridge which arched over the murky water; on the far side, a huge closed oak door led into the castle.

Purposeful ripples on the surface of the water advertised the moat as a dubious choice for skinny-dipping.

Get past the guardian, cross the drawbridge, open the door.

The problems, at least, seemed clear enough.

The dragon fixed me with a golden eye larger than my fridge and moved to stand directly between me and the bridge, but with its body at a slight angle.

If this was a fairy tale, perhaps . . .

I snapped my fingers and gilded armor even brighter than the dragon's eye materialized on my body from my feet up; I heard my clients gasp.

"How did you *do* that?" Tricia wondered.

"I told you. In here, I'm a magician." Still, every time I use the IRS, my powers are different. It takes time, thought, and some luck to find them.

"Shoo," I said to the beast towering above me. "Go away. Bug off."

My words would have had more effect on a Detroit mugger.

"Listen, dragon, you're . . . wailing for a scaling."

Trisha giggled nervously, but the dragon didn't appear to be amused. I tried a few experiments. Mental commands neither moved the animal nor made it vanish and efforts to produce magical lightning only made my sinuses ache.

"This may seem crazy," I said to the clients, "considering our size discrepancy, but I'm going to try the direct approach and give Puff here a mighty shove."

The dragon allowed me to get close enough to touch its scaly leg before it reached down and bit my shoulder.

I jumped back instinctively, yelling with pain and surprise. The sudden shout startled Tricia and Brian into bellowing questions which made Little Mo start barking. A shockwave of alarm. The armor hadn't protected me enough—the thing's mouth had been *hot*. My shoulder felt mangled and burned and I struggled for self-control.

"Damn," I swore. "That hurt! Shut up, Mo. There's a good dog. Tricia? Can you pull my blouse down far enough to see my left shoulder?"

"Yes. Oh my God, it's bruised and red! With *blisters!*"

"Any blood?"

"No. I don't understand how something . . . in *there* can hurt you out here?"

"The mind-body connection is a lot more tangible than people think. Except for my ears, mouth, and lungs, which are in both worlds, I'm essentially *here*."

While I was talking I had a horrible thought: What if the beast had bitten my *head* off? Which gave birth to another question: Why didn't it? It hadn't met me quite head-on, it didn't take my head off . . .

Perhaps Puff was an indirect sort of fellow.

But the kiddy virtual-gloves were definitely off now. I concentrated, and a shining sabre appeared in my right-hand gauntlet. I'd never been able to do *that* before, at least not in that exact way, but I'd never faced a mythological beast either.

"I see a sword," Brian said, "but isn't it a bit small?"

True. The sword was a joke for what I had in mind, but I willed it to grow longer . . . and it did. Its weight stayed impossibly constant.

"Get out of my freaking way, animal, or die," I snapped.

The beast didn't move so I swung the blade, effortlessly separating the reptilian head from the long neck. No gore. The head simply vanished. A bifurcation appeared on the wound, swiftly growing into two independent necks. Then two new heads, half-sized but otherwise identical to the original, appeared on the ends. One head was tilted slightly to the right and the other to the left.

"The old Hydra routine," I muttered. "How conventional."

The dragon was regarding me now with four eyes, none filled with love, and for an unpleasant second, I thought it might charge. Luckily, it did no such thing.

Or was it *bad* luck? I might have dodged around and reached the drawbridge.

Head removal was out, so I tried stabbing the creature in the chest. Silly me. The cut opened up, and out shot a smoky sphere whose core was bright blue flame. I jumped to one side and the peculiar object veered to follow like a guided missile.

"Do something!" Brian yelled.

A pole topped by a shiny umbrella sprouted from my left shoulder—the best I could manage on short notice. The fireball landed on this impromptu shield, making an audible clunk, and knocking me to my knees. Heavy flames? Even shielded, the heat was painful. I managed to shake the damn thing off—it was *sticky*—and it hit the road with a second clunk. There it sat, burning merrily away as if it were homesteading an oxyacetylene leak.

"What the hell!" I shouted repeatedly. When scared, I usually get mad.

Experimentally, I shrank my sword and tried to give the fireball a nudge. It rolled a few inches *towards* me and clung to my sabre so tightly, I was forced to dissolve the sword and materialize a replacement. By now, I was utterly bewildered.

"A diagram with some symbols just appeared on the monitor," Brian stated.

"About time! A diagram of what?"

"I don't know . . . it's already gone. It was animated. Two thick dotted lines came together in the middle of the screen and then they hit and a bunch of thinner dotted lines went off in all directions."

Lord! Such a diagram could represent anything from a billiards trick to a stellar collision! "Please tell me you noticed something else. Anything?"

"I did," Tricia volunteered. "The thickest of the thin lines was labeled with . . . like a 'W' and a number. 3,280."

So! "Was this 'W' *curvy*, by any chance?"

"I guess so."

"Lower-case omega. Good eyes, Tricia! *Thank* you, things are clearing up."

"Not for us!" Brian said.

"Look, when you deal with the subconscious, you deal with mishmash. Somewhere in the back of my brain, I've made some bizarro associations. The initial level of the program we're up against has to be small because the NADB offers such limited space. So my subconscious evidently began thinking *tiny*. This fireball represents an *omega* particle—a subatomic artifact and the heaviest baryon of them all. You can produce them by colliding protons, but they don't hang around all day in normal reality."

"And that number?" Brian continued.

"Electron mass. You'd need that many electrons to balance a see-saw with an omega particle on the other side. And it's negatively charged; did you notice how it moved in my direction when I pushed on it? Even *pushing* is symbolic in these parts." The way it had tracked and clung to me implied that *I* carried a positive charge . . .

"God damn. How do you know all this stuff off the top of your head?"

"Because it's already in the bottom of my head. That diagram was something in my memory, not stored in the NADB."

"But what does it mean?"

"The dragon's chest is the part of the program which does the dirty work. You remember how it inhaled the bonfire? Good data goes in, bad data—heavy and negatively charged—goes out if you try to retrieve the good data. Breathing imagery. Remember these are *my* symbols."

"If the dragon represents programming," Tricia asked slowly, "what does your sword represent?"

I should have been asking myself the same question. "Well . . . what does a sabre do? Divides things, right? Mine has a strong positive charge although I'm not sure why. Whatever, if the sword represents simple division . . . the encryption we're trying to break must be mathematical. Our 'dragon' is probably—"

"How the hell are you supposed to defeat *math*?" Brian griped.

"I've an idea about that, but first . . . "

I made my latest blade grow longer. Then I jumped up and cut off both the dragon's new heads.

Three heads grew back. I removed these and this time five appeared.

"What are you doing?" Brian asked anxiously.

"Don't . . . bug me for a minute please . . . or debug me. I'm keeping count . . . "

One more experiment produced eight heads.

"All right, ladies and generalmen, I've got it. Excalibrate here represents *subtraction* not division and—"

"Subtraction? Minus? Shouldn't your sword have a negative charge?"

"Sounds logical, Brian; but this realm has its own logic."

"Think small and think mishmash. My guess is that bytes here are confused with atoms. I think the sword is minus all right, minus *electrons*. Positive charge."

"Oh."

"Now here's what I learned: our dragon is sadly trite. Originally it had one head. I subtracted it, right? That number was added to the previous and only number in the series so far, one, and two heads appeared. After I cut those off, *that* number was added to the one and we got three. Next, the three got added to the two and presto! Five. Then five and three bought us eight. See? Keep adding each new number of heads to the previous number to derive the next number. It's nothing but the old Fibonacci series. Final test: I'm going to decapitate our friend here to the tune of all eight heads, if I can, and you should see thirteen new ones emerge. Watch."

It made sense. The encryption algorithm needed to be short and sweet yet produce an evasive, non-linear pattern. Nothing head-on and predictable. And the dragon's eyes, I suddenly realized, were shaped like *sunflowers!* Sunflower seeds, like so many things in nature, are spirally distributed according to the Fibonacci series. . . .

Brian was counting out loud. "Thirteen, just like you said. But if heads keep growing back endlessly, how are you supposed to get rid of them all?"

"Solutions, my friends, often lie in coming at problems from another level."

I gave my clients a few moments to ponder the philosophical aspects of my statement, then lengthened my sword and cut the dragon's legs off. The legs, bleeding a thin, clear liquid, fell neatly away from the body and vanished. The beast fell to the ground and became still.

"I figured the legs were constants," I said smugly.

With renewed confidence, I stepped around my vanquished enemy, heading toward the drawbridge. Until my right foot encountered a trickle of dragon blood.

It was more slippery than black ice. My feet went flying and I smashed down on my back hard enough to slap my breath away.

"Are you all right, Emagia?" Tricia asked anxiously. "What happened? Bry? Did you see? Her body twitched and now she's not answering . . . should we press a key?"

I couldn't talk, but I shook my subjective head in denial and hoped that someone would notice. Of course, they were watching *me* now, not the screen.

"She fell pretty hard, honey. I saw it happen. Maybe we should give her just a minute more?"

"I'm counting to ten and if she doesn't say anything, I'm pushing the button. One, two . . . "

On "eight" I finally managed to wheeze a faint, "No." It took five minutes before I was ready to continue.

One thing was troubling. I still had my armor.

Which implied I still needed it.

When I was able to sit up again, I took off a gauntlet and my right boot and felt along the sole with my index finger. It felt incredibly smooth until the remaining "blood" slowly ran off, leaving the sole dry and rough. Slippery and viscous at the same time; very odd . . .

Silicone lubricant from silicon valley?

My back-brain idea of a superfluid? Strange question for the day: What substance would be a superfluid at . . . dream-temperature?

I put my clothes back on, cautiously got to my feet, and approached the bridge. Which looked harmless until I actually stepped on it. The freaking thing threw me backwards so hard, I almost fell again, only this time on my face.

I gathered myself up, and got a running start . . .

Next thing I knew, I was lying in a cozy nest of dragon's heads making an unpleasant discovery: the beast was coming back to life. Thirteen slender necks arose like hyperactive cobras and golden eyes began regarding me from all directions. Each head wasn't much bigger than my own now, but the hundreds of teeth looked remarkably long and pointy.

I got out of there *fast* and made sure to stay beyond snapping range.

"The drawbridge," I bitched, "is a high-speed, moving ramp going the *wrong way*."

"What is it really?" Tricia asked.

"Likely what programmers sometimes call a 'diode.' A connected series of 'goto' instructions. Hard to cross from the wrong side."

"You created a sword," Brian pointed out. "Why not make your own bridge?"

"Because I wouldn't be playing the game and interacting with the challenges. Hey! Here's a thought: What about the dragon-blood? What if it's a semi-conductor? One place you can expect to find silicon: silicone lubricant.

"Listen folks, if I remember my elementary electronics, and I do, semi-conductors work with 'charges' moving in one direction while the 'holes' move the other way. So . . . "

I removed my gauntlet again and filled it with fluid by dragging it along the ground. Then I stood in front of the bridge and carefully poured dragon-blood across my shoulders.

"A semi-conductor," I explained, "moves packets of electrons. Negative charge. Remember what happened when I pushed on the omega particle? If I can coat my body with goo and the bridge tries to push me away . . . well, the logic is a little stretched. We'll just have to see."

I touched the armor over the small of my back with my bare hand. Still dry, so I waited a minute and tried again. This time, it was nice and greasy.

A minute more and my legs were coated. Before the stuff could reach my feet, I jumped, landing on the drawbridge sitting down with my legs straight out in front . . . and BANG!

I was on my back again, my armor dented like a car after a head-on collision and my head spinning like one of the tires.

"You did it!" Brian shouted. "Wow! Are you hurt?"

Sure enough, I was on the good side of the bridge and had evidently smashed into the door and rebounded. I groaned experimentally and decided that the armor had been justified after all . . . but why was I *still* wearing it?

"I'll be all right. Eventually." I struggled up and got my first close look at the door. No dents there. Also no handle or knob and the thing was immovable as a mountain—plus some force kept pushing my hand away.

I retrieved my sword, shrank it to a convenient size and hacked away at the oak. It bounced off and with prejudice. The door had a serious positive charge! Without much hope, I transformed the sabre into an axe and nearly took my leg off. I tried magic next, mental orders, and a tried-and-true method of gaining entrance: knocking. I couldn't hit the thing hard enough to make more than a tap. Even the most inventive swearing failed to get me into the castle.

Worse, when I looked back at the dragon, it was sitting up on little stumps. Somehow the damn constants were regenerating. If I didn't complete the puzzle soon, I had a hunch that a new breed of trouble was headed my way . . .

"I'm running out of ideas, folks, and I'm getting tired. This takes it out of you after awhile. Suggestions are welcome."

Silence.

"I know you're out there, I can hear you blinking."

Brian cleared his throat nervously. "Didn't you use the word 'interdependent' when you were talking about the three parts of the program you're trying to bust?"

"Sure I did. So?"

"You used part of the dragon to cross the drawbridge. Maybe you have to use part of the dragon to open the door?"

"Absolutely!" Out of the mouths of hunks. "Of course I do! Except the solution should require both dragon *and* bridge. Tricia, give him a hug, he's earned it."

But now *I* needed to earn it. Brian had supplied the key, but I needed to figure out which way to turn it.

I looked across the moat to where the symbolic omega particle was still burning on the road of seashells (command seashells?).

My subconscious had made everything so completely obvious and I *still* had managed to miss it!

But the bad news was that, for the next part, I needed to stand in the worst possible place and hope that momentum could overcome attraction. Now I knew why my armor was hanging around.

I tried not to groan as I pulled my visor down over my eyes.

"Fireworks coming, folks, keep your eyes on the screen."

The dragon was watching me thoughtfully and the stumps were much bigger. I reformed my sabre, made it grow outrageously long, and gave it a slight convexity to match the arc of the drawbridge.

Then I lowered the sword and stabbed the dragon in the chest for the second time.

The new fireball rolled far enough to touch the bridge and, being negatively charged, was hurled in my direction like a cannonball on uppers.

No time to dodge. The sphere knocked me over, rolling right over my face. It was *hot*, but it didn't stop to pass the time.

I picked myself up; after this session, I was going to be one purple bruise. But the "particle" was sticking to the door as I'd hoped and the oak was burning brightly while the fireball was dying down. Lovely! Who would've thought that establishing a neutral charge could be a thing of such beauty?

When the fires were gone, so was the door. Inside the castle were stacks and stacks of books . . . the North American Data Base appearing in this waking dream as the ultimate library.

My clients were ecstatic, whooping and cheering, and I felt pretty damn good myself; I'd really wanted to help these people.

"It's us!" Tricia cried.

Us? "What are you talking about?"

"Our own faces! On the monitor! And all the right information! You did it! But I don't understand how. I thought you were going to crack the code and then put in some 'lines' of your own?"

"Someone press a key, please. I'm pooped and it's a bitch to make a subjective finger reach into the normal world."

Brian and Tricia had sobered up somewhat, but their eyes reflected my video-membrane with new enthusiasm. Tricia was grinning at me although her forehead was corrugated with puzzlement.

I returned her smile, leaning back, relaxed and immeasurably relieved; the IRS was still in early development and using it was more of a risk than I'd let on.

"You still don't quite get the nature of immersion-reality, I'm afraid. Solving those three puzzles *was* putting in my own code. We're all done here. Go back to the police. Give them your identity numbers again. Not only will your problems be history, they'll be able to see when and how the changes were made. With some work, they may even get clues about who did this to you."

"So everything is back to normal?"

"Soon as you talk to the cops."

Tricia sighed with relief. "That's incredible! But it's a little strange. It doesn't feel like anything actually . . . happened."

"Right. I'll tell you something. It's going to take the human race time to adapt to the . . . cowardly new world we live in. We've evolved to expect proportional effects. It's always taken physical effort to accomplish things, and now people's lives can be turned upside-down with a few keystrokes. Information has no mass. But listen to me, folks. What happened to you, happened in part because you let yourselves get far too *unconnected*. As far as I'm concerned: I cherish, therefore I am. And what *I* cherish most is *people*."

"We'll never let it happen again," Brian said firmly.

"Good. Human contact: keep in touch. And don't worry about remembering my fee, I'll be sending a bill in due course. And guess what? You've both been so helpful I'm giving you a twenty percent discount. All right? Fantastic luck to you both."

Tricia leaned down to give me a hug before they left and Brian kissed me. Right on the lips! Human contact. I was thrilled to see they were already taking my advice to heart.

four

IS IT CATCHING?

(Biological predictions)

— DAVID GERROLD —

"HOW WE SAVED THE HUMAN RACE"

■ from *With a Finger in My I*, **Ballantine, 1972**

Let's get one thing straight: David Gerrold did *not* predict HIV-AIDS nine years before it came to public attention in 1981. But please consider the nature of HIV-AIDS: it first came to public attention in the homosexual community, it is infamously spread by sex workers, and there have been numerous charges that it was deliberately engineered, even that it was a CIA plot.

Now read "How We Saved the Human Race." There are differences between HIV-AIDS and the "Ledgerton Virus." HIV-AIDS kills. Gerrold's imaginary virus impairs fertility. But there are such powerful similarities that we did not hesitate to include the story in this anthology of predictive science fiction. The discussions of the implications of genetic engineering did not hurt its prospects either.

How We Saved
the Human Race

~

David Gerrold

T EST TRANS CODE
ALPHA ALPHA TAU
QWERTYUIOPASDFGHJKLZXCVBNM1234567890
THE QUICK BROWN FOX JUMPED OVER THE LAZY DOGS.
END TEST
MESSAGE BEGINS HERE
DATE/2037.05.14
FROM/THE UNITED STATES AMBASSADOR TO BRAZIL
TO/ THE PRESIDENT OF THE UNITED STATES
FILE/BRZ9076THX
CODE/ALPHAALPHATAU/20370514.475FGH
STATUS OF DOCUMENT/CLASSIFIED/CODE 475FGH

Mr. President, in plain terms, the answer is no. The government of Brazil absolutely refuses to release the body. There can be no possible negotiation on this. This is an internal matter—they claim—and no other political body will be allowed to intervene. Of course, this is a blatant grab on their part; but there is nothing we can do about it. I am against making any kind of flap.

First of all, world opinion generally favors the Brazilians. Any attempt by us to pressure them would only produce hostile reactions, and that's the last thing we want now. Secondly, they want to take credit for Ledgerton's capture. They found him and they executed him. Or rather, they attempted to. It was unfortunate that the crowd beat them to it. There are those who suggest that the police deliberately let the lynch mob in, but I would discredit that story. They lost twelve of their own in the disorder.

I think we ought to let the Brazilians have the credit. This is not to suggest appeasement, but wisdom. This government is the friendliest one Brazil has had in twelve years and we want to keep it that way. Any pressuring on our part would definitely cool relations, and President Garcia won't bend to pressure anyway. Political reasons. The militant rightists would use such acquiescence as a lever against him. So I think we'd better just make ineffectual noises for now, loud enough to placate our own people, but not loud enough to annoy Juan Pablo Garcia.

By the way, the body will remain on public display for another day and a half. Yes, still hanging from the gallows, bullet holes and all. I've seen it and it's a ghastly sight. Not even Ledgerton deserved what they did to him. You know of course that they castrated him too.

In any case, I have it from Garcia himself that it will be taken down Tuesday and cremated. The ashes will be scattered at sea. No, we can't stop that either.

I wish I could be more encouraging at this time, but all I can do is say that IT's a rotten situation all around. I'll have a more detailed report later. Despite our claims to the contrary, there are still too many people down here who believe the whole thing was a CIA Plot.

For God's sake, this is one time when I hope our official position coincides with the truth.

Sincerely,

2057.05.14/DATELINE: BRAZIL.

Cardinal Silente today dedicated the monument and eternal flame commemorating the martyr Dana Ledgerton. That such a highranking member of the Catholic Church should travel to Brazil for the ceremonies suggests imminent beatification of the martyr. The Cardinal himself said . . .

PSYCHIATRIC INDEX REPORT
COMSKOOL TWELVE, MANWEATHER COMPLEX, CA 91405-0932
May 1, 2003
Dana Ledgerton, DL 551-69-5688, age nine.

Child is unfortunately too smart and too pretty for his own good. Male, age nine, fair skin, pale hair, thin, undersized for age (poor nutrition again, damn these comskool minimums), lives in Comskool Creche. Unfortunately, subject also has advanced intelligence. (Tests enclosed.) Presently enrolled two grades above average for his age level. This physical discrepancy between him and his classmates generates extreme feelings of inferiority, coupled with strong motivation to succeed. Success on mental level increases antagonism between himself and peers, but it is the only arena in which he is fairly matched with his classmates. The kid takes a lot of teasing about being a sissy, and his sense of masculine identification is weak. I'll give odds of ten to one that he's a fag by the time he's twenty.

RECOMMENDATIONS: None. There's nothing we can do. Tough.

SUPERVISOR'S REMARKS: *Dammit, Pete! Can't you be a little more clinical than this?* (signed) H.B.

MAY 9, 2011
LABOR POOL STATUS BOARD, CA 99-5674
UNIT MONITOR FORM JHX-908
DANA LEDGERTON, DL 551-69-5688

Subject is thin, very fair, blond hair. Small for his age. Required to perform eighteen hours of Class IV labor per week in order to support educational demands. Assigned to manual labor in University CafCom.

Designation: busboy.

REMARKS:

Subject discovered in Comskool Personal committing homosexual act with fellow student at age twelve. Referred to PsychStat
who confirmed unit's sexual outlook. No recommendation made. In
accordance with Federal Civil Rights Amendment, subject's sexual
preference has no bearing on his ability to perform Class IV labor.

RECOMMENDATION:

Leave to discretion of local supervisors.

MAY 45, 2035

FROM: FIELD OPERATIVE JASON PETER GRIGG

TO: FBI DIRECTOR WARREN J. HINDLER,

HOOVER CENTER,

WASHINGTON D.C.

FILE: LEDGERTON, DL 551-69-5688

Chief,

Sorry for the sketchiness of this report; I'll have to do a
complete rundown when I get back. This thing is a mess to the
nth power. The Manweather records only go back twelve years.
Before that, it's incomplete and often sketchy. Yes, I know that's
hard to believe, but Manweather was one of the hardest hit during
the sex and protein riots, and, a lot of their records were wiped
clean by the activists.

Attached are copies of the working papers. Here's the
summary:

Ledgerton's birth was an accident. He wasn't wanted, not by
his parents, not by the local board. When he came along, unan-
nounced and unwelcome, the parents were sterilized and sent to
Labor-Module 14, Manweather. The child was transferred to the
Comskool Creche, which had only been open two years at that
time and still had elbow room. However, due to shifting population
pressures, Manweather became one of the densest concentrations
in CA. Within five years, it was a behavioral sink.

Competition wasn't Ledgerton's big thing. He preferred to withdraw into himself. Because his teachers and PsychStats kept telling him how smart he was and how he should be proud of himself, he became narcissistic and introverted. He took a lot of fag-baiting from his classmates, too.

There's a full psych profile in here somewhere. I was lucky to find that. According to the shrink, "Little Dana" wasn't as self-assertive as he should have been and too many of his life choices were made because population pressures forced him into them and he didn't feel like fighting back.

His college career tends to bear this out. He went into bio-chem strictly by accident. It was the only classification still open that he was qualified for. And it was either that or the unskilled labor pool. Nuff said about that.

MAY 24, 2014
UNIVERSITY OF CALIFORNIA AT INDIO
REAGAN HALL
FLOOR MANAGER'S MEMO
SUBJECT: REASSIGNMENT OF ROOMS,
Dana Ledgerton DL 551-69-5688 and Paul-John Murdock PJM 673-65-4532 have been reassigned (at their request) to room 12-32, the "Lavender Hills" section. This leaves rooms 6-87 and 7-54 with only one person in them. Immediate reassignments available for each.

MAY 3, 2015
UNIVERSITY OF CALIFORNIA AT INDIO
PSYCH-STAT REPORT,
CONFIDENTIAL SUBJECT: PAUL-JOHN MURDOCK PJM 673-65-4532
Subject is tall and husky. 6'1", 186 lbs. Fairly well built. Dark hair, curly. Thin face. "Penetrating" eyes—an illusion produced by deep-set sockets and heaviness of eyebrows. Prone to long periods of moodiness and introspection. Theatre arts major.

He has been living for the past year with another male student and the relationship is apparently sexual. However, subject's emotional involvement tends to be shallow. He has a long history of casual sexual encounters with his fellow students, both male and female, and probably would not grieve if this relationship were to end abruptly.

I suspect the continued use of mildly narcotic drugs, including such illegal agents as "Spice," "Pink," and "Harrolin." (No definite proof here.) Subject's manner is lackadaisical and uncaring. Selfish, introverted, narcissistic. Typical T.A. major: more concerned with things on a "higher plane" than with the exigencies of everyday life.

Subject's strongest motivation for continuation of education is the avoidance of the labor draft.

RECOMMENDATION: 1A status.

STATE OF CALIFORNIA, INFORMATION DUP-OUT
APPLICATION FOR CONTRACT TO ENTER STATE OF LEGAL MARRIAGE
DATE: MAY 12, 2015
APPLICANTS:
DANA LEDGERTON DL 551-69-5688
PAUL-JOHN MURDOCK PJM 673-65-4532
LENGTH OF CONTRACT: THREE YEARS.
PURPOSE: Mutual interdependence.
CONDITIONS: Individual property maintenance; dissolution terms non-negotiable. Mutual inheritance. Residence: Reagan Hall, University of California at Indio, room 12-32.
DISPOSITION OF APPLICATION: Granted.
WILLIAM APTHEKER, COUNTY CLERK

HARD COPY FRAGMENT IN FILE, dislocated page, thought to be part of report by investigating agents. (Nature of agency not known.)

"... after his marriage broke up, he remained at the University for another three years. He tried to reconcile the contract several times, but twice he couldn't get in touch with Paul-John and the third time, Paul-John was vague in his reply.

"After that, he concentrated heavily on his studies. He earned a Ph.D. in biochemistry and an M.A. in medicine. They were (in the words of the department head) 'Uninspired degrees'. Meaning he was qualified, but not exceptional.

"Somehow he landed a teaching position and was able to hold onto it for several years. They had him giving the freshman science classes, something nobody else wanted to do.

"What he did on his own time during those years is beyond me, though I suspect he spent a lot of time at the boy-shows."

MAY 32, 2027
COLORADO COLLEGE OF SCIENCE
DENVER, COLORADO
FROM: Dr. Margaret James-Mead
TO: Dept. Head Harlan Sloan
Hal,

If I have to look at that "wispy little thing" wandering around the halls of this college one more day, I think I'll puke. You know who I mean. That man is a disgrace to the institution.

I don't care how you do it, but you've got to get rid of him. If you can't find something on him, make something. If you don't ask him for his resignation within a week, I'll give you mine instead.

Love, Maggie.

May 34, 2027
My dear Dr. Ledgerton,

It is with deepest regret that I must ask you to resign your position with the Denver College of Science. Your record here has been without blemish; however, we find that there is no longer any need for your services and are forced to take this rather unfortunate step.

I assure you that it has nothing to do with your personal life, or the incident with Dr. James-Mead. It is instead a question of . . .

MAY 3, 2029
INTERBEM CHEMICAL RESEARCH
PORTION OF SUPERVISOR'S REPORT

". . . the Ledgerton group seems to have come closest to a workable solution of this problem. They have generated an experimental strain, temporarily designated NFK-98, which appears to combine the functions of both DFG-54 and DFS-09 into one continuous process, rather than the two separate steps we have today.

"Suggest further experimentation along these lines to substantiate the findings and put them into production. The Ledgerton group should be commended. Despite his unappealing manner, Ledgerton is a tireless worker. Morale of the technicians working under him is not as good as it could be, but they do produce usable results.

"The viral research teams should be expanded as soon as possible in order to . . ."

INTERBEM CHEMICAL RESEARCH
MAY 9, 2029
TO ALL EMPLOYEES:
COMPANY FACILITIES ARE NOT TO BE USED FOR PRIVATE RESEARCH PROJECTS WITHOUT FIRST SECURING PERMISSION FROM DEPARTMENT HEADS. IT IS UNDERSTOOD THAT INTERBEM RETAINS THE RIGHT OF FIRST OPTION ON ANY COMMERCIAL APPLICATION OF PRIVATE DISCOVERIES PRODUCED BY INTERBEM EMPLOYEES. REMEMBER, THIS PRIVILEGE IS CONDITIONAL UPON FULFILLMENT OF MINIMUM QUOTAS AND WILL BE REVOKED IF THEY ARE NOT MET.

MAY 1, 2030
FIRST DORIAN CHURCH OF AMERICA

OSCAR WILDE CONGREGATION
CONFIDENTIAL MEMBERSHIP REPORT:

Dr. Dana Ledgerton, employee of InterBem Corporation, age thirty-six. Unmarried.

Dr. Ledgerton was interviewed by the membership committee whose discussion follows. J.M. commented at length that Dr. Ledgerton is thirty-six and physically unappealing. He suggested that the only reason Ledgerton wants to join is because he cannot find sexual partners anywhere else.

K.R. found J.M.'s attitude and phrasing undignified and demeaning.

L.N. said that Ledgerton's primary purpose in joining the church is probably loneliness.

J.M. agreed, but said that loneliness was just another way of saying "horniness."

L.N. insisted that the applicant was basically good intentioned. Lots of people join churches because they are lonely. Why should the Dorians be any different?

K.R. interrupted both of them to speculate on whether or not Ledgerton really did embrace the principles of Dorianism.

Ledgerton was called back into the room then and further questioned. He responded at length and the discussion continued again, while he waited outside.

A.S., visiting minister from the Bay Area, cast his support in favor of Ledgerton. Most people, he said, are not aware of all the precepts of Dorianism when they join, and it would be unfair to hold that against Ledgerton.

A vote was taken then, and Ledgerton was admitted to the membership by a count of 4–1. He was readmitted to the room and sworn to uphold the church and the principles upon which it was founded, that overpopulation is a sin and that all Dorians will devote their whole lives to zero population growth.

Dr. Ledgerton will be presented to the general congregation at the next open meeting.

MAY 39, 2031
INTERBEM CHEMICAL RESEARCH
SUPPLY REQUISITION

Need: Forty hours use of electron microscope for viral research. Private project. After–hours use will be okay. Would appreciate available time as soon as possible.

(signed) D. Ledgerton

MAY 14, 2032
INTERBEM CHEMICAL RESEARCH
SUPERVISOR'S MEMO

Spoke to Ledgerton again today about his after-hours research. He's been working on this one project for nearly a year now, and he has spent nearly 35,000 dollars on it. When questioned how much longer this line of research would continue, Ledgerton declined to say, but seemed to indicate that it would not be much longer.

I asked if he were close to a solution. He replied that he was closer to finding out that there was no solution, but would not go into any further detail. I suspect he does not want to discuss his project. A complete report on the objectives of his program and his findings has been ordered. He has until the end of the month to submit it, at which time it will be evaluated and decided whether or not he will be allowed to continue.

He was upset, but not as much as I expected. Perhaps he is nearing the end of his research after all. He mentioned something about a possible sabbatical later in the year. If he requests it, it is my recommendation that it be granted. His lapse in work has been only recent and may be due to personal problems. Ledgerton has always been a good worker, although his personal manner does leave something to be desired.

MAY 50, 2032
INTERBEM CHEMICAL RESEARCH

REQUEST FOR LEAVE OF ABSENCE
APPLICANT: DANA LEDGERTON DL 551-69-5688
REASON: VACATION, INDEFINITE LENGTH
DISPOSITION OF APPLICATION: GRANTED
REMARKS: (Scrawled in pen.) Good. I never liked him anyway.

MAY 50, 2032
FIRST DORIAN CHURCH OF AMERICA
OSCAR WILDE CONGREGATION
CONFIDENTIAL MEMBERSHIP REPORT:

The membership committee then considered a motion to expel
D.L.

J.M. wanted to go on record as being opposed to D.L.'s membership
in the first place. It was duly noted.

L.N. inquired as to what the charges against. D.L. were.

J.M. said that D.L. has not been faithful to the principles upon
which the credo is based.

K.R. noted that D.L. has been observed almost nightly in the
company of "paid female prostitutes."

L.N. requested amplification of this charge.

J.M. presented receipts made out to D.L. from the Xanadu Pleasure
Corp.

L.N. wanted to know how J.M. got the receipts, but he was ruled
out of order. The issue at hand is D.L.'s transgressions, not J.M.'s source
of information.

L.N. disagreed, saying that we should not be "spying on our
brothers." He was ruled out of order again.

The vote was taken and D.L. was expelled by a count of 4–1. The
general membership will be informed at the next open meeting.

MAY 7, 2036
FIRST DORIAN CHURCH OF AMERICA
OSCAR WILDE CONGREGATION
CONFIDENTIAL MEMBERSHIP REPORT:

L.N. called the special meeting to order at 8:00 PM. The first order
of business was the reconsideration of the expulsion of D.L. four years

ago. In light of recent events, it has become obvious that D.L.'s actions at
that time were not in violation of the basic principles of Dorianism.

If anything, D.L., more than any other member, has done the most
to further the cause of zero population growth.

K.R. noted some additional facts about the situation and a vote was
taken. D.L. was unanimously readmitted to the congregation. He has
not been notified because his whereabouts remain unknown.

It was decided not to apprise either the public or the general
membership of this decision, because of the adverse publicity this might
bring to the church.

MAY 27, 2033
FILE: 639 RADZ
SUBMTTED BY: RESIDENT PHYSICIAN JAMES-TAYLOR RUGG

Mr. and Mrs. Robert D____ came into my office on May 6 of
this year. They have been trying for six months to start a baby and
have had no success. I initiated the Groperson tests as well as a
routine physical examination of each.

Mrs. D____ is in excellent physical condition and well-suited
for child-bearing. Mr. D____ tests out with a normal sperm count
and is in no need of semination-cloning. I'm sure that the rest of
the tests will also turn out negative. I admit it, I'm stumped, and I
pass this case on to the board with all the rest.

WRITTEN IN INK ACROSS THE BOTTOM: *Dammit! This is the*
twenty-third one of these I've seen in the past two months. What the
hell is going on?

(signed) B.V.

2033.05.21/TIMEFAX
. . . SURPRISINGLY, THE ONLY PLACE WHERE THE POPULA-
TION GROWTH HAS KEPT WITHIN ITS PROJECTED LIMITS
HAS BEEN SOUTHERN CALIFORNIA, THE DENSEST URBAN
COMPLEX IN THE COUNTRY. THE STATE SURGEON GENERAL
OFFERED NO EXPLANATION FOR IT, BUT USED THE OCCA-

SION TO CONDEMN ARTIFICIAL ADDITIVES IN THE YEAST CULTURES. HE NOTED AN INCREASE IN THE NUMBER OF MARRIED COUPLES CONSULTING DOCTORS ABOUT THEIR INABILITY TO CONCEIVE AND HINTED THAT THERE MIGHT' BE A CONNECTION.

In Cleveland, Dr. Joyce Fremm discounted this, suggested instead that the California slowdown was a result of its becoming "one giant behavioral stink." When asked if she didn't mean "behavioral sink," Dr. Fremm replied, "I know what I said."

2034.05.03/TIMEFAX

Concern over the so-called "infertility plague" has spread even to the Eastern Bloc nations. The latest cities to report declining birth rates include Moscow, Peking, Hong Kong, Tokyo, Osaka, Hanoi, New Delhi and Melbourne. Earlier in the week, the Paris council met again to report still no success in finding the cause of the decline.

Dr. Joyce Fremm, working out of Southern California Complex, Unit Hospital 43, admitted that her team was no closer to the cause than they had been a year ago. "All we know about it, whatever it is," she said, "is that it keeps people from starting babies." She gave no indication when a solution might be found. While she was speaking, the World Health Organization released a list of an additional fourteen nations whose birth rates have begun to show the initial slowing that indicates the presence of the syndrome.

MAY 9, 2034

MEMO TO: DR. JOYCE FREMM FROM: DR. VICTOR WEBB KING

Joyce,

I don't know how important this is, but it wouldn't hurt to track it down. Out of the last three hundred couples I've interviewed, nearly sixty percent of the men have met their wives and been married only in the past eighteen months. Out of this group, nearly half report occasional premarital visits to a joy house, and nearly a third of all the men we interviewed have had some kind of professional contact.

More important however, is that *at least one partner in every couple has had at least one pre- or extramarital contact with a partner other than wife or husband.*

The former fact is way out of line with the statistical average; the latter implies a definite connection. Could the Xanadu Pleasure Corp be an active vector of the disease?

MAY 11, 2034
MEMO TO: DR. VICTOR WEBB KING
FROM: DR. JOYCE FREMM
(1) We don't know yet that it's a disease.
(2) Make no public announcement of this—especially do not suggest that Xanadu or any other company may be connected with it.
(3) Check it out immediately.

MAY 11, 2034
MEMO TO: DR. JOYCE FREMM
FROM: DR. CARLOS WAN-LEE
Dr. Fremm,

I believe my section has come up with a clue as to the nature of the syndrome. Sperm from one hundred affected men has been compared with the sperm of one hundred unaffected men; i.e. men whose wives have been impregnated within the past two months.

There is a minor but definite difference in the enzyme output of the affected sperm cells. All of the affected men (excepting three with very low sperm counts) had this qualitative difference in their enzyme production. Ninety-three of the unaffected men had normal enzyme production.

We're exploring this further and we'll have a more detailed report at the end of the week.

MAY 30, 2034
REPORT TO THE WORLD HEALTH ORGANIZATION
BY DR. JOYCE FREMM
TRANSCRIPTION OF REMARKS—MOST CONFIDENTIAL

Gentlemen,

We have discovered the cause of the infertility plague, and we believe that it is only a matter of time until we discover the cure.

The cause of the plague is simple: We have been hit by a new kind of venereal disease, a benevolent tyrant, so to speak. It has an incubation period of less than twenty-four hours, and its immediate effects are so mild as to be negligible; perhaps a headache or a mild sense of nausea, that's all; but after that, the victim will pass the infection on to everyone he or she has intimate contact with.

Both males and females are carriers of the disease, creating an ever-increasing reservoir of active infection, with promiscuity its vector.

The disease has no effect on females of the species. To them, it is a benevolent parasite. It lives in the female reproductive tract and minds its own business. Unfortunately, its business is to infect that woman's every male contact.

And each time it does that, it effectively castrates the man. Viability of the sperm cells is reduced to 7 percent of what is considered normal.

The causative agent is a virus. It is a new strain and related to nothing we have seen before. Were it not for the fact that artificial virus tailoring is still such an infant science, I would suspect a vast campaign of virological warfare is being waged against the human race.

The viral bodies live and breed in the cells lining the vaginal wall. During intercourse, the release of certain hormones causes them to become active, and the viral bodies migrate into the male organ—usually through the urethra, but occasionally through a mild, almost unnoticeable rash.

The virus then migrates to the testes, specifically to the sperm-forming cells. The viral DNA chains attack these cells, burrowing into the cell walls, throwing off their protein sheaths and becoming just another hunk of DNA within the cell. Impossible to discover.

The result is small, very small—but very noticeable. The sperm cell no longer "cares."

The average human male ejaculation contains three hundred million sperm cells. Ideally, each of these cells has the capability of being the cell to fertilize the waiting egg; but after being infected by the virus, the quality of the whole ejaculation is changed. The sperm cells still race madly up the fallopian tubes to meet the ovum—but when they get there, they can't fertilize.

You see, each sperm cell carries a tiny amount of an enzyme called hyaluronidase. Hyaluronidase sub-one, that is. No matter what the enzyme is called, though—what does matter is that the virus changes the male so that he no longer produces that enzyme. Instead, he produces something else, some other enzyme. The virus adds a few little acids of its own to the amino chain of the enzyme, and instead of hyaluronidase$_1$ we get hyaluronidase$_2$ —a very different creature altogether.

Hyaluronidase$_2$ is not as active as hyaluronidase$_1$. It takes longer to do its work. Much longer.

Although only one sperm cell is needed for fertilization to occur, three hundred million are provided in order that one will succeed. But because only one is needed, the other 2,999,999 sperm cells must be resisted. For that reason, the cell wall of the human ovum is too strong for any individual sperm cell to break down. Hyaluronidase is the enzyme that breaks down or softens the cell wall, and it takes the combined effort of all the sperm cells to provide enough of the enzyme to soften the wall enough for just one sperm cell to break through. Immediately upon fertilization, a change takes place in the cell wall to prevent other sperm cells from breaking in, a calculated resistance to their pressure.

But, if all those sperm cells are producing hyaluronidase$_2$ instead of hyaluronidase$_1$, fertilization will never take place at all. (Except in very rare cases—statistically insignificant.) The changed enzyme is still an enzyme, and it still works to soften the cell wall of the human egg—but it takes at least ten times longer to do it. And by that time, most of the sperm cells are already dead, dying, or too weak to complete the task of fertilization.

In addition, the ejaculation will also have introduced enough viral bodies into the woman so that if she weren't already, now she too will be infected and will pass the disease on to every subsequent male contact.

Insidious, isn't it?

Other than that, the virus has no effect at all on living human beings—only on the unborn. They stay that way. Unborn.

MAY 47, 2034
SUPPLEMENTARY REPORT, VIRT 897
WHO FILE BVC 675
SUMMARY: The virus, designated VIRT 897, seems to have made its initial appearance on the western coast of the American continent in June or July of 2032, specifically in the area of the Southern California Urban Complex known as Angeles. (colloq. L.A. or "Ellay.") From there it migrated along the heaviest tourist routes, traveling eastward to Denver, St. Louis, Chicago, Dallas, Miami, and scattered parts of the eastern seaboard Urban Complex.

Within six months, it had also appeared and made its effects known in Seattle, Portland, Detroit, Pittsburgh, and scattered areas surrounding. It extended the complete length of the western coast, being specifically virulent in Frisco and Diego counties, as well as in the areas already noted. It spread to Tijuana, Mexico City, and Acapulco. The same trend occurred simultaneously on the eastern coast, with scattered pockets of sterility spreading out from the Boston, York, Jersey, Philadelphia, and D.C. areas of the Urban

Complex. Also affected were Toronto, Montreal, and Quebec, as well as scattered areas surrounding.

At about the same time, it leapt both oceans simultaneously. Tracing the path of the falling birth rate, the disease showed up in London, Paris, Rome, Berlin, Warsaw, Munich, Belgrade, Dublin, Saigon, Seoul, Hanoi, Tokyo, Okama, Osaka, Beijing, Honolulu, Hong Kong, Melbourne, Sidney, Buenos Aires, Caracas, Panama City, Havana, and scattered points on the east African Coast as well as in the Mediterranean and Mid-East areas.

It is obvious that there are too many active vectors by this time, making it increasingly difficult to trace the spreading waves of infection. Not only does the disease move too rapidly, but once the waves of infection overlap, their directions blur.

There is no way to tell at this time whether the origin of the disease was deliberate or accidental or a combination of both.

Detailed analysis charts are enclosed.

MAY 30, 2034
INTERBEM CHEMICAL RESEARCH
MEMO TO: DR. LEON K. HARGER
FROM: SECTION SUPERVISOR VANCE
Dr. Harger,

I've just finished reading the WHO report on the sterility plague and a rather curious anomaly has caught my eye. I'm forwarding it to you to see if you catch it too. If you do, give me a buzz. If not, then forget I said anything.

MAY 30, 2034
INTERBEM CHEMICAL RESEARCH
MEMO TO: ALL DEPARTMENTS
FROM: DR. LEON K. HARGER
Urgent! I need all data pertaining to Dr. Dana Ledgerton DL 551-69-5688 and any and all research that he might have been involved in while he was employed here. Also, anyone knowing

his whereabouts or the itinerary of his sabbatical trip, please contact me immediately. I cannot understate the importance of this information!

MAY 1, 2035
TO: SUPREME COURT JUSTICE DOUGLAS JOSEPH WARREN
FROM: UNITED STATES ATTORNEY GENERAL ALFRED G. WYLER
Dear Doug,
This is strictly *off* the record, and you might want to burn this note after reading it.

I've been talking to the president, and he and I concur that it would be extremely unwise to allow the InterBem Company to be sued merely because Ledgerton was an employee of theirs at the time he constructed the Ledgerton Virus.

Yes, I've studied the briefs in the case. I know that the appealing lawyers make a good case for the company's negligence in not keeping tighter reins on their employees' after-hours research. They also make a good case that Ledgerton would have been unable to construct his artificial venereal disease without the company's research facilities.

However, no matten how good their case is, both the president and I agree that at this time it would be best for all parties if the appeal were turned down. The InterBem Company has been most cooperative with us in *every* area of our investigation, especially in our efforts to develop the artificial enzymes. To allow them to be sued now might destroy them as a viable corporation and would cost us a valuable ally in our fight against this thing.

I don't know if you're <u>familiar</u> with the fact, but my office has registered more than five hundred thousand separate actions against InterBem. That corporation can't afford to be embroiled in this kind of legal feeding frenzy. If you allow this first appeal to be granted, you will be setting a dangerous precedent that might cost the United States a valuable natural resource—i.e. a commercially healthy corporation.

Yes, I know this smacks of pressuring, but this case is too important to allow you to make a decision without knowing the administration's views on it. If you have any questions, don't hesitate to call me.

(signed) Alfred

MAY 7, 2035
FROM: FIELD OPERATIVE JASON PETER GRIGG
TO: FBI DIRECTOR WARREN J. HINDLER,
HOOVER CENTER,
WASHINGTON D.C.
FILE: LEDGERTON, DL 551-69-5688
Chief,

It's my guess that the Paul-John Murdock lead is going to be another dead end and we'll probably have to start digging backward. (I'll try to get up to Manweather Complex before the end of the month, though I don't <u>think</u> I'm going to find much up there.)

We located Murdock in South Frisco, where he's working as a shoe salesman. He has neither seen nor heard of Ledgerton since their post-college days. Apparently, he doesn't miss him either. I get the impression that the only reason they married was so that Murdock could avoid the labor-draft. The full interview tape is enclosed.

On the other side of it, there's some evidence that there was an emotional involvement on Ledgerton's part and that he's been trying to contact Murdock, but without success. We'll continue to monitor Murdock on the off chance that Ledgerton is still trying.

Oh, one more thing. The latest word on Ledgerton hints that he is somewhere in Africa and heading south. But I doubt it. Last week, he was in Scotland.

MAY 14, 2036
THE CONGRESSIONAL RECORD CONGRESSMAN JOHN J. HOOKER; DEM, GEORGIA

Gentlemen, we are presented today with a unique opportunity. The development of the artificial enzyme insures that the human race will not die out—and it gives us the chance to end, once and for all, the population explosion.

We need not manufacture the enzyme indiscriminately, nor need we make it available to every member of the world's population. In fact, even if we wanted to, it would be beyond our technology to service twenty billion individuals.

We are not geared for rehabilitating the human race; we can only provide enough enzyme for a fraction of the people. Dr. Fremm has stated that even if we began a massive synthesis program right now, we would never be able to reach all of those who are infected.

According to Dr. Fremm and others, it is only a matter of time until every man, woman, and child on this planet has the disease. When that happens, the only people who will be able to procreate will be those to whom we provide the enzyme.

Gentlemen, I say to you—here is an opportunity we cannot pass up—historians will condemn us if we allow this golden moment to slip out of our grasp—the chance to optimize the human race, to remake humanity. Therefore, I wish at this time to introduce this bill which would give the government the right to withhold the enzyme from those individuals who are judged to have undesirable genes . . .

(The rest of Congressman Hooker's speech was drowned out.)

MAY 20, 2036
BERKELEY NEW PRESS:
U.S. PLANS RACIAL WARFARE . . . Hooker (The Aardvark)'s plan would be only the first foot in the door. For instance, what

would keep the establishment slime from declaring Negro-ness an "undesirable trait"?

In cities across the nation, Freedom Now groups are planning urban disturbances to demonstrate their opposition to any form of "optimization," which would be only another word for genocide. The right to bear children is a right, not a privilege—and certainly not something that should be legislated. All right-thinking citizens are urged to come this weekend to the Free People's Plaza . . .

MAY 3, 2037
FROM: FIELD OPERATIVE JASON PETER GRIGG
TO: FBI DIRECTOR WARREN J. HINDLER,
HOOVER CENTER,
WASHINGTON D.C.
FILE: LEDGERTON, DL 551-69-5688
Chief,

The monitor on Murdock has turned up an interesting postcard (fax herewith enclosed) postmarked Brazil. Although there's no name signed to it, the content and phrasing could be a code of some sort. Or perhaps a reference to a personal experience known only to Murdock and Ledgerton. It should be checked out by one of our Brazilian operatives as soon as possible. I would appreciate being kept informed on this lead.

2037.05.09/TIMEFAX

. . . The rioters focused particularly on the symbols of establishment control. Four birth control centers in Harlemtown were sacked as well as all but one of the area's ten enzyme control clinics. This outbreak was the worst rioting to hit the city in seven months, and according to Mayor Gilbert Rockefeller, "It does not look as if the end is in sight." Meanwhile, in Washingtontown, the President deplored the nation's growing trend to violence and promised immediate steps to halt it in the future.

With that, he signed into law the controversial Manpower Control Bill . . . .

2037.05.11/ DATELINE:BRAZIL.

Rio de Janeiro. President Garcia today announced the capture of the notorious race-criminal, Dana Ledgerton (Dl 551-69-5688) at Rio de Janeiro Airport. Ledgerton was attempting to board an African-bound flight when Brazilian agents scooped him up. He is being held in Rio indefinitely.

The Brazilian government has announced it intends to try Ledgerton for the crime of genocide, as well as other crimes against humanity. Angry crowds have been milling in the streets of Rio ever since the announcement of Ledgerton's capture was made.

Worldwide reaction to the announcement was immediate. In the United States, the President said . . .

MAY 5, 2040.
REPORT TO THE WORLD HEALTH ORGANIZATION BY DR. JOYCE FREMM
MOST CONFIDENTIAL—TRANSCRIPTION OF REMARKS
Gentlemen,

Our recent studies on the enzyme synthesis program suggest that there is just no way to do what you ask—at least not without massive appropriations—and I, for one, am opposed to it.

(Pause)

If I may continue . . . If I may continue . . . I'll wait . . .

If the delegate from Nairobi will stop calling me a racist slime long enough to listen, I will explain my position. Any appropriations for the enzyme synthesis would have to be made at the expense of other programs and the amount of money needed to do what the delegate from Nairobi wishes us to do would necessitate the closing down of almost every other United Nations Program now in existence, with the exception of the pollution board. And the pollution board is far more important than this!

If I may continue . . . I believe that there is a way to save the human race, but enzyme synthesis is not it. In any case, a few years of minimal breeding will not hurt this planet any. There are about nineteen and a half billion too many people on Earth already.

2041.05.11/TIMEFAX

The Irish civil war, which has been smouldering for more than twenty years, burst into the news again today with the burning of Dublin. The Catholic faction in Ireland continues to charge that the neo-Protestant government is witholding the enzyme from Catholic mothers in an attempt to reduce the number of Catholics in the nation. That charge was echoed across the globe by other minorities in other nations. In Israel, Arab nationals charged the Israeli government with deliberate birth-crimes. The Jewish minority in Russia leveled the same charge against the Kremlin. The Chinese minorities in Malaysia and India have also charged those two governments with witholding the enzyme.

This brings to a total of forty-three, the number of complaints registered with the U.N. Minority Procreation Control Office.

MAY 19, 2041
TO: THE PRESIDENT OF THE UNITED STATES
FROM: WARREN J. HINDLER, HOOVER CENTER
Mr. President,

The situation is becoming more and more serious every day. I have reports coming across my desk to indicate that the activists are planning to step up the number of urban disturbances within the next two months. This nation is headed for civil war unless some way is found to take the steam out of the Anti-Enzyme movement.

I recommend immediate action along the following lines. . . .

MAY 20, 2041
POLICE REPORT, MANWEATHER COMPLEX

At 7:45 PM, Officers J.G. and R.F. investigated a complaint at 1456 Rafferty Avenue, Block 12, Apt 56789. Investigating Officers found Donald Ruddigore in process of assaulting his wife, Alice. Woman had already sustained minor injuries.

Ruddigore explained that his wife had told him she was pregnant. As he had been infected with the Ledgerton Virus some years earlier, he knew that he could not be the father of the child, and he had only begun beating her when she refused to tell him who the real father was.

When questioned, Mrs. Ruddigore insisted that she has never copulated with anyone but her husband. Officer G. suggested that both Ruddigores see a County Clinician before the week was over.

Mr. Ruddigore became abusive at this and had to be forcibly restrained. He was booked at Station 12 (preventive detention) and released the following morning on his own recognizance. Mrs. Ruddigore spent the night at her sister's after being released from the Emergency Hospital, where she was treated for minor scalp injuries.

As he was being taken into custody, Mr. Ruddigore noted that he was "glad that whoever the bastard is, now he's got it too!"

MAY 38, 2041
TO: DR. JOYCE FREMM
FROM: DR. CARLOS WAN-LEE
Joyce,

I've had four physicians call me in the past two days wanting to know if someone is bootlegging enzyme or something. All of them report a number of women (with previously infected husbands) turning up unexpectedly pregnant. Yes, I know it sounds like adultery, but I suspect it is something more. I'd like to talk to you about it in detail. I think we should investigate this. Are you free for lunch?

2042.05.14/DATELINE: BRAZIL.

In Rio today, a crowd of more than ten thousand formed in front of the Ledgerton gallows to hold a memorial service for Dana Ledgerton, who died five years ago on this spot. While Ledgerton's name is still reviled in many parts of the globe, a growing number of people are beginning to realize that not every effect of the Ledgerton Virus is necessarily evil. The Brazilian birth rate, for example, has dropped to a comfortable . . .

MAY 20, 2042
REPORT TO THE WORLD HEALTH ORGANIZATION BY DR. JOYCE FREMM
TRANSCRIPTION OF REMARKS—FOR PUBLIC RELEASE

. . . what has happened is this: The virus has mutated. It wasn't stable. Few viruses are.

We have, in the laboratories, taken the virus through a total of seven different mutations, each of which has a different effect on human fertility. At present, we have no way of stopping the virus completely, but if our early tests hold true, the human race will be able to stop worrying about its birth rate.

Ledgerton Virus sub-one reduces fertility to a scant 7 percent. Variety sub-two, which is currently sweeping the globe, raises that percentage to 53 percent. Certainly not what it was before, but high enough for two very determined people to start a baby, if they wish. The other varieties, which we've produced through careful bombardment of radiation (and other techniques), produce fertility levels ranging from 89 percent normal to 17 percent.

We can expect the virus to keep mutating at least once every four years. This is often enough to keep humanity from developing any kind of immunity to it. Also, it will hold the birth rate down, without keeping it dangerously depressed.

Gentlemen, without knowing it, Dr. Ledgerton seems to have stopped the population explosion.

MAY 43, 2045
TO: THE PRESIDENT OF THE UNITED STATES
FROM: THE SECRETARY OF INFORMATION
Mr. President,

Enclosed are samples of the publicity releases you requested.

You will note that we have taken great pains to minimize Ledgerton's homosexuality. As you said, "It wouldn't do to have an effeminate American hero."

Motivational Research indicates that the need for a new American hero is greater than ever now, especially since the recent Mexican defeat. For that reason, I urge that we initiate this program as soon as possible.

MAY 49, 2045
MINISTRY OF INFORMATION PAMPHLET #354657-098

. . . Single-handedly, this determined little man stopped the population explosion, stopped it dead with a biological brake— then he set that same brake so that it would release gently, allowing the race to maintain itself, but to cease its cancerous growth. When the death rates level off in the next few generations to match the new birth rates, the Earth will enjoy an era of peace and prosperity such as it has never known before . . . .

MAY 4, 2046
TO: THE SECRETARY OF FINANCE
FROM: THE PRESIDENT OF THE UNITED STATES
Dear Jase,

Sorry, but I'm going to have to ask you to quash your economic report on the primary causes of the current depression.

You're probably correct that the economy's continued growth is a direct factor of the nation's population spiral—but we can't suggest that fact publicly without starting a minor panic. (Besides, anything which would reflect negatively on the Ledgerton Program would not be welcome in certain circles.)

I agree with your recommendations though, and if you will circulate copies of your report (privately) to the Vice President and to the Secretary of Commerce, and also to the Secretary of the Treasury, between us we can initiate some of the steps you recommend to keep our financial heads above water.

And the sooner the better. This is an election year and we want to retain control of the House.

MAY 19, 2049
EXCERPT FROM *TODAY'S PSYCHOLOGY*

. . . one of the effects is the disappearance of the term "unwanted child" from the language. There is no such thing any more as an unwanted child. All children are wanted. Just look at the crowd of adults standing by the fence at any playground today.

Of course, not all the cultural changes are so beneficent. For instance, in the past, the pregnancy of an unmarried girl could quite likely have been the result of a mistake. Today, it can only be the result of several nights of steady "mistakes."

However, now that the onus of pregnancy has been removed from intercourse, certain other moral conventions are vanishing. Women are enjoying a sexual freedom even greater than that of the late twentieth century, when use of oral contraceptives first became widespread.

In general, the population of the nation is more birth-conscious than ever before, and one of the side effects has been a reduced tolerance for social and sexual deviants. Homosexuals have been driven out of several cities, and there is reason to believe that this trend will continue for some time. . . .

2050.05.06/TIMEFAX

. . . Found beaten to death in an alley. The man was later identified as Paul-John Murdock, a vagrant. Police suspect the beating death is just one more in a series of "anti-faggot" incidents that have racked Urbana in recent months.

2053.05.10/TIMEFAX

. . . The president announced today a new stamp commemorating the work of Dr. Dana Ledgerton, constructor of the fertility virus. The stamp will go on sale in four days, timed to coincide with the sixteenth anniversary of his death. . . .

— VONDA N. McINTYRE —

"MISPRINT"

■ *Nature*, July 9, 2008.

Wouldn't it be wonderful to have replacement parts that your body wouldn't reject—because they're yours? Scientists are currently working on "tissue printers" (3D printers that produce living tissue) and the first ones are already on the market (so far albeit just for research). Between the precision available with computer-aided design and our current knowledge of how tissues are laid out, we can potentially grow organs on demand.

From organs, it's only a small step to pets and other animals. Vonda McIntyre's story "Misprint" tells of ordering a cat, which is printed on demand. "Misprint" also highlights a problem we have today, namely technological upgrades you don't necessarily want and their unintended consequences. This is a short and satisfying tale, and if it isn't true yet, perhaps it will be in a decade or two.

MISPRINT

~

Vonda N. McIntyre

Fluffy was crying.
Like a baby.

My new cat's name is FluffIII, the third in the Fluffy line, but I call him Fluffy. I'm not sure what I'll call FluffIV, if there is one.

The new cat is supposed to be a normal ordinary catprint, a match to Fluffy, the best cat ever, whom I raised from a kitten. With a catprint, you get a grown cat. That skips the kitten part, which is too bad, but you also skip housetraining. And neutering.

A couple of selection boxes: Neural path—Use the litterbox. A deletion—Testicles.

Correct?

Print.

I never bother with the rest of the form. The non-allergenic Hairless option. Hairless cats are the next ugliest thing to naked mole rats anyway.

And who would tick off "Round Pupils"? Cats should have cat's eyes, slit-pupiled, glow-in-the-dark.

Opushun advertises available Rolydactyly. A cat with opposable thumbs? Forget it. Thumbs are fine for helper animals like dogs or ponies, but with a cat you'd have to add Anxious to Please, a high-performance package (translation: extra cost). They claim it works, but I doubt it. Millennia of domestication didn't produce Anxious to Please in cats.

And if it did, you wouldn't exactly have a cat, would you?

So I chose the standards, ignored the rest, and snapped the order.

A week later—it takes that long to grow enough cells for the printer cartridges—Opushun snapped me back to pick up FluffIII.

The clerk opened the carrier. The Fluffys have long soft grey fur and gold eyes. Their paws look silver in some light. You can change all that, but if I did, I wouldn't exactly have Fluffy, would I?

"He looks perfect! Thank you." I reached into the cat carrier and let him sniff my fingers and rub against my hand. I skritched his ears. I got a little teary. One reason Fluffys are such great cats is they're friendly. They're not anxious to please, but they are, naturally, friendly.

I thumbed for FluffIII and took him home.

But now he was crying.

I jumped up, startled. My work connection broke. I go to another place when I work so I like it to be quiet where I really am.

"Fluffy, nice kitty, what's the matter?"

He looked up from his kitty bed.

"You never talk to me."

He had a perfect Oxbridge accent, that plummy high-class British way of talking.

"I was just talking to you. I talked to you all the way home."

He licked his silver paw and rubbed the tears from his eyelashes. "You call that a conversation? 'Nice kitty, kitty'?"

"I didn't expect you to understand. I didn't expect you to talk back."

"I am not talking back. I am trying to hold a civilized conversation."

"I didn't think cats had civilized conversations," I said.

"Hah," he said. "Or, to be more precise, LOL."

He jumped into my lap,. I cradled him, and he managed to look dignified with his paws splayed all which-way. I petted his belly. The Fluffys have very soft fur.

"We'll have to converse later," I said. "Work calls." I put him back in the kitty bed. Being upset, I expended time and effort to reform the connection.

Fluffy strolled into the room, his furry tail high.

"When's dinner?"

The work connection collapsed.

Before Fluffy could protest, I shoved him into the cat carrier.

"There's been a mistake," I said to the clerk at the Opushun kiosk. I hauled Fluffy out. He glared at me without a word.

"I'm so sorry!" the clerk said. "At Opushun we're anxious to please."

"Can you fix him?"

She frowned, puzzled. "Surely it's already fixed?"

"No, yes, I mean, he came already fixed, that isn't the problem. The problem is . . ." I glanced down at Fluffy. "Tell her the problem."

"That *is* the problem," Fluffy said. "I'm fixed. Can you fix *that*?"

The clerk pretended he wasn't talking.

"Sir, you may exchange any model that's defective."

"Defective!" Fluffy said.

The clerk blinked. For a second I thought she had eyes like Fluffy's but then I blinked and she looked normal again. People's parents don't alterate them outside human traits, usually. Maybe she was wearing mood contacts.

"You see?" I said.

"I'm terribly sorry, sir, I don't."

"He's *talking*."

"Our new development," she said. "It's so popular that we made it standard. At Opushun, we're—"

"—Anxious to please," I said. I hadn't even noticed Conversation so I hadn't opted-out, which would have been an extra charge because they'd have to upgrade the standard by downgrading the upgrade.

"You see?" said Fluffy.

"Can you change him so he doesn't talk?"

Fluffy said something unprintable, which was startling in that accent. The clerk wasn't pretending he couldn't talk—she was ignoring him. That seemed rude. If you're going to create something that talks, you should listen to it.

"I'm so sorry, sir. Alterating a printout is un-cost-effective. But you may certainly make an exchange."

She tried to return Fluffy to the carrier. His claws scrabbled at the flaps. Probably he wished I'd gone for available Polydactyly.

"Wait!" he said, dignity abandoned. "What happens to me?"

"They'll find you a good home," I said. "With somebody who appreciates your finer qualities."

"Prove it!"

"I'm sorry, sir," the clerk said. "It's imprintouted on you. Another client would not be . . . pleased."

Fluffy leaped, flung himself against my chest, and nuzzled my neck, his nose damp and cool. He didn't say anything.

I sighed. "Will you promise not to talk to me when I'm trying to work?"

"I'll . . . try." He sounded more doubtful than anxious.

I took him home.

He isn't exactly Fluffy.

But he's close enough.

— RICHARD A. LOVETT —

"EXCELLENCE"

■ *Running Times*, **May 2009.**

One thing you have to say about sports: "Fair play" is very important. But what does "fair play" mean? Training is obviously okay, even training at high altitude to build up the oxygen-carrying capacity of the blood. But what about taking blood-stimulating hormones to do the same thing? Exercise to build muscle is okay, but taking drugs such as steroids? Having your genes changed, as has been dreamed of since the early 1970s, when researchers first figured out how to move genes from one creature to another?

These questions are vigorously debated, but perhaps we can summarize the debate by saying that there is a sense that it's okay to build one's abilities, but one must pay a price, and the price must be paid up-front. Training is painful. Taking drugs is not; it's the easy way out. And it's not just drugs. There are many enhancement techniques, including gene replacement (or gene-doping), that are going to become common in coming years, and though researchers are working on ways to detect gene-doping and other enhancements, their job will become harder and harder.

Will we judge the use of such enhancements differently if they impose a price on their users, as in the story? Are you on Jefferson Morgan's side? Or not? Would *you* choose to go for glory, or to "be decliningly ordinary for however many years remain"?

EXCELLENCE

◆

Richard A. Lovett

If there's a rule about deals with the devil, it's that you don't realize you're making one at the time. Especially when the devil in question walks with a cane and looks more like Kris Kringle than Beelzebub.

He said his name was August Knox and that he was a researcher working to beat multiple sclerosis, Lou Gehrig's disease, and all the other muscle-wasting disorders the world has ever known. Maybe he was. He was peddling a dream, and you don't look a gift horse too strongly in the mouth.

You remember BALCO, right? Well, suppose BALCO had visited you at age forty-two and asked if you wanted to be a guinea pig for a new product. Kringle/Knox wasn't with BALCO, obviously—they'd been out of business for years—but that's what he was peddling. Test samples of a new product, guaranteed unde-tectable by conventional tests, that would tune up your muscle efficiency not just by enough to roll your performance back to age thirty, but to match you with the best of them.

Could you win an Olympic medal? No guarantee there, but you'd be in the hunt. There was only one catch: If humans were like rats, you'd peak in a year and stay there for eighteen months. Two years, if you were lucky. After that? Well, once the rats had started to decline they'd done so rather precipitously.

"Would I still be able to run?"

"Probably not."

"Hike?"

"Define 'hike."

I told him about my favorite place, a viewpoint called Angel's Rest, 1,500 feet above the river, where I often go to stare into the afternoon sun and try to forget whatever it is that currently needs to be forgotten.

"Is it wheelchair accessible?"

So, what would you do? Go for glory or be decliningly ordinary for however many years remain?

Me, I chose the flame and die. My name's Jefferson Morgan, and ordinary has never been my goal. When I was twelve, I wanted to be a rock star: not just any rock star but the next Lennon. Then my voice changed and I realized not everyone got to sing lead.

A few other things changed too. At twelve, I was a skinny Goth. By the time I was ready to enter college, I was still skinny but I'd grown a new skill: I could run. A lot faster than average, it turned out.

It paid for college.

I was good, but not spectacular—just like my grades. And then I was out, with no real idea what to do next.

And that had pretty much been the story. I kicked around for two decades: tending bar, pumping gas, even mopping floors. I hooked up with a running team where, again, I was good, but not spectacular. Lots of free shoes but no free rent. Then age started to eat at my speed, until Beelzebub/Kringle hobbled up to me at the track one day with his cane and beaming, beady eyes.

Of course, I had to reinvent myself. Nobody would believe a middle-aged guy who suddenly runs like a kid. Luckily, I've always looked young (maybe that's part of why Kringle picked me) and a bit of hair dye and Botox made me younger yet.

Kringle/Knox had a pocketful of fake IDs, so I picked one from Vegas—a great choice for someone who wants to be anonymous. He also planted a few old race results and helped me create a bio. No college, no high school track. If asked, I was a late bloomer who for years had been more interested in training than racing. Every track's got a couple of those guys, and nobody remembers their names. But if I did hit it big, dozens of folks would be sure they'd known me.

It was only after I'd started the treatment that it crossed my mind that with all those fake identities, Knox/Beelzebub probably didn't intend me to be his only product tester. I just hoped I was the only 10,000-meter runner—though for Kringle's sake, too, there'd better not be many others. If he had a whole phalanx of us chasing the same medal, you could bet your sweaty socks that half of us would be willing to wreck what little was left of our lives screaming to the press.

Or maybe the treatment wasn't as good as advertised, and there wasn't that much chance of a Kringle-fest finish. When you get down to it, even deals with the devil are founded on trust.

The treatment took the form of shots. Lots of shots. It was based on gene therapy designed for muscular dystrophy patients, Knox told me as he stabbed enough needles into my quads to make me feel like an inside-out cactus.

For the first few weeks, all the shots did was make me weak.

"It's the virus," he said, having moved from my quads to my hamstrings and then my calves. "It inserts the genes into your muscle cells, and your body sees it as a mild infection. Don't worry, it'll pass."

That's part of what makes it undetectable, he added. The virus was a common one, like the flu or West Nile or some such thing, so while I'd show antibodies for it on a blood test, that didn't mean anything unless the authorities were prepared to reject anyone who'd ever been sneezed on or bitten by a mosquito. "There won't be anything in your blood to show you've been altered," he explained between jabs, "and nobody's going to start requiring muscle biopsies in the near future." He paused. "Though if someone does ask for one, it might be good to refuse. I don't think the genes we're working on would show up, but there's no reason to chance it."

Meanwhile, I started to train. Part of being great is having a good coach, and while Knox hadn't been able to retain the best in the business, the one he found was no slouch. He was just what a talented dark horse like me was supposed to be able to find: good, hungry for victory, but not too good.

I wasn't sure what, if anything, he knew, but Knox made it clear I wasn't supposed to talk to him about the treatments, so I doubted it was much.

Knox was a bit chary on specifics, but no athlete allows that many injections without asking questions. Basically, I was being subjected to two types of changes. One altered my ratio of slow-twitch and fast-twitch muscle fibers. The other had to do with satellite cells, which are kind of like stem cells in your muscles that help them get stronger and recover between workouts. The problem is that they can do this only so many times. After that? Well, that was part of the reason Kringle's treatment wasn't permanent. Most likely, I'd bounce from being a "good" forty-two-year-old to a great pseudo-thirty-year-old, then back to forty-two and on to fifty-two, sixty-two, or worse.

And that, I suppose, is half of why I knew I'd made a deal with the devil.

The other half was that during the treatment stage, with all those injections, it was hard to pretend I wasn't cheating. Not to the world at large, but to myself. Within a few weeks, though, I'd made peace with it. When I was young, the only thing that kept me from being among the best was the (poor) luck of the genetic draw. I'd always had the discipline, toughness, competitive drive. Knox/ Kringle had merely given me what I should have had all along. Back in my rock-star days, if someone had offered to improve my vocal cords, would I have turned it down?

Then I quit worrying at all, because once the injections ceased, I started to improve. I ran a road race and hit a time I'd have loved to have seen when I really was thirty. Twelve weeks later, I ran the best 10K of my life, by a full 90 seconds.

Knox, I decided, was a genius. My coach wasn't much worse. And, whatever else you might think, I'd never worked harder in my life. Kringle had merely redressed nature's imbalance. What I did with it was up to me.

What I did next was stress fracture my tibia. My coach was stunned. "Why didn't you tell me you were prone to these? We weren't even working you all that hard yet."

But the fact was that I'd never before lost more than a few days to injuries, and never to a broken bone.

"We've seen this in a couple of others," Kringle said the next time I saw him, confirming my suspicion I wasn't his only Olympic hopeful, though the others could easily be in different events. "The drugs make your muscles stronger, but not your tendons, ligaments, and bones. They're still your original age, and need time to adapt."

I had to think about that for a while. Not the muscles, bones, tendons, and ligaments bit. That made sense. It was the parts of me not all being the same age that was disconcerting.

It was the first time I'd ever truly felt my years. I don't know about you, but I'd always felt like pretty much the same person at forty-two that I'd been at thirty. Or twenty. I have friends who say they feel like radically different people than even a few years ago, but whomever I was at twenty: That's me.

Now, my muscles were thirty, my bones forty-two, and the essential me still felt like that long-gone twenty-year-old. I just couldn't figure out if I was the young person, the older one, or both at once.

Luckily, physical therapy was the perfect antidote to doubts. That's because it kept me too busy to think. And cross-training, with the top equipment, is amazing. Eight weeks later, when the docs pronounced the fracture healed, I was in nearly as good a shape as before it happened.

You're probably expecting a tale of cheating caught and bad behavior redeemed. It didn't quite work that way. Once we'd gotten over the old-bones surprise, Kringle obviously knew what he was doing. So did my coach. The Olympic trials found me with a series of new PRs, though the stress fracture had set me back enough that in the big event itself, I was fourth (barely even making the Olympic A standard).

Once, I'd have sold my soul simply for that. Now, it felt like defeat. But there's a reason there are Olympic alternates. The third-place finisher developed an Achilles problem—I don't think Kringle/Beelzebub had anything to do with it—and suddenly I was in.

The twenty-year-old me, the one who'd never changed, was ecstatic. The (now) forty-three-year-old me, the one in my bones, and brains, tried (at least briefly) to feel sorry for the guy who'd had to drop out. But the ageless competitor in my guts didn't care. I had reached the spot where, if nature had been fair, I'd have been a generation ago. I could handle that. As I said, this isn't a tale of cheating caught and bad behavior redeemed.

There were twenty-seven of us in the Olympic 10,000, and I was so nervous two days beforehand that I couldn't sleep. It wasn't just that my entire future depended on this: If the rat tests were right, I had no future.

That's when my coach blindsided me.

That's not what coaches are supposed to do. They're supposed to build you up, calm you down, focus you, and point you in the direction of victory. And that's what he thought he was doing.

He did it by telling me a story.

"When I was young," he said, "I was all piss and vinegar, like you." (I've never met a coach who didn't talk in clichés. Maybe everything's been said so many times the non-clichés were long ago used up.) "Then, my wife developed multiple sclerosis. Usually, they give you at least a dozen good years. She only got five. But until the very end, she insisted that I run, and came to all of my meets, even when she was in a wheelchair."

He paused, while I wondered what this could possibly have to do with me.

"This," he said, gesturing to the track, "isn't life. It's a hell of a lot of fun, and I love every minute of it, but in the big scheme of things"—he pursed his lips and blew out a sound, like *pffft*— "it's nothing." He turned back to me. "So, relax. Have fun. Realize that if you don't feel you have to win, you'll run better. And if by some chance you have a bad day . . . well, you've got a whole life yet ahead of you. This is only a small piece of it."

As a guy who'd barely made it into the race, I wasn't expected to be a contender. That made it easy to maintain my thirty-year-old identity because nobody did any of those spotlight profiles on me that the TV folks love to plug into their coverage to mask the fact that long races bore them.

Because I'd not run any races in the weeks since the trials, only my coach, Kringle, and I knew how much I'd continued to improve. I wondered if Kringle had deliberately timed the treatments that way—though having me come up as an alternate, rather than number three on the team, had been cutting it a bit fine. If I won, I'd be the unknown who burst onto the scene: far better than the favorite who lives up to his promise.

He'd never be able to go public with that—but in selling his wares to the next generation of do-anything hopefuls? He'd make sure they knew.

The race came late in the day, a concession to August heat, but not the best thing on the nerves. I much prefer morning races. Here, I had all day to fret and to try to keep away from my coach before he gave me some bromide worse than, "You have all of your life ahead of you." At least now I knew for sure he wasn't a Kringle insider.

But all endless waits eventually end.

I'd like to tell you it was an exciting race: the most dramatic 10,000 in Olympic history. But it was probably pretty ordinary. Thirty-year-old me had the ability to run with the best of them. And while the inner voice in my head might still be the college freshman who'd not yet realized he didn't have world-class speed, forty-three-year-old me had run a lot more races than anyone else on the track. I figured the experience would hold me in good stead now that I finally had the body my unaging inner voice always wanted.

It started as one of those tactical duels. Twenty of us ran in a big pack, where not stepping on someone or getting stepped on are your biggest worries. Nobody wanted the lead, least of all me.

Unfortunately, forty-three-year-old me didn't know what to *do* in that situation. I'd never been fast enough to be caught up in such a thing. In big, important races, there'd always been someone streaking away uncatchably in front. Sometimes lots of someones.

Now, I had the body to streak away—but I didn't know when or whether to try it. So much for all that experience. It had been with a different body.

The laps rolled by and nothing much happened except that a few people dropped out of the lead pack. I had to do something.

Before all of the injections, one thing I could do was kick. Sit back and pounce: that would have been my style. But now that most of my fast-twitch had been converted to slow-twitch, it wouldn't work.

I waited another mile, then took the lead. Before the race, my coach and I had set a target pace, but the pack had been slower than expected, so I knew I had to be faster now. The question was how much.

Within a couple laps, I'd dumped half of the pack, but there were still five left. On the backstretch, I looked up at the big television screen at one end of the stadium and saw myself, closely shadowed by an Ethiopian who'd won last year's world championship and two other guys who'd been here before.

I picked it up again with six laps to go, then again with four, and except for the world champion, the others started to drop off.

Then, with two laps to go, the Ethiopian started to push back.

This was an old game, and I'd always been good at it. Once I passed someone, they stayed passed. But now it didn't work. The Ethiopian pushed harder and when I tried to return the favor, nothing happened. I still managed to stave him off until the last lap, but then he went around me like I was standing still, followed shortly by the other two. If anything, I was slowing down.

I finished totally spent . . . and fifth.

My coach was livid. "What the hell did you think you were doing? First you let yourself get sucked into a slow, tactical duel you can't win, then you take off like a scared rabbit." He drew a big, theatrical sigh, probably trying to remember his own advice about it just being a race. "OK, live and learn. But you ran that thing like a damn teenager."

Knox appeared, and for once he wasn't beaming. "That," he said, "wasn't my fault." Then he turned on his good leg and clomped off.

My coach stared at him, then at me. Belatedly, I wondered why Knox walked with a cane, and what, if anything, my coach knew of it. Was Kringle making his own vicarious effort to redress nature's inequities? Even the devil, I guess, has his reasons.

A week later, my coach resigned. Kringle got me a new one and the next year I took bronze at the worlds, edging the Ethiopian who'd beaten me at the Olympics. But I was fading. Humans, rats . . . apparently we reacted similarly to Kringle's ministrations.

The trail to Angel's Rest isn't long, but I nearly put it off too long. At my prime, I could have popped up it in thirty minutes, barely breaking a sweat. This time it took two hours, and I'd never have made it without a walking stick. But the summit was everything I remembered: a big flat slab of rock, looking straight down on the mile-wide river. Below, a freeway hugged the headland, the monotonous drone of trucks audible even from here. A train rumbled a deeper bass, while downstream, a barge plowed a V-wake through sun-glinted water. Everywhere, it seemed, people were on the move.

Unlike the old days, when this was my private retreat, my brother had come up here with me, in case I needed assistance or (the unspoken fear) rescue.

The only surviving member of my immediate family (we Morgans aren't a long-lived tribe), he'd been the one part of my old life I'd insisted on retaining. But at Kringle's insistence, I'd never let him far into my new life. Mostly, it was easy. He wasn't much of a sports fan, and while I couldn't hide my new name and appearance, I'd just told him I'd done it at a sponsor's request. Not that it mattered: My brother is very much of the don't-ask/don't-tell persuasion.

In my rock-star-dreaming days, he'd wanted to play bass to my lead. Two years older but twenty years more passive, he'd never claimed to resent our never-was stardom. Still, he'd remained in music, and was now a high school band teacher.

I looked down on the cars, moving antlike: linear drones, everyone going where someone else had been. Follow-the-leader from cradle to grave. I had stepped out of line. My brother was sitting on my favorite life-pondering rock, staring into sunlight the color of the medal I'd given so much not to attain.

"Are you happy?" I asked.

He shot me a glance, then looked back to the late-afternoon distance. "Sure."

"No. I mean really, truly happy. Remember when we wanted to be rock stars?"

This time he grinned. "Oh, yeah. After that, I wanted to be an astronaut." His gaze was still on the river. "I grew up. On a ten-point scale, I'm an eight. I'll take it. But you . . . you did live it there for a while, didn't you? Were you happy?"

It was my turn to stare into the eye-numbing goldness. I wondered how much he knew, how much he might have figured out. I wondered if it mattered.

"Good thing it happened before you got sick," he said a few minutes later.

The sun was getting low, and walking down a steep trail isn't as easy as people think. Luckily, we'd brought flashlights. Declining my brother's offer of assistance, I heaved myself to my feet. Then, leaning on my stick, I began the descent into twilight.

five

KEEP WATCHING
THE SKIES!

(Predictions of things to come)

— HAL CLEMENT —

"THE MECHANIC"

■ *Analog*, September 1966.

The first detailed transcription of one person's genetic information cost millions of dollars. Just a few years later, it now costs thousands, and researchers are talking of getting the price down to mere hundreds. Once that happens, everyone will be able to afford to keep a copy of their personal genetic information in a computer file. And from it—perhaps!—a "mechanic" will be able to reconstruct lost body parts or organs.

Unlike the 3D printer which would print new organs outside the body (see Vonda McIntyre's "Misprint" earlier in this volume), Hal Clement's friendly, neighborhood mechanic would regrow your damaged bits and pieces in place. But not yet!

It is also worth mentioning that "synthetic life" such as that discussed in the stay is currently a very active research area.

THE MECHANIC

~❧

Hal Clement

Drifting idly, the *Shark* tended to look more like a manta ray than her name suggested; but at high cruise, as she was now, she bore more resemblance to a flying fish. She was entirely out of the water except for the four struts that carried her hydroplanes; the air propellers which drove her were high enough above the surface to raise very little spray. An orbiting monitor satellite could have seen the vessel herself from a hundred miles up, since her upper hull was painted in a vividly fluorescent pattern of red and yellow; but there was not enough wake to suggest to such a watcher that the wedge-shaped machine was traveling at nearly sixty-five knots.

Chester V. Winkle—everyone knew what the middle initial stood for but no one mentioned it in his presence—sat behind the left bow port of his command with his fingers resting lightly on the pressure controls. He was looking ahead, but knew better than to trust his eyes alone. Most of his attention was devoted to the voice of the smaller man seated four feet to his right, behind the other "eye" of the manta. Yoshii Ishihara was not looking outside at all; his eyes were directed steadily at the sonar display screen which was all that stood between the *Shark* and disaster at her present speed among the ice floes and zeowhales of the Labrador Sea.

"Twenty-two targets in the sweep; about fourteen thousand meters to the middle of the group," he said softly.

"Heading?" Winkle knew the question was superfluous; had a change been in order, the sonarman would have given it.

"As we go, for thirty-two hundred meters. Then twenty-two mils starboard. There's ice in the way."

"Good. Any data on target condition yet?"

"No. It will be easier to read them when we stop, and will cost little time to wait. Four of the twenty-two are drifting, but the sea is rich here and they might be digesting. Stand by for change of heading."

"Ready on your call." There was silence for about a minute.

"Starboard ten."

"Starboard ten." The hydroplanes submerged near the ends of the *Shark's* bow struts banked in response to the pressure of Winkle's fingers, though the hull remained nearly level. The compass needle on the panel between the view ports moved smoothly through ten divisions. As it reached the tenth, Ishihara, without looking up from his screen, called, "Steady."

"Steady she is," replied the commander.

"Stand by for twelve more to starboard—now." The *Shark* swung again and steadied on the new heading.

"That leaves us a clear path in," said the sonarman. "Time to engine cut is four minutes."

In spite of his assurance that the way was clear, Ishihara kept his eyes on his instrument—his standards of professional competence would permit nothing less while the *Shark* had way on her. Winkle, in spite of the sleepy appearance which combined with his name to produce a constant spate of bad jokes, was equally alert for visible obstructions ahead. Several ice floes could be seen; but none were directly in the vessel's path, and Winkle's fingers remained idle until his second officer gave the expected signal.

Then the whine of turbines began to drop in pitch, and the *Shark's* broad form eased toward the swell below as the hydrofoils lost their lift. The hull extensions well out on her "wings" which gave the vessel catamaran-type stability when drifting kissed the surface gently, their added drag slowing the machine more abruptly; and twenty feet aft of the conning ports the four remaining members of the crew tensed for action.

"Slow enough for readings?" asked Winkle.

"Yes, sir. The homing signal is going out now. I'll have counts in the next thirty seconds." Ishihara paused. "One of the four drifters is underway and turning toward us. No visible response from the others."

"Which is the nearest of the dead ones?"

"Fifteen hundred meters, eight hundred forty miles port." Winkle's fingers moved again, The turbines that drove the big, counter-rotating air propellers remained idle, but water jets playing from ducts on the hydrofoil struts swung the ship in the indicated direction and set her traveling slowly toward the drifter. Winkle called an order over his shoulder.

"Winches and divers ready. The trap is unsafetied. Contact in five minutes."

"Winch ready," Dandridge's deep voice reported as he swept his chessboard to one side and closed a master switch. Mancini, who had been facing him across the board, slipped farther aft to the laboratory which occupied over half of the *Shark's* habitable part. He said nothing, since no order had been directed at him, and made no move to uncage any of his apparatus while the vessel was still in motion.

"Divers standing by." Farrell spoke for himself and his assistant after a brief check of masks and valves—both were already dressed for Arctic water. They took their places at either side of the red-checkered deck area, just forward of the lab section, which marked the main hatch. Dandridge, glancing up to make sure that no one was standing on it, opened the trap from his control console. Its halves slid smoothly apart, revealing the chill green liquid slipping between the hulls. At the *Shark's* present speed she was floating at displacement depth, so that the water averaged about four meters down from the hatch; but this distance was varied by a swell of a meter or so. Farrell stood looking down at it, waiting patiently for the vessel to stop; his younger assistant dropped prone by the edge of the opening and craned his neck through it in an effort to see forward.

Ishihara's voice was barely audible over the wind now that the hatch was open, but occasional words drifted back to the divers. "Six hundred . . . as you go . . . four three . . ."

"I see it," Winkle cut in. "I'll take her." He called over his shoulder again, "Farrell . . . Stubbs . . . we're coming up on one. You'll spot it in a minute. I'll tell you when I lose it under the bow."

"Yes, sir," acknowledged Farrell. "See it yet, Rick?"

"Not yet," was the response. "Nothing but jellyfish."

"Fifty meters," called the captain. "Now thirty." He cut the water jets to a point where steerage way would have been lost if such a term had meant anything to the *Shark*, and continued to inch forward. "Twenty."

"I see it," called Stubbs.

"All right," answered the captain. "Ten meters. Five. It's right under me; I've lost it. Con me, diver."

"About five meters, sir. It's dead center . . . four . . . three . . . two . . . all right, it's right under the hatch. Magnets ready, Gil?"

The magnetic grapple was at the forward end of its rail, directly over the hatch, so Dandridge was ready; but Winkle was not.

"Hold up . . . don't latch on yet. Stubbs, watch the fish; are we drifting?"

"A little, sir. It's going forward and a little to port . . . now you're stopping it . . . there."

"Quite a bit of wind," remarked the captain as his fingers lifted from the hydrojet controls. "All right. Pick it up."

"Think the magnets will be all right, Marco?" asked Dandridge. "That whale looks funny to me." The mechanic joined the winchman and divers at the hatch and looked down at their floating problem.

At first glance the "whale" was ordinary enough. It was about two meters long, and perfectly cigar-shaped except where the intake ring broke the curve some forty centimeters back of the nose. The exhaust ports, about equally far from the tail end, were less visible since they were merely openings in the dark gray skin. Integument and openings alike were hard to see in detail, however; the entire organism was overgrown with a brownish, slimy-looking mass of filaments reminiscent both of mold and sealskin.

"It's picked up something, all right," Mancini conceded. "I don't see why your magnets shouldn't work, though . . . unless you'd rather they didn't get dirty."

"All right. Get down the ladder and steer 'em, Rick." Dandridge caused a light alloy ladder to extend from the bow edge of the hatch as he spoke; then he fingered another switch which sent the grapples themselves slowly downward. Stubbs easily beat them to the foot of the ladder, hooked one leg through a rung, reached out with both arms, and tried to steady the descending mass of metal. The *Shark* was pitching somewhat in the swell, and the eighty pounds of electromagnet and associated wiring was slightly rebellious: The youngest of the crew and the only nonspecialist among its members—he was still working off the two-year labor draft requirement which preceded higher education—Rick Stubbs got at least his share of the dirty work. He was not so young as to complain about it.

"Slower . . . slower . . . twenty c's to go . . . ten hold it now . . . just a touch lower . . . all right, juice!" Dandridge followed the instructions, fed current to the magnets, and started to lift.

"Wait!" the boy on the ladder called almost instantly. "It's not holding!"

The mechanic reacted almost as fast.

"Bring it up anyway!" he called. "The infection is sticking to the magnets. Let me get a sample!" Stubbs shrank back against the ladder as the slimy mass rose past him in response to Mancini's command. Dandridge grimaced with distaste as it came above deck level and into his view.

"You can have it!" he remarked, not very originally.

Mancini gave no answer, and showed no sign of any emotion but interest. He had slipped back into his lab as the material was ascending, and now returned with a two-liter flask and the biggest funnel he possessed.

"Run it aft a little," he said briefly. "That's enough . . . I'll miss some, and it might as well fall into the water as onto the deck." The grapple, which had crawled a few inches toward him on its over-head rail, stopped just short of the after edge of the hatch. Mancini, standing unconcernedly at the edge of the opening with the wind ruffling his clothes, held funnel and flask under the magnets.

"All right, Gil, drop it," he ordered. Dandridge obeyed.

Most of the mess fell obediently away from the grapple. Some landed in the funnel and proceeded to ooze down into the flask; some hit Mancini's extended arm without appearing to bother him; a little dropped onto the deck, to the winchman's visible disgust. Most fell past Stubbs back into the sea.

The mechanic took up some of the material from his arm and rubbed it between thumb and forefinger "Gritty," he remarked. "And the magnets held this stuff, but not the whale's skeleton. That means that most of the skeleton must be gone, and I bet this grit is magnetite. I'll risk a dollar that this infection comes from that old 775-Fe-DE6 culture that got loose a few years ago from Passamaquoddy. I'll give it the works to make sure, though. You divers will have to use slings to get the fish aboard, I'm afraid."

"Rick, I'll send the magnets down first and you can rinse 'em off a bit in the water. Then I'll run out the sling and you can get it around the whale."

"All right, sir. Standing by." As the grapple went down again Dandridge called to the mechanic, who had turned back toward the lab.

"I suppose the whale is ruined, if you're right about the infection. Can we collect damages?" Mancini shook his head negatively.

"No one could collect from DE; they went broke years ago—from paying damages. Besides, the courts decided years ago that injury or destruction of a piece of pseudolife was recoverable property damage only if an original model was involved. This fish is a descendant of a model ten years old; it was born at sea. We didn't make it, and can't recover for it." He turned to his bench, but flung a last thought over his shoulder. "My guess that this pest is a DE escapee could be wrong, too. They worked out a virus for that strain a few months after it escaped, and I haven't heard of an iron infection in four years. This may be a mutation of it—that's still my best guess—but it could also be something entirely new." He settled himself onto a stool and began dividing the material from the flask into the dozens of tiny containers which fed the analyzers.

In the water below, Stubbs had plunged from the ladder and was removing slime from the grapple magnets. The stuff was not too sticky, and the grit which might be magnetite slightly offset the feeling of revulsion which the boy normally had for slimy materials, so he was able to finish the job quickly enough to keep Dandridge happy. At Stubbs call, the grapple was retracted; a few moments later the hoist cable came down again with an ordinary sling at its extremity. Stubbs was still in the water, and Farrell had come part way down the ladder. The chief diver guided the cable down to his young assistant, who began working the straps around the torpedo-like form which still bobbed between the Shark's hulls.

It was quite a job. The zeowhale was still slippery, since the magnets had not come even close to removing all the foreign growth. When the boy tried to reach around it to fasten the straps it slithered away from him. He called for more slack and tried to pin it against one of the hulls as he worked, but still it escaped him. He was too stubborn to ask for help, and by this time Farrell was laughing to hard to have provided much anyway.

"Ride him, Buster!" the chief diver called as Stubbs finally managed to scissor the slippery cylinder with his legs. "That's it . . . you've got him dogged now!"

The boy hadn't quite finished, actually, but one strap did seem secure around the forward part of the hull. "Take up slack!" he called up to the hatch, without answering Farrell's remark.

Dandridge had been looking through the trap and could see what was needed; he reached to his control console and the hoist cable tightened.

"That's enough!" called Stubbs as the nose of the zeowhale began to lift from the water, "Hold it until I get another strap on, or this one will slip free!"

Winches obediently ceased purring. With its motion restrained somewhat, the little machine offered less opposition to the attachment of a second band near its stern. The young swimmer called, somewhat breathlessly, "Take it up!" and paddled himself slowly back to the ladder. Farrell gave him a hand up, and they reached the deck almost as quickly as the specimen.

Dandridge closed the hatch without waiting for orders, though he left the ladder down—there would be other pickups in the next few minutes, but the wind was cold and loud. Stubbs paid no attention; he barely heard the soft "Eight hundred meters, seventy-five miles to starboard," as he made his way around the closing hatch to Mancini's work station. The mechanic's job was much more fascinating than the pilot's.

He knew better than to interrupt a busy professional with questions, but the mechanic didn't need any. Like several other men, not only on the *Shark* but among the crew of her mothership, Mancini had come to like the youngster and respect his general competence; and like most professionals, his attitude toward an intelligent labor draftee was a desire to recruit him before someone else did. The man, therefore, began to talk as soon as he noticed the boy's presence.

"You know much about either chemical or field analysis, Rick?"

"A little. I can recognize most of your gear—ultracentrifuge, chromatographic and electrophoretic stuff, NMR equipment, and so on. Is that," he pointed to a cylindrical machine on another bench, "a diffraction camera?"

"Good guess. It's a hybrid that a friend of mine dreamed up which can be used either for electron microphotography or diffraction work. All that comes a bit later, though. One thing about analysis hasn't changed since the beginning; you try to get your initial sample into as many different homogeneous parts as possible before you get down to the molecular scale."

"So each of these little tubes you're filling goes through centrifuge, or solvation, or electrophoresis—"

"More usually, through all of them, in different orders."

"I should think that just looking at the original, undamaged specimen would tell you *something*. Don't you ever do that?"

"Sure. The good old light microscope will never disappear; as you imply, it's helpful to see a machine in its assembled state, too. I'll have some slides in a few more seconds; the mike is in that cabinet. Slide it out, will you?"

Stubbs obeyed, literally since the instrument was mounted on a track. The designers of the *Shark*'s laboratory had made it as immune to rough weather as they could. Mancini took the first of his slides, clipped it under the objective, and took one look.

"Thought so," he grunted. "Here, see for yourself."

Stubbs applied an eye to the instrument, played briefly with the fine focus—he had the normal basic training in fundamental apparatus—and looked for several seconds.

"Just a mess of living cells that don't mean much to me, and a lot of little octahedra. Are they what you mean?"

"Yep. Magnetite crystals, or I'm a draft-dodger." (His remark had no military significance; the term now referred to individuals who declined the unskilled-labor draft, voluntarily giving up their rights to higher education and, in effect, committing themselves to living on basic relief.) "We'll make sure, though." The mechanic slid another piece of equipment into position on the microscope stage, and peered once more into the field of view. Stubbs recognized a micromanipulator, and was not surprised when Mancini, after two minutes or so of silent work, straightened up and removed a small strip of metal from it. Presumably one of the tiny crystals was now mounted on the strip.

The mechanic turned to the diffraction camera, mounted the bit of metal in a clamp attached to it, and touched a button which started specimen and strip on a journey into the camera's interior. Moments later a pump started to whine.

"Five minutes to vacuum, five more for scanning," he remarked. "We might as well have a look at the fish itself while we wait; even naked-eye examination has its uses." He got up from his seat, stretched, and turned to the bench on which the ruined zeowhale lay. "How much do you know about these things, Rick? Can you recognize this type?"

"I think so. I'd say it was a copper-feeder of about '35 model. This one would be about two years old."

"Good. I'd say you were about right. You've been doing some reading, I take it."

"Some. And the *Guppy*'s shop is a pretty good museum."

"True enough. Do you know where the access regions are on this model?"

"I've seen some of them opened up, but I wouldn't feel sure enough to do it myself."

"It probably wouldn't matter if you did it wrong in this case; this one is safely dead. Still, I'll show you; better see it right than do it wrong." He had removed the straps of the sling once the "fish" had been lowered onto a rack on the bench, so nothing interfered with the demonstration. "Here," he pointed, "the reference is the centerline of scales along the back, just a little lighter in color than the rest. Start at the intake ring and count eight scales back; then down six on either side, like that. That puts you on this scale . . . so . . . which you can get under with a scalpel at the start of the main opening." He picked up an instrument about the size of a surgical scalpel, but with a blunt, rounded blade. This he inserted under the indicated scale. "See, it comes apart here with very light pressure, and you can run the cut back to just in front of the exhaust vents—like that. If this were a living specimen, the cut would heal under sealant spray in about an hour after the fish was back in the water. This one . . . hm-m-m. No wonder it passed out. I wonder what this stuff is?"

The body cavity of the zeowhale was filled with a dead-black jelly, quite different in appearance from the growth which had covered the skin. The mechanic applied retractors to the incision, and began silently poking into the material with a variety of "surgical" tools. He seemed indifferent to the feelings which were tending to bring Stubbs' stomach almost as much into daylight as that of the whale.

Pieces of rubbery internal machinery began to litter the bench top. Another set of tiny test tubes took samples of the black jelly, and followed their predecessors into the automatic analyzers. These began to hum and sputter as they went to work on the new material—they had long since finished with the first load, and a pile of diagrams and numerical tables awaited Mancini's attention in their various delivery baskets. He had not even taken time to see whether his guess about magnetite had been good.

Some of the organs on the desk were recognizable to the boy—for any large animal, of course, a heart is fairly obviously a heart when it has been dissected sufficiently to show its valve structure. A four-kilogram copper nugget had come from the factory section; the organism had at least started to fulfill its intended purpose before disease had ended its pseudolife. It had also been developing normally in other respects, as a twenty-five centimeter embryo indicated. The zeowhales and their kindred devices reproduced asexually; the genetic variation magnification, which is the biological advantage of sex, was just what the users of the pseudo-organisms did not want, at least until some factor could be developed which would tend to select for the characteristics they wanted most.

Mancini spent more than an hour at his rather revolting task before he finally laid down his instruments. Stubbs had not been able to watch him the whole time, since the *Shark* had picked up the other two unresponsive whales while the job was going on. Both had been infected in the same way as the first. The boy was back in the lab, though, when the gross dissection of the original one was finished. So was Winkle, since nothing more could be planned until Mancini produced some sort of report.

"The skeleton was gone completely," was the mechanic's terse beginning. "Even the unborn one hadn't a trace of metallic iron in it. That was why the magnets didn't hold, of course. I haven't had time to look at any of the analysis reports, but I'm pretty certain that the jelly in the body cavity and the moldy stuff outside are part of the same life-form, and that organism dissolved the metallic skeleton and precipitated the iron as magnetite in its own tissues. Presumably it's a mutant from one of the regular iron-feeding strains. Judging by its general cellular conformation, its genetic tape is a purine-pyrimidine nucleotide quite similar to that of natural life—"

"Just another of the original artificial forms coming home to roost?" interjected Winkle.

"I suppose so. I've isolated some of the nuclear material, but it will have to go back to the big field analyzer on the *Guppy* to make sure."

"There seem to be no more damaged fish in the neighborhood. Is there any other material you need before we go back?"

"No. Might as well wind her up, as far as I'm concerned— unless it would be a good idea to call the ship first while we're out here to find out whether any other schools this way need checking."

"You can't carry any more specimens in your lab even if they do," Winkle pointed out, glancing around the littered bench tops.

"True enough. Maybe there's something which wouldn't need a major checkup, though. But you're the captain; play it as you think best. I'll be busy with this lot until we get back to the *Guppy* whether we go straight there or not."

"I'll call." The captain turned away to his own station.

"I wonder why they made the first pseudolife machines with gene tapes so much like the real thing," Stubbs remarked when Winkle was back in his seat. "You'd think they'd foresee what mutations could do, and that organisms too similar to genuine life might even give rise to forms which could cause disease in us as well as in other artificial forms."

"They thought of it, all right," replied Mancini. "That possibility was a favorite theme of the opponents of the whole process—at least, of the ones who weren't driven by frankly religious motives. Unfortunately, there was no other way the business could have developed. The original research of course had to be carried out on what you call 'real' life. That led to the specific knowledge that the cytosine-thymine-adenine-guanine foursome of ordinary DNA could form a pattern which was both self-replicating and able to control polypeptide and polysaccharide synthesis—"

"But I thought it was more complex than that; there are phosphates and sugars in the chain, and the DNA imprints RNA, and—"

"You're quite right, but I wasn't giving a chemistry lecture; I was trying to make an historical point. I'm saying that at first, no one realized that anything except those four specific bases could do the genetic job. Then they found that quite a lot of natural life-forms had variations of those bases in their nucleotides, and gradually the reasons why those structures, or rather their potential fields, had the polymermolding ability they do became clear. Then, and only then, was it obvious that 'natural' genes aren't the only possible ones; they're simply the ones which got a head start on this planet. There are as many ways of building a gene as there are of writing a poem—or of making an airplane if you prefer to stay on the physical plane. As you seem to know, using the channels of a synthetic zeolite as the backbone for a genetic tape happens to be a very convenient technique when we want to grow a machine like the one we've just taken apart here. It's bulkier than the phosphate-sugar-base tape, but a good deal more stable.

"It's still handy, though, to know how to work with the real thing—after all, you know as well as I do that the reason you have a life expectancy of about a hundred and fifty years is that your particular gene pattern is on file in half a cubic meter of zeolite mesh in Denver under a nice file number . . ."

"026-18-5633" muttered the boy under his breath.

". . . which will let any halfway competent molecular mechanic like me grow replacement parts and tissues if and when you happen to need them."

"I know all that, but it still seems dangerous to poke around making little changes in ordinary life-forms," replied Rick. "There must be fifty thousand people like you in the world who could tailor a dangerous virus, or germ, or crop fungus in a couple of weeks of lab and computer work, and whose regular activities produce things like that iron-feeder which can mutate into dangerous by-products."

"It's also dangerous to have seven billion people on the planet, practically every one of whom knows how to light a fire," replied Mancini. "Dangerous or not, it was no more possible to go from Watson and Crick and the DNA structure to this zeowhale without the intermediate development than it would have been to get from the Wright brothers and their powered kite to the two-hour transatlantic ramjet without building Ford tri-motors and DC-3s in between. We have the knowledge, it's an historical fact that no one can effectively destroy it, so we might as well use it. The fact that so many competent practitioners of the art exist is our best safeguard if it does get a little out of hand at times."

The boy looked thoughtful.

"Maybe you have something there," he said slowly. "But with all that knowledge, why only a hundred and fifty years? Why can't you keep people going indefinitely?"

"Do you think we should?" Mancini countered with a straight face. Rick grinned.

"Stop ducking. If you could, you would—for some people anyway. Why can't you?"

Mancini shrugged. "Several hundred million people undoubtedly know the rules of chess." He nodded toward the board on Dandridge's control table. "Why aren't they all good players? You know, don't you, why doctors were reluctant to use hormones as therapeutic agents even when they became available in quantity?"

"I think so. If you gave someone cortisone it might do what you wanted, but it might also set other glands going or slow them down, which would alter the levels of other hormones, which in turn . . . well, it was a sort of chain reaction which could end anywhere."

"Precisely. And gene-juggling is the same only more so. If you were to sit at the edge of the hatch there and let Gil close it on you, I could rig the factors in your gene pattern so as to let you grow new legs; but there would be a distinct risk of affecting other things in your system at the same time. In effect, I would be taking certain restraints which caused your legs to stop growing when they were completed off your cell-dividing control mechanisms—the sort of thing that used to happen as a natural, random effect in cancer. I'd probably get away with it—or rather, you would—since you're only about nineteen and still pretty deep in what we call the stability well. As you get older, though, with more and more factors interfering with that stability, the job gets harder—it's a literal juggling act, with more and more balls being tossed to the juggler every year you live.

"You were born with a deep enough stability reserve to keep yourself operating for a few decades without any applied biochemical knowledge; you might live twenty years or ninety. Using the knowledge we have, we can play the game longer; but sooner or later we drop the ball. It's not that we don't know the rules; to go back to the chess analogy, it's just that there are too many pieces on the board to keep track of all at once."

Stubbs shook his head. "I've never thought of it quite that way. To me, it's always been just a repair job, and I couldn't see why it should be so difficult."

Mancini grinned. "Maybe your cultural grounding didn't include a poem called 'The Wonderful One-Hoss Shay.' Well, we'll be a couple of hours getting back to the *Guppy*. There are a couple of sets of analysis runs sitting with us here. Maybe, if I start trying to turn those into language you can follow, you'll have some idea of why the game is so hard before we get there. Maybe, too"—his face sobered somewhat—"you'll start to see why, even though, we always lose in the end, the game is so much fun. It isn't just that our own lives are at stake, you know; men have been playing that kind of game for two million years or so. Come on."

He turned to the bench top on which the various analyzers had been depositing their results; and since Stubbs had a good grounding in mathematical and chemical fundamentals, their language ceased to resemble basic English. Neither paid any attention as the main driving turbines of the *Shark* came up to quarter speed and the vessel began to pick her way out of the patch of ice floes where the zeowhales had been collecting metal.

By the time Winkle had reached open water and Ishibara had given him the clearance for high cruise, the other four had lost all contact with the outside world. Dandridge's chessboard was in use again, with Farrell now his opponent. The molecular mechanic and his possible apprentice were deeply buried in a task roughly equivalent to explaining to a forty-piece orchestra how to produce *Aida* from overture to finale—without the use of written music. Stubbs's basic math was, for this problem, equivalent to having learned just barely his "do, re, mi."

There was nothing to distract the players of either game. The wind had freshened somewhat, but the swells had increased little if at all. With the *Shark* riding on her hydrofoils there was only the faintest of tremors as her struts cut the waves. The sun was still high and the sky almost cloudless. Between visual pilotage and sonar, life seemed as uncomplicated as it ever gets for the operator of a high-speed vehicle.

The *Guppy* was nearly two hundred kilometers to the south, far beyond sonar range. Four of her other boats were out on business, and Winkle occasionally passed a word or two with their commanders; but no one had anything of real importance to say. The desultory conversations were a matter of habit, to make sure that everyone was still on the air. No pilot, whether of aircraft, space vessel, surface ship, or submarine, attaches any weight to the proverb that no news is good news.

Just who was to blame for the interruption of this idyll remains moot. Certainly Mancini had given the captain his preliminary ideas about the pest that had killed their first whale. Just as certainly he had failed to report the confirmation of that opinion after going through the lab results with Stubbs. Winkle himself made no request for such confirmation—there was no particular reason why he should, and if he had it is hard to believe that he would either have realized all the implications or been able to do anything about them. The fact remains that everyone from Winkle at the top of the ladder of command to Stubbs at the bottom was taken completely by surprise when the *Shark*'s starboard after hydrofoil strut snapped cleanly off just below the mean planing water line.

At sixty-five knots, no human reflexes could have coped with the result. The electronic ones of the *Shark* tried, but the vessel's mechanical IQ was not up to the task of allowing for the lost strut. As the gyros sensed the drop in the right rear quadrant of their field of perception, the autopilot issued commands to increase the angle of attack of the control foils on that strut. Naturally there was no response. The dip increased. By the time it got beyond the point where the machine thought it could be handled by a single set of foils, so that orders went out to decrease lift on the port-bow leg, it was much too late. The after portion of the starboard flotation hull smacked a wave top at sixty-five knots and, of course, bounced. The bounce was just in time to reinforce the letdown command to the port-bow control foils. The box curve of the port hull struck in its turn, with almost undiminished speed and with two principal results.

About a third of the *Shark's* forward speed vanished in less than the same fraction of a second as she gave up kinetic energy to the water in front, raising a cloud of spray more than a hundred meters and subjecting hull and contents to about four gravities of acceleration in a most unusual direction. The rebound was high enough to cause the starboard "wing" to dip into the waves, and the *Shark* did a complete double cartwheel. For a moment she seemed to poise motionless with port wing and hull entirely submerged and the opposite wingtip pointing at the sky; then, grudgingly, she settled back to a nearly horizontal position on her flotation hulls and lay rocking on the swell.

Externally she showed little sign of damage. The missing strut was, of course, underwater anyway, and her main structure had taken only a few dents. The propellers had been twisted off by gyroscopic action during the cartwheel. Aside from this, the sleek form looked ready for service.

Inside, things were different. Most of the apparatus, and even some of the men, had been more or less firmly fixed in place; but the few exceptions had raised a good deal of mayhem.

Winkle and Ishihara were unconscious, though still buckled in their seats. Both had been snapped forward against their respective panels, and were draped with sundry unappetizing fragments of the dissected zeowhale. Ishihara's head had shattered the screen of his sonar instrument, and no one could have told at first glance how many cuts were supplying the blood on his face.

The chess players had both left impressions on the control panel of the winch and handling system, and now lay crumpled beside it. Neither was bleeding visibly, but Farrell's arms were both twisted at angles impossible to intact bones. Dandridge was moaning and just starting to try to get to his feet; he and Mancini were the only ones conscious.

The mechanic had been seated at one of his benches facing the starboard side of the ship when the impact came. He had not been strapped in his seat, and the four-G jerk had started to hurl him toward the bow. His right leg had stopped him almost as suddenly by getting entangled in the underpinning of the seat. The limb was not quite detached from its owner; oddly enough, its skin was intact. This was about the only bit of tissue below the knee for which this statement could be made.

Stubbs had been standing at the mechanic's side. They were to argue later whether it had been good or bad luck that the side in question had been the left. It depended largely on personal viewpoint. There had been nothing for Rick to seize as he was snatched toward the bow or, if there was, he had not been quick enough or strong enough to get it. He never knew just what hit him in flight; the motions of the *Shark* were so wild that it might have been deck, overhead, or the back of one of the pilot seats. It was evident enough that his path had intersected that of the big flask in which Mancini had first collected the iron-feeding tissue, but whether the flask was still whole at the time remains unclear. It is hard to see how he could have managed to absorb so many of its fragments had it already shattered; but it is equally hard to understand how he could have scattered them so widely over his anatomy if it had been whole.

It was Stubbs, or rather the sight of him, that got Mancini moving. Getting his own shattered leg disentangled from the chair was a distracting task, but not distracting enough to let him take his eyes from the boy a few meters away. Arterial bleeding is a sign that tends to focus attention.

He felt sick, over and above the pain of his leg; whether it was the sight of Rick or incipient shock he couldn't tell. He did his best to ignore the leg as he inched across the deck, though the limb itself seemed to have other ideas. Unfortunately these weren't very consistent; sometimes it wanted—demanded—his whole mind, at others it seemed to have gone off somewhere on its own and hidden. He did not look back to see whether it was still with him; what was in front was more important.

The boy still had blood when Mancini reached him, as well as a functioning heart to pump it. He was not losing the fluid as fast as had appeared from a distance, but something would obviously have to be done about what was left of his right hand—the thumb and about half of the palm. The mechanic had been raised during one of the periods when first-aiders were taught to abjure the tourniquet, but had reached an age where judgment stands a chance against rules. He had a belt and used it.

A close look at the boy's other injuries showed that nothing could be done about them on the spot; they were bleeding slowly, but any sort of first aid would be complicated by the slivers of glass protruding from most of them. Face, chest, and even legs were slashed freely, but the rate of bleeding was not—Mancini hoped—really serious. The smaller ones were clotting already.

Dandridge was on his feet by now, badly bruised but apparently in the best shape of the six.

"What can I do, Marco?" he asked. "Everyone else is out cold. Should I use—"

"Don't use anything on them until we're sure there are no broken necks or backs; they may be better off unconscious. I know I would be."

"Isn't there dope in the first-aid kit? I could give you a shot of painkiller."

"Not yet, anyway. Anything that would stop this leg from hurting would knock me out, and I've got to stay awake if at all possible until help comes. The lab equipment isn't really meant for repair work, but if anything needs to be improvised from it I'll have to be the one to do it. I could move around better, though, if this leg were splinted. Use the raft foam from the handling locker."

Five minutes later Mancini's leg, from mid-thigh down, was encased in a bulky, light, but reasonably rigid block of foamed resin whose original purpose was to provide on-the-spot flotation for objects which were inconvenient or impossible to bring aboard. It still hurt, but he could move around without much fear of doing the limb further damage.

"Good. Now you'd better see what communication gear, if any, stood up under this bump. I'll do what I can for the others. Don't move Ishi or the captain; work around them until I've done what I can."

Dandridge went forward to the conning section and began to manipulate switches. He was not a trained radioman—the *Shark* didn't carry one—but like any competent crew member he could operate all the vessel's equipment under routine conditions. He found quickly that no receivers were working, but that the regular transmitter drew current when its switches were closed. An emergency low-frequency beacon, entirely separate from the other communication equipment, also seemed intact; so he set this operating and began to broadcast the plight of the *Shark* on the regular transmitter. He had no way of telling whether either signal was getting out, but was not particularly worried for himself. The *Shark* was theoretically unsinkable—enough of her volume was filled with resin foam to buoy her entire weight even in fresh water. The main question was whether help would arrive before some of the injured men were beyond it.

After ten minutes of steady broadcasting—he hoped—Dandridge turned back to the mechanic to find him lying motionless on the deck. For a moment the winchman thought he might have lost consciousness; then Mancini spoke.

"I've done all I can for the time being. I've splinted Joe's arms and pretty well stopped Rick's bleeding. Ishi has a skull fracture and the captain at least a concussion; don't move either one. If you've managed to get in touch with the *Guppy*, tell them about the injuries. We'll need gene records from Denver for Rick, probably for Ishi, and possibly for the captain. They should start making blood for Rick right away, the second enough gene data is through; he's lost quite a bit."

"I don't know whether I'm getting out or not, but I'll say it all anyway," replied Dandridge, turning back to the board. "Won't you need some pretty extensive repair work yourself, though?"

"Not unless these bone fragments do more nerve damage than I think they have," replied Mancini. "Just tell them that I have a multiple leg fracture. If I know Bert Jellinge, he'll have gene blocks on all six of us growing into the machines before we get back to the *Guppy* anyway."

Dandridge eyed him more closely. "Hadn't I better give you a shot now?" he asked. "You said you'd done all you could, and it might be better to pass out from a sleepy shot than from pain. How about it?"

"Get that message out first. I can hold on, and what I've done is the flimsiest of patchwork. With the deck tossing as it is any of those splints may be inadequate. We can't strap any of the fellows down, and if the wave motion rolls one of them over I'll have the patching to do all over again. When you get that call off, look at Rick once more; I think his bleeding has stopped, but until he's on a repair table I won't be happy about him."

"So you'd rather stay awake."

"Not exactly, but if you were in the kid's place, wouldn't you prefer me to?" Dandridge had no answer to that one; he talked into the transmitter instead.

His words, as it happened, were getting out. The *Conger*, the nearest of the *Shark*'s sister fish-tenders, had already started toward them; she had about forty kilometers to come. On the Guppy the senior mechanic had fulfilled Mancini's prediction; he had already made contact with Denver, and Rick Stubbs' gene code was about to start through the multiple-redundant communication channels used for the purpose—channels which, fortunately, had just been freed of the saturation caused by a serious explosion in Pittsburgh, which had left over five hundred people in need of major repair. The full transmission would take over an hour at the highest safe scanning rate; but the first ten minutes would give enough information, when combined with the basic human data already in the *Guppy*'s computers, to permit the synthesis of replacement blood.

The big mothership was heading toward the site of the accident so as to shorten the *Conger*'s journey with the victims. The operations center at Cape Farewell had offered a "mastodon"—one of the gigantic helicopters capable of lifting the entire weight of a ship like the *Shark*. After a little slide-rule work, the *Guppy*'s commander had declined; no time would have been saved, and the elimination of one ship-to-ship transfer for the injured men was probably less important than economy of minutes.

Mancini would have agreed with this, had he been able to join in the discussion. By the time Dandridge had finished his second transmission, however, the mechanic had fainted from the pain of his leg.

Objectively, the winchman supposed that it was probably good for his friend to be unconscious. He was not too happy, though, at being the only one aboard who could take responsibility for anything. The half hour it took for the *Conger* to arrive was not a restful one for him, though it could not have been less eventful. Even sixty years later, when the story as his grandchildren heard it included complications like a North Atlantic winter gale, he was never able to paint an adequate word picture of his feelings during those thirty minutes—much less an exaggerated one.

The manta-like structure of the tenders made trans-shipping most practical from bow-to-bow contact, but it was practical at all only on a smooth sea. In the present case, the *Conger's* commander could not bring her bow closer than ten meters to that of the crippled ship, and both were pitching too heavily even for lines to be used.

One of the *Conger's* divers plunged into the water and swam to the helpless vessel. Dandridge saw him coming through the bow ports, went back to his console, and rather to his surprise found that the hatch and ladder responded to their control switches. Moments later the other man was on the deck beside him.

The diver took in the situation after ten seconds of explanation by Dandridge and two of direct examination, and spoke into the transmitter which was part of his equipment. A few seconds later a raft dropped from the *Conger's* hatch and two more men clambered down into it. One of these proved on arrival to be Mancini's opposite number, who wasted no tune.

"Use the foam," he directed. "Case them all up except for faces; that way we can get them to the bench without any more limb motion. You say Marco thought there might be skull or spine fractures?"

"He said Ishi had a fractured skull and Winkle might have. All he said about spines was that we'd have to be careful in case it had happened."

"Right. You relax; I'll take care of it." The newcomer took up the foam generator and went to work.

Twenty minutes later the *Conger* was on her hydroplanes once more, heading for rendezvous with the *Guppy*.

In spite of tradition, Rick Stubbs knew where he was when he opened his eyes. The catch was that he hadn't the faintest idea how he had gotten there. He could see that he was surrounded by blood-transfusion equipment, electronic circulatory and nervous system monitoring gear, and the needle-capillary-and-computer maze of a regeneration unit, though none of the stuff seemed to be in operation. He was willing to grant from all this that he had been hurt somehow; the fact that he was unable to move his head or his right arm supported this notion. He couldn't begin to guess, however, what sort of injury it might be or how it had happened.

He remembered talking and working with Mancini at the latter's lab bench. He could not recall for certain just what the last thing said or done might be, though; somehow the picture merged with the foggy struggle back to consciousness which had culminated in recognition of his surroundings.

He could see no one near him, but this might be because his head wouldn't turn. Could he talk? Only one way to find out.

"Is anyone here? What's happened to me?" It didn't sound very much like his own voice, and the effort of speech hurt his chest and abdomen; but apparently words got out.

"We're all here, Rick. I thought you'd be switching back on about now." Mancini's face appeared in Stubbs' narrow field of vision.

"We're all here? Did everyone get hurt somehow? What happened?"

"Slight correction—most of us are here, one's been and gone. I'll tell you as much as I can; don't bother to ask questions, I know it must hurt you to talk. Gil was here for a while, but he just had a few bruises and is back on the job. The rest of us were banged up more thoroughly. My right leg was a jigsaw puzzle; Bert had an interesting time with it. I thought he ought to take if off and start over, but he stuck with it, so I got off with five hours of manual repair and two in regeneration instead of a couple of months hooked up to a computer. I'm still splinted, but that will be for only a few more days.

"No one knows yet just what happened. Apparently the *Shark* hit something going at full clip, but no one knows yet what it was. They're towing her in; I trust there'll be enough evidence to tell us the whole story."

"How about the other fellows?"

"Ishi is plugged in. He may need a week with computer regeneration control, or ten times that. We won't be able to assess brain damage until we find how close to consciousness he can come. He had a bad skull fracture. The captain was knocked out, and some broken ribs I missed on the first-aid check did internal damage. Bert is still trying to get him off without regeneration, but I don't think he'll manage it."

"You didn't think he could manage it with you, either."

"True. Maybe it's just that I don't think I could do it myself, and hate to admit that Jellinge is better at my own job than I am."

"How about Joe?"

"Both arms broken and a lot of bruises. He'll be all right. That leaves you, young fellow. You're not exactly a critical case, but you are certainly going to call for professional competence. How fond are you of your fingerprints?"

"What? I don't track."

"Most of your right hand was sliced off, apparently by flying glass from my big culture flask. Ben Tulley from the *Conger*, which picked us up, found the missing section and brought it back; it's in culture now."

"What has that to do with fingerprints? Why didn't you or Mr. Jellinge graft it back?"

"Because there's a good deal of doubt about its condition. It was well over an hour after the accident before it got into culture. You know the sort of brain damage a few minutes without oxygen can do. I know the bone, tendon, and connective tissue in a limb is much less sensitive to that sort of damage, but an hour is a long time, chemically speaking. Grafting calls for healing powers which are nearly as dependent on genetic integrity as is nerve activity; we're just not sure whether grafting is the right thing to do in your case. It's a toss-up whether we should fasten the hand back on and work to make it take, or discard it and grow you a new one. That's why I asked how much you loved your fingerprints."

"Wouldn't a new hand have the same prints?"

"The same print classification, which is determined genetically, but not the same details, which are random."

"Which would take longer?"

"If the hand is in shape to take properly, grafting would be quicker—say a week. If it isn't, we might be six or eight times as long repairing secondary damage. That's longer than complete regeneration would take."

"When are you going to make up your minds?"

"Soon. I wondered whether you'd have a preference."

"How could I know which is better when you don't? Why ask me at all?"

"I had a reason—several, in fact. I'll tell you what they were after you've had two years of professional training in molecular mechanics, if you decide to come into the field. You still haven't told me which you prefer."

The boy looked up silently for a full minute. Actually, be spent very little of that time trying to make his mind up; he was wondering what Mancini's reasons might be. He gave up, flipped a mental coin, and said, "I think I'd prefer the original hand, if there's a real chance of getting it back and it won't keep me plugged into these machines any longer than growing a new one would."

"All right, we'll try it that way. Of course, you'll be plugged in for quite a while anyway, so if we do have trouble with the hand it won't make so much difference with your time."

"What do you mean? What's wrong besides the hand?"

"You hadn't noticed that your head is clamped?"

"Well, yes; I knew I couldn't move it, but I can't feel anything wrong. What's happened there?"

"Your face stopped most of the rest of the flask, apparently."

"Then how can I be seeing at all, and how is it that I talk so easily?"

"If I knew that much about probability, I'd stop working for a living and take up professional gambling. When I first saw you after your face had been cleaned off and before the glass had been taken out I wondered for a moment whether there hadn't been something planned about the arrangement of the slivers. It was unbelievable, but that's the way it happened. They say anything can happen once, but I'd advise you not to catch any more articles of glassware with your face."

"Just what was it like, Marco? Give me the details."

"Frankly, I'd rather not. There are record photos, of course, but if I have anything to say about it you won't see them until the rebuilding is done. Then you can look in a mirror to reassure yourself when the photos get your stomach. No"—as Stubbs tried to interrupt—"I respect what you probably think of as your clinical detachment, but I doubt very strongly that you could maintain it in the face of the real thing. I'm pretty sure that I couldn't, if it were my face." Mancini's thoughts flashed back to the long moments when he had been dragging his ruined leg across the Shark's deck toward the bleeding boy, and felt a momentary glow—maybe that disclaimer had been a little too modest. He stuck to his position, however.

Rick didn't argue too hard, for another thought had suddenly struck his mind. "You're using regeneration on my face, without asking me whether I want it the way you did with my hand. Right?"

"That's right," Mancini said.

"That means I'm so badly damaged that ordinary healing won't take care of it."

Mancini pursed his lips and thought carefully before answering. "You'd heal all right," he admitted at last. "You might just possibly, considering your age, heal without too much scarring. I'd hesitate to bet on that, though, and the scars you could come up with would leave you quite a mess."

Stubbs lay silent for a time, staring at the featureless ceiling. The mechanic was sure his expression would have been thoughtful had enough of the young face been visible to make one. He could not, however, guess at what was bothering the boy. As far as Mancini could guess from their work together there was no question of personal cowardice—for that matter, the mechanic could not see what there might be to fear. His profession made him quite casual about growing tissue, natural or artificial, on human bodies or anywhere else. Stubbs was in no danger of permanent disfigurement, crippling damage, or even severe pain; but something was obviously bothering the kid.

"Marco," the question came finally, "just where does detailed genetic control end, in tissue growth, and statistical effects take over?"

"There's no way to answer that both exactly and generally. Genetic factors are basically probability ones, but they're characterized by regions of high probability which we call stability wells. I told you about fingerprints, but each different situation would call for a different specific answer."

"It was what you said about prints that made me think of it. You're going to rebuild my face, you say. You won't tell me just how much rebuilding has to be done, but you admitted I *could* heal normally. If you rebuild, how closely will you match my original face? Does that statistical factor of yours take over somewhere along the line?"

"Statistical factors are everywhere, and work throughout the whole process," replied Mancini without in the least meaning to be evasive. "I told you that. By rights, your new face should match the old as closely as the faces of identical twins match each other, and for the same reason. I grant that someone who knows the twins really well can usually tell them apart, but no one will have your old face around for close comparison. No one will have any doubt that it's you, I promise."

"Unless something goes wrong."

"If it goes wrong enough to bother you, we can always do it over."

"But it *might* go really wrong."

Mancini, who would have admitted that the sun might not rise the next day if enough possible events all happened at once, did not deny this, though he was beginning to feel irritated. "Does this mean that you don't want us to do the job? Just take your chances on the scars?" he asked.

"Why do scars form, anyway?" was the counter. "Why can't regular, normal genetic material reproduce the tissue it produced in the first place? It certainly does sometimes; why not always?"

"That's pretty hard to explain in words. It has to do with the factors which stopped your nose growing before it became an elephant's trunk—or more accurately, with the factors which stopped your overall growth where they did. I can describe them quite completely, and I believe quite accurately, but not in basic English."

"Can you measure those factors in a particular case?"

"Hm-m-m, yes; fairly accurately, anyway." Stubbs pounced on this with an eagerness which should have told the mechanic something.

"Then can't you tell whether these injuries, in my particular case, will heal completely or leave scars?"

"I . . . well, I suppose so. Let's see; it would take . . . hm-m-m; I'll have to give it some thought. It's not regular technique. We usually just rebuild. What's your objection, anyway? All rebuilding really means is that we set things going and then watch the process, practically cell by cell, and correct what's happening if it isn't right—following the plans you used in the first place."

"I still don't see why my body can't follow them without your help."

"Well, no analogy is perfect; but roughly speaking, it's because the cells which will have to divide to produce the replacement tissue had the blueprints which they used for the original construction stamped 'production complete; file in reference storage' some years ago, and the stamp marks covered some of the lines on the plans." Mancini's temper was getting a little short, as his tone showed. Theoretically his leg should not have been hurting him, but he had been standing on it longer than any repairman would have advised at its present stage of healing. And why did the kid keep beating around the bush?

Stubbs either didn't notice the tone or didn't care. "But the plans—the information—that's still there; even I know that much molecular biology. I haven't learned how to use your analysis gear yet, much less to reduce the readings; but I can't see why you'd figure it much harder to read the plans under the 'file' stamp than to work out the ability of that magnetite slime to digest iron from the base configuration of a single cell's genes."

"Your question was why your body couldn't do it; don't change the rules in the middle of the game. I didn't say that *I* couldn't; I could. What I said was that it isn't usual, and I can't see what will be gained by it; you'd at least double the work. I'm not exactly lazy, but the work at best is difficult, precise, and time-consuming. If someone were to paint your portrait and had asked you whether you wanted it on canvas or paper, would you dither along asking about the brand of paint and the sizes of brushes he was going to use?"

"I don't think that's a very good analogy. I just want to know what to expect—"

"You can't *know* what to expect. No one can. Ever. You have to play the odds. At the moment, the odds are so high in your favor that you'd almost be justified in saying that you know what's going to happen. All I'm asking is that you tell me straight whether or not you want Bert and me to ride control as your face heals, or let it go its own way."

"But if you can grow a vine that produces ham sandwiches instead of pumpkins, why—" Mancini made a gesture of impatience. He liked the youngster and still hoped to recruit him, but there are limits.

"Will you stop sounding like an anti-vivisectionist who's been asked for a statement on heart surgery and give me a straight answer to a straight question? The chances are all I can give you. They are much less than fifty-fifty that your face will come out of this without scars on its own. They are much better than a hundred to one that even your mother will never know there's been a controlled regeneration job done on you unless you tell her. You're through general education, legally qualified to make decisions involving your own life and health, and morally obligated to make them instead of lying there dithering. Let's have an answer."

For fully two minutes, he did not get it. Rick lay still, his expression hidden in dressings, eyes refusing to meet those of the man who stood by the repair table. Finally, however, he gave in.

"All right, do your best. How long did you say it would take?"

"I don't remember saying, but probably about two weeks for your face. You'll be able to enjoy using a mirror long before we get that hand unplugged, unless we're remarkably lucky with the graft."

"When will you start?"

"As soon as I've had some sleep. Your blood is back to normal, your general pattern is in the machine; there's nothing else to hold us up. What sort of books do you like?"

"Huh?"

"That head's going to be in a clamp for quite a while. You may or may not like reading, but the only direction you can look comfortably is straight up. Your left hand can work a remote control, and the tape reader can project on the ceiling. I can't think of anything else to occupy you. Do you want some refreshing light fiction, or shall I start you on Volume One of 'Garwood's Elementary Matrix Algebra for Biochemists?' "

A regeneration controller is a bulky machine, even though most of it has the delicacy, and structural intricacy possible only to pseudolife—and, of course, to "real" life. Its sensors are smaller in diameter than human red blood cells, and there are literally millions of them. Injectors and samplers are only enough larger to take entire cells into their tubes, and these also exist in numbers which would make the device a hopeless one to construct mechanically. Its computer-controller occupies more than two cubic meters of molecular-scale "machinery" based on a synthetic zeolite framework. Mating the individual gene record needed for a particular job to the basic computer itself takes nearly a day; it would take a lifetime if the job had to be done manually, instead of persuading the two to "grow" together.

Closing the gap between the optical microscope and the test tube, which was blanketed under the word "protoplasm" for so many decades, also blurred the boundary between such initially different fields as medicine and factory design. Marco Mancini and Bert Jellinge regarded themselves as mechanics; what they would have been called a few decades earlier is hard to say. Even at the time the two had been born, no ten Ph.D.'s could have supplied the information which now formed the grounding of their professional practice.

When their preliminary work—the "prepping"—on Rick Stubbs was done, some five million sensing tendrils formed a beard on the boy's face, most of them entering the skin near the edges of the injured portions. Every five hundred or so of these formed a unit with a pair of larger tubes. The sensors kept the computer informed of the genetic patterns actually active from moment to moment in the healing tissue—or at least, a statistically, significant number of them. Whenever that activity failed to match within narrow limits what the computer thought should be happening, one of the larger tubes ingested a single cell from the area in question and transferred it to a large incubator—"large" in the sense that it could be seen without a microscope—just outside Rick's skin. There the cell was cultured through five divisions, and some of the product cells analyzed more completely than they could be inside a human body. If all were well after all, which was quite possible because of the limitations of the small sensors, nothing more happened.

If things were really not going according to plan, however, others of the new cells were modified. Active parts of their genetic material which should have been inert were inerted, quiet parts which should have been active were activated. The repaired cells were cultivated for several more divisions; if they bred true, one or more of them was returned to the original site—or at least, to within a few microns of it. Cell division and tissue building went on according to the modified plan until some new discrepancy was detected.

Most of this was, of course, automatic; too many millions of operations were going on simultaneously for detailed manual control. Nevertheless, Mancini and Jellinge were busy. Neither life nor pseudolife is infallible; mutations occur even in triply redundant records. Computation errors occur even—or especially—in digital machines which must by their nature work by successive-approximation methods. It is much better to have a human operator, who knows his business, actually see that connective tissue instead of epidermis is being grown in one spot, or nerve instead of muscle cells in another.

Hence, a random selection of cells, not only from areas which had aroused the computer's interest but from those where all was presumably going well, also traveled out through the tubes. These went farther than just to the incubators; they came out to a joint where gross microscopic study of them by a human observer was possible. This went on twenty-four hours a day, the two mechanics chiefly concerned and four others of their profession taking two-hour shifts at the microscope. The number of man-hours involved in treating major bodily injury had gone up several orders of magnitude since the time when a sick man could get away with a bill for ten dollars from his doctor, plus possibly another for fifty from his undertaker.

The tendrils and tubes farthest from the damaged tissue were constantly withdrawing, groping their way to the action front, and implanting themselves anew, guided by the same chemical clues which brought leukocytes to the same area. Early versions of the technique had involved complex methods of warding off or removing the crowd of white cells from the neighborhood; the present idea was to let them alone. They were good scavengers, and the controller could easily allow for the occasional one which was taken in by the samplers.

So, as the days crawled by, skin, and fat and muscle and blood vessels, nerves and bones and tendons, gradually extended into their proper places in Stubbs' face and hand. The face, as Mancini had predicted, was done first; the severed hand had deteriorated so that most of its cells needed replacement, though it served as a useful guide.

With his head out of the clamp, the boy fulfilled another of the mechanic's implied predictions. He asked for a mirror. The man had it waiting, and produced it with a grin; but the grin faded as he watched the boy turn his face this way and that, checking his appearance from every possible angle. He would have expected a girl to act that way; but why should this youngster?

"Are you still the same fellow?" Mancini asked finally. "At least you've kept your fingerprints." Rick put the mirror down.

"Maybe I should have taken a new hand," he said. "With new prints I might have gotten away with a bank robbery, and cut short the time leading to my well-earned retired leisure."

"Don't you believe it," returned Mancini grimly. "Your new prints would be on file along with your gene record and retinal pattern back in Denver before I could legally have unplugged you from the machine. I had to submit a written summary of this operation before I could start, even as it was. Forget about losing your legal identity and taking up crime."

Stubbs shrugged. "I'm not really disappointed. How much longer before I can write a letter with this hand, though?"

"About ten days; but why bother with a letter? You can talk to anyone you want; haven't your parents been on the visor every day?"

"Yes. Say, did you ever find out what made the *Shark* pile up?"

Mancini grimaced. "We did indeed. She got infected by the same growth that killed the zeowhale we first picked up. Did you by any chance run that fish into any part of the hull while you were attaching the sling?"

Rich stared aghast. "My gosh! Yes, I did. I held it against one of the side hulls because it was so slippery. . . . I'm sorry . . . I didn't know—"

"Relax. Of course you didn't. Neither did I, then; and I never thought of the possibility later. One of the struts was weakened enough to fall at high cruise, though, and Newton's Laws did the rest."

"But does that mean that the other ships are in danger? How about the *Guppy* here? Can anything be done?"

"Oh, sure. It was done long ago. A virus for that growth was designed within a few weeks of its original escape; its gene structure is on file. The mutation is enough like the original to be susceptible to the virus. We've made up a supply of it, and will be sowing it around the area for the next few weeks wherever one of the tenders goes. But why change the subject, young fellow? Your folks have been phoning, because I couldn't help hearing their talk when I was on watch. Why all this burning need to write letters? I begin to smell the proverbial rat."

He noticed with professional approval that the blush on Rick's face was quite uniform; evidently a good job had been done on the capillaries and their auxiliary nerves and muscles. "Give, son!"

"It's . . . it's not important," muttered the boy.

"Not important . . . oh, I see. Not important enough to turn you into a dithering nincompoop at the possibility of having your handsome features changed slightly, or make you drop back to second-grade level when it came to the responsibility for making a simple decision. I see. Well, it doesn't matter; she'll probably do all the deciding for you."

The blush burned deeper. "All right, Marco, don't sound like an ascetic; I know you aren't. Just do your job and get this hand fixed so I can write—at least there's still one form of communication you won't be unable to avoid overhearing while you're on watch."

"What a sentence! Are you sure you really finished school? But it's all right, Rick—the hand will be back in service soon, and it shouldn't take you many weeks to learn to write with it again—"

"What?"

"It is a new set of nerves, remember. They're connected with the old ones higher up in your hand and arm, but even with the old hand as a guide they probably won't go to exactly the same places to make contact with touch transducers and the like. Things will feel different, and you'll have to learn to use a pen all over again." The boy stared at him in dismay. "But don't worry. I'll do my best, which is very good, and it will only be a few more weeks. One thing, though—don't call your letter-writing problem my business; I'm just a mechanic. If you're really in love, you'd better get in touch with a doctor."

— CHARLES SHEFFIELD —

"SKYSTALK"

■ *Destinies*, **August 1979**.

Russian space pioneer Konstantin Tsiolkovsky was the first—in 1895!—to propose what we now call a "space elevator," a strong cable extending from the ground to orbit, and even beyond, to a counterweight that stabilizes the whole construction. In 1979, the late Arthur C. Clarke, the science fiction writer famed for predicting communication satellites (albeit not in fiction), built a novel, *The Fountains of Paradise*, around the concept. Quite coincidentally, Charles Sheffield published his shorter story, "Skystalk," at about the same time.

Currently, NASA is running a competition to develop the technology needed to build a space elevator. See Jeremy Hsu, "NASA's Space Elevator Games Challenge Research Teams to Beam Up the Energy" (http://www.popsci.com/technology/article/2009-10/nasas-space-elevator-games-challenge-you-beam). It may not be long before you can ride an elevator to space!

SKYSTALK

~꙯

Charles Sheffield

Finlay's Law: Trouble comes at three AM.

That's always been my experience, and I've learned to dread the hand on my shoulder that shakes me to wakefulness. My dreams had been bad enough, blasting off into orbit on top of an old chemical rocket, riding the torch, up there on a couple of thousand tons of volatile explosives. I'll never understand the nerve of the old-timers, willing to sit up there on one of those monsters.

I shuddered, forced my eyes open, and looked up at Marston's anxious face. I was already sitting up.

"Trouble?" It was a stupid question, but you're allowed a couple of those when you first wake up.

His voice was shaky. "There's a bomb on the Beanstalk."

I was off the bunk, pulling on my undershirt and groping around for my shoes. Larry Marston's words pulled me bolt upright.

"What do you mean, on the Beanstalk?"

"That's what Velasquez told me. He won't say more until you get on the line. They're holding a coded circuit open to Earth."

I gave up my search for shoes and went barefoot after Marston. If Arnold Velasquez were right—and I didn't see how he could be—then one of my old horrors was coming true. The Beanstalk had been designed to withstand most natural events, but sabotage was one thing that could never be fully ruled out. At any moment, we had nearly four hundred buckets climbing the Stalk and the same number going down. With the best screening in the world, with hefty rewards for information even of *rumors* of sabotage, there was always the small chance that something could be sneaked through on an outbound bucket. I had less worries about the buckets that went down to Earth. Sabotage from the space end had little to offer its perpetrators, and the Colonies would provide an unpleasant form of death to anyone who tried it, with no questions asked.

Arnold Velasquez was sitting in front of his screen down at Tether Control in Quito. Next to him stood a man I recognized only from news pictures: Otto Panosky, a top aide to the president. Neither man seemed to be looking at the screen. I wondered what they were seeing on their inward eye.

"Jack Finlay here," I said. "What's the story, Arnold?"

There was a perceptible lag before his head came up to stare at the screen, the quarter of a second that it took the video signal to go down to Earth, then back up to synchronous orbit.

"It's best if I read it to you, Jack," he said. At least his voice was under control, even though I could see his hands shaking as they held the paper. "The President's Office got this in over the telecopier about twenty minutes ago."

He rubbed at the side of his face, in the nervous gesture that I had seen during most major stages of the Beanstalk's construction. "It's addressed to us, here in SkyStalk Control. It's quite short. 'To the Head of Space Transportation Systems. A fusion bomb has been placed in one of the out-going buckets. It is of four megaton capacity, and was armed prior to placement. The secondary activation command can be given at any time by a coded radio signal. Unless terms are met by the president and World Congress on or before 02.00 U.T., seventy-two hours from now, we will give the command to explode the device. Our terms are set out in the following four paragraphs. One —' "

"Never mind those, Arnold." I waved my hand, impatient at the signal delay. "Just tell me one thing. Will Congress meet their demands?"

He shook his head. "They can't. What's being asked for is preposterous in the time available. You know how much red tape there is in intergovernmental relationships."

"You told them that?"

"Of course. We sent out a general broadcast." He shrugged. "It was no good. We're dealing with fanatics, with madmen. I need to know what you can do at your end."

"How much time do we have now?"

He looked at his watch. "Seventy-one and a half hours, if they mean what they say. You understand that we have no idea which bucket might be carrying the bomb. It could have been planted there days ago, and still be on the way up."

He was right. The buckets—there were three hundred and eighty-four of them each way—moved at a steady five kilometers a minute, up or down. That's a respectable speed, but it still took almost five days for each one of them to climb the cable of the Beanstalk out to our position in synchronous orbit.

Then I thought a bit more, and decided he wasn't quite right.

"It's not that vague, Arnold. You can bet the bomb wasn't placed on a bucket that started out more than two days ago. Otherwise, we could wait for it to get here and disarm it, and still be inside their deadline. It must still be fairly close to Earth, I'd guess."

"Well, even if you're right, that deduction doesn't help us." He was chewing a pen to bits between sentences. "We don't have anything here that could be ready in time to fly out and take a look, even if it's only a couple of thousand kilometers. Even if we did, and even if we could spot the bomb, we couldn't rendezvous with a bucket on the Stalk. That's why I need to know what you can do from your end. Can you handle it from there?"

I took a deep breath and swung my chair to face Larry Marston.

"Larry, four megatons would vaporize a few kilometers of the main cable. How hard would it be for us to release ballast at the top end of the cable, above us here, enough to leave this station in position?"

"Well . . ." He hesitated. "We could do that, Jack. But then we'd lose the power satellite. It's right out at the end there, by the ballast. Without it, we'd lose all the power at the station here, and all the buckets too—there isn't enough reserve power to keep the magnetic fields going. We'd need all our spare power to keep the recycling going here."

That was the moment when I finally came fully awake. I realized the implications of what he was saying, and was nodding before he'd finished speaking. Without adequate power, we'd be looking at a very messy situation.

"And it wouldn't only be us," I said to Velasquez and Partosky, sitting there tense in front of their screen. "Everybody on the Colonies will run low on air and water if the supply through the Stalk breaks down. Dammit, we've been warning Congress how vulnerable we are for years. All the time, there've been fewer and fewer rocket launches, and nothing but foot-dragging on getting the second Stalk started with a Kenya tether. Now you want miracles from us at short notice."

If I sounded bitter, that's because I *was* bitter. Panosky was nodding his head in a conciliatory way.

"We know, Jack. And if you can pull us through this one, I think you'll see changes in the future. But right now, we can't debate that. We have to know what you can do for us *now*, this minute."

I couldn't argue with that. I swung my chair again to face Larry Marston.

"Get Hasse and Kano over here to the Control Room as soon as you can." I turned back to Velasquez. "Give us a few minutes here. While we get organized. I'm bringing in the rest of my top engineering staff."

While Larry was rounding up the others, I sat back and let the full dimensions of the problem sink in. Sure, if we had to we could release the ballast at the outward end of the Stalk. If the Beanstalk below us were severed we'd have to do that, or be whipped out past the Moon like a stone from a slingshot, as the tension in the cable suddenly dropped.

But if we did that, what would happen to the piece of the Beanstalk that was still tethered to Earth, anchored down there in Quito? There might be as much as thirty thousand kilometers of it, and as soon as the break occurred it would begin to fall.

Not in a straight line. That wasn't the way that the dynamics went. It would begin to curl around the Earth, accelerating as it went, cracking into the atmosphere along the equator like a billion-ton whip stretching halfway around the planet. Forget the carrier buckets, and the superconducting cables that carried electricity down to the drive train from the solar power satellite seventy thousand kilometers above us. The piece that would do the real damage would be the central, load-bearing cable itself. It was only a couple of meters across at the bottom end, but it widened steadily as it went up. Made of bonded and doped silicon whiskers, with a tensile strength of two hundred million Newtons per square centimeter, it could handle an incredible load—almost two-thirds of a billion tons at its thinnest point. When that stored energy hit the atmosphere, there was going to be a fair amount of excitement down there on the surface. Not that we'd be watching it—the loss of the power satellite would make us look at our own survival problems; and as for the Colonies, a century of development would be ended.

By the time that Larry Marston came back with Jen Hasse and Alicia Kano, I doubt if I looked any more cheerful than Arnold Velasquez, down there at Tether Control. I sketched out the problem to the two newcomers; we had what looked like a hopeless situation on our hands.

"We have seventy-one hours," I concluded. "The only question we need to answer is, what will we be doing at this end during that time? Tether Control can coordinate disaster planning for the position on Earth: Arnold has already ruled out the possibility of any actual *help* from Earth—there are no rockets there that could be ready in time."

"What about the repair robots that you have on the cable?" asked Panosky, jumping into the conversation. "I thought they were all the way along its length."

"They are," said Jen Hasse. "But they're special purpose, not general purpose. We couldn't use one to look for a radioactive signal on a bucket, if that's what you're thinking of. Even if they had the right sensors for it, we'd need a week to reprogram them for the job."

"We don't have a week," said Alicia quietly. "We have seventy-one hours." She was small and dark-haired, and never raised her voice much above the minimum level needed to reach her audience—but I had grown to rely on her brains more than anything else on the station.

"Seventy-one hours, if we act *now*," I said. "We've already agreed that we don't have time to sit here and wait for that bucket with the bomb to arrive—the terrorists must have planned it that way."

"I know." Alicia did not raise her voice. "Sitting and waiting won't do it. But the total travel time of a carrier from the surface up to synchronous orbit, or back down again, is a little less than a hundred and twenty hours. That means that the bucket carrying the bomb will be at least *halfway* here in sixty hours. And a bucket that started down from here in the next few hours —"

"—would have to pass the bucket with the bomb on the way up, before the deadline," broke in Hasse. He was already over at the Control Board, looking at the carrier schedule. He shook his head. "There's nothing scheduled for a passenger bucket in the next twenty-four hours. It's all cargo going down."

"We're not looking for luxury." I went across to look at the schedule. "There are a couple of ore buckets with heavy metals scheduled for the next three hours. They'll have plenty of space in the top of them, and they're just forty minutes apart from each other. We could squeeze somebody in one or both of them, provided they were properly suited up. It wouldn't be a picnic, sitting in suits for three days, but we could do it."

"So how would we get at the bomb, even if we did that?" asked Larry. "It would be on the other side of the Beanstalk from us, passing at a relative velocity of six hundred kilometers an hour. We couldn't do more than wave to it as it went by, even if we knew just which bucket was carrying the bomb."

"That's the tricky piece." I looked at Jen Hasse. "Do you have enough control over the mass driver system to slow everything almost to a halt whenever an inbound and an outbound bucket pass each other?"

He was looking doubtful, rubbing his nose thoughtfully. "Maybe. Trouble is, I'd have to do it nearly a hundred times, if you want to slow down for every pass. And it would take me twenty minutes to stop and start each one. I don't think we have that much time. What do you have in mind?"

I went across to the model of the Beanstalk that we kept on the Control Room table. We often found that we could illustrate things with it in a minute that would have taken thousands of words to describe.

"Suppose we were here, starting down in a bucket," I said. I put my hand on the model of the station, thirty-five thousand kilometers above the surface of the Earth in synchronous orbit. "And suppose that the bucket we want to get to, the one with the bomb, is here, on the way up. We put somebody in the inbound bucket, and it starts on down."

I began to turn the drive train, so that the buckets began to move up and down along the length of the Beanstalk.

"The people in the inbound bucket carry a radiation counter," I went on. "We'd have to put it on a long arm, so that it cleared all the other stuff on the Stalk, and reached around to get near the upbound buckets. We can do that, I'm sure —if we can't, we don't deserve to call ourselves engineers. We stop at each outbound carrier, and test for radioactivity. There should be enough of that from the fission trigger of the bomb, so that we'll easily pick up a count when we reach the right bucket. Then you, Jan, hold the drive train in the halt position. We leave the inbound bucket, swing around the Stalk, and get into the other carrier. Then we try and disarm the bomb. I've had some experience with that."

"You mean we get out and actually climb around the Beanstalk?" asked Larry. He didn't sound pleased at the prospect.

"Right. It shouldn't be too bad," I said. "We can anchor ourselves with lines to the ore bucket, so we can't fall."

Even as I was speaking, I realized that it didn't sound too plausible. Climbing around the outside of the Beanstalk in a space suit, twenty thousand kilometers or more up, dangling on a line connected to an ore bucket—and then trying to take apart a fusion bomb wearing gloves. No wonder Larry didn't like the sound of that assignment. I wasn't surprised when Arnold Velasquez chipped in over the circuit connecting us to Tether Control.

"Sorry, Tack, but that won't work—even if you could do it. You didn't let me read the full message from the terrorists. One of their conditions is that we mustn't stop the bucket train on the Stalk in the next three days. I think they were afraid that we would reverse the direction of the buckets, and bring the bomb back down to Earth to disarm it. I guess they don't realize that the Stalk wasn't designed to run in reverse."

"Damnation. What else do they have in that message?" I asked. "What can they do if we decide to stop the bucket drive anyway? How can they even tell that we're doing it?"

"We have to assume that they have a plant in here at Tether Control," replied Velasquez. "After all, they managed to get a bomb onto the Stalk in spite of all our security. They say they'll explode the bomb if we make any attempt to slow or stop the bucket train, and we simply can't afford to take the risk of doing that. We have to assume they can monitor what's going on with the Stalk drive train."

There was a long, dismal silence, which Alicia finally broke.

"So that seems to leave us with only one alternative," she said thoughtfully. Then she grimaced and pouted her mouth. "It's a two-bucket operation, and I don't even like to think about it—even though I had a grandmother who was a circus trapeze artist."

She was leading in to something, and it wasn't like her to make a big buildup.

"That bad, eh?" I said.

"That bad, if we're lucky," she said. "If we're unlucky, I guess we'd all be dead in a month or two anyway, as the recycling runs down. For this to work, we need a good way of dissipating a lot of kinetic energy—something like a damped mechanical spring would do it. And we need a good way of sticking to the side of the Beanstalk. Then, we use two ore buckets—forty minutes apart would be all right—like this . . ."

She went over to the model of the Beanstalk. We watched her with mounting uneasiness as she outlined her idea. It sounded crazy. The only trouble was, it was that or nothing. Making choices in those circumstances is not difficult.

One good thing about space maintenance work—you develop versatility. If you can't wait to locate something down on Earth, then waste another week or so to have it shipped up to you, you get into the habit of making it for yourself. In an hour or so, we had a sensitive detector ready, welded on to a long extensible arm on the side of a bucket. When it was deployed, it would reach clear around the Beanstalk, missing all the drive train and repair station fittings, and hang in close to the outbound buckets. Jen had fitted it with a gadget that moved the detector rapidly upwards at the moment of closest approach of an upbound carrier, to increase the length of time available for getting a measurement of radioactivity.

He swore that it would work on the fly, and have a better than 99 percent chance of telling us which outbound bucket contained the bomb—even with a relative fly-by speed of six hundred kilometers an hour.

I didn't have time to argue the point, and in any case Jen was the expert. I also couldn't dispute his claim that he was easily the best qualified person to operate the gadget. He and Larry Marston, both fully suited up, climbed into the ore bucket. We had to leave the ore in there, because the mass balance between in-going and outbound buckets was closely calculated to give good stability to the Beanstalk. It made for a lumpy seat, but no one complained. Alicia and I watched as the bucket was moved into the feeder system, accelerated up to the correct speed, attached to the drive train, and dropped rapidly out of sight down the side of the Beanstalk.

"That's the easy part," she said. "They drop with the bucket, checking the upbound ones as they come by for radioactivity, and that's all they have to do."

"Unless they can't detect any signal," I said. "Then the bomb goes off, and they have the world's biggest roller-coaster ride. Twenty thousand kilometers of it, with the big thrill at the end."

"They'd never reach the surface," replied Alicia absentmindedly. "They'll frizzle up in the atmosphere long before they get there. Or maybe they won't. I wonder what the terminal velocity would be if you hung onto the Stalk cable?"

As she spoke, she was calmly examining an odd device that had been produced with impossible haste in the machine shop on the station's outer rim. It looked like an old-fashioned parachute harness, but instead of the main chute the lines led to a wheel about a meter across. From the opposite edge of the wheel, a doped silicon rope led to a hefty magnetic grapnel. Another similar arrangement was by her side.

"Here," she said to me. "Get yours on over your suit, and let's make sure we both know how to handle them. If you miss with the grapple, it'll be messy."

I looked at my watch. "We don't have time for any dry run. In the next fifteen minutes we have to get our suits on, over to the ore buckets, and into these harnesses. Anyway, I don't think rehearsals here inside the station mean too much when we get to the real thing."

We looked at each other for a moment, then began to suit up. It's not easy to estimate odds for something that has never been done before, but I didn't give us more than one chance in a hundred of coming out of it safely. Suits and harnesses on, we went and sat without speaking in the ore bucket.

I saw that we were sitting on a high-value shipment—silver and platinum, from one of the Belt mining operations. It wasn't comfortable, but we were certainly traveling in expensive company. Was it King Midas who complained that a golden throne is not right for restful sitting?

No matter what the final outcome, we were in for an unpleasant trip. Our suits had barely enough capacity for a six-day journey. They had no recycling capacity, and if we had to go all the way to the halfway point we would be descending for almost sixty hours. We had used up three hours to the deadline getting ready to go, so that would leave us only nine hours to do something about the bomb when we reached it. I suppose that it was just as bad or worse for Hasse and Marston. After they'd done their bit with the detector, there wasn't a thing they could do except sit in their bucket and wait, either for a message from us or an explosion far above them.

"Everything all right down there, Larry?" I asked, testing the radio link with them for the umpteenth time.

"Can't tell." He sounded strained. "We've passed three buckets so far, outbound ones, and we've had no signal from the detector. I guess that's as planned, but it would be nice to know it's working all right."

"You shouldn't expect anything for at least thirty-six hours," said Alicia.

"I know that. But it's impossible for us not to look at the detector whenever we pass an outbound bucket. Logically, we should be sleeping now and saving our attention for the most likely time of encounter—but neither one of us seems able to do it."

"Don't assume that the terrorists are all that logical, either," I said. "Remember, we are the ones who decided that they must have started the bomb on its way only a few hours ago. It's possible they put it into a bucket three or four days ago, and made up the deadline for some other reason. We think we can disarm that bomb, but they may not agree—and they may be right. All we may manage to do is advance the time of the explosion when we try and open up the casing."

As I spoke, I felt our bucket begin to accelerate. We were heading along the feeder and approaching the bucket drive train. After a few seconds, we were outside the station, dropping down the Beanstalk after Jen and Larry.

We sat there in silence for a while. I'd been up and down the Stalk many times, and so had Alicia, but always in passenger modules. The psychologists had decided that people rode those a lot better when they were windowless. The cargo bucket had no windows either, but we had left the hatch open to simplify communications with the other bucket and to enable us to climb out if and when the time came. We would have to close it when we were outside, or the aerodynamic pressures would spoil bucket stability when it finally entered the atmosphere—three hundred kilometers an hour isn't that fast, but it's a respectable speed for travel at full atmospheric pressure.

Our bucket was about four meters wide and three deep. It carried a load of seven hundred tons, so our extra mass was negligible. I stood at its edge and looked up, then down. The psychologists were quite right. Windows were a bad idea.

Above us, the Beanstalk rose up and up, occulting the backdrop of stars. It went past the synchronous station, which was still clearly visible as a blob on the stalk, then went on further up, invisible, to the solar power satellite and the great ballast weight, 105,000 kilometers above the surface of the Earth. On the Stalk itself, I could see the shielded superconductors that ran its full length, from the power satellite down to Tether Control in Quito. We were falling steadily, our rate precisely controlled by the linear synchronous motors that set the accelerations through pulsed magnetic fields. The power for that was drawn from the same superconducting cables. In the event of an electrical power failure, the buckets were designed to "freeze" to the side of the Stalk with mechanical coupling. We had to build the system that way, because about once a year we had some kind of power interruption—usually from small meteorites, not big enough to trigger the main detector system, but large enough to penetrate the shields and mess up the power transmission.

It was looking down, though, that produced the real effect. I felt my heart begin to pump harder, and I was gripping at the side of the bucket with my space-suit gloves. When you are in a rocket-propelled ship, you don't get any real feeling of height. Earth is another part of the Universe, something independent of you. But from our position, moving along the side of the Bean-stalk, I had quite a different feeling. We were *connected* to the planet. I could see the Stalk, dwindling smaller and smaller down to the Earth below. I had a very clear feeling that I could fall all the way down it, down to the big, blue-white globe at its foot. Although I had lived up at the station quite happily for over five years, I suddenly began to worry about the strength of the main cable. It was a ridiculous concern. There was a safety factor of ten built into its design, far more than a rational engineer would use for anything. It was more likely that the bottom would fall out of our ore bucket than that the support cable for the Beanstalk would break. I was kicking myself for my illogical fears, until I noticed Alicia also peering out at the Beanstalk, as though trying to see past the clutter of equipment there to the cable itself. I wasn't the only one thinking wild thoughts.

"You certainly get a different look at things from here," I said, trying to change the mood. "Did you ever see anything like that before?"

She shook her head ponderously—the suits weren't made for agility of movement.

"Not up here, I haven't," she replied. "But I once went up to the top of the towers of the Golden Gate Bridge in San Francisco, and looked at the support cables for that. It was the same sort of feeling. I began to wonder if they could take the strain. That was just for a bridge, not even a big one. What will happen if we don't make it, and they blow up the Beanstalk?"

I shrugged, inside my suit, then realized that she couldn't see the movement. "This is the only bridge to space that we've got. We'll be out of the bridge business, and back in the ferry-boat business. They'll have to start sending stuff up by rockets again. Shipments won't be a thousandth of what they are now, until another Stalk can be built. That will take thirty years, starting without this one to help us—even if the Colonies survive all right, and work on nothing else. We don't have to worry about that, though. We won't be there to hassle with it."

She nodded. "We were in such a hurry to get away it never occurred to me that we'd be sitting here for a couple of days with nothing to do but worry. Any ideas?"

"Yes. While you were making the reel and grapnel, I thought about that. The only thing that's worth our attention right now is a better understanding of the geometry of the Stalk. We need to know exactly where to position ourselves, where we'll set the grapnels, and what our dynamics will be as we move. I've asked Ricardo to send us schematics and layouts over the suit videos. He's picking out ones that show the drive train, the placing of the superconductors, and the unmanned repair stations. I've also asked him to deactivate all the repair robots. It's better for us to risk a failure on the mainte-nance side than have one of the monitoring robots wandering along the Stalk and mixing in with what we're trying to do."

"I heard what you said to Panosky, but it still seems to me that the robots ought to be useful."

"I'd hoped so, too. I checked again with Jen, and he agrees we'd have to reprogram them, and we don't have the time for it. It would take weeks. Jen said having them around would be like taking along a half-trained dog, bumbling about while we work. Forget that one."

As we talked, we kept our eyes open for the outbound buckets, passing us on the other side of the Beanstalk. We were only about ten meters from them at closest approach and they seemed to hurtle past us at an impossible speed. The idea of hitching on to one of them began to seem more and more preposterous. We settled down to look in more detail at the configuration of cables, drive train, repair stations, and buckets that was being flashed to us over the suit videos.

It was a weary time, an awful combination of boredom and tension. The video images were good, but there is a limit to what you can learn from diagrams and simulations. About once an hour, Jen Hasse and Larry Marston called in from the lower bucket beneath us, reporting on the news—or lack of it—regarding the bomb detection efforts. A message relayed from Panosky at Tether Control reported no progress in negotiations with the terrorists. The fanatics simply didn't believe their terms couldn't be met. That was proof of their naivety, but didn't make them any less dangerous.

It was impossible to get comfortable in our suits. The ore buckets had never been designed for a human occupant, and we couldn't find a level spot to stretch out. Alicia and I passed into a half-awake trance, still watching the images that flashed onto the suit videos, but not taking in much of anything. Given that we couldn't sleep, we were probably in the closest thing we could get to a resting state. I hoped that Jen and Larry would keep their attention up, watching an endless succession of buckets flash past them and checking each one for radioactivity count.

The break came after fifty-four hours in the bucket. We didn't need to hear the details from the carrier below us to know they had it—Larry's voice crackled with excitement.

"Got it," he said. "Jen picked up a strong signal from the bucket we just passed. If you leave the ore carrier within thirty-four seconds, you'll have thirty-eight minutes to get ready for it to come past you. It will be the second one to reach you. For God's sake don't try for the wrong one."

There was a pause, then Larry said something I would never have expected from him. "We'll lose radio contact with you in a while, as we move further along the Stalk. Good luck, both of you—and look after him, Alicia."

I didn't have time to think that one through—but shouldn't he be telling me to look after her? It was no time for puzzling. We were up on top of our bucket in a second, adrenalin moving through our veins like an electric current. The cable was whipping past us at a great rate; the idea of forsaking the relative safety of the ore bucket for the naked wall of the Beanstalk seemed like insanity. We watched as one of the repair stations, sticking out from the cable into open space, flashed past.

"There'll be another one of those coming by in thirty-five seconds," I said. "We've got to get the grapnels onto it, and we'll be casting blind. I'll throw first, and you follow a second later. Don't panic if I miss—remember, we only have to get one good hook there."

"Count us down, Jack," said Alicia. She wasn't one to waste words in a tight spot.

I pressed the digital readout in my suit, and watched the count move from thirty-five down to zero.

"Countdown display on Channel Six," I said, and picked up the rope and grapnel. I looked doubtfully at the wheel that was set in the middle of the thin rope, then even looked suspiciously at the rope itself, wondering if it would take the strain. That shows how the brain works in a crisis—that rope would have held a herd of elephants with no trouble at all.

I cast the grapnel as the count touched to zero, and Alicia threw a fraction later. Both ropes were spliced onto both suits, so it was never clear which grapnel took hold. Our bucket continued to drop rapidly towards Earth, but we were jerked off the top of it and went zipping on downwards fractionally slower as the friction reel in the middle of the rope unwound, slowing our motion.

We came to a halt about fifty meters down the Beanstalk from the grapnel, after a rough ride in which our deceleration must have averaged over seven Gs. Without that reel to slow us down gradually, the jerk of the grapnel as it caught the repair station wall would have snapped our spines when we were lifted from the ore bucket.

We hung there, swinging free, suspended from the wall of the Stalk. As the reel began to take up the line that had been paid out, I made the mistake of looking down. We dangled over an awful void, with nothing between us and that vast drop to the Earth below but the thin line above us. When we came closer to the point of attachment to the Beanstalk wall, I saw just how lucky we had been. One grapnel had missed completely, and the second one had caught the very lip of the repair station platform. Another foot to the left and we would have missed it altogether.

We clawed our way up to the station rim—easy enough to do, because the gravity at that height was only a fraction of a G, less than a tenth. But a fall from there would be inexorable, and we would have fallen away from the Beanstalk, with no chance to reconnect to it. Working together, we freed the grapnel and readied both lines and grapnels for reuse. After that there was nothing to do but cling to the side of the Beanstalk, watch the sweep of the heavens above us, and wait for the outbound ore buckets to come past us.

The first one came by after seventeen minutes. I had the clock readout to prove it, otherwise I would have solemnly sworn that we had waited there for more than an hour, holding to our precarious perch. Alicia, seemed more at home there than I was. I watched her moving the grapnel to the best position for casting it, then settle down patiently to wait.

It is hard to describe my own feelings in that period. I watched the movement of the stars above us, in their great circle, and wondered if we would be alive in another twenty minutes. I felt a strong communion with the old sailors of Earth's seas, up in their crow'snests in a howling gale, sensing nothing but darkness, high-blown spindrift, perilous breakers ahead, and the dipping, rolling stars above.

Alicia kept her gaze steadily downwards, something that I found hard to do. She had inherited a good head for heights from her circus-performer grandmother.

"I can see it," she said at last. "All ready for a repeat performance?"

"Right." I swung the grapnel experimentally. "Since we can see it this time, we may as well throw together."

I concentrated on the bucket sweeping steadily up towards us, trying to estimate the distance and the time that it would take before it reached us. We both drew back our arms at the same moment and lobbed the grapnels towards the center of the bucket.

It came past us with a monstrous, silent rush. Again we felt the fierce acceleration as we were jerked away from the Beanstalk wall and shot upwards after the carrier. Again, I realized that we couldn't have done it without Alicia's friction reel smoothing the motion for us. This time, it was more dangerous than when we had left the downbound bucket. Instead of trying to reach the stationary wall of the Stalk, we were now hooked onto the moving bucket. We swung wildly beneath it in its upward flight, narrowly missing contact with elements of the drive train, and then with another repair station that flashed past a couple of meters to our right.

Finally, somehow, we damped our motion, reeled in the line, slid back the cover to the ore bucket and fell safely forward inside it. I was completely drained. It must have been all nervous stress—we hadn't expended a significant amount of physical energy. I know that Alicia felt the same way as I did, because after we plumped over the rim of the carrier we both fell to the floor and lay there without speaking for several minutes. It gives some idea of our state of mind when I say that the bucket we had reached, with a four megaton bomb inside it that might go off at any moment, seemed like a haven of safety.

We finally found the energy to get up and look around us. The bucket was loaded with manufactured goods, and I thought for a sickening moment that the bomb was not there. We found it after five minutes of frantic searching. It was a compact blue cylinder, a meter long and fifty centimeters wide, and it had been cold-welded to the wall of the bucket. I knew the design.

"There it is," I said to Alicia. Then I didn't know what to say next. It was the most advanced design, not the big, old one that I had been hoping for.

"Can you disarm it?" asked Alicia.

"In principle. There's only one problem. I know how it's put together, but I'll never be able to get it apart wearing a suit. The fingerwork I'd need is just too fine for gloves. We seem to be no better off than we were before."

We sat there side by side, looking at the bomb. The irony of the situation was sinking in. We had reached it, just as we hoped we could. Now, it seemed we might as well have been still back in the station.

"Any chance that we could get it free and dump it overboard?" asked Alicia. "You know, just chuck the thing away from the bucket."

I shook my head, aware again of how much my suit impeded freedom of movement. "It's spot-welded. We couldn't shift it. Anyway, free fall from here would give it an impact orbit, and a lot of people might be killed if it went off inside the atmosphere. If we were five thousand kilometers higher, perigee would be at a safe height above the surface—but we can't afford to wait for another sixteen hours until the bucket gets up that high. Look, I've got another idea, but it will mean that we'll lose radio contact with the station."

"So what?" said Alicia. Her voice was weary. "There's not a thing they can do to help us anyway."

"They'll go out of their minds with worry down on Earth, if they don't know what's happening here."

"I don't see why we should keep all of it for ourselves. What's your idea, Jack?"

"All right." I summoned my reserves of energy. "We're in a vacuum now, but this bucket would be airtight if we were to close the top hatch again. I have enough air in my suit to make a breathable atmosphere in this enclosed space, at least for long enough to let me have a go at the bomb. We've got nearly twelve hours to the deadline, and if I can't disarm it in that time I can't do it at all."

Alicia looked at her air reserve indicator and nodded. "I can spare you some air, too, if I open up my suit."

"No. We daren't do that. We have one other big problem—the temperature. It's going to feel really cold in here once I'm outside my suit. I'll put my heaters on to maximum, and leave the suit open, but I'm still not sure I can get much done before I begin to freeze up. If I begin to lose feeling in my fingers, I'll need your help to get me back inside. So you have to stay in your suit. Once I'm warmed up, I can try again."

She was silent for a few moments, repeating the calculations that I had just done myself.

"You'll only have enough air to try it twice," she said at last. "If you can't do it in one shot, you'll have to let me have a go. You can direct me on what has to be done."

There was no point in hanging around. We sent a brief message to the station, telling them what we were going to do, then closed the hatch and began to bleed air out of my suit and into the interior of the bucket. We used the light from Alicia's suit, which had ample power to last for several days.

When the air pressure inside the bucket was high enough for me to breathe, I peeled out of my suit. It was as cold as charity in that metal box, but I ignored that and crouched down alongside the bomb in my underwear and bare feet.

I had eleven hours at the most. Inside my head, I fancied that I could hear a clock ticking. That must have been only my fancy. Modern bombs have no place for clockwork timers.

By placing my suit directly beneath my hands, I found that I could get enough heat from the thermal units to let me keep on working without a break. The clock inside my head went on ticking, also without a break.

On and on and on.

They say that I was delirious when we reached the station. That's the only way the press could reconcile my status as public hero with the things that I said to the president when he called up to congratulate us.

I suppose I could claim delirium if I wanted to—five days without sleep, two without food, oxygen starvation, and frostbite of the toes and ears, that might add up to delirium. I had received enough warmth from the suit to keep my hands going, because it was very close to them, but that had been at the expense of some of my other extremities. If it hadn't been for Alicia, cramming me somehow back into the suit after I had disarmed the bomb, I would have frozen to death in a couple of hours.

As it was, I smelled ripe and revolting when they unpacked us from the bucket and winkled me out of my suit—Alicia hadn't been able to reconnect me with the plumbing arrangements.

So I told the President that the World Congress was composed of a giggling bunch of witless turds, who couldn't sense a global need for more bridges to space if a Beanstalk were pushed up their backsides—which was where I thought they kept their brains. Not quite the speech that we used to get from the old-time returning astronauts, but I must admit it's one that I'd wanted to give for some time. The audience was there this time, with the whole world hanging on my words over live TV.

We've finally started construction on the second Beanstalk. I don't know if my words had anything to do with it, but there was a lot of public pressure after I said my piece, and I like to think that I had some effect.

And me? I'm designing the third Beanstalk; what else? But I don't think I'll hold my breath waiting for a Congressional Vote of Thanks for my efforts saving the first one.

ABOUT THE AUTHORS

～

G regory Benford has published more than twenty books, mostly novels. Nearly all remain in print, some after a quarter of a century. His fiction has won many awards, including the Nebula Award for his novel *Timescape*. A winner of the United Nations Medal for Literature, he is a professor of physics at the University of California, Irvine. He is a Woodrow Wilson Fellow, was Visiting Fellow at Cambridge University, and in 1995 received the Lord Prize for contributions to science. He won the Japan Seiun Award for Dramatic Presentation with his seven-hour series, *A Galactic Odyssey*. His 1999 analysis of what endures, *Deep Time: How Humanity Communicates across Millennia*, has been widely read. A fellow of the American Physical Society and a member of the World Academy of Arts and Sciences, he continues his research in both astrophysics and plasma physics. Time allowing, he continues to write both fiction and nonfiction. Recently he began a series on science and society with biologist Michael Rose, published on the Internet at Amazon.com Shorts—you can visit this site at http://www.benford-rose.com/

Cleve Cartmill (1908–1964) specialized in writing science fiction short stories. He's best known for what is sometimes referred to as "the Cleve Cartmill affair," when his 1944 story "Deadline" attracted the attention of the FBI due to its detailed description of a nuclear weapon similar to that being developed by the highly classified Manhattan Project (see the "Deadline" headnote for more information). Before writing for pulp magazines, he held a number of jobs, including newspaperman, radio operator, and accountant. Many of his earliest stories, written at the beginning of World War II, were published in John W. Campbell's magazines *Unknown* and *Astounding Science Fiction*. Outside of his writing career, he was best known for being the co-inventor of the Blackmill system of high speed typography. His son, Matt Cartmill, is currently a Professor of Biological Anthropology at Boston University.

Thomas A. Easton is a member of the Science Fiction and Fantasy Writers of America and a well-known science fiction critic (he wrote the book review column for *Analog* for thirty years). He holds a doctorate in theoretical biology from the University of Chicago, teaches at Thomas College in Waterville, Maine, and writes textbooks for McGraw-Hill on Science, Technology & Society, Environmental Science, and Energy & Society. Over the years he has published about fifty science-fiction and fantasy short stories and ten sf novels, of which his favorites are *Sparrowhawk* (Ace, 1990), *Silicon Karma* (White Wolf, 1997), and *The Great Flying Saucer Conspiracy* (Wildside, 2002).

David Gerrold is the author (and father of) *The Martian Child*, basis for the 2007 movie starring John Cusack, Amanda Peet, and Bobby Coleman. He's also known as the creator of *Star Trek*'s tribbles, *Land of the Lost*'s sleestak, and his own much more terrifying Chtorrans in *The War Against The Chtorr*. He's published more than fifty books, including *When HARLIE Was One, The Man Who Folded Himself*, and *Jumping Off the Planet*. In his spare time, he redesigns his website, www.gerrold.com.

Jeff Hecht is a science and technology writer who concentrates on fiber optics and lasers, including consulting on fiber optics, lasers, and optical technology. In his copious spare time, he writes science fiction. His books include *Beam: The Race to Make the Laser*, *Understanding Fiber Optics* (now in its fifth edition), and *City of Light*, a history of the development of fiber optics. His shorter articles have been published in *Optics & Photonics News*, *Analog Science Fiction and Fact*, *Laser Focus World*, and *New Scientist*. His short fiction has been published in *Nature*, *Interzone*, *Isaac Asimov's Science Fiction Magazine*, and many others.

Murray Leinster (1896–1975) was the pseudonym for William Fitzgerald Jenkins, a consummate professional who wrote for a wide number of venues during his varied career. Although he wrote more than forty novels during his fifty-year career, it is for his short fiction, including stories such as "The Lonely Planet," "First Contact," and "Sidewise in Time," for which he is best remembered. Fascinated with the idea of an alternatives to reality as we or his protagonists know it, he pioneered the concept of a multiple points along one time continuum, or the simple concept of parallel worlds. Well-regarded in the science fiction community, he was the Guest of Honor at the twenty-first World Science Fiction Convention in 1963.

Richard A. Lovett is the author of thirty-five science-fiction stories and more than 2,700 nonfiction articles. A prolific contributor to *Analog*, he has won five AnLab Awards and one Sigma (Russian translation) award. He has written nearly as many science articles for *Analog* as he has science-fiction stories. In "real" life, he writes for a living for a publication list that includes *New Scientist*, *Science*, *Psychology Today*, *National Geographic News*, and many large newspapers. A veteran of Greenland's 100–mile Arctic

Circle (cross-country ski) Race, he has also coauthored a book on cross-country skiing.

Vonda N. McIntyre is the author of many novels, including *Dreamsnake*, which won both the Nebula Award and the Hugo award for best science-fiction novel, and has been published in thirteen languages, including Japanese and Polish. She has written two screenplays, *The Moon and the Sun* (which also became a novel published by Pocket Books) and *Illegal Alien*. She also wrote *The Starfarers Series* (*Starfarer, Transition, Metaphase*, and *Nautilus*), as well as a *Star Wars* novel, *The Crystal Star*, and novelized the screenplays for the *Star Trek* movies *The Wrath of Khan*, *The Search for Spock*, and *The Voyage Home*. Other novels by her include *The Exile Waiting*, *The Entropy Effect*, *Superluminal*, and *Barbary*. Her collection, *Fireflood & Other Stories*, includes the Nebula award-winning "Of Mist, and Grass, and Sand," plus ten other stories. With Susan Janice Anderson, she edited *Aurora: Beyond Equality*, an anthology of humanist science fiction by Ursula K. Le Guin, James Tiptree, Jr., A. R. Sheldon, Marge Piercy, David J. Skal, P.J. Plauger, and others. She has twice been writer-in-residence at Clarion West, the Seattle daughter of the original Clarion, Pennsylvania, writers, workshop. She has spoken at Rutgers University, Antioch West, the University of Washington, the Harbourfront International Author's Festival, and the Melbourne Writers, Workshop. She was a judge for the first James Tiptree, Jr., Memorial Award.

Edgar Allan Poe (1809–1849), while a mainstay of literature today, and the recognized creator of the modern genres of horror and mystery fiction, spent much of his life chasing the public and literary acclaim he craved. He first began publishing his poems during his time in the U.S. Army, including an early collection, *Tamerlane and Other Poems*, which was printed under the byline "A Bostonian." In 1831, Edgar decided to try making a living as an author, and was the first well-known American to attempt to make a living solely through his writing. His only full-length novel, *The Narrative of Arthur Gordon Pym of Nantucket*, was published in 1838 to wide review and acclaim, although Poe saw little profit from his work. The year after saw the appearance of his first short story collection, *Tales of the Grotesque and Arabesque*, which received mixed reviews and sold poorly. Even the publication of one of his most famous works, "The Raven," in 1845, which gained him widespread acclaim, only paid him nine dollars for the poem itself. Unfortunately, Poe's health declined until his death under mysterious circumstances on October 7th, 1849.

Robert Sheckley (1928–2005) was born in Brooklyn, New York, and raised in New Jersey. He went into the U.S. Army after high school and served in Korea. After discharge he attended NYU, graduating with a degree in English. He began selling stories to all the science-fiction magazines soon after his graduation, producing several hundred over the next several years. His best-known books in the science-fiction field are *Immortality, Inc.; Mindswap;* and *Dimension of Miracles*. He had produced more than sixty-five books throughout his career, including twenty novels and nine collections of his short stories, as well as his five volume *Collected Short Stories of Robert Sheckley*, published by Pulphouse. In 1991 he received the Daniel F. Gallun award for contributions to the genre of science fiction, and in 2001 he was given the Author Emeritus award by the Science Fiction Writers of America.

Charles Sheffield (1935–2002) was born in England and educated at St. John's College, Cambridge. He is a Past-President and Fellow of the American Astronautical Society, a Fellow of the American Association for the Advancement of Science, a Past-President of the Science Fiction Writers of America, a Fellow of the British Interplanetary Society, a Distinguished Lecturer for the American Institute of Aeronautics and Astronautics, and a Member of the International Astronomical Union. His forty-one published books include best-sellers of both fact and fiction. He authored more than a hundred technical papers on subjects ranging from astronomy to large-scale computer systems, and served as a reviewer of science texts for the *New Scientist*, *The World & I*, and the *Washington Post*. His writing awards included the Hugo, the Nebula, the Japanese Seiun Award, the John W. Campbell Memorial Award, and the Isaac Asimov Memorial Award for writing that contributes significantly to the public knowledge and understanding of science. He was the creator and main author of the Jupiter (TM) line of science fiction for young adults, and authored or co-authored the first four books of that series. His 1999 book, *Borderlands of Science*, explored the boundaries of current science for the benefit of would-be writers.

Harry Clement Stubbs (1922–2003), who wrote under the pen name Hal Clement, had his first novel, *Needle*, published in 1950, and wrote carefully extrapolated, fully-realized novels of alien worlds and detailed hard science fiction ever since. Through such novels as *Mission of Gravity*, *Ocean on Top*, and *The Nitrogen Fix*, his humans, and more importantly his aliens, remained true to their desires and wants, and their evolution as well. Ever since his first story, he has also written excellent shorter fiction as well, the best of which has been collected in *The Best of Hal Clement*.

Regularly published in *Analog Science Fiction and Fact* beginning with the story featured in this collection, Rajnar Vajra has found writing science fiction and fantasy the ideal expression of his imagination, intellect, and love for the human race and its enormous potential. When Rajnar isn't teaching, composing or performing music, cooking, or practicing one of several contemplative disciplines, he is most often working on writing projects such as editing a Ph.D. thesis in chemistry, constructing story lines and dialog for a computer-gaming company, or developing his own stories and novels. He paints, usually in acrylics, as a

ABOUT THE AUTHORS · 311

hobby. Strangely, with all that free time he has, he hasn't done much painting lately.

James Van Pelt writes and teaches in western Colorado. During the school year he teaches English at both Fruita Monument High School and Mesa State College. His fiction has appeared in numerous publications, including *Analog Science Fiction and Fact*, *Asimov's*, *Realms of Fantasy*, and *Weird Tales*. His nonfiction work has appeared in *Tangent* magazine. In 1999 James was a finalist for the John W. Campbell Award for Best New Writer. Several of his stories have received Nebula and Stoker recommendations, including two pieces that made the preliminary Nebula ballot. His stories have been listed on the honorable mention lists in both Datlow and Windling's *The Year's Best Fantasy and Horror* and Dozois' *The Year's Best Science Fiction*. His stories have also been reprinted in Dozois' *The Year's Best Science Fiction* for the twentieth and twenty-first editions, David Hartwell's *Year's Best Fantasy #3*, and Stephen Jones's *Mammoth Book of Best New Horror*, both the fifteenth and sixteenth editions. His short story, "The Last of the O-Forms" was a 2004 Nebula finalist. Currently he is working on a new novel that he hopes to complete some time soon.

Herbert George Wells (1866–1946) was a British novelist, journalist, sociologist, and historian, whose various science fiction stories have been filmed many times. The best known of his almost fifty novels, *The Time Machine* (1895), *The Invisible Man* (1897), and *The War of the Worlds* (1898), ensured his place in the pantheon of science fiction writers. Although Wells' novels were highly entertaining, he also tried to spur debate about the future of mankind through several of his works. His novel, *In the Days of the Comet* (1906), was about a giant comet that nearly hits Earth, but its tail gases cause changes in human behaviour. However, in *The Shape of Things to Come* (1933), he failed to anticipate the importance of atomic energy, although in *The World Set Free*

(1914) a physicist manages to split the atom. Near the turn of the century Wells switched to literary novels with *Love and Mr. Lewisham* (1900), and *Kipps* (1905), his literary critique of English society that strengthened his reputation as a serious writer. In later years Wells's romantic and enthusiastic conception of technology turned more doubtful. His bitter side is seen early in the novel *Boon* (1915), which was a parody of Henry James. After World War I, Wells published several non fiction works, among them *The Outline of History* (1920), *The Science of Life* (1929–39), written in collaboration with Sir Julian Huxley and George Philip Wells, and *Experiment in Autobiography* (1934). He also entered politics, and in the early 1920s was a Labour candidate for Parliament. Wells lived through World War II in his house on Regent's Park, refusing to let the blitz drive him out of London. His last book, *Mind at the End of Its Tether* (1945), was about mankind's future prospects, which he'd always viewed with pessimism. He died in London on August 13, 1946.